Praise for *The Serpent and the Scorpion*

"Of course I'm fascinated with early-twentieth-century women and Ursula Marlow is a shining example of the Oxford-educated woman before WWI. Suffragette and business owner, she becomes a player on the world stage. The book sweeps from the steamy bazaars of Egypt to proper English drawing rooms as Ursula battles international intrigue and her own sensuous nature. Dorothy Sayers would be proud of her Oxford sister."

—RHYS BOWEN, AWARD-WINNING AUTHOR OF
THE MOLLY MURPHY AND ROYAL SPYNESS MYSTERIES

"*The Serpent and the Scorpion* is an evocative, wise, and affecting book, which also just so happens to be a page turner. I can't wait to see more of Ursula and Lord Wrotham. May this series continue forever!"

—CHARLES FINCH, AUTHOR OF
THE CHARLES LENOX MYSTERIES

"Ursula Marlow is a true woman of daring; a gorgeous suffragette with the mind of Hercule Poirot and the spunk and daring of Nellie Bly. She's the perfect match against assassins, Bolsheviks, and spies in this exciting adventure laced with intrigue and romance."

—SUZANNE ARRUDA, AUTHOR OF THE JADE DEL
CAMERON MYSTERY SERIES, INCLUDING *The Serpent's
Daughter* AND *The Leopard's Prey* (JANUARY 2009)

"*The Serpent and the Scorpion* is an absolute delight. Clare Langley-Hawthorne has once again captured Edwardian London in deft strokes. Forward-thinking Ursula Marlow is a character readers will want to meet again and again; her wit, intelligence, and compassion are irresistible."

—TASHA ALEXANDER, AUTHOR
Elizabeth: The Golden Age

PENGUIN BOOKS

THE SERPENT AND THE SCORPION

Clare Langley-Hawthorne was raised in England and Australia. She was an attorney in Melbourne before moving to the United States, where she began her career as a writer. She lives in Oakland, California, with her family. *The Serpent and the Scorpion* is the second book in the Ursula Marlow series.

The *Serpent* and the *Scorpion*

AN **Ursula Marlow** MYSTERY

Clare Langley-Hawthorne

PENGUIN BOOKS

PENGUIN BOOKS
Published by the Penguin Group
Penguin Group (USA) Inc., 375 Hudson Street, New York, New York 10014, U.S.A. •
Penguin Group (Canada), 90 Eglinton Avenue East, Suite 700, Toronto, Ontario,
Canada M4P 2Y3 (a division of Pearson Penguin Canada Inc.) • Penguin Books
Ltd, 80 Strand, London WC2R 0RL, England • Penguin Ireland, 25 St Stephen's
Green, Dublin 2, Ireland (a division of Penguin Books Ltd) • Penguin Group (Australia),
250 Camberwell Road, Camberwell, Victoria 3124, Australia (a division of Pearson
Australia Group Pty Ltd) • Penguin Books India Pvt Ltd, 11 Community Centre,
Panchsheel Park, New Delhi–110 017, India • Penguin Group (NZ), 67 Apollo
Drive, Rosedale, North Shore 0632, New Zealand (a division of Pearson New Zealand
Ltd) • Penguin Books (South Africa) (Pty) Ltd, 24 Sturdee Avenue, Rosebank,
Johannesburg 2196, South Africa

Penguin Books Ltd, Registered Offices:
80 Strand, London WC2R 0RL, England

First published in Penguin Books 2008

10 9 8 7 6 5 4 3 2 1

Publisher's Note
This is a work of fiction. Names, characters, places, and incidents either are the product
of the author's imagination or are used fictitiously, and any resemblance to actual per-
sons, living or dead, business establishments, events, or locales is entirely coincidental.

LIBRARY OF CONGRESS CATALOGING IN PUBLICATION DATA
Langley-Hawthorne, Clare.
The serpent and the scorpion : an Ursula Marlow mystery / Clare Langley-Hawthorne.
    p. cm.
ISBN 978-0-14-311339-3
1. Inheritance and succession—Fiction.   2. Young women—Fiction.   3. Great
Britain—History—Edward VII, 1901–1910—Fiction.   4. Murder—Fiction.
I. Title.
PS3612.A584S47 2008
813'.6—dc22   2008015696

Printed in the United States of America
Set in Goudy Old Style with Jennifer and Flourish

For Mum

Acknowledgments

I owe a debt of gratitude to all those who provided me with valuable research, advice, and unfailing support. Without them, my writing would be languishing in a drawer somewhere. As always, a huge thank-you to my parents, who are always willing to read the manuscript one more time, to my mother-in-law, Marie, who provides support from afar, to my husband for making it all financially viable, and to my twin sons, Samuel and Jasper, for proudly telling everyone that Mummy is a writer.

I am privileged to have Randi Murray as my agent and Alicia Bothwell as my editor and am grateful for their wise counsel and passionate commitment to my work. I also need to thank: Brett Kelly, my previous editor; Ann Day, my publicist at Penguin; and Hilary Redmon, my editor (and enthusiastic supporter) while Ali was on maternity leave. I feel extremely fortunate to be surrounded by such an amazing group of accomplished women.

Thank you to Professor Yossi Ben Artzi and his assistant, Riva Friedman, at the University of Haifa for advising me on early-twentieth-century settlements in Palestine. Professor Ben Artzi's grandparents settled in Hartuv, thankfully without any murder or mystery, but nevertheless they provided me with a seed of inspiration for the story. I am also grateful for Margot Badran's insight on the nascent feminist and nationalist movements in Egypt, Phil Jarrett's timely input on the airplanes of the day, and the historian at the RAC's practical advice on motorcars in Britain in 1912. I need to write another series of books to do justice to all the information my experts provided me.

Finally, I still owe so much to my writing group, who helped launch Ursula Marlow into print. I continue to be grateful for all their support and send a huge thank-you to Winifred for her much-needed input and advice on the first draft of *The Serpent and the Scorpion*.

The Serpent and the Scorpion

Prologue

The Blériot monoplane circled above the bleached, dry valley. To the east the Judean hills crumpled and folded beneath the deep blue sky, like a golden sable coat left carelessly in the sun.

The pilot shouted and pointed to the ground below. The woman in the rear seat replied, but her words were soon lost in the wind. The plane rolled, the wheels tipped, and they started the rough descent, finally bouncing along the sand and stones before coming to a halt beside a small wooden watchtower. The pilot clambered out of the plane and placed two blocks against the wheels. Once the beat of the propellers was gone, the air was silent. The pilot assisted his female passenger down before taking off his goggles and smoothing back his blond hair. Her face remained shrouded in the hood of her cloak, which she kept drawn in close, despite the heat of the midday sun.

In the distance, at the edge of the valley, was a huddle of houses, barely visible except for the reflection of whitewashed walls in the sun. Out of the corner of his eye, the pilot saw a rider approaching, a cloud of dust his only companion. The rider slowed when he was about twenty feet away, dismounted, and walked toward them cautiously. He had a rifle slung across his back, and a round of bullets across his chest. A pistol in a leather holster hung off his belt at the hip. He wore shabby loose-fitting trousers and a short narrow jacket. On his head was perched a brightly woven *kippah*. He had a long beard, black curly hair, and two dark ringlets hung just above his ears.

"Wait for me no more than one hour." The woman passenger spoke to the pilot in imperious, heavily accented English.

The pilot nodded; her instructions to him had been quite clear. *Ask no questions.*

The rider remounted the horse, then swung the woman up to sit behind him. As they left, the pilot turned back and walked over to his plane. He slid his hand lovingly over its cloth-covered wood frame before grabbing a canvas bag from the cockpit. He then propped himself up on a boulder, took out his compass, and proceeded to check the map for the return journey to Jaffa.

An hour and a half later his female passenger returned. She did not seem surprised that he had waited longer than the appointed hour, nor that he did not question the reason for her delay. She did not guess, however, that it was her very countenance that had silenced him. Gone was her glorious pomposity, gone was her haughty tone. She looked like a lost and forgotten child, with eyes that reflected such anguish that the pilot could think of no words to say.

The return flight to Jaffa was turbulent. An early *hamsin* swirled up from Egypt, turning the late-afternoon sky from blue to topaz. By the time they landed on the makeshift airstrip near the orange groves east of the German Colony, a thick, sand-stung twilight had descended. Her driver was waiting by a black horse-drawn carriage. A sudden gust of wind rattled the carriage door and ruffled the horses' manes. The pilot and the woman said their good-byes, raising their voices to be heard above the rising sandstorm. She paid him generously for both his services and his silence. As she pulled away in the carriage, he caught a final glimpse of her white face staring out into the darkness.

Early the next day she sailed out on a steamship bound for Alexandria. The boat slipped the moorings, slid back in the sleek clear water, and made its way out of the harbor just as the sun began to rise above the port of Jaffa. She stood on the deck, wrapped in the shawl her mother had given her the day they left Russia. Its soft deep hues mirrored the blue of the morning sky. She shielded her eyes as the sun came into fiery view, creating a halo of bright light around the houses and towers of the old port.

Without a word she made her way through the throng of passengers and down belowdecks to her cabin. The morning sun streamed through the portholes, forming pools of light on the floor beneath her feet. She passed her husband in the narrow hallway. He reached out to take her hand, but she shook her head and walked on by. Bitter disappointment registered on his face as he retreated into the shadows.

Once in her suite, she removed her shawl, splashed some cool water on her face from a blue-and-white ceramic jug, and sat down at the wooden desk beneath the window. All her movements were mechanical and deliberate, without expression or emotion. She held her head in her hands but could not cry. She remained sitting there, alone in the gathering light, for nearly an hour before picking up the gold-tipped fountain pen that lay on the desk. She shook the pen and with quiet deliberation began to write on a piece of cream-colored paper.

> *Dearest sister,*
>
> *I write to you from Eretz Yisrael with great urgency and despair. I dare not tell anyone what I have learned, not even Peter. But you, my dearest sister, you are the only one I can trust. It is you I must confide in.*
>
> *What I have just discovered could get me killed. . . .*

A month later Katya Vilensky was dead.

Part One
England

One

The banner over the fireplace read "New Year Greetings 1912." Made of die-cut embossed paper and strung up with red ribbon, the words, encircled by roses and angels, were suffused in the golden light of the fire beneath. Ursula Marlow wrapped her ermine stole tightly around her and sighed. She didn't feel much like celebrating tonight. Although it was almost two years since her father's murder, this festive season seemed worse than the last. Having lost her mother to tuberculosis when she was just three, Ursula was used to feeling wistful at this time of year, but the last few weeks she had felt the absence of family acutely. Tonight, surrounded by the elite of London society, she felt more alone than ever. Her father's absence was like a steel blade that slid into her abdomen. Its cold, sharp tip could never entirely retract—one flinch, one unbidden recollection, and the blade pierced her anew.

The host of the party, Lady Catherine Winterton, came past and gave Ursula's arm a quick squeeze. "The punch isn't that bad, I hope!" she said.

Ursula gave her a weak smile in reply.

"You just caught me alone with my thoughts," she answered, and Lady Winterton's eyes softened. Ursula knew Lady Winterton from the local branch meetings of the Women's Social and Political Union, and not for the first time, she envied her friend's ability to navigate both the world of London society and the world of the militant suffragettes. Lady Winterton, with her simple periwinkle gown, immaculately coiffed chestnut hair, and angular features, was just as poised and elegant in either world. She was only five years older than Ursula, but already she seemed more at ease with herself than Ursula was ever likely to be. Lady Winterton did not appear to suffer Ursula's constant inner struggle between the demands of society and her social conscience.

"Well, don't spend too much time with them," Lady Winterton replied lightly. "If he can't be here, at least welcome the New Year knowing that he will return."

Without waiting for Ursula to respond, Lady Winterton drifted off into the tide of guests making their way into the drawing room. Besides their affiliation with the WSPU, both Ursula and Lady Winterton had imprudent relationships in common. At the tender age of nineteen, Lady Winterton had eloped with a penniless Irish peer, much to her family's dismay. Her husband's death three years later, however, had managed to mitigate the scandal, and Lady Winterton, with her family's support, had cast off the stigma of an inopportune marriage and converted herself into one of society's most sought-after young widows.

Ursula had no such talent. Her staunch defense of her suffragette friend Winifred Stanford-Jones against accusations of murder was still the subject of derision and censure. The fact that Laura Radcliffe, daughter of one of Ursula's father's close friends, Colonel Radcliffe, had been the murder victim as well as Winifred's lover had only fueled further speculation as to Ursula's motives in the case. Even her father's death at the hand of the murderer was insufficient to garner society's sympathy. What sealed Ursula's fate was not that she discovered the identity of the murderer, nor that he had been her fiancé, Tom Cumberland, it was that she had the temerity to drag a man of Lord Wrotham's stature and reputation into her "sordid little mess." Whereas Lady Winterton had accepted her role in society, Ursula continued to rail against its expectations. She had taken over her father's business, continued to maintain her suffragette and socialist views, and, worse still, had refused to countenance marriage.

Lady Winterton's words, nonetheless, provoked a pang of sympathy. She understood their double meaning. Lady Winterton's husband may not have been a suitable match for the wealthy daughter of an earl, but Ursula knew he had been the love of her life. His death cast as much of a pall over Lady Winterton's life as Ursula's father's death continued to do over hers. As Lady Winterton alluded, even if Lord Wrotham could not be here tonight, at least he was alive.

The warmth of the fireplace beckoned, and Ursula moved across to stand in the recess formed by the protruding chimney breast beside the glazed red tile overmantel. The room was getting crowded, and the air was thick with smoke and conversation. Out of the corner of her eye she saw Christopher Dobbs enter the room. Coarsely featured and dark-haired like his father, Obadiah Dobbs, Christopher (or "Topper" to his friends) was a permanent fixture in society's new young set. On his arm was a pale young girl with limpid blue eyes and painted red lips.

"Lady Winterton's standards must really be dropping," Ursula muttered.

Christopher Dobbs had taken over operations of the Dobbs Steamship Company following his father's nervous collapse the previous year—a collapse precipitated by the police investigation into the death of Laura Radcliffe and Robert Marlow, Ursula's father. Obadiah Dobbs's attempts to blackmail his business associates, revealed by this investigation, fueled endless speculation as the press tried to uncover the secrets Dobbs had planned to unveil. These secrets surrounded the fate of a young naturalist, Ronald Henry Bates, who had served on an expedition to Venezuela led by Colonel Radcliffe and financed by Ursula's father. The revelation that Bates had not died as previously thought, but had survived and was taking his revenge on the children of those associated with the expedition, caused Dobbs to suffer a nervous breakdown. Ursula suspected that

Christopher Dobbs blamed her for both his father's condition and his subsequent business troubles and she was understandably wary.

"Have you sought refuge here too?" A heavily accented voice interrupted Ursula's thoughts.

Ursula turned quickly and found herself facing a pair of dark, intense eyes. A woman about the same age as herself observed her with an enigmatic smile.

"Is it really that obvious?" Ursula asked.

"That you are unhappy? No. That you are an outsider? Yes."

The directness of the reply was unsettling.

"Can I ask what you mean by that exactly?" Ursula demanded.

The lady inclined her head slightly. "I meant no offense. Only I feel that you, just as I, do not belong here."

Ursula noticed the cut of the lady's rich burgundy dress and the sparkle of the diamonds and rubies that adorned her neck. There was something indefinable yet nonetheless exotic about this woman—the way her black hair was coiled above her head, the sallow smudge beneath her deep-set eyes, the curve of her hips accentuated by a dress that defied the current fashion with its tightly corseted waist. As her gaze returned to the lady's face, Ursula realized that she too was under scrutiny.

"By your dress, I can see that you are wealthy," the lady said bluntly, and Ursula flushed. The lady remained unaffected by Ursula's obvious embarrassment. Instead she continued, "That is a dress by Poiret, is it not?"

Her French pronunciation was impeccable.

Ursula nodded.

"I lived in Paris when I was a girl and used to dream of owning such a dress," the lady replied. "Now I, like you, have the money to possess such things. Though I've learned that money alone is not sufficient—it does not buy dreams, nor does it guarantee happiness."

Ursula watched as the fire flickered in the grate. An ember shifted, and a blue-yellow flame flared and died. She exhaled slowly. Money could not bring her father or mother back from the grave. It couldn't give her the freedom she craved or the man she loved.

The lady studied Ursula's face. "You are clearly wealthier than many in the room," she murmured. "Yet I sense you are not one of them. . . . You are not 'of the blood,' I think. . . ."

Ursula flushed. "I wasn't born into the aristocracy, if that's what you mean, no."

The lady nodded vigorously. "As I suspected. An outsider. I am Jewish, of course, which automatically makes me so, but I am also Russian and the daughter of a grain merchant." Ursula was graced with a sudden smile. "So you see, I will never be one of them," the lady concluded with an imperious flourish, gesturing to the crowd of guests that had filled the room.

"Well," Ursula replied in kind, "as the daughter of a mill owner and the granddaughter of a coal miner, I don't have much chance either."

"Then you and I will just have to become friends."

"Yes," Ursula replied. "I suppose we will," and she held out her hand to introduce herself formally.

"Katya Vilensky," the lady replied in turn. "My husband is standing over there by the doorway."

Ursula looked over and saw two men deep in conversation. One was tall and dark, with a neatly trimmed mustache and downcast eyes. He was fiddling with the chain of the gold fob watch in his waistcoat pocket. The other was an octogenarian with thinning white hair, leaning heavily on a silver-tipped cane. The name of Vilensky was well known in business circles. He was, after all, one of the most influential financiers in the city. Ursula, however, had not yet met him and she viewed both men with interest.

"Don't look so worried," Katya interjected. "He's not the one with the cane." Ursula had to laugh, and her spirits rallied for a moment. She tucked her arm in Katya's. "Mrs. Vilensky," she said, "I can tell we're going to get along famously. But first, I have to ask, what is your view on votes for women?"

Ursula soon found herself embroiled in a passionate discussion with Katya on the merits of the vote and whether it could provide the engine for true social change in England. Ursula concluded that she and Katya were alike in many ways. They were both struggling to assert their independence and uncertain about what the future held.

Katya told Ursula about her childhood—how she and her family fled Odessa for Paris, only to witness both her mother and father succumb to influenza in the winter of 1896. Katya was just sixteen years old when she and her sister were forced to leave school and become *mécaniciens* at a nearby garment factory.

"Having grown up around mills and factories all my life, I can imagine it must have been a hard existence." Ursula's voice was full of compassion.

"We survived," Katya replied simply. "We were luckier than most. I met Peter when I was nineteen. I was attending a Zionist meeting in the Marais—that's the Jewish quarter in Paris—and he was one of the speakers. I asked many questions, so many that he drew me aside after the meeting. We were married less than a month later."

"Gosh!" Ursula exclaimed involuntarily. "You didn't waste any time!"

Katya's smile faded. "Yes, many people have suggested that it was Peter's money that I fell in love with so quickly, but it wasn't. I simply knew the moment I met him that he was the man I was to marry. The fifteen years between us didn't matter. The fact that I was poor did not matter. At least, it didn't used to. . . ." Katya stopped.

Ursula shifted uncomfortably from one foot to the other.

"My apologies." Katya recovered briskly. "But I wonder sometimes if rumors have a way of getting into someone's blood and poisoning it."

Ursula frowned, unsure how to respond. Katya's mood seemed to switch suddenly, but Ursula, who was herself the subject of endless speculation and gossip, felt compelled to empathize. She understood all too well the toxic power of rumors. She was about to enquire further when Katya, in yet another mood shift, demanded to know about Ursula's family instead.

"My mother died when I was very young," Ursula said quietly. "I don't remember much about her." As always, she felt a pang of regret as she said these words. In many ways it was a lie. She could still conjure up the scent of orange blossom, the touch of her mother's kiss upon her cheek, or the remembrance of her smile. Ursula blinked. It was discomfiting how easily a stranger's question could reawaken those childhood memories.

"What about your father?" Katya asked.

Ursula took a deep breath. "He was killed."

"Killed?!" Katya's voice dropped to a hoarse whisper. "But of course, Robert Marlow. I remember now." She caught Ursula's hand in hers. "You need say nothing more, I read enough in the newspapers."

"What's all this about newspapers?" Lady Winterton's voice interrupted them. "I never believe anything I read anymore! Lord Northcliffe has ruined the noble profession of journalism once and for all." Lord Northcliffe was arguably the most powerful newspaper proprietor in Britain. His newspapers were constantly fueling public fear of the so-called "German Peril."

"I'm not sure it was ever very noble, but thanks all the same," Ursula responded. Before the events that took her father from her, it had been Ursula's dream to be a journalist—an ambition that remained unsatisfied. After her father's death, she had assumed control of his textile empire, and in doing so gave up that aspiration.

Ursula turned and introduced Katya to Lady Catherine Winterton.

"I've only met your husband up until now," Lady Winterton replied with a smile. "But as I see that you and Ursula are already friends, I feel sure you and I will be too. Has she convinced you to come to our local WSPU branch meeting on Monday?"

Katya laughed. "She has."

"Excellent!"

As Lady Winterton turned to Ursula, her finely sculptured features creased into a frown. "I had hoped that Lord Wrotham would be back in time to be here . . . ," she prompted.

"He's still abroad." Ursula's reply was swift. Lady Winterton's eyes narrowed for a moment before she flashed Ursula another wide smile.

"This must be the third time in as many months. I can't think what a barrister like him would be doing over there!"

"He has a number of international clients that demand his attention," Ursula answered cautiously. Even she didn't know the full extent of Lord Wrotham's duties as a 'gentleman negotiator' for the British government, and she was acutely aware that, given the clandestine nature of most of his recent trips abroad, she should be careful not to divulge too much. "I'm sure he is very busy with his legal cases," she finished lamely.

"No doubt," Lady Winterton answered dryly.

Ursula's face reddened. She knew she sounded naive.

Katya turned to Ursula as Lady Winterton walked away and opened her mouth to speak.

Ursula held up her hand. "Don't ask," she said. "Let's just say that Lord Wrotham is yet another reason why I'll never be accepted as one of *them*."

Katya raised her eyebrows but said nothing.

Out of the corner of her eye, Ursula saw Christopher Dobbs approach Peter Vilensky, and her countenance darkened. She felt conflicted about Vilensky. His wife seemed to be a kindred spirit, but what of her husband? Since Peter Vilensky had opened his checkbook, the Dobbs Steamship Company had grown exponentially and now represented one of the most important shipping companies in the Mediterranean. Ursula was well aware of the magnitude of the investment Vilensky had made. It had saved the company from ruin. Given all that had happened in the past, Ursula was not sure she could ever quite forgive Vilensky for helping Obadiah Dobbs's son become one of London society's wealthiest young men.

Katya followed Ursula's gaze, and her eyes narrowed. "Ah," she announced blandly. "I see Mr. Dobbs has found my husband."

Ursula looked at her swiftly. This was hardly the tone she expected from the wife of someone so closely associated with Christopher Dobbs.

"Don't look so surprised," Katya responded. "I saw how you reacted when he first arrived. And you need not be concerned. Although many of my compatriots have reached the Holy Land aboard Dobbs's ships, I still cannot bring myself to trust the man."

Ursula blinked.

"I'm sure you are aware that conditions across Russia are very difficult. My husband has provided funds for several agricultural settlements—we call them *moshavot*—situated just outside Jaffa. Dobbs's ships have transported nearly one hundred men, women, and children to a new life in Palestine. Unlike my husband, however, I am not deceived by Mr. Dobbs or his charm. I do not believe he does anything except serve his own interests."

Ursula was about to respond when Peter Vilensky looked up from his discussion with Dobbs and signaled for Katya to join them. Katya sighed. "I must go," she said, clasping Ursula's hand. "But I am glad to have found another outsider with whom to view the world."

"Me too," Ursula answered, noting the resignation in Katya's voice.

"I hope to see you Monday," Ursula urged. "At the WSPU meeting?"

"I will try. We are in the midst of making preparations for another trip to Palestine. My husband and Baron Rothschild are considering a new land trust, and it is important for us to visit. We are hoping to visit Egypt en route back to England."

"Why, I'm going to Egypt in a few weeks—for business, I'm afraid, not pleasure. Perhaps we will also see each other there?" Ursula caught sight of Peter Vilensky signaling again, this time a flash of irritation passing across his face.

"I would like that very much, but now I really must go." Katya's eyes flickered between her husband and Ursula. She kissed Ursula gently on both cheeks. "May the new year bring you health, happiness, and continued wealth."

"For you, too," Ursula replied. She could feel the tension in Katya's embrace. Ursula was uneasy. Peter Vilensky's summons was so peremptory—as if his wife was little more than a servant, to be summarily ordered to do whatever he chose. It annoyed her, but Ursula had learned by now not to display such feelings in public. Instead she reflected, once again, on the repressive nature of marriage.

Katya joined her husband and Christopher Dobbs, leaving Ursula standing alone beside the fire. Mrs. Pomfrey-Smith, an old friend of her father's, soon sought her out, and Ursula endured her gossip and advice for nearly half an hour ("Ursula, no man, not even Lord Wrotham himself, is going to abide a woman telling him that he's wrong; that's the problem with educating you young women—you will disagree with people all the time! Mark my words, a man is much happier hearing you discuss redecorating the sitting room than he is hearing about votes for women. . . .").

As midnight approached, Lady Winterton gathered her guests in the vaulted entrance hall of her Kensington home. Ursula found herself uncomfortably wedged between Mrs. Pomfrey-Smith and Brigadier Galbraith as she watched Lady Winterton ascend the stairs and stand next to the grandfather clock on the landing. They waited as the clock struck twelve. A violinist appeared at the top of the stairs and began to play. The crowd responded in turn, and soon the hall resonated to the strains of "Auld Lang Syne." Lady Winterton waved her champagne glass and bid them all Happy New Year.

A draft of cold air crossed the hall and lifted the fringe on the bottom of Ursula's dress. She turned, craning her neck to see above the crowd of heads, but no one had entered through the front door. There was only Lady Winterton's footman, standing in the narrow portico. His countenance seemed prescient somehow, silent and grave. Hardly a good omen, Ursula thought bleakly, for the year that lay ahead.

TWO

A week later, Ursula Marlow and Winifred Stanford-Jones sat side by side on the high-backed Mackmurdo sofa. Winifred, with her navy trousers and striped shirt, shoes off and feet propped up on the low ottoman, looked like a young man contemplating life through the haze of cigarette smoke. In fact, she was Ursula's good friend and fellow suffragette. They had met at Oxford University, and while both shared a passion for politics and writing, Winifred preferred drafting political manifestos to journalism. She also owed Ursula her life. Without Ursula's determination to clear her name, Winifred would have spent her life as a patient at Broadmoor, an asylum for the criminally insane.

Winifred extinguished the cigarette in the small ceramic ashtray on the side table and immediately lit another. Ursula had banned her from smoking her pipe inside ("such a ghastly smell, Freddie!"), so Winifred had to be content with her Gauloises. Ursula, in her stylish afternoon dress by Cheruit and dark auburn hair coiled about the nape of her neck, presented a total contrast to Winifred's mannish figure. It was as if Hades and Persephone had risen from the underworld to sit side by side in an English parlor.

Ursula looked up from her notes and stretched her arms above her with a yawn. She had recently finished redecorating the front parlor, and she surveyed it with satisfaction. Finally, almost two years after her father's death, she could call Chester Square *her* home. She had had the whole house repainted, new drapes and furniture ordered; she'd even arranged for the servants' quarters to be refurbished. The only room that remained in its original state was her father's study. Apart from removing a number of his files to be archived, Ursula couldn't bear the thought of changing anything in his room. It provided her with both a poignant reminder of him and a place of sanctuary. She could often be found there, curled up in her father's armchair, on a rainy Sunday afternoon, drawing comfort from the familiarity of his books and belongings.

The front parlor had been painted eggshell blue, and the fireplace, once white marble, was now adorned with glazed green and blue tiles. On the east wall hung two paintings by Wassily Kandinsky, maelstroms of color and bold black lines. Instead of the plush velvet drapes her father had favored, silvery damask curtains now adorned the bay windows. On the mantel was the Liberty Tudric pewter bowl Lord Wrotham had given her and a green Farnham pottery vase filled with tall white tulips.

"We're accepting twenty-five apprentices to start with," Ursula said. "The room isn't large, but it's well ventilated, and we can fit three long tables in through here. We can then set up the cutting room next door and put in a row of sewing machines, like so—" She pointed to the pencil-drawn map that lay in her lap. "The nursery annex will go here, next to the cafeteria. There's a formidable local lady, Mrs. Murchison, who'll run both of these for me. She used to work at a Dr. Barnado's orphanage in Birkdale." She looked at Winifred eagerly. "So what do you think?"

"Hmm . . . ," Winifred replied, drawing on her cigarette.

"Oh, Freddie! You know it's a good plan. These aren't women with many options. I can provide them with a basic wage, child care, and vocational training as well as one hot meal a day. I don't know of any other place that would offer this—not to these women. Most of the factories in the area wouldn't even spare them the time of day!"

Ursula had read about the pioneering work by Cadbury and had resolved to try in her own small way to emulate it by setting up a factory in Oldham in which women who had "fallen on hard times" could get the opportunity to work and receive training as seamstresses. Such women included those whose husbands had deserted them and who had young children still to clothe and feed. There were also women who, for whatever reason, found themselves without any family or support. Ursula had visited the local workhouses as a child and had been horrified by what she had seen. She was now determined to offer an alternative for poor women such as these—somewhere they could find employment and receive not only a decent wage and a meal but also a place for their children to be looked after.

Winifred broke into a wide but guarded smile. "It's a splendid plan, Sully. I just wonder how you're going to convince 'that lot' to go along with it." Winifred used the pet name she had given Ursula while they were at Somerville College, Oxford.

Ursula knew "that lot" referred to Lord Wrotham and Gerard Anderson, two of her father's most trusted friends who now, in capacity of trustee and financial adviser, still held much of the power over her father's estate.

"Oh, let me worry about them." Ursula replied airily.

"I'm not worried about Anderson—you can manage him all right. It's Lord Wrotham I'm not so sure about."

Ursula abruptly got to her feet and walked over to the bay window that overlooked Chester Square. It had been a bleak winter, despite Christmas with Winifred's aunt in Yorkshire, but today, at least, the rain had stopped. The sun, however, remained stubbornly trapped behind the low, leaden clouds. There had hardly been a clear, dry day since Ursula returned to London to attend Lady Winterton's New Year's Eve party.

"Don't be angry," Winifred responded to the unspoken rebuke. "You know exactly what I mean."

Ursula rubbed her nose.

"Sully," Winifred then said in gentler tones, "it's been a really tough year for you. What with the strikes and accidents at the mills and factories. I just want you to choose your battles carefully. And as for Lord Wrotham, well—" Winifred paused for a moment. "Are you sure you really know what you're doing?"

"Getting myself into even more scandal, that's for sure," Ursula responded nonchalantly, but her face belied her tone.

Winifred rose from the sofa and walked over to her friend. She placed a hand on her shoulder, but Ursula continued to stare resolutely out of the window.

"Why must it always come down to marriage?" Ursula finally asked.

Winifred leaned against the wall and folded her arms. "Because for a man like Wrotham, it always does." The Seventh Baron Wrotham and eminent King's Counsel, Lord Oliver Wrotham was one of the many peers of the realm who had to earn his living to preserve his family estate, Bromley Hall, from financial ruin. Since Venezuela, Ursula's relationship with Lord Wrotham had gone from "complicated" to "fraught" as he wrestled with society's censure over their unlikely romantic liaison and its failure to materialize into matrimony.

"But I'm just finding out what it means to be me—not my father's daughter, not somebody's fiancée, but *me*. I want to learn how to do it on my own. Otherwise, no one's going to respect me, no one's going to believe I actually succeeded in running my father's business. Not if I'm married to him."

"No need to convince me. You know my views on the whole marriage thing."

"I know." Ursula sighed.

"But even if I felt differently, I would understand why you need more time. After what happened with Tom . . ."

Ursula shivered at the unwelcome reminder of her onetime fiancé, Tom Cumberland—the man who had murdered her father. The man who had tried to murder her. Ursula blinked. Even today, she could not forget the image of the judge, in his ivory wig and black-and-red gown, as he leaned over, staring at the prisoner, and delivered his sentence. *You will be taken from hence to a lawful prison, and from thence to a place of execution, and there you will be hanged by the neck until you are dead.* Ursula had sat transfixed by these words, even as the crowd in the public gallery began to disperse. Even as Winifred, with tears in her eyes, urged her to leave. She had sat, cold and numb, as all those around her departed. It wasn't until Lord Wrotham, who had been seated behind the prosecutor, rose and came over to her that the trance was broken. His voice, low and calm, had washed over her. She had then stood up, clasped his hand, and together all three of them had left the court.

Winifred tapped her arm gently. "That was thoughtless of me. I shouldn't have reminded you."

"It's all right," Ursula replied, rubbing her temples. The unbidden image of Tom, standing in the dock, however, remained in her mind. "It's not like either of us are likely to forget."

Winifred looked away. The revenge Tom had exacted on behalf of his father had affected her just as badly as it had Ursula. Accused of murdering her female lover, Winifred still bore the emotional scars of her time spent in Holloway Prison awaiting trial. She owed Ursula and Lord Wrotham a debt of gratitude too great to ever be repaid, for finding out the truth and gaining her acquittal. All she could do was remain Ursula's steadfast friend.

A familiar gray Daimler come to a halt at the curb outside. Winifred glanced at Ursula and, seeing her look of surprise, gave Ursula's hand a tight squeeze.

"That's my cue to leave," Winifred said in low tones. "We can speak more at tomorrow night's committee meeting. We're at Lady Winterton's, remember—and be careful, the police are keeping a close watch on our activities now." As members of the militant WSPU, Winifred and Ursula were under increased scrutiny, especially since the start of the WSPU's window-smashing campaign.

"Don't worry," Ursula replied as she watched the familiar tall, lean frame get out of the motor car. "I think I can manage to avoid the likes of Inspector Harrison." Harrison was the detective who had led the investigation into the deaths of Laura Radcliffe, Cecilia Abbott, and Ursula's father, Robert Marlow. He was also the man who had arrested Winifred on charges of murder.

Winifred kissed her on the cheek. "Harrison's been promoted, my dear; he's now got bigger things to worry about than us, like German spies and the invasion of England!"

Ursula remembered that six months ago, after having been promoted to chief inspector, Harrison had seemingly disappeared from the ranks of the Metropolitan Police. Rumor had it that he was now a member of the Special Branch of Scotland Yard.

A knock at the door dismissed all thoughts of Chief Inspector Harrison from her mind.

Biggs, Ursula's butler, entered the parlor and announced, "Lord Wrotham to see you, Miss."

Really, Biggs could be such a martinet sometimes.

Lord Wrotham walked through the doorway, immaculately dressed in a navy pin-striped suit, round collar, and flawlessly executed necktie. Tall and self-possessed, he exuded such total confidence that it always seemed, whether he was in a court of law, the House of Lords, or here in Ursula's parlor, that he owned the room. His physical presence, perfectly proportioned and sleek, had a potent effect on Ursula. She felt the irresistible pull of his attraction.

"I told Biggs not to worry with introductions," Lord Wrotham said with the ghost of a smile. "I think you know who I am by now."

He took three strides into the room before he saw Winifred and stopped short.

"Miss Stanford-Jones," he said coolly, and Ursula sensed with annoyance his disapproval.

"Why, Lord Wrotham, we were just discussing our campaign to fire-bomb the Houses of Parliament!" Winifred replied without hesitation. Lord Wrotham's countenance darkened. "Actually," she continued with a half smile on her face, as if it amused her to see that her association with Ursula still irked him, "I was just leaving."

Ursula accompanied Winifred to the door as Biggs left to collect Winifred's square-topped Derby hat and long, loose coat. She kissed Winifred lightly on the cheek as she murmured her goodbye. After Winifred bid Lord Wrotham breezy adieu, Ursula closed the door behind her and stood for a moment with her back to him.

"I thought you weren't due back for another week," she ventured. Ursula remembered their last meeting, the night before he was due to leave for the Balkans on his clandestine mission for the British government, and wasn't sure how to react to him now.

"Our talks did not go as well as we had hoped," Lord Wrotham responded. "I came straight here from Liverpool Street station."

Ursula detected a weariness in his tone that immediately roused her pity. She turned round swiftly. "You sound awfully tired."

He was still standing in the middle of the room, arms crossed. His gray-blue eyes took aim at hers. She felt like a defendant in the dock, waiting for him to make his closing argument. She knew him well enough by now to recognize that his self-control rarely faltered, and she could not bear it. She wanted to shatter his resolve, and yet when she recalled their last conversation, when she thought of her angry refusal ("I will not be forced into marriage just because society demands it!"), she wanted only to be in his arms and seek forgiveness.

She started to walk toward him but hesitated and stopped.

"I missed you," was all she said.

He turned away quickly.

"Damn it!" he cursed, and Ursula took some satisfaction that his composure had already snapped. "I can't do this, Ursula," he said angrily as he walked over and gripped the mantel with both his hands. "I can't go back to the way it was."

Ursula walked over to the fireplace and stood beside him, blinking back her tears. He leaned over to gaze into the cold, empty grate. She and Winifred had been so engrossed in their discussions, they had failed to notice the fire dying out.

"Nothing has changed since I left," he continued. "I told you that I needed an answer. My reputation cannot survive much more of this. We must be married or be done with it. You may be able to flout society's conventions, but I cannot afford to do so. My good name and reputation are all that I have."

Ursula placed her hand on his arm, feeling the soft, light brush of his cashmere suit jacket as he pulled away. She could see the edge where his round-tabbed collar attached to his white linen shirt as he readjusted the gold tie pin on his crimson necktie.

"I never wanted to place your reputation in jeopardy," she said quietly. "But I don't understand why you cannot wait. I just need more time to—"

"Time to what?" he interrupted her sharply. "Time to reconcile yourself to the appalling prospect of being married to me? I don't want that, Ursula, and well you know it."

He started to pace up and down the edge of the room. Ursula could hear the strike of his oxford shoes on the wooden floor beating out an uneasy rhythm to the silence between them, and her head started to ache. "I just need more time," she repeated, staring bleakly into the fireplace.

She heard him approach and felt the warmth of his hand through the light woolen weave of her dress as he pressed it against her shoulder.

He kissed her softly on the nape of her neck.

"Your hesitation is my answer."

Ursula swung round to face him. She gripped his hands in hers. "It is not my answer!" she retorted fiercely.

"Neither is your previous assertion that you love me but cannot marry me."

"But it's true." Her voice sounded small.

"It may be true," he responded, "but it's not enough for me."

Three

After hours in front of the long trestle tables lined with duplicating machines, cranking out copies of *Votes for Women*, Winifred pulled Ursula aside and asked if she would stay for a meeting with Lady Winterton. Preparations were under way for Mrs. Pankhurst to speak at the following Monday afternoon meeting at the London Pavilion, but Ursula was preoccupied with the breach between her and Lord Wrotham, as well as her upcoming business trip to Egypt. Nevertheless, for Winifred's sake, she agreed to stay.

Winifred perched on the edge of a wooden desk, her boots propped up on one of the chairs, and signaled for Ursula and Lady Winterton to take a seat.

"Thanks for staying," she began. "I've been asked by Christabel Pankhurst to chat with you both about a project we need help with. This"—Winifred held up a piece of paper—"is a communication sent to our sisters in Portsmouth. It uses our usual codes and gives details of a protest on Thursday, coinciding with Churchill's inspection of the Royal Naval Dockyards."

Ursula frowned; she was not aware of plans for any such protest, and she was only vaguely aware that the WSPU had taken to using special codes to thwart the police.

"It was only a test," Winifred confirmed. "We wanted to see whether the police were intercepting our messages. As you know, the police continue to watch us closely—they've been seen photographing us at events—even in Holloway Prison—and we're growing worried they may be mouting efforts to infiltrate our ranks and preempt our activities."

"What happened with the test message?" Lady Winterton asked.

"We believe it was intercepted and decoded. We know that the local police were planning to bring in additional men as a precaution." Winifred pulled out her pipe from her jacket pocket and proceeded to stuff it with tobacco. "I think this shows that we urgently need to address the issue of secrecy in our communications; otherwise, the police may soon be able to discover and preempt our every move."

Lady Winterton shifted in her chair. "Not an idea I would relish," she commented.

"No," Ursula agreed.

"The Pankhursts want us to try come up with a better system—but we must do so in complete secrecy. It is vital that we do not disrupt WSPU operations or, more important, let anyone who may be a police informer find out what we're doing."

Mrs. Emmeline Pankhurst and her daughter Christabel were the leaders of the WSPU and proponents of the new wave of militancy.

Winifred prodded the bowl of her pipe with her finger and waited for the news to sink in.

"Now Mrs. P and Christabel have already made it clear that we are entering a new phase of militancy," Winifred added. "The WSPU needs a strategy that uses the element of surprise, even shock, to our advantage."

Ursula chewed her lip thoughtfully. "What do you propose?" she asked.

"You are two of the smartest women I know," Winifred responded, lighting her pipe. "Lady Winterton, I'm sure we can put your linguistic skills to good use."

Having had an excellent tutor as a child, Lady Winterton was fluent in French and German as well as Russian (her mother's family was related, after all, to the tsarina's family). She was also proficient in translating ancient Greek and Latin. Ursula always thought Lady Winterton would have made an excellent scholar, but her family disapproved of university education.

"And Sully," Winifred continued, "I seem to recall you got interested in ciphers at Somerville. . . ."

Ursula had studied political history at Somerville College at Oxford, and in her second year had become interested in Mary, Queen of Scots, and the secret code she had used to communicate with her conspirators in the plot to incite rebellion and assassinate Queen Elizabeth I.

"I was only dabbling!" Ursula protested. "I'd hardly call it anything more than that!"

"Well, it's better than nothing," Winifred retorted.

Ursula rubbed her eyes. "I do remember asking my father once, and he told me about the Vigenère cipher. I can't say I remember much more about it—except that it remained indecipherable until the middle of last century."

"Your father knew about ciphers?" Lady Winterton asked.

"A little, I suppose. He was certainly concerned about the potential for industrial espionage, but as far as I'm aware he never actually employed a cipher in his business communications."

"Given some of your recent problems with his mills and factories, maybe you should think about doing so yourself," Lady Winterton observed.

"Perhaps," Ursula conceded. "But I have learned one thing from all that I've read—almost every cipher to date has been broken. Freddie"—she turned back to face Winifred—"what makes you think we could come up with anything better?"

A curl of smoke rose from Winifred's pipe. "It's worth at least trying. I still have contacts with some other groups who have explored similar issues."

"You mean anarchists and Bolsheviks?" Lady Winterton interjected with distaste.

Winifred merely shrugged. "You needn't worry, I won't drag you into any of that sort of thing."

"I should hope not," Lady Winterton retorted. "Some of us have reputations to keep."

Winifred's eyes narrowed, but Ursula intervened quickly.

"Now is hardly the time," she chided. "We need to work together, not create more divisions." Ursula was fully aware that the WSPU contained many different social elements, often in conflict over the degree of militancy, the power of the Pankhursts, and not least, the influence of socialism. Winifred was a strong supporter of Sylvia Pankhurst's desire to ally female suffrage with other social equity issues. Lady Winterton, however, was true to her own class. She wanted the vote, but she didn't subscribe to any socialist ideals.

"Will you at least work with me?" Winifred asked after a pause. "See if we can try to develop a more secure means of communicating with our sisters? It could make the difference between future success and failure."

"Of course," Ursula replied without hesitation. "You know I'll help you, Freddie, any way that I can."

Lady Winterton seemed reticent, but eventually she too nodded.

"I won't be able to do anything for a while," Ursula reminded Winifred. "I'm not back from Egypt until April."

Winifred pulled out a small notebook and pencil from her skirt pocket and began to write. "That reminds me, here is the name of someone who may be useful to contact—Mrs. Mahfouz. She has started a nascent movement to push for universal suffrage. She's also married to an Egyptian nationalist, so she believes Britain must first withdraw from Egypt. She has written some pieces for the Women's Press, so I think it would be useful to speak to her."

"Thank you," Ursula said as she folded the piece of paper. "I will definitely try to contact her."

"She may be able to share the nationalists' experience with keeping communications secret," Winifred agreed before flicking open the fob watch she wore tucked into her waistcoat.

"Who knows, I may even get an interview out of all this," Ursula said, rising to her feet. "Maybe I'll finally get asked to write an article for *Lady's Realm* that deals with something other than the latest fashion in hats!"

"We'd better go," Winifred cautioned them. "Another meeting is starting at three fifteen, and I don't want to raise any suspicions. But first"—she eyed them with a grin—"let's make sure the police aren't already waiting for us outside."

Part Two

Egypt

Four

Mena House Hotel, Giza, Egypt
MARCH 1912

Ursula stood beneath the arched window watching the sun set behind the Pyramids of Giza. The twilight, starlit and blue, was scented with jasmine. She inhaled deeply and sighed as she leaned against the balcony that overlooked the fragrant gardens below. Ursula had been staying at Mena House for two weeks now and had come to love the early evening, when the heat of the day began to dissipate and the blue-black shadows crept across the desert. A soft breeze fluttered the hem of her crepe de chine evening dress. She closed her eyes and breathed in the night.

For the first time in ages, she felt briefly free of the burdens of the past. Although it was well known that she had come to Egypt to secure cotton supplies for her Lancashire mills, no one knew of her fierce struggle to keep her father's textile empire intact. Few knew about the Laura Radcliffe case or the lengths to which Ursula had gone to save Winifred from the gallows. Even fewer cared that she, a wealthy heiress of barely twenty-four, militant suffragette, and member of the Fabian Society, had had the audacity to reject Lord Oliver Wrotham's marriage proposal. Nobody in Egypt was interested in such things—everyone had their own secrets to keep.

Ursula opened the palm of her hand and looked again at the photograph. It was really nothing more than a cheap souvenir, but it brought back memories of a pleasant afternoon spent exploring the Giza plateau with Katya Vilensky. The photograph had been taken only two weeks ago by an enterprising sheik who, in his flowing black cloak and red tarboosh, had followed them from the hotel. It captured them up close, framed in the background by the recumbent Sphinx. From her sensible khaki skirt and white shirt to her wide-brimmed straw hat and the freckles visible on her cheeks and nose, there was no mistaking Ursula for being anything but English. Katya, however, with her embroidered white dress, headscarf, and dark brooding eyes, looked even more exotic in the photograph than in real life.

Ursula had known Katya for only a brief few months since New Year's Eve, but had delighted in being with a strong, independent woman like herself. Katya had arrived in Egypt a week after Ursula, and became a welcome ally at the nightly functions and parties first in Alexandria and later in Cairo. Weary of her negotiations, Ursula reveled in Katya's love of literature and art. Ursula's presence also seemed to lift the air of melancholy surrounding Katya, as if in each other's presence the pain of the past was forgotten.

Ursula gripped the photograph tightly. A wave of nausea swept over her. With Katya's death, the past she had tried to set aside again intruded. She felt the old pain of loss, the old feelings of despair, and a palpable sense of horror that still sickened her. How could it not? Her father's death was never far from her thoughts, and she had been with Katya in the Khan el-Khalili bazaar that day. She had seen Katya die. It was not something to be ignored or forgotten, despite what the Egyptian authorities urged her to do.

Katya had been looking for scented oils to take back to England for her sister, and Ursula had accompanied her, eager to procure some attar of roses for herself. When questioned about her sister, Katya responded with a jerk, noting that her husband's disapproval precluded them from maintaining regular contact. Ursula and Katya had decided to forgo the fashionable shops of Emad al-Din in favor of the historic bazaar. They walked along the crowded, narrow passageways, past the vendors sitting atop their mastabas, the stone steps in front of their tiny shops.

Katya and Ursula were just passing under a vaulted gateway and making their way down the Sikkit al-Badistan when they became separated as a group of young men, clad in long brown cloaks and white turbans, swarmed about them, shouting and calling out in the confusion. At first Ursula was amused. One man's monkey climbed up onto her shoulders, and she delighted in placing a ripe date in its tiny paws. Another man waved a tray filled with brass and copper vessels in front of her.

Beneath the covered canopy and the projecting windows of the upper floors, with their delicate latticework, the air was dusty and dim. Hazy sunbeams filtered slowly to the ground. Ursula tried to catch a glimpse of Katya, but all she could see were jostling images, flashes of white cloth and dark eyes, and the monkey with its red jeweled waistcoat jumping up and down, clapping its paws. She called out Katya's name and weaved her way between the men, finally catching sight of her amid the tumult and swirling dust. Ursula saw a flutter of concern in Katya's eyes, and she pointed to the monkey with a laugh. Katya's eyes, however, widened with fear. Something, Ursula realized, was terribly wrong.

Ursula shrugged the monkey off her back and pushed her way through the crowd. She heard a shrill cry of pain and was seized by panic as she fought to move forward against the noise and chaos. Dust and grit stung her eyes. She was making little headway, for the men were suddenly massed before her like a human wall, their limbs outstretched, torsos rigidly repelling any advance. Ursula called out Katya's name again as she struggled against the men, but she could not see or hear her. Then, as suddenly as they had arrived, the crowd began to disperse. Ursula became disoriented as they scattered about her, shouting and raising their fists in the air. Caught off balance, she stumbled to her knees and her hat fell off. By the time she got to her feet and shook the dust from her skirt, the men had vanished.

The laneway was now eerily empty. Even the shopkeepers had left their mastabas and closed the wooden doors to their stalls. All that remained was a lone donkey boy, his braying charge, and an elderly beggar asleep on the steps of the mosque of Sayidna Hussein. Ursula looked around wildly. In her confusion it took her a few minutes to realize that slumped against one of the wooden stalls was the body of Katya Vilensky. At first Ursula thought she had merely fainted, until she saw the bloodstain soaking through her white embroidered dress. And this brought it all back—her father lying in her arms, his eyes looking up at her as the life left him. At first Ursula could not move; the horror of death held her once more in its thrall, and she was powerless. She stood rooted to the ground until a voice within her, with a sudden and terrible calm, urged her to Katya's side. She rushed over and knelt down beside the body, listening first for her breath then laying her trembling fingers against Katya's pale, exposed neck. There was no sound of breath. There was no beat beneath her fingertips. There was only the heat and the taste of sweat upon her lips.

"Miss, will you not take some of this?" Julia's voice intruded upon her thoughts.

Ursula clutched the photograph and tried to clear her mind.

Julia was standing in the archway, clad in her lady's maid's outfit—black dress and white pinafore—holding a bottle of Boots Pure Drug Company Sleeping Draught in her hands.

Ursula turned around and shook her head. "No, truly, Julia. That stuff is absolutely vile. I'm sure I'll be fine."

Since the terrible events in the Khan el-Khalili bazaar, Ursula had found it almost impossible to sleep. Night after night she tried without success to vanquish the images of Katya's and her father's deaths from her mind. But the images always returned, refusing to let her rest.

"I'll be going to bed in a few minutes. Don't worry about me." Ursula tried to sound reassuring, but Julia looked unconvinced. "It's late," Ursula continued; "you need to get a good night's rest."

Since arriving in Egypt Julia had served as both Ursula's lady's maid and her companion. The prospect of accompanying Ursula had thrilled Julia for a time, but now that their return to England was fast approaching, she seemed reassured by the fact that, back in London, she would be relieved of such a role.

Julia opened her mouth to protest.

"You've already laid out everything for tomorrow," Ursula said, pointing to the linen suit laid out carefully across the chaise longue. "So please, get some sleep. I'll see you in the morning."

Reluctantly Julia placed the sleeping draught down on the bedside table with a murmured "Just in case you change your mind" and took her leave, retreating to the adjoining room.

Ursula leaned her head against the railing. She found herself going over and over those last conversations with Katya, trying desperately to make sense of her death. The Egyptian authorities had refused to widen their investigations. To them it was an obvious political act. Katya, stabbed by unknown assailants in Cairo's Khan el-Khalili bazaar, was nothing more than a victim of circumstance, a pawn in the Egyptian nationalists' plan to disrupt English rule. Ever since the assassination of Egypt's prime minister Boutros Ghali in February 1910, the Cairo police had been monitoring nationalist activities. Katya's death provided them with an ideal opportunity to detain a number of suspected members for questioning. Given Katya's nationalist sympathies and her Russian rather than English origins, Ursula found it hard to believe that her death was politically motivated. How would her death have served those fighting against English colonial rule? An editorial in the nationalist paper *Al-Liwa* by the leader of the Nationalist Party denied any knowledge of or responsibility for what occurred. The Egyptian authorities, however, refused to countenance any alternative theory, and Ursula was left to brood over her doubts alone.

Ursula remembered Katya's words the morning of her death. They had been sitting on the hotel's terrace, looking across the gardens. Katya had a faraway look in her eyes. "It's incredible, is it not," she began in her heavily accented English, "how easily dreams can be made"—she waved a hand toward the Great Pyramid of Khufu—"when you have power over so many lives." Her expression darkened as she continued. "But what to do when you realize you are powerless? When the dream is not what it seems. What if the costs are too high, and yet you can do nothing?"

Ursula was just about to dismiss the comment as nothing more than pensive reflection when she saw the raw anguish on Katya's face. She leaned across the table and clasped her friend's hand.

"What is it?" Ursula cried.

Katya moved her hand away quickly. "Nothing." She wiped her eyes with her napkin, but Ursula could see her scrutinizing the terrace to see if anyone was watching them. "Please." Katya looked at her with a startling intensity. "Forget I said anything. It is no longer safe. . . ."

In the week since that terrible day, Ursula had tried in vain to comprehend what had occurred. Attacks on Western women in Cairo were rare, despite concerns over the rise in anti-European feeling. Ursula was also puzzled by Peter Vilensky's reaction to his wife's death. Although in the short time she had known him he had always presented a cold, austere countenance, the absence of any real outpouring of grief at his wife's death shocked her. Peter Vilensky had merely made the necessary arrangements to have his wife's body buried in her beloved Palestine with clinical calculation and entered the initial seven days of the Jewish mourning period of shivah.

Ursula shook her head. It wouldn't do to fuel Julia's concerns any further by staying out on the balcony all night, worrying about Katya's death. She took a few steps back, but the sound of voices in the garden below drew her to the balcony rail once more.

Beneath the lights she recognized the tall figure of Hugh Carmichael and the balding, florid countenance of Ambrose Whittaker, engaged in conversation. Though almost old enough to be her father, Hugh Carmichael cut a dashing figure in his evening suit and white silk bow tie. After three weeks' acquaintance, she was used to seeing his nonchalant stride as well as hearing his soft San Franciscan drawl. The owner of one of the largest shipyards in England and a self-confessed adventurer, Hugh was in Egypt to indulge in his latest obsession—flying. Despite his casual manner, Ursula had found a surprising adherent in Hugh. A widower still devoted to the memory of his English wife, who had been an avowed pacifist and suffragette, Hugh treated Ursula just as he treated his male business colleagues. They had developed an easy and respectful rapport, untainted by the sexual tension Ursula usually encountered in her business dealings.

Next to him Ambrose Whittaker, his thinning hair swept across his forehead, looked every inch the Anglo-Egyptian official. Although he was an adviser to the Ministry of Interior and a reputed expert on Alexandrian art, Ursula considered him an all-round pompous idiot.

"There's a new man in town," Whittaker began. "Keen as mustard to speak to you. He's looking into that dreadful incident in the Khan el-Khalili."

Ursula edged closer to the rail.

"I don't know why he'd want to speak to me," Hugh replied, tossing his cigarette aside. "I wasn't even there."

Whittaker proffered him another cigarette from a silver case. "That's just the thing, old boy; looks like this new man's taking over the investigation, and I guess he wants to know what your story is."

"What my story is—" Hugh's voice rose with irritation. "I hardly think there's a story for me to tell. He should be speaking to Miss Marlow on that score, though from what she's told me, there was too much confusion in the bazaar to see anything much. So there really is nothing to say, is there, *old boy*." Hugh's emphasized these final words sarcastically.

"Oh, I don't know." Whittaker shrugged and stepped out of the lamplight. He was trying to sound nonchalant, but Ursula was not deceived.

"Come on, man, out with it!" Hugh replied. "You're obviously not here for an idle chat."

"It's really nothing—just wanted to give you a heads-up if the chief inspector should ask you anything. He's arriving tonight, don't you know. And from what I've heard, he's quite an important man in Scotland Yard these days."

"I thought the Egyptian authorities said it was a political matter which *they* were handling internally."

"Of course, of course . . . No need to get riled up, old boy. The chief inspector just happened to be in Cairo and came forward to offer his assistance. You know how we British are—just want to make sure we dot all the i's and cross all the t's."

"As I said, what's it to me?"

Ursula frowned; the chill in Hugh's response was unexpected.

"You might want some time to think through your story."

"Again, what's with the 'my story'? There isn't any story to tell."

Whittaker coughed politely, and paused before saying in low tones that Ursula strained to hear, "But you must be aware of the rumors . . ."

"Rumors?"

Ursula felt the tension rise. She was well aware of the stories swirling about Cairo society concerning Hugh Carmichael and Katya Vilensky.

"Yes, reports of a . . ." Whittaker hesitated for a moment before continuing, ". . . liaison between you and Mrs. Vilensky. That she was on her way to meet you when she was attacked in the bazaar. Surely you must be aware of these?"

Hugh fell silent.

"Let me give you some advice," Whittaker said. "Steer clear of Peter Vilensky for a while. He's heard all the tittle-tattle, and let's just say he's concerned. Given his very special relationship with the British government, that makes me very concerned. I want to see his fears put to rest. So if you were to discredit these innuendos, perhaps by telling the chief inspector that your affections were engaged elsewhere, well then, that might put paid to the whole thing."

"Tell him that my affections were engaged elsewhere?" Hugh replied with exasperation. "You test a man's patience to the absolute limit!"

"Now, now," Ambrose Whittaker reproached him mildly. "Don't get your back up. Only trying to help. I just know if I was in your shoes, I wouldn't want Scotland Yard sniffing around my personal affairs—never know what might come out."

Ursula sensed Hugh stiffen. The atmosphere between them, already tense, suddenly became acrimonious.

"Some secrets are better left buried. Don't you think?" Whittaker said.

"So what do you suggest? I insinuate that Miss Marlow and I are somehow involved?"

Ursula's eyes narrowed, and she straightened up.

"Well," Ambrose Whittaker replied slowly, "given her reputation in London, it would hardly come as a surprise."

That night, Ursula slept fitfully despite taking some of the sleeping draught left out for her. At first she had been angry and then, by turns, humiliated and depressed. The brief respite she had enjoyed before Katya's death was now well and truly broken. She felt weighed down again by the pressures of London, the necessity of conforming to society's expectations, and her failure to be able to do so. The strain of trying to make her own way as an independent businesswoman while remaining true to her socialist and suffragette principles had already taken its toll. Now she felt an additional humiliation—that a man such as Ambrose Whittaker had no compunction about impugning her reputation galled her. Though she believed Hugh Carmichael would never countenance Ambrose Whittaker's suggestion, she was angry that she could be exposed to the possibility of such a scandal. Why could she not be a man, able to make her way in the world on her own terms, without the threat of censure merely because of her own determination and passion?

Ursula tossed and turned in bed until mental exhaustion finally forced sleep upon her. She dreamed she was lying beside a river, gazing up at the sky. Two men came and lifted her into their arms. One was Alexei, a lover she had not seen in years. The other man's face was shrouded in shadow. Alexei whispered in her ear that it was time she returned. Ursula struggled against his grip, but as she looked below, as she saw the deep, dark depths of the river, she gave in and let the undertow take her from his arms. She felt the icy water seep into her skin as she drifted along. She saw her father's body float past, saw a man rise from the riverbank in a halo of fire. Slowly she started to emerge from the water. She struggled to the shore, her limbs heavy and her dress sodden. The man from the shadows was standing in the distance. She cried out to him, but he turned and walked away. The river was forgotten. The sense of water was forgotten. The sun bore down. The sand burned beneath her toes. She was left parched and alone.

Ursula's eyelashes quivered. The morning sun was streaming in through the lattice shutters of her room, and her mouth felt dry and dusty. Her eyes opened. She was awake, with the taste of sand, like the bitter taste of death, still on her tongue.

Five

Ursula stood with her back to the sun and, using the winding key, prepared the film on her Kodak Brownie camera to take the next shot. She held the camera firmly against her body, looked down into the viewfinder, and scanned the landscape. The mounds of limestone, rocks, and sand slowly began to take shape in the wash of light. In the distance lay the pyramids of Abusir and Giza on the horizon. To the southeast the step pyramid of Sakkara rose from the sandy plain, and beyond that the palm trees bordering the green valley of the Nile. Ursula steadied the camera, adjusted the shutter, and then held her breath for a moment as she pushed down the lever to take the photograph. Satisfied, she looked up and wound the film on once more, ready for the next exposure.

"Miss Marlow!" the unmistakably plummy English voice of Ambrose Whittaker called out from a distance. Ursula ignored him and pretended to fiddle with the camera instead.

"I say, I didn't know you were interested in photography!"

Ursula sighed and knelt down to place the camera in her khaki knapsack.

"Out alone again?" This time his voice was insidious. Whittaker had walked up and was now standing right behind her. Ursula stood up quickly.

"Julia is unfortunately feeling unwell. I advised her to remain in her room for the day to recover," Ursula replied, without turning around.

"I had no idea Julia's stomach was so obliging."

Ursula turned and looked at him shrewdly. In that one comment, the mask of cheerful bonhomie dropped, and she caught a glimpse of the real Ambrose Whittaker.

"I'm taking some photographs for an article I'm writing. *Lady's Realm* wants a story about my perceptions of Egypt, and I thought I might include some photographs. Perhaps I'll juxtapose the pyramids with the street urchins in the back streets of Cairo and entitle it 'The Path of Progress'?"

Ambrose Whittaker flushed at her remark, sensitive to any criticism of the British presence in Egypt. Ursula was about to continue when she spied, rising over the nearest sand dune, the dreadful yet all too familiar sight of an English tourist party on the loose. Each perched on a donkey, wielding a commanding stick, and shaded by a wide-brimmed hat, the tourists stared at her with unified amazement.

"Let me introduce you to my guests," Ambrose Whittaker said with a sly smile. "I'm showing them the sights personally."

"Miss Marlow!" An exclamation came from one of the ladies in the tourist party as she edged her donkey forward from the rear of the group. Ursula stifled a groan. The lady was Mrs. Millicent Lawrence, a Scottish vicar's wife whom Ursula had met at a salon in Alexandria. Despite their common political agenda to achieve votes for women, Ursula had found Millicent's sense of colonial superiority over the Egyptian women unbearable. She was also dismayed by Millicent's dogmatic crusade against all forms of what she called "moral corruption." Accompanying Mrs. Lawrence were two women, one bespectacled and thin, the other stout with flaming red hair. They were both dressed, inappropriately given the fine weather, in black serge wool skirts. Millicent Lawrence had spoken of two Methodist missionaries who were accompanying her home after two years in the Sudan. Ursula could only assume that the two women on donkeys were these. They both stared at her with faint disapproval as they were introduced in turn, and Ursula suspected that Mrs. Lawrence had already told them of her "unsavory" past.

"Mrs. Lawrence, what a pleasant surprise," Ursula replied with a deadpan expression. "When did you arrive in Cairo?"

"Only yesterday, but I managed to convince Whittaker here to take me on a tour of Giza and Sakkara today. Tomorrow he's promised to join our little party on a tour of the Church of the Virgin. Coptic churches are fascinating, don't you think?!"

"Indeed," Ursula responded blandly, trying to think of some means of extricating herself from Whittaker and his party. She had already told the dragoman who had brought her to Sakkara to leave, and she hadn't spied Hugh Carmichael, whom she was expecting to meet, as yet.

The distinctive whirr of an airplane engine overhead caused everyone to look up. Silhouetted against the sky was Hugh's Blériot monoplane, circling as it descended to land. Despite the presence of Whittaker and his companions, Ursula felt a surge of adrenaline as she saw the airplane dip across the sky.

"An exciting but rather dangerous pastime, don't you think?" Ambrose Whittaker commented. "You heard, of course, about Mr. Carmichael's copilot."

"Yes, I did." Ursula's eyes narrowed as she regarded Whittaker closely. "Hugh told me. An accident in Palestine. Tragic. I believe the other plane was totally destroyed."

"Luckily Mr. Carmichael's still rich enough to own not one but two of the world's finest airplanes."

"I guess so."

Hugh had brought both airplanes to Egypt in preparation for a series of test flights across the Libyan Desert. His plan, he told Ursula, was to enter next year's air race from Egypt to England. "Assuming," he had noted dryly, "that both I and my business are still living." Carmichael Shipyards in Newcastle had been plagued by recent industrial problems, and Ursula had heard rumors that Hugh's earlier, riskier forays into petroleum were faltering. The loss of his copilot had hit him hard, and Ursula had even heard him speak of abandoning flying altogether.

"Ever thought about going up in one?" Whittaker asked.

"Yes," Ursula replied candidly. She thought the idea of flying quite exciting.

"Really, Miss Marlow, that would hardly be seemly!" Mrs. Lawrence interjected, perspiration trickling down her ruddy face.

The donkeys, bored by the wait, shuffled in the sand. Miss Violet Norton and Miss Emerence Stanley, the Methodist missionaries, exchanged glances but remained mute.

Ursula turned west toward the Djoser complex. "Well, that's where I'm headed, so I'd better be off," she started to say, but Whittaker, immune as always to the snub, beamed. "Excellent, just where we were headed! Come along, Milly, mustn't dawdle, we have a great deal to accomplish today."

"Right-oh, Whittaker. Lead on!"

Ursula was forced to trudge through the sand beside the donkeys conveying Whittaker and Mrs. Lawrence. The missionary ladies followed in silence.

Shards of pottery dotted the sand, tiny remnants of ancient Egypt that only hinted at the riches that lay beneath in tombs and shafts. There was such feverish anticipation associated with every archaeological dig that Ursula couldn't help but feel the lure of the past with every footfall. She only wished she could stay in Egypt longer, unhurried by business concerns, and learn more about the digs that seemed to set up daily among the ancient ruins. Instead, as they reached the entrance wall to the complex, Ursula focused once more on the questions surrounding Katya's death and turned to Whittaker.

"Have you seen Mr. Vilensky?" she queried. She hadn't seen him since the days that followed Katya's death.

"I met with him yesterday about donating some of his private collection to the museum. I believe he is in the process of finalizing his plans to return to London," Whittaker responded.

"I thought he may have gone back to Palestine," Ursula ventured.

Whittaker cast her a sideways glance. "He was lucky we could even make the arrangements for Mrs. Vilensky in time. If he wasn't such an important fellow, I doubt we could have managed it. It's their custom, you know, to arrange the burial within twenty-four hours. We had to get a dispensation from a local rabbi to delay the matter by just a few days to transport the body. I had to really pull strings to arrange it all."

"I'm sure Mr. Vilensky is exceedingly grateful," Ursula replied evenly. "I must confess, though, I was surprised by the speed with which everything happened. I thought the Egyptian authorities or local coroner would have wanted to wait to examine the body further."

Whittaker coughed. "Oh, that wouldn't have been the done thing at all—besides, it was clear what happened. No need to upset Vilensky further. Although I must say the chap from Scotland Yard was most put out when I told him on the telephone that the body was long gone."

Ursula shivered involuntarily. The way Whittaker described Katya Vilensky dispassionately as "the body" chilled her.

"I'd heard that Scotland Yard was now involved," Ursula said. "Bit unusual, isn't it? I thought this was a local political matter. Shouldn't this chap of yours have contacted me by now, to discuss what happened that day in the bazaar?"

Ambrose Whittaker sniffed disdainfully. "The chief inspector is conducting some discreet inquiries in an unofficial capacity. No doubt he will speak to you when he is good and ready. I wasn't aware that anyone else knew he was here yet. How did you find out?"

"Oh, you know, I have my sources," Ursula replied airily, but she noted the change in Ambrose Whittaker's behavior. He was wary of her now.

"Goodness gracious me!" Millicent Lawrence interrupted their conversation with a shriek. "That man must be absolutely mad!"

Hugh Carmichael, piloting his plane, executed a dramatic dip before slowly descending for a near-perfect landing on a stretch of sandbank west beyond the step pyramid. The young local mechanic who always followed him rode across the sand on a white Arabian colt. Ursula bit her lip. Hugh's recklessness had begun to worry her greatly. She had heard that since his wife's death two years ago, Hugh had taken up all sorts of dangerous pastimes—racing experimental motor cars, flying planes, even alpine climbing—to the point where he had frittered away a great deal of his fortune on such pursuits. Katya and his copilots' deaths seemed to have brought out the very worst in him, and Ursula wondered whether Hugh cared now whether he lived or died.

"Shall we go see Mr. Carmichael?" Ambrose Whittaker gestured with his hand. "After all, that is why you are here, is it not, Miss Marlow?"

Ursula bit her tongue and restrained herself before replying, with a disingenuous smile, "How clever you are! I was indeed planning to meet Mr. Carmichael here. He's promised me a flying lesson before I return to England."

"Oh, my," Millicent Lawrence said faintly.

"Of course he did," Whittaker answered smoothly. "And I would hate to see you disappointed. Will you be attending tonight's celebrations at the club?"

Ursula returned another smile. "Of course. Will the chief inspector, what's his name, be there?"

"Chief Inspector Harrison will indeed be there," Whittaker replied as smoothly as before. His eyes watched for her reaction closely.

Ursula's mouth went dry.

"But of course," she murmured.

"Miss Marlow is well acquainted with the chief inspector." Ambrose Whittaker turned to a bemused Millicent Lawrence. The missionary ladies exchanged glances once more. "He investigated the murder of her father a year or so ago," Whittaker explained.

"I'm hardly likely to forget that, now am I?" Ursula responded, mustering all her self-control to ensure her tone remained even.

"And if you will excuse me, I must go and see about that flying lesson. Good day, Mr. Whittaker." Ursula gave him a perfunctory nod. "Good day, Mrs. Lawrence"—she turned to the twin missionary sisters—"Miss Norton, Miss Stanley."

Ursula hitched her narrow skirt up and, with a kick of her flatheeled suede shoes, stomped off across the desert.

Hugh was bending over, inspecting the plane's diagonal wire bracing and bamboo skid tail, when he heard Ursula approach. The mechanic, ignoring Ursula, knelt down to check the landing gear that appeared, to Ursula at least, to consist of little more than a pair of bicycle wheels connected by a wooden beam.

"Have you got a death wish?" she exclaimed. "You just about gave us all a heart attack!"

"Saw you with Whittaker and his party," Hugh commented, ignoring her concern. "Bit of a surprise."

"Well, it wasn't by choice, I can tell you," Ursula retorted. "That man's like a bad penny—always turning up when you least expect or want."

Hugh straightened up, pulled out a handkerchief from his trouser pocket, and wiped his hands. "So, I'm guessing this isn't a social call."

"No, it isn't. I wanted to ask you something—now that Whittaker and his party have finally left."

"Oh?" Hugh ran his fingers through his salt-and-pepper hair, sending dust into the air.

"Yes, I overheard you and Whittaker talking last night."

"That's unfortunate. But no need to worry, sweetheart, I'm not about to start any rumors about us."

"As if I should think you would," Ursula retorted. "Whittaker's an idiot."

"Whittaker may be a lot of things, but an idiot isn't one of them."

Ursula shielded her eyes against the sun. It was barely spring, yet she was already perspiring beneath the sun's glare.

"So I see you suspect, like I do, that things are not what they seem."

Hugh gazed out across the expanse of sand. To the west the retreating figures of Whittaker and his party gave him pause.

"I'm not sure what I think, and that's the truth."

"But you don't believe that Katya's death was political, do you?"

Hugh did not reply.

Ursula crossed her arms. She wanted to delve deeper and understand what Hugh was keeping from her. Ever since Katya's death, he had been distant and distracted. "Remember that night in Alexandria," she started, trying to introduce the subject as delicately as she could, "at Khedive Abbas Hilmi's cocktail party? Katya wanted to leave early, because of something Peter Vilensky said. Do you remember?"

Hugh kicked the sand and nodded.

"Well, I noticed you went after her. I was talking to Eugenie Mahfouz, but I could tell Peter was angry, yet he made no attempt to follow you."

"It was nothing. Katya was upset, that's all."

Ursula regarded him closely. "I think there was something else, something she told you." Hugh kicked his shoe in the sand again. "No, don't try and shrug it off, Hugh! Ever since then, there was a change in your relationship with Katya. I'm just not sure what it was—"

"How do you know it wasn't what everyone else thought—simply an affair?"

"I think I know you better than that," Ursula replied simply. "And despite her husband's suspicions, I know Katya loved him. So I never believed the rumors. I do, however, think you found something out that night."

Hugh ran his hands along the frame of the airplane, avoiding her gaze.

"Can't you tell me what it was?" Ursula pleaded. "All I want is to find out what really happened. To understand why Katya died. She was a good friend, even though I didn't know her long. Don't you think I owe it to her to find out the truth?"

"You don't owe her anything."

"But—"

"No, let me finish. This isn't something you can get involved in. All I know is that anyone associated with Katya has to be very careful. I suspect my copilot was not, and that was why he died. I don't think it was an accident, any more than I think that Katya was the victim of political extremists. But I'm going to keep my suspicions to myself, because I don't want to involve you in whatever mess Katya found herself in. No, Ursula, I'm serious—I think that as long as we leave well alone, we'll be okay. But if we start snooping—well, I consider Whittaker's words last night a warning. Vilensky is a powerful man. We'd do best not to cross him."

Ursula opened her mouth to speak, but when she saw the look on Hugh's face, she changed her mind. "You're really worried, aren't you?" she said quietly.

Hugh made no reply. He merely signaled the mechanic, who pulled a pair of goggles and a headscarf from a leather satchel and tossed them over to her.

"Put those on, and I'll take you up for a spin."

Ursula picked up the scarf and shook the sand off.

"I can't change your mind?"

"As Whittaker said, some secrets are better left buried."

"But surely you trust me?" Ursula exclaimed.

"Miss Marlow, I would trust you with my life. That's why we need to leave well enough alone. You are too much like my late wife, Iris, God rest her soul, for me to allow anything to happen to you."

From above, the pyramids of Sakkara were awe-inspiring and forbidding. The Blériot airplane seemed so insubstantial and flimsy that Ursula felt as if she were flying in little more than a kite made of cloth, wood, and wires. Hugh, with his hand on the bell-shaped control stick and his feet steering the plane with the foot pedals, seemed oblivious to the surge of fear and panic that rose within her. Ursula clung to the wooden bracing and tried not to think about the emptiness, that space between the sky and the ground, beneath her feet.

The experience of flying was surreal, exciting, and terrifying. The wind pressed against her cheeks, and, as the plane slowly banked to the north, she had to quickly shield her eyes from the glare of the late-afternoon light.

"That was amazing," she told Hugh after they landed at the airstrip at Heliopolis, north of Cairo. "I cannot even begin to describe it." She pulled off the goggles and headscarf and shook her head.

"Sure beats traveling by donkey," he answered with a grin, but Ursula knew it was forced. She sensed a conflict within him. The shadows lengthened; the light was dying. Ursula looked out across the airstrip, watching as Hugh removed his goggles, adjusted his collar, and signaled for his driver to take them back to the hotel. Since the accident in Palestine that had claimed the life of his copilot, Hugh always insisted that his driver follow and meet him where he landed. Hugh's plane was stored in one of the hangers beside the airstrip, and as they made their way to the motor car, Ursula noticed that though his face remained relaxed, his smile never reached his eyes.

That evening a reception was being held at the Khedival Sporting Club to celebrate the day's gymkhana. As she sat in the enclosed landau, Ursula was already dreading the evening. She was tired of the arrogance and insularity of the English in Egypt. She sat back in the leather seat and closed her eyes.

Last summer she had wanted nothing more than for time to stand still. Now she wished the present would simply disappear. She wanted to be lying on green English grass once more, gazing up at a blue, cloud-edged sky. Last summer at Bromley Hall, seat of the Wrotham family, she had experienced one of the few perfect days of her life. She had been there a month, and Mrs. Pomfrey-Smith (whom Lord Wrotham had insisted come as her chaperone) was ensconced in the dowager's private parlor playing bridge, leaving Ursula free to spend the afternoon just as she pleased. It had been one of the hottest summers on record, and Ursula decided to walk to one of her favorite places on the entire estate, the ornamental lake that bordered Rockingham Forest, to cool off. Accompanied by Lord

Wrotham's two collies, Charles and Edward, she had set out with nothing more than a knapsack containing her Brownie camera and a copy of Lord Tennyson's poems.

She arrived at the lake just as the sun reached its peak, bathing the grass embankment in light. She threw the knapsack to the ground and tore off her shoes and silk stockings. Even in her lightest white dimity dress, her limbs felt heavy and listless. She lay down in the grass, feeling the sun's warmth on her exposed arms, and gazed up at the sky, the dark fringes of the oak leaves, the wisps of clouds above. She let her eyes wander and her mind drift, and a drowsy sun-filled numbness took hold. It was perfect. She felt a reckless abandonment, an urge to fling her clothes to the ground and plunge into the lake's icy waters, when, like the image from a painting by John Singer Sargent, he came into view. Lord Wrotham stood over her for a moment, framed against the sun, before kneeling beside her.

"Isn't it glorious?" she said.

He stroked her face. "'And all his world worth for this, / To waste his whole heart in one kiss / Upon her perfect lips.'"

"Tennyson?" Ursula murmured.

Casting a glance to the book of poems that lay open on the grass, its pages fluttering in the summer breeze, Lord Wrotham smiled. "Sir Lancelot and Queen Guinevere," he replied, so softly that his words, barely louder than a rustle of the wind, drifted across her face, as he leaned over and kissed her.

The carriage came to a halt with a jolt, and the dream was lost. Ursula snapped open her eyes as the present, in all its dark confusion, returned. She drew herself up with a sigh and opened the carriage door. The hem of her slender dinner gown caught on the straps of her delicate white shoes, and she had to lift the narrow folds of silk aside to step out of the carriage.

It was already half past nine, and the post-gymkhana festivities were in full swing. Many of the army officers were still in their afternoon boaters and cream-colored suits, singing and toasting the success of their horses in the day's equestrian events. Mingling among the crowd were the club servants, with their turbans and flowing white gowns, each holding a silver platter of wineglasses and cana-pés aloft. All of this was accompanied by the strains of Elgar's Symphony No. 1 drifting in as the orchestra played outside.

Ursula entered the pavilion and, with a gentle tug of the light transparent sleeves that extended to her wrists, prepared herself for the evening. Millicent Lawrence was standing by the entrance, holding forth for all to hear about the success of her husband's mission in Rhodesia. Ursula hurried past to the far corner of the room, avoiding Ambrose Whittaker, who was making a beeline for the buffet table along the way. Upon the white-clothed table was a lavish spread of assorted meats: game pie, roast beef, and lamb chops. From her final vantage point Ursula grabbed a glass of champagne and surveyed the room discreetly. She hated coming to these events. At least in London she used to have Lord Wrotham by her side. She admonished herself to try to forget him once and for all. Had he not delivered her an ultimatum—marry him or be done with him?

Ursula saw Chief Inspector Harrison enter, in his evening suit, looking decidedly uncomfortable in such salubrious surroundings. His eyes met hers, and they both gave the barest hint of acknowledgment. The last time Ursula had seen Harrison was the day the jury found Tom guilty of her father's murder. As the jury delivered its verdict, a cheer arose from the public gallery, and Ursula looked up to see Harrison leaving quietly by the rear door. There had been no acknowledgment, no indication that they were even acquainted, just the briefest of looks exchanged as he turned before leaving. It seemed strange to be standing across from him and to be reminded of that look. Ursula suddenly felt very weary.

She made her way over to one of the long buffet tables with an elaborate centerpiece filled with blue water lilies. She popped a can-apé in her mouth, eyeing the tower of *chaud-froid du poulet* with some distrust, and then reached for another glass of champagne.

"Ursula, *ma chérie!*" Eugenie Mahfouz came over and enveloped Ursula in a hug. "I've been reading all about your friends in London—

they are creating quite the commotion." Even the French daily newspaper in Egypt, *La Réforme,* was reporting the WSPU's latest window-smashing campaign on Regent Street. Ursula returned Eugenie's embrace warmly while saying with some surprise, "What on earth are you doing here?"

Eugenie Mahfouz was the only daughter of a wealthy French merchant who had settled near Alexandria. Married to a prominent Egyptian writer who was well known for his views on what he called the "English occupation" of Egypt, she was one of the few Western women to assimilate into Egyptian society. She maintained segregated harems, or living quarters, when she moved to her husband's home in Alexandria and converted to Islam. Ursula had contacted her on Winifred's advice and had soon discovered that Eugenie was also one of Egypt's most famous hostesses, allowing European women to visit her salons during the winter season. It was only because of her mother's family connections that Eugenie could gain entry to the notoriously racially prejudiced Khedival Sporting Club. Nonetheless, given her views on the English colonial presence in Egypt, Ursula was surprised at Eugenie being there.

"I received your message," Eugenie whispered in her ear. "And I have made the inquiries you asked for—can we talk?"

"Outside maybe, but not here," Ursula said as she pulled away. As always, Eugenie presented an incongruous juxtaposition of cultures. She first appeared to be a classic French beauty, with her wide almond-shaped eyes and aquiline nose. On closer observation, however, this image seemed to shimmer and recast itself. Suddenly one was struck by the smoky rim of kohl beneath her eyes, the richness of the raw silk of her modest dress, and the jangle of gold bangles encircling her arms. Now she appeared rather like one of the ancient queens of Egypt, caught midstride in the hieroglyphs in a tomb.

Eugenie caught Ursula's face in her hands. "You look tired beyond words. I insist you come back with me to Alexandria so you can rest."

"Oh, how I wish I could," Ursula responded. "But I have only a few more weeks left before I must return home to England. I will be in Alexandria for three days next week to finalize matters at the Cotton Exchange, though. May be we could meet up then."

"I must at least take you to Pastroudi's for afternoon tea," Eugenie said as she steered Ursula in the direction of the door out onto the terrace. "So tell me"—she dropped her voice to a whisper once more—"what is a member of Scotland Yard's Special Branch doing investigating Mrs. Vilensky's death?" Eugenie inclined her head toward Chief Inspector Harrison.

Eugenie was nothing if not well informed.

"I'm not sure," Ursula replied in a low voice. "Whittaker told me that the chief inspector just happened to be in Cairo and is assisting the Egyptian authorities in what he describes as a routine investigation into Katya's death."

"And hens have teeth," Eugenie said sarcastically.

"Quite," Ursula replied.

Eugenie looked around quickly. "I tried to speak to Harvey Pasha, commandant of the Cairo police, but he refused to talk to me. Said I had to go through Whittaker or this man Harrison. Something is terribly wrong, my friend."

"I know," Ursula replied, taking Eugenie by the arm. "Tell me what you have found out."

Ursula and Eugenie squeezed through the crowd that was gathered near the door to the terrace. As they passed, Ursula caught snatches of conversation, mostly centered around the day's gymkhana, interspersed with the occasional comment on weightier concerns such as the possibility of home rule for Ireland, and the recent coal miners' strike in England. Italy's bombardment of Tripoli was also a topic of some contention, for there were some in the British Army who feared it might spark a "holy war" against Western imperialist interests in the region. For many of the guests, the world seemed very uncertain.

A couple of army officers, in their regimental finery, stepped aside for Eugenie and Ursula as they approached the doorway, and continued their conversation.

"Churchill's got the right idea, don't get me wrong," the older man said to his companion. "It's naval power that's the key."

They drew on their cigars and nodded. Winston Churchill was the First Lord of the Admiralty. Ursula took a dim view of Churchill's jingoism as well as his antisuffrage views and had to restrain herself from making any comment as she walked by. The younger man looked at her keenly, and she felt rather like one of the horses in the day's gymkhana, sized up for both breeding and potential. The older man leaned over and whispered something in the other man's ear. The younger man sniffed. "Pity," he said with disdain. Ursula flushed.

She and Eugenie walked onto the terrace that overlooked the expansive gardens, polo fields, tennis courts, and croquet lawns. The scent of oleander and roses filled the air. The gymkhana was over, and apart from the occasional servant rushing to and fro to replenish provisions, there was no one to disturb them.

"Katya's death was not a political matter. You have my assurance on that," Eugenie began, "but the British have detained a number of innocent people for questioning, which has angered a number of my husband's friends. Luckily, so far no one is advocating any reprisals."

Ursula took hold of Eugenie's hand. "I know this must be very hard for you."

"It is a difficult time," Eugenie acknowledged. "Especially for those of us who advocate a peaceful means of obtaining independence from Britain."

"Do any of your friends have any idea who may have been responsible for Katya's death?"

Eugenie's face was grave. "No. Peter Vilensky is, of course, a very powerful man. As with many bankers, he is heavily involved in securing loans to the British and other imperialist governments. He is also very close to that man Whittaker, whom I have long suspected is involved in more than just the Ministry of Interior."

"What do you mean?"

"No one has ever had any real evidence, but many of us believe Whittaker is more than what he seems."

"Like what?" Ursula prompted.

"No one's entirely sure but he seems to have surprising influence. We're never sure whether he is acting on behalf of the British government. There are even rumors of arms trading. These days it's hard to keep up with all the political and military intrigue."

"Who knows what Whittaker is up to?" Ursula commented. "But I cannot imagine Peter Vilensky involved in anything like that."

Eugenie shrugged. "Even if he was, why would Katya be killed?"

"Katya may have heard the rumors," Ursula reminded her.

Eugenie shrugged, unconvinced. "I doubt that Whittaker would concern himself with Katya."

"Unless she threatened to disclose publicly what she had found out?"

"Perhaps . . . but—"

"Mrs. Mahfouz!" Ursula interrupted loudly. She had suddenly noticed Ambrose Whittaker and Chief Inspector Harrison approaching them from the other side of the pavilion. "You can't believe how grateful I am for your kind invitation. I haven't explored the Museum of Greco-Roman Antiquities—shall we set up a time when I am in Alexandria? Oh, and have you seen the latest edition of *La Gazette du Bon Ton?* I can't believe sprigged muslin may be returning—I swear we shall all look like milkmaids by summer!"

Whittaker raised an eyebrow as he passed by.

"Come and see me in Alexandria," Eugenie whispered, planting a kiss on each of Ursula's cheeks. "We can talk more there."

"Miss Marlow." Chief Inspector Harrison held out his hand. Ursula, amused, reached out and shook it. Whittaker stood next to Harrison and smoothed back his thinning hair.

Eugenie took her leave, shooting both men an arched stare.

Ursula looked at Harrison and said, "A bit anticlimactic, don't you think?" Harrison fingered his mustache, unsure of how to respond.

"I mean, our meeting like this," Ursula explained. "I half expected to be woken in the middle of the night and dragged off to the British Agency for questioning. Isn't that how you chaps operate?"

Harrison knew better than to take the bait.

"Aren't you a little far from your usual territory?" Ursula continued, taking a quick sip of her champagne. "I thought East End anarchists and German spies were now your sort of thing?"

Harrison accepted a tall glass of Pimm's from one of the servant's trays that passed by.

"I admit my remit has widened since we last met, Miss Marlow, but there's no need for concern. I am not here to search for any German spies."

"Well, that's a relief," Ursula responded drily.

"Perhaps we could speak alone for a moment?" Harrison said evenly. "Whittaker, would you mind?"

Ursula noticed that Harrison's East End accent, which used to creep through, was now totally suppressed.

"Not at all, old chap!" Whittaker replied blithely. "I'll see you back inside,"

Once Whittaker had left, Ursula allowed Harrison to light her a cigarette as they stood side by side, gazing out over the polo field. She was amused. A year ago Harrison would have been horrified to see a woman smoking.

"How have you been?" Harrison began cautiously.

"Fine," Ursula replied blandly. "Apart from witnessing another murder, of course."

"His lordship was very concerned to hear about that," Harrison responded, and held up his hand quickly before she could react. "Don't worry, he didn't send me here. . . . I merely meant that we had been in communication since my arrival in Cairo. He is aware of what happened to Mrs. Vilensky."

"I'm not sure I understand. What has Lord Wrotham got to do with any of this?" Ursula asked, taking a long drag on her cigarette to suggest her indifference as to the answer.

"No interest, except obviously in your well-being," Harrison replied as he smoothed down his neatly trimmed mustache. "As for the Vilensky matter, well, it's probably best not to talk too much about it here." Harrison tossed aside his cigarette. "Are you available to meet tomorrow?"

"But I thought this was an internal political matter?"

Harrison shrugged. "I'm conducting a routine follow-up. Nothing more."

"Really?" Ursula didn't bother to hide her skepticism. "So tell me, why would a member of the Scotland Yard's Special Branch be interested in conducting a routine follow-up?"

Harrison ignored her. He merely raised his drink and smiled.

"Mr. Vilensky is a powerful man," he replied.

"Yes, he is."

"Powerful men have powerful friends."

"Yes," Ursula replied carefully. "They can also have powerful secrets."

Six

The following morning, Harrison arranged for Ursula to visit
a private house on Rhoda Island, southwest of central Cairo.
He was accompanied by a young Egyptian in a cream suit
and red fez, who remained silent and implacable as he stood in the
corner of the room while they spoke. Ursula sat on the huge be-
cushioned divan beneath the lattice-screened window, her body almost consumed by the polished cottons and silks that surrounded
her. Her simple white frock seemed flimsy and insubstantial in contrast to the elaborate decoration of the inlaid marble and fretwork
that adorned the high-ceilinged room.

Harrison started by asking Ursula to describe the scene at the bazaar
on the day Katya died, taking out a tan-and-black notebook from
his jacket pocket. He scribbled his notes in it with the lead of a half-
chewed pencil. He was particularly concerned about whether Ursula
could describe any of the men who had been in the bazaar that day.

Ursula screwed up her eyes but could recall only a sea of indistin-
guishable faces, the flash of dark eyes, and the swirl of white cloth.

"I really only remember the man with the monkey—and it's not
like that's a rare sight in downtown Cairo. But I would describe him
as bigger than the other men—stockier, I mean. Yes. And although

he had brown eyes, I remember thinking that he didn't look like one of the fellahin—I'm not exactly sure why I thought that, but I did." Ursula leaned back on the divan. "Not much help, I'm afraid. Told as much to the Egyptian authorities—I mean, it all happened so quickly. There was so much confusion. I see a blur of faces, nothing more. Maybe if I saw some of them again I'd recognize them, but I really can't be sure."

Harrison simply nodded. "It's to be expected. The men were creating a diversion—and it worked."

Ursula's lips pursed. Recounting the story had made her feel like a half-witted young girl, easily distracted by something as obvious as a performing monkey.

"You said you believed Katya was concerned about her own safety?" Harrison prompted.

"Yes," Ursula replied, and she recounted the conversation she'd had with Katya the morning of her death. Harrison didn't seem to hold much stock in her theory, but Ursula continued. "Look, I know it sounds absurd, but I sensed that Katya was looking out for someone. Watching to see who was there. And I don't just mean her husband, although Peter Vilensky did make a thorough nuisance of himself, following her just to make sure she wasn't having some secret affair with Hugh Carmichael. Really, that man was the limit!"

Harrison raised his eyebrows and Ursula continued on a more rueful note. "I sound like one of those penny romances, seeing shadows in every corner, but, Chief Inspector, I really do think there was something that Katya had found out, something she had discovered, that made her believe her life was in danger."

"And what do you think she had discovered?"

"Don't you know? Isn't that why you're here?" Ursula demanded.

Harrison shook his head. "I told you before this is a routine matter, nothing more."

Harrison's eyes wouldn't meet hers. Ursula knew him well enough to know that he would not be drawn out yet.

"Just make sure justice is served," Ursula responded quietly. "Someone must be brought to account for her death, and I want to ensure that justice is done. You waited too long last time, and my father and Cecilia died as a result. Do not make the same mistake again."

Ursula's reference to the deaths of her father and Cecilia Abbott made Harrison flinch. "Believe me, Miss Marlow, I am well aware of the risks. But these are difficult times—we may well be at war sooner than you think. My priorities are different now—England's security is under threat—but I promise you, I will not lose sight of what needs to be done to solve Katya Vilensky's death."

"You know her death had nothing to do with the nationalists!" Ursula began, hoping that she might be able to find out more using this line of inquiry.

"Let me worry about that," Harrison interrupted. "But I can assure you the British government has been watching a number of secret societies since Boutros Ghali's assassination that may have connections to the incident in the Khan el-Khalili."

"It wasn't a mere incident," Ursula interrupted coldly. "It was the murder of a young woman. My friend."

Harrison sighed. "Please, Miss Marlow, just be patient. There are far bigger things at stake here. The British Empire may be at risk."

"So it's my patriotic duty not to investigate Katya's death, is that what you're telling me?" Ursula's self-control was rapidly diminishing.

"No." Harrison's response was smooth, though there was an unspoken threat beneath it. "To be honest," he continued, "I think you have better things to be worrying about—like keeping your father's business from collapsing around you." Noticing her shock, he continued, "Yes, I know about the attacks on your mills and factories. That's what you should be focusing on—because, believe me, there are few policemen inclined to help a suffragette rabble-rouser when she's in business difficulties."

Harrison's words hit her hard. Ursula got to her feet and summoned all her self-control. "I've heard enough threats for one day," she said with an imperious glare. "If you don't mind, Chief Inspector Harrison, I think it's time that I end our little chat, enlightening though it has been, and return to my hotel."

Harrison had his Egyptian associate escort Ursula downstairs and arrange for a carriage to return her to Mena House. As it pulled up at the hotel, Ursula saw Hugh Carmichael walking quickly along the path that led to the gardens. She opened her mouth to call out, but something about his demeanor and the fury of his stride made her stop. She hesitated for a moment before climbing out of the carriage. Peering round, she spied Peter Vilensky standing by the hotel entrance, watching as Hugh retreated down the path. He straightened his jacket, smoothed back his dark brown hair, and then signaled for his motorcar to be brought round. Ursula turned back and sank down in her seat. There were getting to be too many secrets in this place.

The next day, Ursula returned to Mena House after a morning spent on the Giza plateau. She needed time away from people and had found a degree of solace walking among the ruins of the great pyramids—although she could hardly say she was ever really alone. No matter where she wandered, there were always the familiar outstretched hands and the call for baksheesh. Then there were the vendors of so-called antiquities and fossils, supposedly from the sands near Zawiyet el-Aryan. Each and every one Ursula dismissed with a wave of her hand, clutching her trusty Baedeker guide in the other.

As Ursula entered the Mena House gardens and made her way along the magnolia-lined path, she looked up to see Peter Vilensky approaching. His skin looked pallid in the harsh sunlight, a bleak contrast to his dark, neatly trimmed beard, black mourning suit, and wide-brimmed hat. According to Jewish custom, Peter Vilensky had been in near seclusion, refusing all social engagements until his initial seven days of sitting shivah were over. Ursula hesitated for a moment, knowing that their paths would cross and wondering whether she should broach the subject that had been on her mind.

Peter Vilensky saw Ursula and waited as she drew near, regarding her with guarded dark eyes.

"Miss Marlow," he said tersely.

"Mr. Vilensky, it is good to see you."

Peter Vilensky eyed her suspiciously, and Ursula felt her face flush. Nevertheless, she plowed ahead.

"I was speaking with Mr. Whittaker, and he told me that Chief Inspector Harrison was helping with the investigation. That must be a great relief to you—he is a fine, capable detective. You see, I have dealt with him before—" If she had expected this would draw him out, she was mistaken.

"Really," was all Vilensky replied.

There was an awkward pause, but Ursula was determined to continue.

"I know this must sound terribly impertinent," she began with feigned embarrassment. "But I was just wondering, have all of Katya's belongings been packed up and sent away?" She fiddled with the edge of one of her cotton gloves.

"Why do you ask?" Vilensky demanded.

"It's nothing really, only Katya and I exchanged some books, and I wanted to make sure I returned hers, and also—I hope this doesn't sound too rude—but I'd like to retrieve my books as well. There are some lovely books of poetry that were a gift to me. . . ." Ursula's voice trailed off awkwardly.

Peter Vilensky scowled, his face even harsher than before.

"All our books are being packed into the trunks. . . . Some of Katya's may still be out, but I haven't the time to arrange for anyone to go through them. I hardly think Katya's maid, who cannot speak or read English, would be able to—"

"Oh, I'd be quite happy to sort through them myself," Ursula interrupted. "With your approval, of course."

Peter Vilensky's face did not alter.

"It really would be no bother at all," Ursula continued brightly, noting how he was clenching and unclenching his hands.

"I suppose that will be . . . yes . . . all right," Vilensky said. "Just arrange it with the hotel staff, and they can also deal with Katya's maid. I have more important things to concern myself with than some trifling books lent to my wife." He said the word *wife* with bitterness.

"I'll arrange it for this afternoon then, thank you," Ursula replied.
Vilensky's curt nod was both an acquiescence and a dismissal.

Ursula was escorted to the Vilenskys' suite by the hotel manager,
Baron de Radowkasky, who held the keys aloft with disdain. With the
end of the Egyptian "season," he was busy making arrangements for a
Cook & Sons tour group that was departing for Alexandria the following morning, and was unimpressed by the interruption to his day.

"Please tell Mr. Vilensky how very grateful I am for this opportunity. I won't be more than a few minutes, I assure you, and then I
will return the keys immediately."

The hotel manager bowed. "Mr. Vilensky has graciously made
his late wife's maid available to assist you, should you require it. He
told me all of the books are in the bedroom."

"Thank you. I'm sure I will be able to manage."

The hotel manager waved her into the room and left with another bow. Katya's maid, a timorous girl of eighteen, stood meekly
beside one of the divans that graced the suite's living room.

"Nadia," Ursula said kindly, "I'm sure you must have a lot of
packing to finish. Please don't worry about assisting me. It will take
me no time at all to find the books I need."

Nadia, with a blank face that suggested she had only understood
part of what Ursula was saying, scurried off and soon left the suite
with a pile of laundry in her arms.

Ursula walked into the bedroom, which was a replica of her own.
The curtains were open, and a slight breeze filtered in through the
filigree latticework surrounding the open window, filling the room
with the scent of jasmine from the garden below. Above the bed was
a lavish mural with inlaid mother-of-pearl.

On the bed, Katya's clothes had been folded and stacked, ready to
be packed, with great care and obvious tenderness. Ursula ran her fingers across the blue shawl she had seen Katya wear many mornings.
The sensation was like running her hands across a shallow pond, the
silk was so soft and cool. Ursula walked over to the bureau, which was
piled high with books and magazines. On the chair there was also a

series of portfolios, photographs, and large bound books. Buried amid the stack of books by the bed were the books she had loaned Katya—Rupert Brooke's *Poems*, which had been published the previous year, a volume of *Selected Poems* by Matthew Arnold that Lord Wrotham had given her for Christmas, and a translation of Baudelaire's poetry.

Ursula carefully placed the books Katya had lent her on top of those piled high on the chair. Katya had been excited to introduce Ursula to a recent translation of Pushkin's poetry as well as a novel by Tolstoy translated into English by Constance Garrett.

Ursula scanned the room, wondering if she could find anything to suggest an explanation for Katya's unease in the days before her death. Everything, however, apart from her books and clothes, had been removed. Reluctant to leave, Ursula picked up her books and slowly made her way past the closed double doors that led into Peter Vilensky's adjoining suite.

Once upstairs in her own suite, she threw the books onto her bed and sat down heavily in the rattan armchair beneath the window.

"Oh, Miss—I wasn't expecting you back so soon." Julia was sitting on the bed, mending one of Ursula's shirts. She spoke while still holding the pins in her mouth. "Would you like me to help you change for afternoon tea?" At teatime, the terraces of Mena House were always crowded with guests and tourists.

"No, that's all right," Ursula answered distractedly. "Let me just sit for a while."

"The trunks are nearly all packed. Would you like me to set out the mauve day dress for tomorrow?"

"Hmm?" Ursula looked at Julia blankly. "Oh, sorry, yes, the mauve will be fine."

"Do you want me to take these, Miss?" Julia pointed to the books that lay scattered on the bed.

"What? No, leave them for the moment. They can be stowed in the top of my trunk. But you can certainly pack the rest of my books. All the arrangements are finalized. We leave on the afternoon train Wednesday. That should give us enough time to finish packing. Oh, and here, can you return these keys to the hotel manager?"

"Yes, Miss." Julia bobbed a curtsy. "And Miss, the post arrived—I've popped the letters on the top of the bureau for you."

"Thank you, Julia," Ursula replied as Julia withdrew.

Ursula rose and crossed over to the bureau beside the bed. There were two letters waiting for her—one from Gerard Anderson, her financial adviser, and one from Winifred, whom Ursula expected was back in London after a lengthy lecture tour around Ireland on the topic of "socialism and the working woman." Ursula glanced at Anderson's letter quickly. He expressed relief that Ursula had secured contracts for next year's cotton supply but remained concerned as a recent strike at the Victoria and Rochdale mills had already caused the loss of two major contracts. Anderson urged Ursula to return home as soon as possible to discuss what he termed "the increasingly precarious" financial situation of some of the factories and mills in Lancashire. Ursula folded his letter up carefully, feeling the burden of living up to her father's expectations more acutely than ever.

She took some comfort in reading Winifred's letter, a six-page missive in her distinctively bold handwriting. After providing a hilarious account of the travails of traveling in Ireland, she turned to more serious matters—the arrest of more than one hundred of their "sisters" following the attacks on Regent Street.

> I returned, having missed out on all of the adventure, to discover that Christabel has fled the country. Mrs. P and the Pethick-Lawrences are due to stand trial on conspiracy charges no less. No chance of persuading Lord W to intercede on their behalf I'm sure. Imagine the scene in the Criminal Court if that ever happened!
>
> I know. I know . . . you don't want to hear any more about him, but I have to say I read about his recent performance in the House of Lords on the subject of home rule for Ireland and I had to admire his oratorical skill (if not his sentiments!).
>
> So, when are you coming home, my dear?
>
> London's a frightful bore without you. We all miss you at Clements Inn—although half of our local committee are enjoying

*a little holiday in Holloway Prison at the moment—the rest of us
are holding tight!*
  All my love,
  Freddie

Ursula put down Winifred's letter with a smile. Although her
breezy epistle bolstered her, it was not enough to raise her spirits
entirely. For that she needed a few quiet moments to sit and im-
merse herself in poetry. She held up the green cloth pocket-sized
book of Matthew Arnold poems she had lent Katya and, propping
up the pillows on the bed, cushioned herself against them and started
to read. She immediately saw that Katya had marked her place in
the book with a postcard from Palestine. Ursula turned to the page
and ran her fingers along the outside of the postcard. It was a poignant reminder of a friend.

Katya had been reading Matthew Arnold's poem "Dover Beach,"
and Ursula read it slowly, feeling a growing despondency. So much for
lifting the spirits, she thought ruefully. But then she looked at the
postcard more closely, turning it over and over again in her hands.
Apart from the printed description, "Jaffa Gate, Jerusalem," there was
only one handwritten word: *Hartuv*. Something stirred inside Ursula,
but she couldn't place the feeling. She leaned back on the pillows and
closed her eyes. Did this postcard offer any clue about Katya's death?
Or was it nothing more than a bookmark?

An hour later Ursula was downstairs in the small hotel library
seated at a wooden desk beneath one of the many decorative wooden
window grilles, or *mashrabiyyah*, that graced the hotel. A small pile
of guidebooks were stacked on the table beside her. Ursula felt confident that the reference to Hartuv was most likely a person or a
place, and had started with the most obvious resource—the hotel's
collection of Baedeker guides. Head bent, she was sifting her way
through the Baedeker guide to Palestine and Syria when, in the section that detailed the route from Jaffa to Jerusalem, she found a
brief reference to a place called Hartuv. The entry read: "A colony
of Bulgarians (pop. 95) founded in 1896 a little below *Sara* (ancient

Zoreah). *Sara* and *Hartuv* can be seen on a hill to the left. This is where the mountains now begin." Ursula leaned back in her chair and rubbed her eyes, pondering the possible significance to Katya of this small Jewish colony.

It was nearly midnight, and Ursula sank deep into the warm water of her bath. The hotel was silent, Julia asleep, and through the latticework shutters a pale moonlight filtered in, leaving soft folds of light across the silk dressing gown she had thrown carelessly over the wicker chair beneath the window. Ursula lay in the bath, gazing at the ceiling fan whirring away noisily above her head. She felt melancholic, and strangely forsaken. The water lapped over the side of the bath as she moved her leg. Ursula closed her eyes and slid her face under the water. She thought of her father and his unfulfilled dreams, of Lord Wrotham and his dashed expectations. She ached for the past. Why did she feel as though nothing she had achieved mattered anymore—that she had failed all those around her? Ursula blinked back her tears. Matthew Arnold's "Dover Beach" always had a similar effect on her. She felt as though she too was standing on the shore, gazing across the straits, watching the certitude of peace, of happiness, retreat with the tide.

Seven

rsula left Julia at Le Metropole hotel and made her way down to Alexandria's inner harbor to watch the steamers leaving the quays that lined the western side of the bay to the Arsenal. After her business at the Cotton Exchange, she had come to see Peter Vilensky, who was returning to London via Marseilles on the French steamer *Caledonien*. Something inside her impelled her to watch him depart. In some small way perhaps she was bidding Katya a final good-bye—the haste with which her body had been taken for burial had prevented her from doing so until now.

The quays were bustling with people, carriages, motorcars, and trams. There were fishing trawlers unloading their catch, yachts attempting to moor, and the sleek, tall-funneled ocean liners that plied the Mediterranean port with tourists, sounding their horns. In her navy-and-white-striped suit and wide-brimmed white straw hat, Ursula was hardly inconspicuous, but whether out of prudence or merely a fit of pique, she held back from the quay, watching at a distance the passengers' embarkation via the gangway.

The steamer was due to leave at three o'clock, and Peter Vilensky was one of the last passengers to board. Despite Ursula's many requests, he had refused to meet with her to answer any questions regarding his wife or settlements such as Hartuv. He arrived in a Renault motorcar and took his time boarding as an entourage of butlers and maids handled arrangements for the luggage to be taken on board. Ursula noticed that Katya's lady's maid, Nadia, was crying, and that in her hand she held a small leather suitcase, which she was clinging to as if her life depended upon it. She expected that once the ship reached Europe, Nadia, now that her mistress was dead, would have to fend for herself.

As Ursula stood watching the proceedings from beneath the brim of her wide hat, she caught sight of a tiny squirrel of a man heading quickly toward the customs house. He darted in and out of the crowd, past crates filled with bananas and packing cases stuffed with straw and artifacts, even a motorcar being hoisted aboard by a huge steel winch. He wore a blue suit and Panama hat and looked like one of the many clerks that worked for the major shipping lines. The man seemed rushed and uncomfortable, but as he hurried past the *Caledonien*, he took a moment to look up and caught sight of Vilensky strolling along the gangway. Ursula immediately sensed the intense scrutiny with which the shipping clerk regarded Vilensky. For a moment she thought Peter Vilensky was going to call out, but it passed without either man saying a word. Intrigued, Ursula decided to follow the man in the Panama hat. The man was walking briskly, but Ursula had managed to catch up to him by the time he reached the customs house.

"Excuse me!" Ursula called out as the man opened the glass-fronted door. The man ignored her and continued walking across the foyer. It was dark and cool inside, a haven from the chaos of the port.

"Excuse me! Do you speak English?" she shouted again, and the men at the front counters looked up. The man paused in midstep; he clearly did not want to make a scene in the middle of the customs house.

He turned round. "Yes, yes. I speak English. What can I help you with?" His tone was polite, and his eyes would not meet hers.

"Do you know Mr. Vilensky?" she asked. "I saw you at the steamer, and I wondered . . ."

"Of course, of course. Very important man. I don't know him well. No, not well . . ." The man finished on a hesitant note, peering at Ursula anxiously. "Why do you ask?"

"You heard about his wife, then?" Ursula prompted.

"Yes . . . but I really must be getting back. Yes, must be getting back."

"I was wondering if I could ask you some questions,"

"Questions?! Questions?! No, no . . ." The clerk turned away and hurried toward the wood-paneled door that led to the customs offices at the rear of the building.

Ursula followed him quickly. She caught the door with her hand before it closed.

"I'm sure Mr. Vilensky would be most upset if he heard that you had refused to help me," Ursula said, hoping that the threat of displeasing an extremely powerful man such as Peter Vilensky would have an impact. "I'm his private secretary, and as you can see, he is leaving today for Britain. He has sent me here urgently, to follow up on his wife's previous enquiries." The lies rolled easily off her tongue.

The shipping clerk stopped in his tracks. After a momentary hesitation he then peered over his shoulder and gestured for her to follow him quietly.

"What has he told you?" the clerk asked anxiously, after almost pushing Ursula into his tiny office and closing the door.

"As I said, he asked me to follow up on something his wife was investigating," Ursula lied, uncertain where such a ruse might lead her.

The clerk sat down in his chair heavily.

"She only came to see me the once, and I . . . I couldn't be of much assistance. . . ."

Ursula demurely took a seat, trying to conceal the pounding of her heart in her chest.

"Just tell me everything you told Mrs. Vilensky."

The shipping clerk chewed his lip nervously.

"It was many weeks ago," he protested weakly. "I'm not sure I can remember all that she—"

"Tell me everything," Ursula urged.

The clerk opened the bottom drawer of his desk and rummaged in it for a few moments.

"She asked only about the *Bregenz*," he said, his voice muffled as he rummaged still further.

The clerk pulled out a leather-bound ledger and set it down on the desk with a thump. "I could only provide her with minor details."

"Go on," Ursula replied firmly.

"The *Bregenz* took on further cargo and passengers at Port Said bound for Jaffa and then Smyrna. I only showed her the entry I had in our register."

The clerk's fingers drummed as he kept the ledger closed.

"Can you show me the entry?" Ursula asked

The clerk watched her carefully. "You said Mr. Vilensky knows you are here?"

Ursula got up and walked around the desk. She traced her finger across one of the maps on the wall.

"Why can't you tell me?" she asked softly. "Was Mrs. Vilensky afraid? Are you afraid too? Is that why you don't want to tell me?"

The man's face was inscrutable. Ursula remained silent, waiting to see how he would respond.

The clerk licked his lips and opened the ledger.

"The *Bregenz*," he said. "Here is the entry—please don't ask me for anything more."

Ursula bent over to read the entry. The clerk pointed to the middle of the page to an entry written in blue ink. The date was December 29, 1911. The entry read: "Master: Captain Murphy, appointed to the vessel 1910. Steel twin screws steamer; 2 decks; fitted with electric light and refrigerating machinery. Accommodation for 30 passengers. Water ballast. 7,524 tons gross. Construction: 1901, Carmichael & Co. Ltd., Tyneside. Owners: Dobbs Steamship Co. Ltd. Port of registry: Liverpool." Ursula made a mental note to follow up the connection to Dobbs, although it was hardly surprising, given the number of ships operated by Dobbs's company in the Mediterranean.

"She was bound for Jaffa and then Smyrna," the clerk said. "Carrying mainly cargo, but I believe there were twelve passengers who embarked at the port of Thessaloniki."

"Did Mrs. Vilensky tell you why she was interested in this ship?" The man shook his head.

"No." His response was unconvincing.

"What did she tell you?" Ursula asked gently, but he would not meet her eyes.

"Nothing. Now please, you must go."

Ursula heard the desperation in his voice, his dormant fears now laid bare.

"Are you sure there's nothing more you can tell me?" she asked.

The clerk put the ledger away and urged her to leave. Ursula opened her mouth to protest, but his fears seemed to escalate with each minute she remained.

"What if I came back tomorrow?" she asked from the doorway, but there was no reply.

The clerk busied himself in the paperwork on his desk, and she accepted, at least for now, that their interview was over.

Ursula walked down the corridor back toward the foyer. A group of officials in formal frock coats and hats passed her by without comment. A lone clerk remained at the front counter, and she nodded to him as she passed. Ambrose Whittaker was coming through the front door to the customs house as she exited. He tipped his hat politely, saying, "Poor Mrs. Lawrence is in a bit of a flap about some artifacts that were confiscated when she arrived, so I have accompanied her to Alexandria to help sort it all out."

It seemed a remarkable coincidence that Whittaker should be at the customs house, but Ursula was well aware that this was the time of year when many British vacationers were returning home from Egypt. Alexandria seemed to be full of English travelers, and she suspected Whittaker had to spend a great deal of his time placating travelers frustrated by the Egyptian customs bureaucracy.

"Just smoothing some ruffled feathers," Whittaker continued. "But I trust we can expect the pleasure of your company at tonight's little soiree? It's really the last for the season." Ursula forced a polite smile and a nod. "Good, then I trust I will be seeing you there tonight." She was in no mood for Ambrose Whittaker's inane conversation.

Outside, the bright gold light was a sharp contrast to the dark coolness of the customs house. Ursula felt uneasy. The shipping clerk's behavior puzzled her, just as Katya's once had. Why should Katya have wanted information about a ship that had departed over three months ago? What information could she have possibly gained that would have made her feel that her life was in jeopardy? None of it made any sense.

That afternoon Ursula decided to visit Eugenie Mahfouz to see whether her investigations had yielded anything further regarding Katya's death. The Mahfouz residence was a modest limestone villa in the heart of fashionable Alexandria. Eugenie Mahfouz kept to the old Egyptian traditions, however, and Ursula's driver stopped at the door that led through to the courtyard and the women's quarters, at the rear of the residence. Ursula had been here before and needed no guidance as she navigated across the courtyard, through the curtained doorway, and up the stairs to the harem. One of the Sudanese eunuchs who served as a servant met her at the door at the top of the stairs.

"Good afternoon, Mehmed," Ursula said with a smile. "Is Mrs. Mahfouz available?"

The servant nodded his head. "Please wait here, I will let her know you are here."

"Thank you," Ursula replied.

Only a few minutes passed before the door was reopened by Eugenie herself, and Ursula was welcomed with open arms into the elaborate antechamber that led to the women's parlor. Eugenie was wearing a long gray dress and a silvery light cloak that seemed to shimmer about her. Once again Ursula was struck by the duality that surrounded Eugenie's life. Despite her European origins, Eugenie seemed to have accepted the situation as a necessary part of assimilating to her husband's way of life in Egypt. As always, there was a fleeting image of a young Egyptian woman, veiled with kohl-rimmed eyes, only to be superimposed on another image—this time of *la belle époque*, conjured up by the peek of a dark curl from beneath Eugenie's veil, the curve of her waist, and the unmistakable smell of Guerlain's *L'Heure Bleue* perfume.

"I am pleased you have come," Eugenie said quietly. "I will tell you what I have learned about Katya." She moved a box of Groppi chocolates from the table. "Mehmed!" she called out. "Bring us more tea!"

First, Ursula told Eugenie what had transpired at the customs house earlier in the day and about the postcard inscription she had found amid Katya's belongings.

"I have heard nothing about a place called Hartuv or of a ship called the *Bregenz*," Eugenie commented when Ursula finished. "It seems odd that Katya would be interested. But then, what about this incident makes any sense to us? Ah, thank you, Mehmed. Here, Ursula, you should try some of the *gâteau aux fruits*. It is my mother's recipe."

Ursula settled back in her seat, and Eugenie began to speak. "After we met last week, I made inquiries through a friend of mine, Aminah Nasif. She is heavily involved in the Red Crescent society, helping repatriate refugees from the Italian-Libyan conflict. She met Katya briefly at one of their charity dinners. Aminah told me that Katya asked about helping fund a relief center. What was interesting was that Katya also mentioned providing money to a relief group with definite nationalist sympathies."

Ursula frowned. "But that totally undermines the theory that nationalists targeted Vilensky—I mean, why would they bite the hand that feeds them?"

Eugenie nodded vigorously. "I agree. But unfortunately, that is all I have discovered so far. Apart from Vilensky's donations to the museum, I haven't heard anything of interest to us. You are aware, of course, of Vilensky's relationship with Whittaker, but that seems to relate solely to governmental matters. Then there are the extensive loans to the Dobbs Steamship Company, but I am sure you know all about those."

Ursula's jaw tightened at the mention of Christopher Dobbs's company. She rubbed her temples with her fingers. Any reference to Dobbs always made her uneasy, but now she was also frustrated. She couldn't put all the elements together to make any coherent story. Was Whittaker somehow involved? Was the British government concerned over Katya's influence in funding nationalist extremists? Neither of these possibilities seemed plausible, and they hardly explained Chief Inspector Harrison's interest in the matter. If the government had countenanced Katya's death, they'd hardly send someone in to investigate it further. And what was Katya's interest in Hartuv or the *Bregenz*?

The soiree Ambrose Whittaker referred to was a charity ball to raise money for a new dispensary for poor women and children hosted by the khedive Abbas Helmy II at the El-Salamlek Palace overlooking Montazah Bay. Ursula, wearing a deep green Poiret dress, felt conspicuous as an unaccompanied female. At least here there were continentals and members of Egypt's most notable families, unlike at the exclusively English domain of the Khedival Sporting Club in Cairo. Ursula was speaking with a Belgian archaeologist when she was drawn into a debate with a wealthy Greek merchant on the recent war in Libya. Just as the two men began discussing the use of aerial bombardment, Ursula caught sight of three other women arriving. As soon as she recognized them, Ursula extricated herself from the discussion, grabbed a glass of wine, and retreated to the terrace that overlooked Montazah Bay and the busy port of Alexandria.

"Sorry, sweetheart," Hugh Carmichael said as he appeared from behind one of the potted palms. "Seems like we both had the same escape plan in mind!"

"With the likes of Millicent Lawrence, Violet Norton, and Emerence Stanley, can you blame me?" Ursula replied.

"I thought I saw them in there—surrounding the punch bowl like coyotes at a water hole," Hugh said.

"Those three are worse than Macbeth's witches. If I have to spend one more moment listening to their moralizing and condemnation, I think I will throw up."

"Well, so long as you throw up inside, I won't object." Hugh replied.

They both stood for a moment, enjoying one of the few moments of levity they'd shared in recent weeks.

Ursula watched as the sun began to set, casting an orange glow across the long, dark sea edge.

"Is it my imagination, or does it seem unusually busy for this time of evening?" she asked. "I thought most of the steamers would have left by now." She pointed to the row of steamer funnels.

"I guess it's not every day that a lowly shipping clerk blows his brains out in the customs office," Hugh replied. "Whittaker tells me that passengers have been held up for hours."

"What happened?" Ursula asked hoarsely.

"No one's sure. But the poor man's dead—that's one thing for certain. Whittaker said the man was apparently in financial trouble."

"Whittaker said?" Ursula asked sharply.

"Yes," Hugh answered with a sideways glance. "You should know by now that Whittaker is always one step ahead of the rest of us."

Ursula made no reply, but there was a bitter taste in her mouth.

"Are you feeling all right?" Hugh asked.

Ursula steadied herself. "Yes . . . I think, I think I'll just go inside for a moment, if you don't mind."

"Feeling unwell, Miss Marlow?" Ambrose Whittaker called out through the open French doors. Ursula couldn't even bring herself to look at him.

"Miss Marlow is fine," Hugh replied evenly, his eyes fixed on hers. "No need to concern yourself."

As soon as Whittaker's back was turned, Hugh's demeanor changed. He looked at Ursula with apprehension and said, "Let me take you back to your hotel."

"Thank you," Ursula replied, still dazed. "I think that would be for the best."

As she turned, a young servant, little more than a boy, approached. He was dressed in a white robe and holding a telegram in his slender dark hands.

"Miss Marlow?" he said, and Ursula nodded blankly. Seeing her expression, Hugh gave the messenger a couple of piasters and took the telegram. "Do you want me to open it?" he asked gently. Ursula shook her head, but her heart was sinking. Ever since the events of two years ago, she dreaded telegrams. With trembling hands, she opened the envelope and stared at the words, which seemed to jump and blur before her eyes.

"Bad news?" Hugh asked.

Ursula handed the telegram from Lord Wrotham to him mechanically. The telegram confirmed her worst fears. It was indeed bad news.

> *Fire at Oldham factory STOP Young woman inside*
> *dead STOP Return immediately STOP*

Ursula swayed. First the news of the shipping clerk's death, and now this. To leave, with Katya's death still hanging over her, seemed unthinkable, and yet Ursula knew she had to return to England as soon as possible. Given all her recent business trouble, a death at one of her factories could ruin her.

"I have to leave for England immediately," she said numbly.

"Well, let's get you back to your hotel first."

Hugh took her arm as they walked back through the assembled guests.

Ursula tried to ignore Ambrose Whittaker as they passed, but the image of that afternoon at the customs house forced her to look. He lit a cigar and threw the end that he had clipped off aside. His disdain angered her, but she showed no emotion as she passed him. She could have sworn, however, that as she turned and bid her hosts good-bye, she saw him smile.

Ursula returned to her hotel to find Julia waiting anxiously in her bedroom suite, looking unusually pale and agitated

"As soon as they told me there was a telegram for you, I knew it was something terrible!" Julia wailed. "I told 'em they had to find you quick smart!"

"You did the right thing," Ursula responded distractedly. "I just need to collect my thoughts and work out what's the best way to get back to England as soon as possible."

"I'll go and speak with my agent at the docks," Hugh called out from the doorway. "I think the Marienbad sails for Brindisi in the morning."

He had already left by the time Ursula responded with a mute nod of her head.

"Oh, Miss," Julia said helplessly. "Can I get you something? You look right poorly, you do!"

"No." Ursula was slowly recovering her senses. "Let's just concentrate on getting things organized. I must write to Mrs. Mahfouz and the chief inspector. . . ." Ursula's voice drifted off as she mulled over what was to be done.

"That reminds me—Mrs. Mahfouz sent this around for you. It arrived just after you left for the party."

Julia pulled out an envelope from the apron pocket and handed it to Ursula.

Ursula opened it quickly.

The police came soon after you left this afternoon, and I was told in no uncertain terms to desist from making any further inquiries about Katya or Peter Vilensky. As you know, my husband cannot risk any further police scrutiny, and so, ma chérie, it may be some time before I can find out anything more. In the meantime, please be careful. My husband sends you a warning: Do not focus so much on the serpent lest you miss the scorpion.

Part Three

England

Eight

Yorkshire, England
APRIL 1912

The monoplane landed in a field of grass on the Earl of Hattersley's estate in Yorkshire. A friend of Hugh Carmichael and fellow airplane enthusiast, the earl was quite prepared to set aside a section of his vast estate to provide an airstrip for local pilots and aviation aficionados. It was supposedly spring, but Ursula could see little sign of winter ending. There were no new buds on the hedgerows or blossoms in the trees. Even the daffodils, usually the first signal of spring approaching, were absent. Ursula climbed out of the plane, clad in a pair of overalls and a long, hooded cloak. She threw back the hood and took off the goggles, grateful finally to be able to remove the wretched things.

In her quest to return to England as soon as possible, she had been forced to leave Julia in Alexandria. The day after Lord Wrotham's telegram arrived, the morning they were due to sail, Julia had awoken feverish and ill. Ursula, concerned about Julia's condition worsening on the sea voyage home, with mixed feelings accepted Mrs. Millicent Lawrence's offer for Julia to accompany her and Misses Norton and Stanley home the following week. Hugh Carmichael reorganized his business plans so he could join Ursula aboard the Austrian Lloyd steamer ship the *Marienbad*, leaving for Brindisi that morning. From there they traveled by train to Calais. Originally headed to France to undertake a series of test flights with his friend Louis Blériot, he offered instead to pick the plane up in Calais and fly Ursula across the English Channel. She was back in England in less than a week.

Cold, grimy, and exhausted, Ursula was beginning to question the wisdom of that decision. Twilight was approaching, and the dull gray light of England oppressed her already. Unwittingly she found herself searching for Lord Wrotham's familiar face, but there was only Samuels, Ursula's chauffeur, standing dutifully by "Bertie," the silver Rolls-Royce, waiting for her return. In the half-light, with Samuels's solemn garb and the motorcar standing silent, Ursula was suddenly reminded of her father's funeral.

Hugh tapped her on the arm and bid her a hasty good-bye. He wanted to make it to Newcastle before the light faded entirely. With the assistance of three of the earl's footmen, Hugh climbed into the airplane; the propellers rotated, and the engine engaged. After bumping along the makeshift airstrip, the plane was soon airborne once more.

"Miss Marlow," Samuels said, "it is good to have you back with us."

"It is good to be back, despite the circumstances," Ursula replied, mustering a smile. She slipped into Bertie's backseat. The leather was cold and uninviting.

Ursula had heard the news of the tragedy of the *Titanic* while aboard the *Marienbad* and having known a number of those who had perished, she was glad to be safely home. She shivered when she thought of the men who had considered it unnecessary to provide enough lifeboats for all their passengers, irrespective of their class. Had she, too, become complacent in her wealth, arrogant enough to think nothing could sink her?

"Any messages for me?" Ursula asked, unable to conceal the wistfulness in her voice.

Samuels turned round and handed her a sheaf of papers.

"We didn't have time to inform anyone, Miss, since we received your telegram only this morning, but his lordship dropped this off for you a couple of days ago. It's his notes on the incident in Oldham."

Samuels read her face and answered before she could even ask the question. "Lord Wrotham hasn't been by Chester Square or Gray House, and Mrs. Stewart said we should wait and ask you first before we sent word of your arrival. . . ." Samuels's voice dropped off uncertainly.

Ursula mustered a weak smile. "No matter."

"Mrs. Norris is taking care of the arrangements at Gray House, and Bridget came up by train this morning," Samuels continued. Mrs. Norris, Ursula's old nanny, had remained on as caretaker of her old home in Lancashire, Gray House, after the Marlow family moved to London.

"No need for you to worry. I'm sure everything will be fine. Drive on. It'll be a few hours before we'll be at Gray House. I'll read Lord Wrotham's notes in the car." It didn't take her long to become acquainted with what had happened at the Oldham factory. As always, Lord Wrotham was brief and to the point but even his stoic, matter-of-fact report could not dispel her anguish.

Ursula slumped back into her seat, the notes crumbling in her lap as she gazed out, preoccupied, at the gray-green landscape.

That night, after arriving late at Gray House, Ursula slept in the green bedroom that had been hers as a child. Bridget, one of the parlor-maids, had already lit the coal fire in the room and placed an earthen-ware hot water bottle between the sheets. With the warmth of the room and the familiarity of her childhood furniture surrounding her, Ursula fell into a deep and languid state that hovered on the verge of sleep but never quite crossed over. She kept thinking about Lord Wrotham's notes and his concern (written as a terse postscript) that the fire was further evidence of possible industrial espionage. Her body was heavy and her senses dulled, but she could not rest. The clock on the mantel struck one, then two in the morning, and still she was held suspended. Her mind refused to quiet, and all the while, as her worries intensified and her languorousness became an oppressive torpor, she kept seeing a pair of cool blue-gray eyes, in a face masked by shadows, watching and waiting as if expecting her to speak.

Ursula stepped gingerly over the fallen beam. The air grew thick with the acrid smell of smoke as her leather boots trod heavily on the piles of ashes beneath her feet. So this was all that remained, she thought bitterly, of her much cherished project. Ursula's ambition had been to provide employment to those women whom society had discarded. Now her dreams had been reduced to nothing more than soot and ash.

George Aldwych, previously the foreman of the nearby Oldham mill, had been in charge of overseeing the Oldham Garment Factory. Ursula saw him now, bent over a charred piece of machinery, trying to see if anything was salvageable. He looked pensive and tired. His beard, normally ginger, was streaked with black. George's habit of stroking his beard when he was thinking had clearly taken its toll.

"I'm sorry you had to return under these circumstances," George called out.

"So am I, though it is good to see you again, George. So much has happened, it seems like I've been away years, rather than six weeks."

"Aye, it certainly seems longer than that," George agreed as he sifted through the ashes.

"Where did they find the girl?" Ursula asked.

George rose from his knees. "They found the body over there in the back," he replied.

"Can you show me?"

"If you insist, Miss, but there ain't much to see now. They took the body away over a week ago."

"Still, I'd like to see where she was found. She was my responsibility. I need to know what happened to her."

"Aye. Poor lass . . . well, follow me, then. She was found through 'ere."

Ursula followed George through the open doorway and into a room that had once served as the cafeteria.

He pointed to a clearing in the ashes and debris. "That's where she was, all curled up like she was just sleepin'."

Ursula walked over and crouched down near the spot.

"Who was she?"

"Arina Petrenko. She was one of the girls hired to help train the others."

"I vaguely remember her. She was Russian, wasn't she?"

"Yes, though you'd not know it. Said she moved here when she were a lass and she were almost as English as you and I. Not sure she even spoke Russian anymore."

"Do we know why she was here that late at night?"

"No. We're still waitin' to hear what the police think. At first I just thought it was a ragamuffin or summat like that, but now we know it was Arina. Poor girl chose the wrong time to be in here, that's for sure." George's mouth twisted.

"What time did the fire start?" Ursula asked.

"Oh, they reckon it musta started around half past ten. The fire brigade were called then, anyways, but by the time they arrived they couldn't save the place."

"Who called the fire brigade?" Ursula asked as she stood up.

George poked around in the pocket of his jacket. "Mrs. Entwistle . . . lives round the corner on Henry Street." George pulled out a scrap of paper. "Yes, here we are. She said she phoned at quarter to eleven."

Ursula gazed up into the sky through what was left of the factory roof. "Run through the day again for me. You were the one who closed up as usual, right?"

"That's right. The whistle blew at five thirty. Same as usual. All the girls clocked off—I was there, so I would 'ave seen if anyone was skiving off in the back. Anyway, I did my usual rounds—checking on the machinery and such. Then I locked up around six. Same as I always do."

"And there was no one in the factory then?"

"No, as I said, all the girls had clocked off their shift."

"After you locked up, what did you do?"

"Same as always. Went to the Dog and Duck for a pint or two, then went home—it'd be around half past seven by then or eight—and had my tea."

"And you had the keys with you?"

"I always have 'em. Keep 'em in the drawer in the kitchen."

Ursula put her hands on her hips. "No one else has access to the keys?"

"No—except you, of course, Miss."

"Well, I know I didn't let the poor girl in—what about other people? Had the keys gone missing recently?"

"No."

"So she must have broken in."

"Looks that way."

"Hmm . . ." Ursula frowned. "It all seems very strange. Why would Arina break into the factory at night? Why did she not escape after the fire broke out? Had she set the fire? Was she disgruntled with working here?" Ursula reeled off the questions, knowing that George had few, if any, answers.

"I guess we just 'ave to wait until the coroner's inquest . . . though Arina were a good worker. She had no complaints that I heard."

Ursula remained thoughtful. "I think I should pay the coroner a visit. I need to find out as much as I can about what happened here."

"Right you are, Miss. I can take you to Dr. Mortimer's if you'd like."

"No need. Samuels is waiting outside. Just tell me where I can find this Dr. Mortimer."

"Barrow Street. Number fourteen. He lives with his sister above the consulting rooms."

"In the meantime, why don't you ask around a bit? See if anyone knows why Arina was here. I can't believe it's been over a week, and no one's come forward with any more information. As you said, there's nothing here at all that would explain what happened."

"None. She had no papers. No money. Nothin'. Her roommate nicked off just after the police came to tell her about Arina. No one knows where she's gone."

"Well, we can only hope that the police have found something out by now—really, you wonder how a girl can simply vanish without anyone knowing how or why. But first, to the coroner—let's see what he has to say."

Ursula carefully climbed over the debris and made her way out of the factory. She called out to Samuels, who was waiting beside Bertie, chatting with some of the locals. He hastily grabbed his cap, opened the rear door for her, and nodded as she told him where he needed to take her next.

"Dr. Ainsley Mortimer." He spoke with a slight hesitation before holding out his hand to shake hers. "I assume you are . . . Miss . . . Miss Marlow." Ursula noticed he paused carefully over his words, as if quieting a stutter.

"Please just call me Ursula. I'm here to ask you some questions about the girl that was brought in about a week ago—the one who died in the fire at my Oldham factory, I mean."

Ainsley Mortimer nodded his head and looked grave. "Perhaps you should come inside and sit down. I'm not sure I can say much— I'm awaiting the pathologist's report for the inquest—but I'd be happy to tell you as much as I'm able." He gestured to her to enter the room and followed her into his study, closing the glass-paneled door behind him.

"Please take a seat." He hesitated once more. "The surroundings aren't quite what you are used to, I'm sure . . . but we like to think it's comfortable enough."

"I'm sure this will be fine," Ursula said, embarrassed that she should have prompted such a comment. Her voice drifted off as she looked about the room, which was filled with almost every conceivable scientific instrument, along with piles of papers and books that lined not only the bookshelves but also the floor and the top of the large wooden desk in the middle of the room. A skeleton hung from a post in the corner of the room, the bones of the feet and toes resting on a large pile of leather-bound books with macabre titles such as *A Hand-Book of Post-Mortem Examinations and of Morbid Anatomy* and *A Popular Treatise on the Remedies to Be Employed in Cases of Poisoning and Apparent Death.*

Ursula went to sit down in a high-backed chair that appeared to be available for guests—and whose upholstery was clean, if a little threadbare.

"I don't usually have to share my seat with a skull, though, I must admit," she said with a rueful smile, picking up the offending item and placing it on the desk.

"Sorry about that," Dr. Mortimer said, and then, eyeing the specimen jar containing a dissected heart that was serving as a paperweight, he began to apologize further, insisting that they had best discuss the case in his sister's office instead.

"You must think me a frightful mess. . . . My sister is forever telling me off for leaving this room in such a state. She doesn't see patients up here, of course; the consultation rooms are down the hall," Dr. Mortimer finished lamely, a curl of brown hair springing over his left eye despite his efforts to smooth it back.

"Here is perfectly fine," Ursula reassured him, barely suppressing a smile. "So your sister works with you—is she a nurse, then?" Ursula asked as she sat down on the chair. Dr. Mortimer picked over a pile of papers to make his way over to his desk.

"She's a physician, actually." He sat down. "First of us to follow my father into the profession. She graduated from the University of Manchester in 1905. She was one of the first women to do so. I graduated the following year." Ursula noticed how his gaze never left hers. Clearly he was waiting to gauge her reaction.

"Impressive," Ursula replied. "I'm looking forward to meeting her."

"As she is, too—she is a great admirer of yours."

Ursula's eyebrows rose in surprise. Dr. Mortimer's eyes crinkled as he smiled.

"We are not so backward as to be entirely ignorant of your goings-on, Miss Marlow." Ursula flushed, confused as to his true meaning. She was wary now, having met many people who relished the opportunity to dig up scandal and innuendo where she was concerned.

Seeming to sense her confusion, he frowned. "I didn't mean . . . ," he started, but before he could complete his sentence, the office door was flung open by a tall, lanky woman in a pale green pinafore. The sleeves of her white shirt were rolled up to the elbows, and her hair, which was the same light brown color as Dr. Mortimer's, was coming loose from the chignon at the nape of her neck. There was no mistaking them for anything other than brother and sister.

"I thought I would find you here. . . . Really, Ains, you are the limit! Fancy inflicting this pigsty on Miss Marlow. Now, then, I want you to both come along with me. Nancy's popped the tea on, and we have a nice fire going in the lounge. I just saw our last patient—batty old Mrs. McCaffey, worst luck! But I managed to send her on her way with a tincture of valerian. We should be quite comfy and private in there, and Ains can give you all the information you need about that poor girl."

Ursula sat stunned by the onslaught of words.

"Well?" Dr. Mortimer's sister asked, with an impatient gesture at her brother. Ainsley rose from his seat.

"Miss Marlow, my sister Eustacia."

Ursula got up and, still dazed, shook her hand. Eustacia grabbed her arm with a smile. "Come along, then," she said. "Let's get you out of this mess and into somewhere more salubrious. Ains, why don't you ask Nancy to bring out some jam roll as well. I'm famished."

Ainsley chuckled. "As you can see, Miss Marlow, both of us must fall into line. I'll be with you shortly. In the meantime, Stacie— maybe you could take this file with you? It has all my notes from the postmortem."

"Right-oh!" Eustacia took the file from him and started to lead Ursula out of the room and down the hallway. "Our father was coroner, you know. . . . It was his dying wish that Ainsley follow in his footsteps. It took him a few years to decide, but now he's one of the few coroners in the country with medical and legal experience. Didn't he tell you he also studied law? Typical! Anyway, better him than me, as coroner, I mean. I'd rather be taking care of the living any day of the week!"

Ursula followed Dr. Eustacia Mortimer into the lounge and sat down.

Eustacia looked at her squarely as she perched herself on the edge of the other armchair. "So," she said abruptly, "why do you think these things are happening to your business? I've been keeping an eye out in the local newspapers, and it seems like this must be the fifth or sixth incident in as many months. Is it because you're a woman, do you think?"

Ursula was taken aback by her directness, but she answered in kind.

"I think that probably has something to do with it, but there's no evidence of a concerted attack on my business, so we may never know for sure."

Eustacia rubbed her nose thoughtfully. "I think men are threatened by a successful, educated, and beautiful woman like yourself. No one could call me attractive, so at least I have that in my favor."

Ursula wasn't sure how to react, but Eustacia's mouth quivered and broke into a wide grin. They both laughed, just as Ainsley Mortimer walked in bearing a tray with teacups, a brown teapot, and a plate of jam roll.

He frowned. "I'm not sure there was anything in the file that was amusing."

"No, of course not." Eustacia straightened her face quickly.

Ainsley took the file as Eustacia poured the tea and, with a hesitant cough, put on his glasses and began to read.

"The deceased, whom the police have formally identified as Arina Petrenko of 1 Back Gladstone Street, was a twenty-three-year-old female of Russian Jewish descent. She was found on the premises of the Oldham Garment Factory at . . . well I'm sure you know the address, Miss Marlow. I'm not really sure how much information you want."

"Ains, do get on with it!" Eustacia interrupted him.

"Right, yes. Well . . . in my report I note that due to the condition of her bodily remains, I could not provide any reliable estimate of the time of death, though it seems from what we know of her movements to have occurred sometime between six and ten o'clock that night. Nor could I definitively identify the cause of death. That being said, I did infer from the lack of suppuration of some of the remaining injured surfaces and lack of evidence of smoke inhalation in the (admittedly poor condition) bronchial passages that Arina Petrenko was already dead at the time of the fire. Though scant evidentiary remains preclude me from making any final pronouncement, it would appear, from the medical evidence available, that the fire may be eliminated as a proximate cause of death. I have sent tissue samples and other evidence to the pathologist for more detailed examination. Without further evidence, however, I can make no determination whether her death was accidental, self-inflicted, or a result of a deliberate and malicious act. I therefore recommend a full coronial inquiry to address the issues identified."

Ainsley snapped the file closed and looked up at Ursula. "I'm still waiting to hear more from the pathologist and the local police to see if they have any further evidence that could assist us. Of course I've had the dickens' own job trying to hurry things along. The local rabbi has been quite distressed by the delay in getting the poor girl buried."

"Thank you, Dr. Mortimer, for being so forthcoming. But can I just clarify one point? If I heard you correctly, you believe Arina was dead before the fire broke out?"

"Yes—yes, I do."

"Was there anything else at all—off the record, of course—that could explain how or why she died?"

"Well, I've spared you all the minute medical details—they can be pretty gruesome—but in short, no. As I said, I'm still waiting on information from the pathologist. It's a pity we couldn't get Spillsbury—he's the chap who helped on the Crippen case." Ainsley sighed. "Anyhow, the inquest is currently scheduled for next Friday."

"Any idea what sort of fire it was?"

Ainsley looked thoughtful. "A petrol fire, most likely. Generates a tremendous amount of heat, which would account for the condition of the body. Oh, I'm sorry, Miss Marlow. . . ."

Ursula's face was white.

"Oh, Ains, really! Now, Miss Marlow just you have another cuppa." Eustacia reached over and poured Ursula another cup of tea. "You'll feel much better."

Ursula sipped her tea gratefully. "Anything else?" she asked hoarsely.

"Well, we have to wait for the inquest, obviously, but I reckon that unless your girls were sewing petrol-soaked dresses, this fire was no accident."

As she clambered into Bertie's backseat, Ursula asked Samuels to drive her to the Oldham police station. George had told her the name of the sergeant assigned to the case, but Ursula wasn't sure what kind of reception she would get. In her experience, most policemen weren't too keen on having a woman "poking her nose" into their investigations.

They arrived at the small redbrick police station on Barn Street just as the afternoon sun was dipping behind the rows of terraced houses. Ursula quickly checked the watch she carried on a gold chain about her neck. It was nearly four o'clock.

Once out of the car, Ursula straightened her skirt and adjusted her hat before entering the police station. A young redheaded constable stood behind the desk, and he greeted her with a faint look of both recognition and bemusement.

"I'd like to see Sergeant Barden, please," Ursula announced, placing her gloves on the desk.

"And you are?"

She regarded this disingenuous request with arched eyebrows.

"Miss Ursula Marlow."

The constable exchanged glances with an older policeman walking out the swing doors by the main desk.

"Why d'yer want to speak to Barden?" the older man queried.

"I own the factory on Beasdale Street where that poor young girl died. In the fire. I have just arrived and would very much like to assist as best I can on this case. Is Sergeant Barden around?"

"No, he's not. Been called down to London." The man gestured toward the constable behind the desk. "You can leave a message, if you'd like."

"Thank you," Ursula murmured. She had a sense that the death of a factory girl was not one of the top priorities for the Oldham police. As if reading her thoughts the older man swiveled his head and with a baleful stare said, "We've got two in t'cells from last night drunk and disorderly and four robberies in the last week. We're short staffed as is." Ursula's hands twitched—surely the death of a young woman, even one as lowly as Arina, merited more compassion and attention than this.

The older policeman turned back to the young constable. "Tell Henry I need him to go out to Legget's farm; they've reported some missing sheep. Looks like the Ramsbottom twins are up to no good again."

"Yes, sir," the young constable answered, avoiding Ursula's gaze.

The older man left the station, and Ursula took out her card to write a note to Sergeant Barden. It seemed ridiculous that she should have traveled all the way to Gray House, only to find the sergeant had been summoned to London. She quelled her frustration, however, and wrote a polite message reiterating her commitment to providing whatever assistance she could to the police investigation.

"I knew your father when I was but a lad," the constable said, taking the note from her. He bit his lip. "God bless 'im. It were terrible, wot happened."

"Yes, it was," Ursula responded sadly. Her father's death was never far from her thoughts.

With her visit to the Oldham police station cut short, Ursula decided to visit the address Dr. Mortimer had given for Arina Petrenko. Back Gladstone Street lay on the edge of Oldham, and apart from recalling that there were several disused coal pits near there, Ursula was unfamiliar with the area.

As Samuels drew up alongside a dilapidated cottage, Ursula soon realized that "home" this most certainly was not. She hadn't seen such rural poverty since she was a child. She felt the mud thick beneath her feet as she stepped out of the motorcar, and had to put on her long navy blue cardigan to ward off the chill wind that swept across the moorland from the Pennines, rattling the windows and doors.

As she approached the front door of the cottage, a lady in an apron appeared from round the back, a wailing child in one arm and a laundry basket in the other. From the farmhouse on the hillock above, a border collie came running out, barking furiously.

"Oh, shut yer gob, Shep!! I said shut it!!"

The dog stopped barking and slunk off with its tail between its legs. The woman glared at Ursula.

"There's no use knockin'!" she called out. "They ain't there no more. All cleared off, more like, when they heard about the girl."

"You mean Arina?" Ursula replied.

"Can't say I knows wot 'er name was. But she weren't from round 'ere, that's for sure. None of 'em were."

"I'm Ursula Marlow," Ursula said, approaching her.

"Don't know that I care who you are!" the lady responded. The baby in her arms stopped crying and glared at Ursula mutinously.

"I own the factory that was destroyed in the fire."

"So?" The lady looked Ursula up and down, as she stood there in her white apron and brown shawl. Ursula reflected she probably could have said she was the queen of England and gotten just the same response.

"I wondered if you knew where Arina's roommate may have gone."

"She left sudden like, middle o't'other night. No idea where she went. But she were foreign like t'other girl."

"Did she work in town?"

The woman eyed her suspiciously before answering. "I reckon she worked at the colliery. My son Len works there. He'd know more."

"And where is Len?"

"He's workin'. Gets off at half six."

"I'd like to come by and speak with him. I'm trying to find out as much as I can about the girl who died in the fire. Arina Petrenko was her name. Do you mind if I go inside and take a look?"

The lady sniffed disdainfully. "I guess so. We never had much to do wi' them. But they paid their rent regular, so we didn't ask any questions."

"You live in the farmhouse up there?" Ursula pointed to the stone cottage on the hill.

The woman narrowed her eyes. "Aye, we do an'all."

"Then if you don't mind, I'd like to take a look inside their cottage and then come up and speak to your son. Would that be all right?"

"I reckon so." The lady didn't wait for Ursula to reply before turning and hoisting the child into her arms. She pushed open the door to the cottage and let Ursula in.

The baby in her arms started to cry again, and without another word the lady left, hauling the laundry basket up the muddy embankment that led to the farmhouse.

Ursula peered inside the doorway. The cottage smelled musty and damp. There was still the faint aroma of singed embers in the air. Without lights, the front room was dim and dank, even though the walls were wallpapered in a gaudy rose-and-leaf pattern. The room was bare, except for an iron-grated fireplace and a single wooden chair left in the middle of the room. Carefully Ursula made her way through and up the narrow stairs to the bedrooms above. The ceiling was low, and Ursula had to bend over as she reached the top of the stairs. There were two bedrooms upstairs. One had two single beds, each made of wrought iron that had been painted white and was now peeling. Ursula lit the gas lamp on the wall beside the bedroom door. The light hissed before emitting a smoky yellow glow. Ursula entered the room and looked around. Given the distinct lack of interest conveyed by the Oldham police, she doubted that their examination of Arina's room had been very thorough, so she scanned the room to see what might have been missed.

Some scattered pamphlets lay on the floor beneath the window, and she walked over to give them a closer look. She recognized them immediately as recent editions of the English socialist journal the *People*, as well as a number of pamphlets written by Lenin. Alexei had introduced her to journals and pamphlets just like these back in 1908.

Alexei Prosnitz had come to England after the failure of the St. Petersburg revolution of 1905. The son of one of Winifred's tutors at Oxford, he was a fervent member of the Russian Social Democratic Party and follower of Lenin. He had also been Ursula's lover—a fact she would rather not be reminded of, even after the passage of nearly four years.

Ursula's eyes soon adjusted to the jaundiced light, and she began to scan the room for any clues to why Arina might have been killed. She thumbed through the pamphlets, but they appeared to be nothing out of the ordinary. She tapped on the floorboards and walls, but likewise there was no evidence of any secret hiding place.

Ursula rubbed her chin. It was damp in the room and she knew from growing up in the north that most working-class families could not afford to light the fires in the bedrooms except when someone was ill. It was more than likely that Arina and her housemate spent their winter evenings huddled around the fireplace in the front room rather than upstairs in the cold, so Ursula made her way back downstairs. She discovered that both fireplaces, in the front room and the kitchen, had been swept clean. "Damn and blast," she muttered, standing in the kitchen with her arms firmly crossed. Her mind clicked over as she gazed around the bare, flagstone kitchen. There were rickety wooden shelves (all empty), a cracked ceramic sink, and the shallow grated fireplace; a heavy, cast-iron stove squatted against the rear wall. Taking her ivory-handled comb out of her cardigan pocket, Ursula opened the door of the stove and peered inside. A cloud of soot and ash rose as she poked around. Beneath the charred wood and ashes, she discovered what appeared to be fragments of paper that had not completely burned.

Gingerly Ursula tried to lift these using the tapered handle of the comb. She pulled out a handkerchief from her pocket with her other hand and awkwardly spread it out on the floor. She then placed the fragments carefully on the crisp white linen and leaned over to see if she could make out anything from them. They appeared to be the remnants of a handwritten letter, but it was hard to decipher much besides the fact that the letter was in Cyrillic script and was almost totally destroyed. Ursula peered over to see if there were any further fragments in the stove, but none remained. Carefully folding the handkerchief with the letter fragments inside, she placed it in her skirt pocket, got to her feet, and tried to dust off the ash, instead leaving a long streak of black across her skirt.

"Arina fell in with a bad lot." The sound of a man's voice behind her made her jump. Ursula spun round to come face to face with a short, stocky man dressed in threadbare brown pants and open-necked shirt. "Them Bolsheviks or whatever they're called. She and her friends were always talking to the union representatives at t'collieries and t'mills." Ursula presumed this must be the son of the landlady.

"It's Len, right?"

He nodded.

"And you called her Arina, so you knew her?"

He nodded again. "Talked wi'her a few times. Parents died when she were but a lass. She told me she'd been in England about ten year now."

"And did you know her roommate?"

"Didn't have much to do wi'er. Name was Natasha or summat like that. Worked in the colliery office. Then there were a couple o' lads who I saw come by. Not for a few months though, now. Don't know who they was but I reckon they were Bolshies too—"

"Do you know if they left anything behind that would help explain why Arina was in the factory the night of the fire?"

"Police came and took stuff the day after the fire. Then Natasha cleared off that night. Think she was terrified of the police."

"Why was she afraid of the police?" Ursula queried.

Len's face became guarded. "How should I know? Only a few days before the fire, they complained that someone had broken in and messed the place about a bit. I told 'em they should go to the police, but they refused. Said they didn't trust 'em."

"After meeting some of your local constabulary, I can't say I blame them."

Len shrugged. "Arina's lot gave us no trouble, so I didn't worry about it at the time."

"Now, of course, one has to wonder whether the break-in had anything to do with the fire or Arina's death," Ursula murmured thoughtfully. "Did they tell you if anything had been taken?"

Len shook his head. "No one said nothing about anything being taken."

"Pity. Do you have any idea where Arina's roommate may be now?"

"I've heard nowt about 'er."

Ursula suppressed a sigh.

"Did you happen to see Arina the night of the fire?"

"Me mam said she saw her come home same as usual. Didn't notice anything else, but then we're not ones for pryin', and at night, with all the bairns to feed and get ready for bed, none of us would have been watchin' for anyone."

"No, of course not," Ursula replied before digging out a card and pen from her jacket pocket. "But if you do think of anything that may be useful, please let me know." She wrote the address for Gray House on the card. "I feel it is my responsibility to find out as much as I can about this poor girl's death."

"Me mam said you owned the factory," Len said tentatively.

"Yes, that's right."

"Bloody funny thing for a woman to do," he said with a sniff, and walked out of the room.

Nine

London

APRIL 1912

The following evening, after a day spent with the local factory inspector and union representative, Ursula traveled back to London by train. Samuels arranged for her motorcar Bertie to be placed on a special train car to accompany their return. Christopher Dobbs was holding a cocktail party, and Ursula felt compelled to accept the invitation, despite Arina Petrenko's death in Oldham. Her attendance was intended to reassure all London society that Marlow Industries was in no way threatened by what had occurred.

She carefully placed the letter fragments she had found in a silver box, planning to get the Cyrillic script translated while back in London. When she was with Alexei she had known many Russians, but since that time she had fallen out of contact with all his comrades. She would now have to depend on Winifred to try to find a translator for her, one who they could rely on to be both trustworthy and discreet.

She greeted Biggs and Mrs. Stewart with relief—at least they remained, as always, stalwart in the face of all adversity. A stack of business correspondence awaited her in the study but once she had dealt with the worst of it, Ursula finally found a moment to call Winifred. Sitting at her father's desk, her finger beating out a nervous rhythm on the lid of the silver box, Ursula bent over the receiver and waited for Winifred's deep, masculine voice to answer.

"Freddie," Ursula began.

"Sully! When did you get back from Egypt?!"

"Late last week, but things . . . things have been rather awkward."

"I read about what happened to the Oldham factory. I've left messages for you all over the place!"

"Sorry, Freddie, but it's been an absolute nightmare." Ursula hesitated.

Winifred, as if sensing her discomfit, answered somberly, "I know. What can I do?"

Ursula exhaled. At least Winifred could be relied upon to help.

"The coroner says that the girl, Arina Petrenko, was already dead before the fire—so we're looking at a murder investigation."

"And if I know you, Sully, you're already undertaking your own inquiries."

"Well, I'm hardly going to place my faith in the Oldham police, now, am I? Not when it's my father's business that's at stake."

"Your business now," Winifred gently reminded her.

"Of course," Ursula answered, too preoccupied to notice the reproach.

"What do you need me to do?" Winifred asked.

"I found a fragment of paper, possibly a letter, in Russian, which I need translated. There's not much, maybe a couple of sentences, but it may be important. I don't know anyone anymore. Could you find someone? Someone we can trust?"

"As good as done. I've still got contacts. You want me to come round now and get it?"

"No, I've got to get ready—Dobbs is holding a cocktail party this evening, worse luck. But I can't afford to miss it. I have to hold my head up tonight and prove I've not been broken by this. Christopher Dobbs may be a thundering bore, but I don't trust him as far as I can spit. I intend to keep an eye on him."

"Like father, like son, eh?"

"Something like that," Ursula answered.

What had once been a Georgian town house had been converted by Dobbs over the last year into a house befitting a wealthy bachelor eager to impress society. From the rich wallpaper to the maritime paintings, everything was deliberately planned to evoke the image of Dobbs as a man who had helped make the British Empire what it was today. None of this impressed Ursula, for her tastes were far less ornate, but nonetheless she recognized and respected the power that Dobbs was trying to convey.

Framed against the Moorish fretwork of Dobbs's ornate entrance hall, Ursula, in her draped gown by Doucet, could have stepped out of the French magazine *Gazette du Bon Ton*—from the soft folds of her diaphanous dress to her satin coat edged with silver fox and the black ostrich feather in her hair, every inch the model of Parisian haute couture. Christopher Dobbs, in a sleek black tuxedo, stood by the doorway to his opulent ballroom, welcoming his guests. His eyes narrowed as he threw her an appraising glance, but Ursula refused to lose her composure.

"Ursula!" Christopher held out his hand to clasp hers. "You look positively ravishing! It seems only yesterday you were running around Gray House in your pinafore and pigtails."

Ursula ignored his condescending tone. Instead she smiled charmingly and replied pleasantly, "The new place looks splendid. You've achieved so much since I've been in Egypt." If, she thought to herself, achievement means converting a decent Georgian town house into a monstrosity of lavish and vulgar tastes.

Dobbs's butler, Jeffries, moved forward to take Ursula's coat. It slid off easily with a shrug of her shoulders to reveal the neoclassical lines of her oyster gray dress. The delicate citrine and peridot necklace about her throat shimmered in the electric light.

Christopher Dobbs tightened his smile, clearly not deceived by Ursula's disingenuous compliment. His attention quickly moved on to his other guests as Ursula entered the ballroom scanning the crowded room to see who had been invited. There were Gerard and Elizabeth Anderson, of course, standing next to one of Christopher's latest acquisitions, a painting of Nelson's ship *Victory* at Trafalgar. Daniel Abbott was here without his wife, and judging from the awkwardness of his gait, Ursula surmised he had already been drinking for some time. In addition to her late father's erstwhile associates, there was a multitude of London's most successful businessmen and their wives or mistresses. Christopher Dobbs also loved to be surrounded by the music-hall set— he found the gaiety girls a particularly successful enticement for the aristocrats and military men with whom he wished to become better acquainted. With the thick cigar and cigarette smoke, glasses of champagne and whiskey, and a pianist playing ragtime, the room had the atmosphere of a private men's club rather than a cocktail party.

Ursula made her way into the ballroom and spent the next hour mingling and chatting with those she knew. She felt the disapproving stares of many of the guests: her status of female businesswoman and suffragette was sufficient cause for raised eyebrows in much of London society, but here she also felt the pall of a different kind of condemnation among Dobbs's guests—the denunciation of an "educated" woman. As a result, Ursula felt detached and uneasy. She cradled her glass of champagne in one hand and carefully mounted the stairs that led to the balcony overlooking the ballroom. She needed a place that would allow some circumspection as well as relief from the tedium of conversation with the likes of Brigadier Galbraith and his "lady friend," Doris Arkwright (known as Dolly Starbright every Saturday night at the Trocadero). Ursula leaned against the marble balustrade and closed her eyes for a moment.

"A penny for them . . . ," Hugh Carmichael said coming up behind her.

Ursula turned her head in astonishment. "Hugh, what on earth are you doing here?"

Hugh joined her and, with a gesture to the masses below, said, "I've come for the spectacle of it all."

Ursula raised her eyebrows. "I thought you would be at home by now."

Hugh's face clouded over. "I wish I were. But Dobbs here," he continued with a pointed look at Christopher Dobbs, "has just made an offer for one of my shipyards."

Ursula frowned. "I didn't think your shipyards were for sale."

"They're not," Hugh replied curtly. "But the bankers are closing in, and Dobbs knows it. My manager sent word of his offer as soon as I arrived . . . which is why I'm here."

"You're not telling me you're actually thinking of accepting him!"

"Never." Hugh's response was grim. "But I thought I had better see what I was up against."

Ursula looked at Hugh with concern. "What does Dobbs want with a Newcastle shipyard?"

"Dreadnoughts, it would seem. Rumor has it he's angling for a contract to build 'em. Taking advantage of the naval buildup against the German threat and all that."

Ursula let her mind tick over the import of his words.

"Iris would have insisted that I reject his offer in the strongest terms possible," Hugh continued.

Of course, Ursula remembered, Iris had been a pacifist. She would never have countenanced the use of her family's shipyards to build a warship.

"I understand. Please let me know if there's anything . . ." Ursula's voice trailed off as she saw him enter the ballroom below. It had been over three months, but the physical impact of his presence was as potent as ever. Hugh Carmichael's gaze followed hers to the tall, aristocratic man in immaculate evening clothes.

"Lord Wrotham, I presume."

Ursula roused herself and nodded. Hugh patted her shoulder. "It's time I went and met my enemy face to face. Looks like you are preparing to do the same."

Ursula drained her champagne glass and gave him a weary smile. "Something like that," she admitted. Hugh took his leave and started walking back down the staircase.

Ursula's hands gripped the balustrade. Her throat grew tight, so constricted that she could hardly breathe. She had to will herself to defy the panic that rose within her, to vanquish the surge of desire he aroused. But she hadn't expected him to be here, and she could not stem the breach. He looked up and caught sight of her. The ambush was complete.

Ursula quickly stepped back and retreated into the dim recesses of the book-lined mezzanine. Christopher Dobbs had purchased the entire library of an earl he had forced into bankruptcy. Although Ursula despised him for it, she could not help but admire the wealth of the collection. Now, surrounded on all sides by books, she found momentary sanctuary. She inhaled and exhaled slowly. She needed to recover her self-possession quickly; the last thing she wanted was to generate any more gossip.

Ursula returned to the balcony and then descended the wide staircase into the ballroom. The staircase was filled with people. She caught snippets of conversations, fragments of images. Champagne glasses, cigarettes, feathers—the flash of fine jewelry. By the time she reached the foot of the staircase, she had regained at least the appearance of equanimity. Lord Wrotham, standing by the wide marble fireplace, started to approach her. With a calm, determined stride she joined him, noting out of the corner of her eye that Christopher Dobbs was watching them closely. I will not be intimidated by these men, she admonished herself, and bid Lord Wrotham a serene good evening.

His countenance, as always, was impassive.

"I was not aware that you had returned from Egypt." Wrotham paused with quiet deliberation, but the unspoken censure was evident in his tone.

Ursula flushed. "I only returned only a couple of days ago, and went straight up north."

"I see."

"Mr. Carmichael kindly allowed me to accompany him across the Channel in his airplane. He's a pilot, you know. . . . Julia is still en route from Egypt with the rest of my things. When I got your message about the accident in Oldham, I knew I had to return as quickly as possible."

"You came by plane—"

"Across the Channel, yes." Ursula waited for his disapproval, but his expression remained neutral.

She couldn't bear it—the strain of their conversation, the chill in his tone. It was as if they were strangers.

"Why, Miss Marlow!" The shrill, unmistakable voice of Mrs. Eudora Pomfrey-Smith interrupted her thoughts.

Ursula thought she saw Lord Wrotham wince. In the last few years before Ursula's father's death, Mrs. Pomfrey-Smith had been his mistress. She now regarded herself as Ursula's personal confidante and adviser on all things related to "polite society."

Mrs. Pomfrey-Smith tucked her arm through Ursula's with a conspiratorial smile. "I've been talking to Mr. Carmichael. My dear, you have been having some adventures. Returning from Egypt and crossing the Channel in an airplane, of all things! Why, it will be the talk of the town!"

Ursula barely suppressed a groan. She should, of course, have guessed that her trip would soon generate quite a sensation. "Mrs. Pomfrey-Smith, I didn't expect to see you here." She thought it was best to ignore the subject of her arrival.

"Oh, Topper has been so good to me. After your father died." Mrs. Pomfrey-Smith's eyes suddenly filled with tears. Ursula found it irritating that she should make such a display of herself in public. "I was totally at a loss, but Topper's return from India has given me quite the new lease on life. I am determined to find him a suitable match. You know"—she leaned in with a sly smile—"you really must come to my salons more often." Mrs. Pomfrey-Smith shot Lord Wrotham a sly look. "As trustee for your father's estate, I'm sure Lord Wrotham would agree on the necessity of you marrying well."

"Indubitably," Lord Wrotham responded drily, and Ursula flushed again.

"Your concern for my marital well-being is most commendable," Ursula said, "but I'm sure I am quite capable of taking care of that particular matter on my own."

"Really?" Mrs. Pomfrey-Smith replied, her tone sharpening. "Doesn't seem that way to me."

Ursula fell silent, feeling the weight of Lord Wrotham's stare upon her. His eyes, watchful and guarded, never left her face. She wanted to pull him aside and confide in him all her concerns over Katya's death and the events in Oldham, but she knew she had to deal with these on her own. Under his scrutiny she felt her self-assurance falter, but she endeavored to maintain the appearance of calm despite the irritating presence of Mrs. Pomfrey-Smith.

Thankfully, Mrs. Pomfrey-Smith spied an old acquaintance from her days in India, providing both Lord Wrotham and Ursula the opportunity to extricate themselves from her and each other's company. Ursula found refuge beside one of the tall French windows that led out onto the garden terrace. She grabbed another glass of champagne from the tray proffered by one of the footmen and took a swift gulp. As she did so, she could hear Christopher Dobbs on the terrace, holding forth on his favorite topic—the possibility of a war with Germany.

"We all know war is coming; we may as well be helping England build her military power and resources to meet the German threat now. There's money to be made, yes, but there's also the real chance that Germany could act sooner than we think. England needs to be prepared. I'm just seeking the opportunity to be of help in that."

Ursula felt slightly sick. He sounded so dispassionate, so calculating—as if war should not be measured in people's lives but in armaments and machines.

"I mean, I don't deceive myself that I can compete with the likes of Vickers, but with war coming, there's plenty of work to be done."

"There's no disputin' that," came the emphatic voice of Brigadier Galbraith.

"And naval power will be critical. It'll be the dreadnoughts that win us this war, mark my words."

"Undoubtedly—so when are we likely to see the new shipyard up and running?"

"Just as soon as I can persuade Hugh Carmichael to hand over the papers."

"Is that really likely?"

"Well, he may have no choice. He's already defaulted on his loan. I've made him a fair offer. Unless another buyer comes forward, which is highly unlikely, I don't see what else he can do."

"And if he refuses?"

"My solicitor has it all in hand. We've even retained the services of one of the most eminent lawyers in the country. If we have to, we'll go to court and force the issue, but I really don't think it will come to that. Hugh Carmichael is a sensible man—I'm sure we can make him see reason."

Ursula bit her lip. She would have to warn Hugh Carmichael about Dobbs.

"Good thing his wife ain't around anymore—Quaker, don't you know. Bloody pacifists—if they had their way, England would soon be at the mercy of the Hun!"

Ursula sighed. Clearly Dobbs had surrounded himself with likeminded men. She would have to tread carefully. Trying to shake off her fears, she returned to the party and for the next two hours found herself engaged in a strange kind of dance. She and Lord Wrotham circled each other; the more she tried to avoid him, the more she found her gaze locking on his. They made no move to speak with each other again, but it was as if the room became ever smaller—drawing them closer and closer to each other in an ever-narrowing spiral.

Ursula felt lightheaded. Too much champagne, no doubt. But with this came a giddy recklessness that took all her strength to restrain. Each of her senses pricked. If she closed her eyes she could feel his warmth, she could smell his cologne, she could taste his kiss. The heat, the chatter, and the smoke whirled around her. She knew she had to leave.

Ursula walked swiftly to the entrance hall. Out of the corner of her eye she spied Christopher Dobbs mounting the staircase up to the balcony.

"I wouldn't bother waiting for him to say your good-byes." A drunken figure stumbled past her, and Ursula turned to see Daniel Abbott lurch toward the billiards room. He hadn't been the same since his daughter Cecilia's death. "Brought back a little something to keep him company—from India, don't y'know," he said, tapping a finger on his nose. "Name's Lilliani or some such thing."

"That's enough, Daniel." Lord Wrotham's distaste was evident, but Daniel Abbott didn't even acknowledge Wrotham's sudden arrival; he merely flashed Ursula an inane grin and continued on his way.

Before Ursula could utter a word, the footman returned, bearing her satin coat.

"Please, allow me," Lord Wrotham said, taking the coat and placing it around her shoulders. Was she deceiving herself, or was there a momentary hesitation as his long, tapered hands smoothed down the collar, and she felt his breath against her neck?

"Thank you," she said with a calmness that belied the thumping of her heart in her chest.

"Your coat, my lord." The footman returned and handed over Lord Wrotham's black cashmere evening coat.

"Would you like me to call you a cab, or is your driver waiting?" the footman addressed them both, as if they were leaving together. Before Ursula had a chance to rectify his misapprehension, Lord Wrotham started to speak. In cool, measured tones he informed the footman that there were two cars waiting outside. "If you would be so kind as to inform Miss Marlow's driver that she is ready, I will wait here. My driver knows to return at eleven-thirty, so I expect he will be arriving shortly."

"Of course, my lord." The footman bowed, with no outward indication of discomfiture at his mistake. He grabbed an umbrella from the elephant foot stand and ducked out the front door to find Samuels.

Lord Wrotham shrugged on his evening coat without another word. Ursula, with her back still to him, waited, determined to remain to all outward appearances poised and composed. Inside, however, the alcohol and the closeness of his presence produced a heady combination. She fought off her desire, fought off the reckless urges that stirred within her. She needed the cool night air to bring her back to her senses.

"It may be prudent to wait a few minutes after I have left." Ursula heard her voice as if from afar. It sounded dull and deadened. "I would hate to cause any further scandal by us being seen leaving at the same time."

He made no reply. She refused to look at him for fear that her actions would contradict all the restraint of her words. As a result, she could not gauge his reaction.

The footman returned and offered to shelter her under his umbrella to her car.

"Good night, Lord Wrotham." Ursula turned and spoke from the doorway. Their eyes met briefly before she turned away, as the tears started to prick.

"Good night, Miss Marlow," he responded coolly.

Ursula got into the back of Bertie and flung her head back against the seat.

"Wait," she instructed Samuels, trying to regain her composure. "Please, just wait a few minutes."

"Of course, Miss."

Ursula closed her eyes and listened to the sound of the motor idling. She didn't know why she was waiting, only that she needed some time to think, to release the tension that her emotions had built inside her. She fought back the tears, angered by her own weakness.

Samuels said nothing, but she sensed, as he saw Lord Wrotham's Daimler pull up, that he was uncomfortable. Ursula banged her head back lightly against the leather seat—what was she doing?

She saw Lord Wrotham climb into the rear seat of the motorcar. She saw the blue-orange flame as he lit a cigarette and the pale blue smoke rising as he leaned back in the seat. The Daimler pulled away from the curb and drove off.

"Miss," Samuels ventured.

Ursula was silent for a moment. Her thoughts were tangled and confused. The giddy spin of emotions threw her off balance.

"Brook Street," she said rashly. She no longer cared about self-control or restraint.

Samuels hesitated before nodding and with the grind of the gears maneuvered the motorcar out onto St. Michael's Street.

The rain grew heavier, and drops beat at the windows with a ferocity that mirrored the intensity of her own inner struggle. She felt as though she had been heaved through a storm surge and left stranded, smashed and vulnerable, against a seawall.

Samuels drew up along Brook Street, stopping just short of number 36, as Ursula had instructed. She could just make out Lord Wrotham's butler Ayres struggling with his umbrella against the wind and rain as he raced out to greet Lord Wrotham, who was alighting from the motorcar. Ursula leaned forward in her seat. She mentally willed him to look at her, to see her in the darkness and give her a sign, any sign, to show her what she should do next. But Lord Wrotham appeared to neither see her nor seek her out. The front door closed quickly, and Ursula was left waiting in the car to decide what she should do. "What a god-awful mess I've made of it all," she muttered, and placed her head in her hands.

Samuels looked at her in the rearview mirror but made no comment.

Ursula was just about to tell him to drive her to Chester Square when she saw Lord Wrotham appear in the doorway.

He stood in the rain, still in his evening coat without any umbrella. With slow deliberation he turned to look down the street toward her. The rain lashed down, and in the darkness he was barely visible. But still, she knew he was waiting for her to make her move.

Later she would blame her recklessness on an excess of champagne.

"Take Bertie home, Samuels," Ursula said slowly as she reached for the rear door handle. "I'll make my own way back to Chester Square."

Samuels glanced at her again through the rearview mirror, but merely nodded and said, "Certainly, Miss Marlow."

Ursula stepped out of the motorcar and into the rain. Beads of raindrops stung her face and her arms. Her satin coat became slick and clung to her torso. She neither noticed nor cared. She walked toward him with unsteady steps. Apart from the streetlamps, Brook Street was dark. There were no lights in the windows, no signs of life except the noise of her heels on the pavement and the relentless rain.

He made no effort to approach her. He waited for her to reach him, and once she was there, they both merely stood and let the rain wash over them.

Finally he took her hand and led her inside.

"I told Ayres to retire for the night," he murmured. "We're alone."

The first kiss was tentative. His lips lightly brushed hers as he closed the door behind them. He wiped the raindrops from her cheeks before reaching back and releasing her hair from its golden clasp. The black ostrich feather fell to the ground, and her hair, coiled and wet, tumbled down. He led her to the foot of the staircase. She started to peel off her coat, and he kissed the nape of her neck. He smelled of a cool, spring night and the rain.

She let her coat fall to the floor, her arms bare and wet, and he led her up the stairs in silence. He did not kiss her again until they reached the landing. This time, it was long and lingering. Ursula kicked off her drenched silk shoes and let each tumble, one then the other, down the stairs. Warmth flooded through her. He guided her into the bedroom and drew her in close. She could feel his heart beating through his rain-soaked clothes. Beneath his coat and jacket, his waistcoat and shirt were dry and warm. She leaned against his chest as his fingers found the satin edging of her dress and began unhooking the back clasps one by one. The fire in the bedroom was the only source of light, and as she turned from him she caught sight of her reflection in the mirror above the fire, bathed in the firelight's soft glow.

Her oyster gray dress slid to the floor, leaving her standing in her embroidered chemise and lace-edged corset, feeling suddenly vulnerable. His fingers lightly traced the outline of her necklace. She watched him in the mirror's image, his movements mesmerizing. He slowly unclasped the necklace and unhooked her corset. He took off his jacket, his waistcoat, wing collar, and tie. He walked over to the tall chest of drawers and laid these down. He placed her necklace carefully next to the silver brush set and then, with a flick of his wrist, removed his cufflinks and cuffs. The ritual of his undressing was itself tantalizing. Time seemed to hover and buzz in her ears. She removed her corset and sat down on the hand-carved canopy bed. He was masked from view by the thick velvet drapes as she bent over to unroll her silk stockings. Blood rushed to her head as she looked up. She tasted his kiss and let the deep, dark, yearning take her.

Ursula was awakened by the morning light on her face, caught and refracted in the mirror above the now-cold fireplace. She blearily rubbed her eyes and adjusted her senses to the unfamiliarity of the room. It seemed as though she had last been here in a dream, and she wasn't entirely sure, until she heard the horn from the delivery van below, that she wasn't still sleeping. Then the realization of what she had done hit her. She rolled over gently and saw that he was still asleep. Facedown on the feather-filled pillow, his dark hair obscuring his eyes, he looked like a sleeping knight in a Pre-Raphaelite painting. She wanted to run her fingers along his exposed skin, feel his smooth, cool body beneath her hands. It took all her willpower not to touch and wake him. But then she sat up and hugged her knees tight. The impact of last night hit with sudden force. God, how could she have been so stupid?!

She gingerly extricated herself from the tangle of sheets and crept across the room, careful to avoid being seen through the open curtains of the front window. She crouched down and retrieved her undergarments and dress before walking past him to the door that led to the bathroom. She walked in and closed the door quietly behind her before hastily dressing herself. "Damn and blast!" she muttered as she tried to tie her corset and wriggle into her dress, which by now was a crumpled mess. As she surveyed the result in the mirror, she groaned. How on earth was she going to escape unnoticed in this state?

She blinked back her tears and then doused her face with the cold water from the basin. There was a faint knock on the door that led to the hallway. Ursula froze before she heard Ayres's unmistakable sniff. She opened the door a fraction and saw him standing on the landing, holding one of her day dresses in his hands.

"I took the liberty of arranging for this to be brought over. Samuels is waiting at the rear entrance. Will you be staying for breakfast?"

Ursula stared at Ayres in amazement, the full import of his words barely sinking in.

"If you would like, Sarah, our scullery maid, can come and assist you. Unfortunately, we do not have a lady's maid on staff at present."

"Obviously," Ursula replied drily, recovering her wits.

She then took the dress from him and thanked him for his foresight. "No need to have Sarah come up. Please tell Samuels I'll be down shortly. I won't be staying for breakfast."

Ursula closed the door. Even she had to admit there was no small element of farce about her situation. She sobered up soon enough when she thought of Lord Wrotham's reaction and the possibility of further scandal. She dressed quickly, coiling her hair in a loose plait to keep it off her face before, gripping the sides of the basin, she began to comprehend fully the ramifications of last night's recklessness.

Ursula lay in her bath, gazing at the ceiling. She tried to clear her mind, but last night remained too vivid, too visceral, for her to push it aside. She had arrived home to find the household heavy with disapproval. As Bridget ran her bath, Ursula overheard Mrs. Stewart, the housekeeper, whispering to Biggs, "She'll be the absolute ruin of us! Her dear father would be turnin' in his grave if he knew. And his lordship all ready to wed her but she, brazen as you like, refusing to have a bar of it! I never did see anything like it in all my life!"

Biggs's response had both surprised and saddened her. She could imagine him stiffening as she heard his fierce whisper: "Mrs. Stewart, hold your tongue! Miss Marlow is mistress of the house, and we should respect her as such. Don't you be going fueling gossip belowstairs!" She hated the thought that Biggs felt the need to defend her.

As she sank back into the water, she realized she could hardly expect the household to put up with very much more. Her position in society was tenuous as it was—only her wealth kept her immune from total censure. If the attacks on her businesses continued, that wealth could very well be in jeopardy. Ursula closed her eyes and fought back tears. She owed it to her father's memory to own up to her responsibilities.

As Julia was still en route to England, Bridget assisted Ursula in getting dressed. She was also busy packing for Ursula's return journey to Oldham, planned for the following day. Ursula wanted to leave as soon as she had given Winifred the letter fragments to be translated. She was anxious to meet with the local police to see how their investigation into Arina's death was progressing. So far Sergeant Barden had not responded to her message. She would have liked to have left earlier, but a phone call from Gerard Anderson soon after she arrived home that morning meant she had further business to attend to before she left. Her heart was filled with dread, for Anderson had sounded grim on the phone. She only hoped that the fire at Oldham hadn't fueled further speculation that her takeover of her father's business was failing.

Bridget was terribly excited at the prospect of being elevated to the status of lady's maid, even if it was for only a week. She fussed around Ursula like an enthusiastic kitten.

"Oh, Miss, a whole set of dresses arrived just last week for you. Mrs. Stewart said you'd probably like your gray and rose linen suit for today, so I laid that out for you."

"Thank you, Bridget, that sounds perfect."

Ursula was in no mood for small talk, but one look at Bridget's excited face, and she hadn't the heart to be less than enthusiastic. She therefore let Bridget choose a boat-necked blouse to wear underneath and a necklace, earrings, and hair comb to match the neatly trimmed day suit. When she had finished, she even allowed Bridget to select a brooch to pin on her jacket.

Ursula met Biggs as she descended the stairs. He was on his way up, bearing a silver tray.

"Tell Samuels that we will need to leave early tomorrow if we are to make it to Whalley by the evening," she said. "He may as well put the trunks in Bertie tonight. Bridget's nearly finished packing them."

"You have a visitor. I've told him to wait in the front parlor," Biggs said abruptly.

"A visitor—who is it?" She felt a mounting sense of dread at the thought of a confrontation with Lord Wrotham. She wasn't prepared to see him yet. She wasn't even sure what she was going to say when she did see him at all.

"His card, Miss." Biggs handed her the tray, his face inscrutable.

Ursula took hold of the small white printed card and turned it over. It was handwritten in a scrawl she hadn't seen in over four years. Suppressing her astonishment, she merely nodded and continued down the stairs. Only when she reached the bottom did she grip the balustrade, revealing her disquiet.

She walked down the hall to the door leading to the front parlor. With a deep breath she turned the handle, opened the door, and entered.

"Alexei Prosnitz. You are the very last person I expected to see."

Ten

Alexei sat hunched on the sofa, his workman's clothes disheveled, his dark, curly hair looking wild and unkempt. He had placed his wire-rimmed glasses precariously on the dainty side table next to him and was rubbing his eyes as Ursula entered the room and saw him.

"*Lapushka*," he cried in the deep, melancholic voice she remembered all too well. "It is good to see you." He picked up and put on his glasses before he rose to his feet.

"I never thought I'd see you again," Ursula replied and closed the door. She had dreamed of this moment so many times, especially in the months that followed his departure, that she was taken aback by the calm normalcy of their meeting. It was hard to believe that four years had passed since he had left, and yet here he was once more, just as she had imagined. He even called out to her using the endearment he had always used, *lapushka*. If this had been one of her old dreams, however, she would have rushed into his arms, but instead she remained rooted to the ground, unable and unwilling to move.

"I heard about your father. I am so very sorry." Alexei approached her as he spoke.

"You could have sent a letter," Ursula said with a deadpan expression. "It would have been faster."

Alexei hesitated for a moment, midstep. He frowned, obviously unsure of her meaning.

"Papa died two years ago, Alexei. Don't you think it's a little late for condolences?"

He moved toward her. "Forgive me." His hand touched her lightly on the cheek. "You are even more beautiful than I remember."

Ursula brushed his hand aside.

"What are you doing here?" she demanded, though not without a twinge of regret as she noted his wounded expression and the dark circles under his eyes.

"You look as if you slept in those." She pointed to his crumpled trousers.

"I did," Alexei confessed, and Ursula flushed. She knew she sounded cold and abrupt, but she couldn't seem to stop herself. She was angry that Alexei assumed he could simply walk back into her life. After last night, his presence just added to her inner turmoil and confusion.

Ursula pointed to the sofa. "Please," she said, softening her tone. "Sit down before you collapse. You look terrible." Alexei nodded and sat down on the sofa with a sigh.

Ursula settled herself in the high-backed armchair opposite him.

"So you won't even sit beside me?"

"I'm fine where I am," Ursula replied, crossing her arms. "Why don't you start by telling me why you're back in England."

Alexei lay back on the sofa and closed his eyes. "Why I am back? Not, why I have come back to you?"

"You haven't come back to me, Alexei . . . so don't even try to pretend that you have." Ursula's voice grew sharp.

"I find you much changed, *lapushka*."

Ursula pursed her lips but made no reply.

Alexei leaned forward. "I hear you have found yourself an aristocrat for a lover. Who would have thought? I guess it is easy to forget your principles when you are an heiress looking for marriage."

"I am not looking for marriage, and my personal affairs are no longer any business of yours. You relinquished the right to know *anything* about me the day you walked out that door!" Ursula pointed an emphatic finger at the door leading from the parlor.

"I did not leave you. I left only to join comrade Lenin."

Ursula jumped to her feet. "Damn it all, Alexei, what game is this? What do you want from me? You can't just waltz back into my life after four years and expect me to drop everything for you!" She couldn't believe how quickly being around him roused all the old confusions and turmoil.

"I can't go back to that . . . ," she continued, more to herself than to him.

"I am not asking you to," Alexei said with maddening calmness. "Forgive me for intruding. I am tired, that is all, and I had no one else to turn to, so I came to you. You, who meant so much to me all those years ago. Though it now seems a lifetime ago. . . ." He patted the seat beside him on the sofa. "Please sit next to me, *lapushka*. Let me explain why I am here."

Ursula stood for a moment, arms crossed once more. "Why didn't you go to Anna?"

Anna Prosnitz was Alexei's mother.

"She has her own troubles. I did not want to burden her with mine."

Ursula knew that Anna was under intense police scrutiny for her involvement in the WSPU and suspected anarchist groups. She hesitated, but his face, which looked drawn and exhausted, stirred her compassion. She walked over and sat beside him.

Alexei took her hand in his and began to talk, his head bowed slightly as his story unfolded.

"I came back to England out of a sense of duty to a comrade. Do you remember Kolya Menkovich? You would have met him at the Rose and Anchor at our meetings. No? Well, it is of no matter. I have known him since we were at university together in St. Petersburg. He remained in England when I left for Geneva, organizing strikes in the north. In January he decided it was time to join us and arrived in Prague. Soon after the Party Congress he fell ill—pleurisy in both lungs. He died three weeks later."

Alexei inhaled sharply, evidently remembering Kolya's death all too clearly. He soon regained his composure and continued. "I am here because he wanted me to return and find his lover—the woman he had left behind in England. He wanted her there with him at the end, but it was too late. So what else could I do? I promised Kolya as he lay dying that I would look after her. So I returned to England. . . ." Alexei hesitated again.

"Go on," Ursula prompted him.

"I smuggled myself aboard a steamer bound for Liverpool from Antwerp. But by the time I arrived, it was too late. A worse fate had befallen poor Arina."

"Arina?" Ursula said sharply. "You don't mean to say this man's lover was Arina Petrenko?"

"Yes."

Ursula looked at Alexei sharply. The incredible coincidence immediately raised her suspicions.

"So then you know that she died in a fire in one of my factories."

"Yes, I know. But please, listen. Before you jump to any conclusions, let me try to explain it to you."

Ursula opened her mouth to interrupt him, but stopped as she caught sight of his face.

"I arrived in Oldham the night of the fire. I took the tramway and went to Arina's lodgings on the outskirts of town. But she did not return home. No one did. So I returned to town and booked into the railway hotel. I was at a loose end and decided to see the factory that you had established. Anna had, of course, written and told me what you had done."

Ursula raised her eyebrows. Anna's antipathy toward Ursula was well known. She was surprised she had told her son anything about the factory.

"So I went there, and by now it was close to eight o'clock. The factory was of course locked. I walked around the streets for a while and then returned to the hotel. When I awoke the next morning, I heard about the fire and the rumors of a young girl being pulled from the ashes. I had no idea it was Arina until I returned to her house the next morning. Her roommate, Natasha, was in a terrible state. She told me Arina was missing, but she refused to go to the police. You know how it is, *lapushka*, for those of us who have endured brutal treatment at the hands of the tsarist police in Russia. While I was at the house, a policeman arrived. I had to hide upstairs, but when I came down, Natasha's face was white . . . she told me it was Arina who had perished in the fire."

Ursula rubbed her nose. Alexei's taste for the dramatic had certainly not diminished over time.

"Natasha told me the police were looking for witnesses who may have seen a 'foreign'-looking gentleman outside the factory earlier that evening. The description they gave was of me."

"So someone saw you outside the factory?"

"Yes. I had to leave Oldham as quickly as I could. I couldn't risk being taken in for questioning. And as you can see I had nowhere else to go."

"Did Natasha go with you?" Ursula asked.

Alexei shook his head. "I don't know where she went."

Ursula sighed. "You really should go to the police and clear things up. Tell them you had nothing to do with what happened. Otherwise they'll be spending countless hours on a wild goose chase looking for you."

Alexei looked at her intently. "You know that I cannot risk being found by the police."

Ursula bit her lip. She wasn't sure what to do. She knew that when he left England four years ago, Alexei had been under investigation for inciting "agitation" among workers across the country.

"I panicked. I didn't know what to do. So I came to you. It took a while. I had to accept rides from strangers or walk most of the way, but I had to find somewhere safe. . . ."

Ursula didn't doubt his fears were real. There were a number of influential people in the government and at Scotland Yard who would like nothing better than to see Alexei Prosnitz silenced in jail.

"But you say you saw nothing suspicious at the factory that night?"

"I saw nothing."

"You didn't see anybody there? No sign of a break in perhaps? Or a light on?"

Alexei shook his head. "My mother told me you were quite the detective."

Ursula scowled at his flippancy. It was difficult for her to gauge whether what he said was true. So many years had passed since she had last been around him. She found her judgment clouded by the uncertain emotions his return had aroused. Alexei always did have a way of embellishing the truth till it was little more than fiction.

"I am in England to achieve a great many things. Fulfilling my duty to Kolya was one of these, but there are others," Alexei said carefully. "Things that are vital for the future of the Bolsheviks and for the global class struggle. Things that cannot be brought to the attention of the Metropolitan Police."

Ursula sat in silence, weighing up his story. He stared down at his hands, his dark curls spilling over his forehead. The minutes ticked away on the mantel clock.

"What can I do?" Ursula finally asked quietly.

Ursula left Alexei in the front parlor thumbing through the latest copy of the *Strand Magazine*. Closing the door carefully behind her, she went into the study and lifted the telephone receiver. She hesitated for a moment and stared down at the desk, trying to collect her thoughts. The operator answered, and with a deep breath she asked to be connected to Miss Stanford-Jones.

"Freddie," Ursula said. "I have another favor to ask, one that may make things a bit tricky. . . ."

"Sully, you know better than to even ask. Fire away, old bean. Whatever you need!" came Winifred's swift response.

"It concerns Alexei."

Winifred went silent.

"He's back in England,"

"Ah . . ."

"And he needs help."

"Now there's a surprise," Winifred responded with sarcasm.

"And to make matters worse, he may be involved in what happened at Oldham. I can't say anything more at the moment, but he needs somewhere to stay. Somewhere the police won't find him. It's a lot to ask, I know . . . but Freddie, I need your help."

Ursula waited, knowing that what she was asking was of immense personal risk. Winifred had already been to Holloway Prison for her suffragette activities and falsely accused of Laura Radcliffe's murder; Ursula could well imagine that Winifred wanted to avoid any unnecessary police entanglements.

"There's no one else I can turn to," Ursula said, and she could hear the desperation in her voice.

"Of course, Sully," Winifred replied quickly. "Just tell me what you want me to do."

"Freddie, I owe you a huge debt of gratitude. . . . I know I ask far too much of you—"

"Sully, it is I who you owe you a debt!" Winifred responded. "But I do have just one question," she said, dropping her voice. "Do you really think he may be involved in the death of that girl in Oldham?"

Ursula watched as the rain pounded against the window. Two years ago she had faced a similar dilemma when Winifred had telephoned her in the middle of the night, asking for her help. That time Winifred had been accused of murdering her female lover, and Ursula had been determined to clear her name.

"With you," Ursula replied slowly, "I was so sure. I knew you were innocent."

"And with Alexei?" Winifred prompted.

"With Alexei, I don't know. Deep down I know he couldn't have been involved, not in the death of a girl, not in a fire in my own factory . . . and yet . . ."

"And yet?"

"I know he is holding something back."

Winifred was quiet for a moment. "Sully," she said, "trust your instincts. Bring him to my place. Whatever happened, whatever Alexei's involvement, I know you can work this out."

Ursula made Alexei leave by the servants' stairs and had Samuels wait in the rear lane in Bertie. She and Alexei climbed in the back, and Ursula instructed Samuels to fasten the top down securely to obscure them from the neighbors' prying eyes.

Samuels drove them up Grosvenor Place and Park Lane before turning onto Oxford Street, where they continued until they reached Tottenham Court Road. He then weaved through the streets and squares of Bloomsbury before stopping outside Winifred's new abode in Woburn Square. The memories associated with Laura Radcliffe, Winifred's murdered lover, had been too great, and Winifred had moved a month after her acquittal. Her aunt had helped her lease a ground-floor flat complete with basement kitchen and laundry room, small garden, and two bedrooms. Insisting on her own independence, Winifred refused her aunt's offer to provide additional funds for a live-in maid, but used her own meager earnings to support a local girl, Mary, to come in a couple of mornings a week to help. The result was that Winifred had been forced to become quite domesticated, much to Ursula's amusement (and her dismay, after tasting some of Freddie's baking efforts).

Winifred was waiting for them, and as soon as Bertie drew up outside she opened the front door and ushered them in quickly.

"Freddie!" Alexei hailed her with a smile.

"Alexei." Winifred's face was impassive.

"Now, now," Ursula chided gently. "Let's put the past behind us, Freddie." Ursula knew that Winifred had never forgiven Alexei for leaving as he did. Nor would she forgive him for the heartbreak he had inflicted on Ursula. Ever the staunch defender, Winifred seemed determined to make her censure felt.

"Of course," Winifred responded coolly.

Ursula led Alexei into the front parlor and threw her hat and gloves down onto one of the armchairs. Books and papers were strewn all over the room.

"Sorry about the mess," Winifred said lightly, removing a pile of pamphlets from one of the chairs and motioning for Alexei to sit. Ursula seated herself beneath the window while Winifred perched on the piano stool.

"So, I've set up a camp bed downstairs. You're next to the kitchen, I'm afraid, but if we are to keep you secreted away it's best you aren't seen upstairs. As you know, we're right in the middle of our suffrage campaign, so there'll be heaps of women coming in and out. . . . So if you are to stay, you'll have to abide by three conditions."

"And they are?" Alexei sat back in the chair with a smirk.

Winifred leaned forward. "First, you must remain downstairs at all times. If you need anything, let Mary know, and she'll come to me. Mary's a good sort and won't breathe a word of you being here. She's used to all our cloak-and-dagger stuff."

"So I gather you, like my dear mother, are still involved with the Pankhursts."

"Of course!"

"You can't really believe that your current tactics will achieve anything, can you? I mean, you're never going to win the vote for women by throwing stones in a few West End shops, or setting fire to pillar-boxes—"

"And this coming from a man who once tried to dynamite the tsar's yacht at Cowes and ended up with fried fish instead," was Winifred's sarcastic reply.

Alexei flushed darkly. "I just think that if you are dedicated to action, to militancy, to achieve your goals, you need to operate like an army," he retorted. "You need discipline and experience. Look at you. Three of your leaders are in jail. Christabel has fled to France and seems to spend her time shopping along the Champs-Elysées or sipping wine in Montmartre. From what I've heard, half your committees have no idea how to throw a stone so it will actually hit a target. Face it, Freddie you're losing the fight."

"And what do you suggest?"

"Rise up. Organize. Demand universal suffrage for all men and women and redistribution of wealth from the rich to the poor. The issues are broader than just votes for women. We could be on the verge of a worldwide revolution. Female suffrage is meaningless when weighed against the global class struggle!"

"Can we leave this discussion for later? Please!" Ursula interrupted sharply. "We have a dead girl in Oldham. We have police sniffing around for proof that Alexei was involved. Let's focus on what needs to be done here and now. Once this is all over, we can have the luxury of debate—but not now!"

"Sorry," Winifred said with a rueful smile, and Ursula felt a pang of nostalgia. There was a time when all three of them could be found sitting in Anna's parlor, arguing over suffrage and socialism. Those days seemed glorious, innocent, almost naive now. Ursula closed her eyes for a moment, trying to expel the memories from her mind.

"So what is the second condition?" Alexei crossed his arms and leaned back in the chair.

"The second condition is, no visitors." Alexei raised one eyebrow. "No, I mean it," Winifred continued. "Nothing will give the game away more than if my house suddenly becomes the focal point for the entire London Bolshevik population."

Alexei shrugged. "And the third?"

"The third condition is that you will ensure that nothing is done that will harm Sully in any way. And by that I mean, nothing that will injure her business, nothing that will injure her reputation, and nothing, absolutely nothing, that will make her regret all that she has done for you. Let me be clear. You are here because of Sully. Because she asked me. Cross her, injure her, and I will march into Scotland Yard myself and tell them who you are. . . . Do I make myself clear?"

Alexei reddened again. "Yes, and believe me, I will do nothing to harm either of you. I am in both your debt."

There was an awkward pause. The room seemed to darken as the clouds grew heavy and the rain started once more. Winifred reached over and turned on the standard lamp beside the piano.

Ursula got up to leave. "I really must be heading off. I have a meeting with Anderson in half an hour, and then I have to get ready to return to the North tomorrow."

Winifred bent over and readjusted the cuffs of her trousers. They were coming loose from her ankle-high boots. "I'll see you out." Her voice was muffled. She straightened up. "You," she instructed Alexei, "stay here."

Alexei raised an eyebrow. As Ursula passed him, he tried to reach out and kiss her hand. Ursula pulled her hand away sharply and without another word left the room.

As they approached the front door, Ursula pulled Winifred aside and gave her the handkerchief containing the letter fragments.

"Here are the pieces. Why don't you call me later, once you've found a translator? Until we find out more, I don't want Alexei to know anything about the letter."

Winifred placed the handkerchief in her jacket pocket and nodded. "I'll call you tonight when I get the chance and am sure Alexei isn't around. Let's hope it gives you some clue as to what happened to that poor girl."

"Let's hope," Ursula responded grimly. All she wanted was time alone to think things through and initiate further inquiries. She still hadn't found any answers to the mystery surrounding Katya's death in Egypt. The frustration of the two unsolved murders was weighing heavy on her mind.

Samuels was waiting outside, leaning against Bertie and engrossed in the latest *London Illustrated News*.

As he spied her walking toward him, Samuels shoved the paper under his arm and came round to open the rear door of the motorcar.

Ursula responded with a smile as she tucked in her skirt, sat down, and swung her legs inside.

Samuels closed the door, cranked the engine vigorously a few times to get Bertie's engine going, and then climbed into the driver's seat.

"Straight to the city, then, Miss?" The offices of Anderson & Stowe were on Threadneedle Street.

"Yes," Ursula replied and settled back into the leather seat as Samuels maneuvered Bertie out and onto the street.

Gerard Anderson was on the telephone when Ursula arrived, and she bided her time in the large wood-paneled meeting room, staring out of the window and tapping her gloves on her skirt to a nervous rhythm. She watched as the red and black omnibuses, horse-drawn carriages, and tan and green motorcars all vied for the road as pedestrians, men in their bowler hats, women in their straw hats, and flower sellers with their baskets all weaved and ducked as they tried to cross the busy street. Ursula was so intent on her own thoughts and watching the scene below that she never noticed the knock on the door. It wasn't until she turned round, with a preoccupied sigh, that she saw Lord Wrotham entering the room, followed by Gerard Anderson.

"Ursula, my dear!" Anderson called out as he approached her. "I saw you last night at Topper's but we really didn't get a chance to chat. Take a seat, take a seat. I heard about Egypt. Good news about the supply, but I was sorry to hear about your friend. When Elizabeth and I visited in '96 such an incident would have been unheard of—what is the world coming to, eh?!"

"What indeed." Ursula sat down across the table from Lord Wrotham. She was not deceived by Anderson's tone—he was nervous, which could only mean he had bad news to impart.

"I didn't realize Lord Wrotham was going to be here," Ursula began.

"As trustee, Anderson felt it was necessary for me to attend," Lord Wrotham interjected before she could finish. "I received his note just this afternoon. If I had known earlier, I would, of course, have told you."

You mean, if I hadn't walked out on you this morning, Ursula thought despondently.

"But of course," she replied smoothly, keeping a close rein on her emotions. "So then"—she turned her attention to Anderson—"tell me the bad news."

Anderson set down a manila folder and tapped it thoughtfully.

"Not bad news at all, my dear—more what I would call 'an interesting development.' One that could prove most advantageous to you."

"Go on." Ursula remained unconvinced.

"This morning I received a formal offer for your father's entire estate. All the companies, mills, and factories. The offer is to purchase everything outright."

Ursula's face remained rigid.

"Given our recent industrial concerns, it is a very generous offer indeed. I have the details in front of me."

"Who, pray tell, is the interested buyer?"

"Christopher Dobbs."

Ursula's head jerked back.

"Now, then," Anderson said hurriedly, "before you fly off the handle, let me remind you that this is, after all, business. None of us should let personal animosity toward Obadiah cloud our judgment."

Obadiah Dobbs, Christopher's father, had only threatened to blackmail them all over the death of her father.

Ursula could barely contain her anger.

"The offer provides an ideal opportunity," Lord Wrotham started to say.

"An ideal opportunity for what?" came her choked response. "For me to give up my father's dreams for his empire? To admit I could not succeed?"

"Not at all," Anderson interjected gently, but his normally ruddy face was redder than ever.

"It would enable you to do what you've always wanted to do," Lord Wrotham replied, his tone remaining neutral and calm, even though all color had drained from his face. "You could be a reporter or a writer. With this kind of money, unencumbered as it will be, you will be able to live as you wish and answer to no one. There will be no boards of directors, no union chiefs, no protracted contract negotiations. If you accept this offer, you can be free—"

Anderson coughed. "Of course, as per your father's will, the money would remain in trust until you marry or turn thirty-five. But as you know, your trustee is very supportive of your desire for a career. A gal must have her hobbies, after all."

Ursula looked at Anderson, contempt drawing her lips into a straight, immutable line. "I cannot accept this," she replied slowly and coldly. "My father would have been horrified by the prospect of selling. He worked his entire life to build this empire. I'm not about to let his dream die with me."

"But Ursula, you know how things look. We've lost three contracts already due to industrial issues in the North. The accident at the Oldham factory has everyone worried—can we meet our contracts? Can we guarantee the safety of our workers? You know the sort of thing."

"My answer is still no."

Anderson ran his chubby fingers through his hair.

"Dobbs will have to find another way to expand his empire," Ursula said coldly. "The thought of him making a profit out of supplying armaments used to kill and maim sickens me."

"If war comes, you may want to change that view," Anderson replied.

"If war comes," Ursula retorted, "the last thing we should all be thinking about is money."

She gathered up her gloves and rose to her feet, forcing Lord Wrotham and Gerard Anderson to rise also.

"We should talk about this some more. You shouldn't dismiss his offer without further consideration." Anderson said anxiously.

Ursula gave him a withering look. "It is incumbent upon me to fulfill my father's wishes. I cannot imagine he would want his empire carved up."

"He would have been a pragmatist," Lord Wrotham said as he walked over and held open the door. "He would have accepted, when the time came, the need to consolidate and sell. As trustee I am duty bound to act in your best interests and I urge you to reconsider. If you insist on pursuing this strategy, well . . . it could ruin you."

Ursula froze in midstep. Lord Wrotham's hand was still on the door, and as she stood in the doorway, she could barely contain her rage.

"I would have thought you, of all people, would have supported me in this," she hissed.

He stepped back. "Ursula, I—"

She didn't give him time to finish, but straightened up, tugged on her gloves, and stalked past. It wasn't until she was walking down the staircase that she realized, as she steadied herself on the wooden balustrade, that she was trembling.

Ursula sat curled up in her father's armchair, starched collar unbuttoned, her tie askew, a cup of tea clasped in both her hands. She had taken off the jacket of her gray and rose suit and was now wearing a comfortable, loose-fitting tunic and cardigan over her blouse. Her hair had started giving her a headache, so she had removed all her hairpins so her dark auburn hair cascaded down her back, tied loosely together by a thin red ribbon. She sat lost in her thoughts, with papers strewn across her father's desk. His photograph stood prominent in a silver frame. Stiff and formal in his morning suit and top hat, Robert Marlow looked so assured and confident. She fingered the pendant she wore about her neck, wishing her father was still with her. Wishing her mother had not died when she was but a little girl. She was in danger of wallowing in self-pity when the telephone rang.

She picked up the earpiece and leaned into the receiver.

"I've found you a translator. For what it's worth," Winifred said.

"Go on. . . ."

"He couldn't make any sense of it at all. I mean, it was only a fragment, but even the parts we have make no sense. It's probably written in some kind of code."

"Did the translator have any idea what kind of code was being used?"

"No. The parts he could make out were just gibberish."

Ursula chewed the lid of her fountain pen.

"I copied it all down for you. Why don't we meet at that café near the station tomorrow and discuss it further, before you get your train? Hold on, oh, I'd better go, Alexei is calling out from downstairs. I can't believe he's been here less than twenty-four hours, and already Mary and I are running after him."

"But, Freddie—," Ursula started to say, but Winifred had already hung up. Ursula put the telephone receiver down and leaned back in her chair with a groan of frustration. She scrubbed her eyes and was trying to collect her thoughts when a gentle rap on the study door roused her once more.

"Come in," Ursula called out.

Biggs entered and stood silently in the middle of the room. Ursula looked at him expectantly. "Yes?"

"Lord Wrotham to see you, Miss. I've had him wait in the front parlor."

Ursula looked down at her tea.

"Tell him I am indisposed."

Biggs' face was inscrutable.

"I . . . I just can't face him right now, Biggs," she admitted, raising her eyes briefly before looking down at her cup once more.

"No need to explain, Miss. I'll go tell him."

"Thank you, Biggs; you are my savior as always."

Biggs bowed slightly, but she could see a shadow of concern passing over his face as he turned and left. Ursula put down her tea. The belt of her gray knitted cardigan had come loose. She bent her head and closed her eyes. She had to summon all her strength and pull herself together. Self-pity, she admonished herself, was a luxury she could not afford.

There was another knock at the door.

"Yes?" Ursula heaved a sigh.

Biggs entered once more, this time holding an envelope.

"His lordship wanted me to give you this." Biggs handed over an envelope. On it was Lord Wrotham's elegant writing. *Miss Ursula*

Marlow. She opened the envelope, and a pair of peridot earrings almost fell out onto her lap. They were the ones she had worn to Christopher Dobbs's party. The ones she had taken off at Lord Wrotham's house.

There was no message.

Eleven

The next morning Ursula sat at the breakfast table reading the *Times*, eating a triangle of toast spread thickly with Cook's homemade marmalade. After an unsettled night, she was now determined to pull herself out of the mire of despondency and make a fresh start. A silver teapot sat on the sideboard, steam rising from the spout. Ursula reached over, picked up her bone china cup, and raised it to her lips, temporarily engrossed in reading the headlines. They were a welcome distraction from her thoughts.

The trial of the Pethick-Lawrences and Mrs. Pankhurst on charges of conspiracy in relation to the demonstrations and window-smashing in March was due to start in the next few weeks. Lady Winterton had already left messages telling both Ursula and Winifred that she suspected that the police raid on Clements Inn would have uncovered evidence of the WSPU's codes. Winifred was still eager to pursue the issue of developing new codes or even a cipher, but Ursula was too preoccupied by recent events to be of any assistance. The only code she was interested in was the one that could decipher the letter fragments found in Arina Petrenko's room.

Although Ursula would have liked to stay in London for the WSPU trial and attend the public gallery to show her support, with all that was happening she knew her place was in the North. Ursula knew many of her sisters doubted her resolve, and there were mumblings of her lack of commitment to militant action. Her failure to serve time in Holloway Prison only reinforced these views. Ursula felt torn; she believed passionately in the cause of female suffrage, yet it was difficult, given her position in society, to devote her time and energy to militant activity that seemed to be turning the tide of public opinion against them. Her financial contribution to the WSPU, however, had managed to stave off any overt criticism—for now.

Ursula drummed her fingers on the table, mentally admonishing herself once more not to get distracted by self-pity. She took another piece of toast from the toast rack and smothered it in butter and marmalade, took a bite, and turned her attention to the morning's post. Before breakfast she had already written to Eugenie Mahfouz to see if she had found out anything further about either Hartuv or the *Bregenz*. To date she had received no response to her inquiries from the Admiralty or Peter Vilensky (whom she had written no fewer than three times).

She sifted through the post quickly, first to ascertain whether Peter Vilensky had replied to any of the letters she had written him, and then, when it was clear he had not, to see what invitations had been delivered. There was a request to attend a private viewing of the Royal Academy's Summer Exhibition and an invitation from Mrs. Pomfrey-Smith to attend her Empire Day ball. Then there was a note from an old friend from Ursula's Oxford days, asking if she would join them in their private box at Lord's for the Eton-Harrow cricket match. Ursula loathed cricket, professing it to be the "most boring sport in all history," but she hadn't seen Sadie in over a year, so she put this invitation to one side for further consideration. In addition to these, there was a letter from Baroness Kohn regarding her debating circle, three catalogs from Paris, a meeting schedule for the Fabian Society, and last, a letter from Sir Huxtable Smythe requesting an article on the "fine art of hairdressing" for *Lady's Realm* magazine. Ursula groaned and took another sip of tea. So much for ever having a career as a serious journalist. With a loud sigh, she returned to reading the newspaper.

Finishing her breakfast, Ursula rang for Bridget, who arrived to retrieve the breakfast items.

Bridget was aglow with excitement.

"Ooh, Miss, Mrs. Stewart said she got one of them postcards from Julia. From Holland. Lovely it was."

"Did Julia sound well?" Ursula asked with interest and a small pang of guilt. She hoped Julia wasn't going demented traveling with Mrs. Millicent Lawrence and her party.

"Well . . ." Bridget mused for a moment. "She quoted scripture, which impressed Cook no end."

Ursula looked at Bridget quizzically.

"I didn't know Julia was prone to that sort of thing."

"Well, she did say that she was learnin' a heap from the Lawrences. Said Mr. Lawrence's sermons were a highlight of the trip."

Ursula stifled her horror. Had Julia, stuck with the Lawrences, suddenly found religion en route back to England?

"Anyways, she's hoping to be back at the end of next week. So she tells Mrs. Stewart."

"It will be lovely to have Julia back," Ursula responded with a smile. Bridget's face looked uncertain, and Ursula, sensing the reason why, reached out her hand and patted Bridget's arm.

"Not that you haven't made an excellent lady's maid, Bridget."

Bridget beamed as she picked up the silver toast rack and Ursula's cup and saucer and placed them on her tray.

"Can you ask Mrs. Stewart and Biggs to come in? I need to check on the arrangements for my return to Gray House."

"Yes, Miss."

"Oh, and make sure you've packed my mackintosh in the trunk. I have a feeling there won't be many fine days like today up north."

"Yes, Miss." Bridget bobbed a curtsy and left the room.

Biggs and Mrs. Stewart entered a few minutes later.

"Now then, Mrs. Stewart, I'm trusting you to hold the fort while

I'm gone. Just check the mail and relay any telephone messages. Particularly from Miss Stanford-Jones—she's helping me on a project at the moment." Ursula paused, knowing Mrs. Stewart would hardly consider Alexei a suitable "project" for her to be involved in at all. "Biggs, tell Samuels to bring Bertie round in about ten minutes. I have a few errands to run before we leave for the North, so we will be leaving later than anticipated. Are you and Bridget taking the eleven o'clock train?"

"Yes, Miss, and I sent instructions yesterday, so Mrs. Norris should have everything prepared for your arrival."

"Excellent," Ursula replied, and dismissed them both with a grateful smile. Everything was now set for Biggs and Bridget to meet her at Gray House, leaving Mrs. Stewart to take care of the house in Chester Square. In the meantime she had two visits to make before she saw Winifred—both of which could prove disastrous. As she waited for Samuels to draw up outside, she straightened her small brimmed hat, pulled on her white cotton gloves, and steeled herself for what she was about to do.

Ursula's first visit was to Temple Chambers. She asked Samuels to drop her at Inner Temple Lane so she could walk through the Inner Temple to Kings Bench Walk and Lord Wrotham's chambers. Instead, she had barely passed the Temple church when she caught sight of Lord Wrotham, in full wig and gown, making his way back from the Royal Courts of Justice. Trailing behind him was St. John Eyres, another barrister who often acted as Lord Wrotham's junior. Behind him in turn was Alistair Fenway, Ursula's father's solicitor, struggling to keep up, his arms full of books. Fenway was accompanied by a young articled clerk, looking harried as he tried desperately to find something in a stack of papers.

"Barnaby, have you found the reference yet?" The junior barrister's voice was high with anxiety.

"Still looking, sir!" the articled clerk responded desperately, sending a plume of papers into the air. Lord Wrotham strode forth, oblivious to all the commotion. Ursula hung back, unsure whether to proceed or not. As she watched Eyres, Fenway, and the articled clerk start to pick up the papers scattered about the ground, she realized Lord Wrotham's had disappeared from view. Ursula took a deep breath and hastened to catch him up.

She hurried past Fenway, fearing he would look up and recognize her, but he was too immersed in the chaos to even notice. "Barnaby," he was saying in an exasperated voice, "His Lordship is going to be most put out if we have to tell him that we have no idea which case His Honor was referring to—I mean, really!"

Ursula caught sight of Lord Wrotham again as he paused by the entrance to the Inner Temple Gardens. He looked at his pocket watch impatiently, no doubt realizing that Fenway and his junior were lagging behind.

Ursula opened her mouth to call out, but before she could, another voice drew Lord Wrotham's attention, one she recognized with shock from Egypt.

"My lord, apologies for being so early, but I wondered whether we might have a quiet word before our luncheon at Lansdowne House."

Lansdowne House was the seat of Lord Lansdowne, leader of the Conservatives in the House of Lords. Ursula ducked inside the filigree wrought-iron gate and into Inner Temple Gardens, keeping out of sight.

"Mr. Vilensky," Lord Wrotham replied. "By all means, we can speak before luncheon. I'm just waiting on my . . . oh, here they are . . . Eyres, Fenway, meet me back in my chambers at two and have those case notes ready. Mr. Vilensky and I have a meeting with Lord Lansdowne and need to prepare."

"But of course," Fenway murmured.

Ursula crept along the gravel path and tried to overhear what Peter Vilensky had to say. Lord Wrotham's back was to the garden, his black barrister's gown flapping in the wind. Peter Vilensky stood beside him in a formal black frock coat. From Ursula's vantage point they looked like two crows, sinister and sleek, preening themselves in the sun.

"First of all, thank you for your condolence card. It was most unexpected." Peter Vilensky's tone was deferential. "I hadn't realized your connection to Miss Marlow."

He lapsed into an awkward silence.

"What can I help you with?" Lord Wrotham inquired. "You are welcome to accompany me to chambers . . . or we can talk here. Whichever you prefer. You are aware, of course, of what our meeting with Lord Lansdowne concerns?"

"Yes, and you have my pledge of full financial support. No, what I need from you is of a more personal nature. . . ."

Lord Wrotham coughed politely. "Then by all means, let us wait until we are in my chambers to discuss it."

"Thank you. I feel I ought to say at the outset, however, that I hope you have not received a false impression of me from Miss Marlow," Vilensky said.

"Please, do not concern yourself. I assure you I have received no reports from Miss Marlow to form any impression."

"Only I did not realize that you were . . ."

There was another awkward silence.

"Trustee of her father's estate?"

"I'm sorry, my lord, there seems to be have been some confusion," Vilensky responded. "For I had heard that Miss Marlow . . ."

"Yes?" Lord Wrotham prompted. Ursula heard the warning note in his voice, but it went unheeded by Peter Vilensky.

"That Miss Marlow was your fiancée."

"Really." Lord Wrotham's response was deadpan. "Whatever gave you that idea?"

Ursula had gone to Temple Chambers hoping to explain her recent behavior to Lord Wrotham, but hearing his conversation with Peter Vilensky had thrown those plans into disarray. She still wasn't sure what to make of it all. What was the personal matter Peter Vilensky alluded to? Did it have anything to do with Katya's death? What proposal was he supporting for Lord Lansdowne? A year ago she would not have hesitated; she would have gone to Lord Wrotham and demanded her answers. Now, with the gulf between them widening, she no longer knew what to do.

Instead, Ursula continued on to her next meeting and was presently sitting in Bertie outside Christopher Dobbs's house near Holland Park, trying to get her thoughts in order.

"Do you still want to wait, Miss?" Samuels asked with a quick glance at Ursula in the rearview mirror. Ursula bit her lip; it was already eleven o'clock. She had to decide whether she was going to go through with meeting Christopher Dobbs.

"Yes," she replied, gathering her skirts. "I expect this won't take long."

Ursula opened the car door and stepped out onto the pavement.

As she gave Dobbs's footman her calling card, she noted with distaste Dobbs's recent acquisition of a tiger-skin rug in the hallway. The footman led her to the front parlor to wait. Standing next to one of the reproduction Chippendale chairs, she gazed about the room, trying to formulate what she was going to say. She had taken a chance that Christopher Dobbs was still in London for there were rumors he was already planning to tour Carmichael Shipyards. Arriving unannounced, she might catch him off guard and be able to assess what he was really up to in offering to buy Marlow Industries.

Above the fireplace was a painting of Napoleon in Egypt, and beneath this a line of invitation cards was propped up against the mantel. Ursula could not resist taking a look. One invitation in particular caught her eye—it was from the First Lord of the Admiralty, Winston Churchill.

"Not bad after only eighteen months at the helm of the Dobbs Steamship Company," Christopher Dobbs called out from the doorway. His voice still betrayed the lilt of his Liverpool upbringing.

"Not bad at all," Ursula replied, continuing to peruse the invitation cards. "Although your father was not without connections himself."

"Yes, but even he would admit I've expanded our family's horizons beyond measure."

"Indeed," Ursula responded coolly before turning to face him.

Christopher Dobbs stood in the center of the room, wearing dark gray flannel trousers, a wing-tipped shirt, and a somber tie. Over his suit he wore a loose velvet jacket with a quilted silk collar. Entirely inappropriate for the time of day, it did denote a casual indifference to her presence and, Ursula suspected, a deliberate attempt to disconcert her.

Dobbs walked over to his desk in the rear corner of the room and flipped open the silver cigarette box. He motioned for her to join him, but Ursula refused with a decorous shake of her head.

"So I'm guessing you're here to discuss my little offer for Marlow Industries," Dobbs said as he took a seat behind the desk and looked at her confidently.

"Yes," Ursula replied, taking a seat on the long chesterfield sofa. "I thought a face-to-face meeting might help me decide."

"Decide?" Christopher Dobbs countered with a smile. "But I thought you had already rejected the offer."

"Yes." Ursula smiled. "But a woman can always change her mind."

Dobbs watched her closely.

"For example, I think I will have one of those cigarettes after all—are they Turkish?"

"No, Woodbines—I'm afraid my days at sea left me with a taste for them."

"Then I think I will have to decline after all," Ursula responded with feigned sweetness as she leaned back against one of the brocade cushions on the sofa. "How is your father, by the way? I meant to ask after him the other night, but I did not get the chance."

Dobbs continued to watch her closely. "My father is feeling much better," he said.

"I'm pleased to hear it. What does *he* think about you buying Marlow Industries?"

"What does he think? He thinks it's a capital idea, of course, but I hardly think you are here to discuss my father's views."

"No, I'm here to reiterate my total rejection of your offer, in person."

"I doubt the trustee of your father's estate agrees with you."

"I am aware of his views on this matter."

"He could decide to overrule you."

"Oh, I think we both know he won't do that."

Dobbs threw the cigarette butt in a ceramic ashtray on the desk and started to fidget with the paperweight on his desk, a brass replica of HMS *Victory*. "Miss Marlow, what are you really doing here?" he asked, with a barely suppressed irritation that Ursula found quite satisfying. She noticed his glance flick to the grandfather clock in the corner of the room, and wondered whether he was expecting someone to arrive soon, someone he did not wish her to meet.

"I'm trying to work out what kind of creature you are," she responded enigmatically.

"What the bloody hell is that supposed to mean?!"

Ursula smiled. "Just something a friend of mine warned me about in Egypt. I'm just trying to piece it all together. Dobbs Steamship Company. Carmichael Shipyards. My factories. It doesn't quite fit together yet."

"Well, I wouldn't worry your pretty little head about it. I doubt for a woman like you it will ever 'quite fit' together."

Ursula gathered up her skirt and got to her feet. "Oh, believe me, I'll make sense of it all soon." She flashed him a grim smile. "And I'll work out if it's you who is behind all the trouble at my mills and factories. I'll figure it out all right, and when I do—"

Christopher Dobbs rose and walked around the desk. Ursula was suddenly reminded of Eugenie Mahfouz's warning.

"And when you do?" he said insolently.

"I'll know if you are the serpent or the scorpion."

Ursula had Samuels drive Bertie round the block and come to a halt just on the periphery of Holland Park, keeping Dobbs's house just in sight. As instructed, Samuels kept the motor running.

"Wait here for a bit," she told Samuels. He looked at her quizzically in the rearview mirror, but she gave no explanation. She wanted to see who Dobbs was expecting. It was nearly midday, and the sun was starting to make Ursula feel uncomfortably warm in her formal day suit and hat. It was one of the few sunny days in an otherwise soggy spring. She took the opportunity to remove her jacket, and when she looked up, a motorcar was pulling up outside Dobbs's house.

Ursula watched closely. The motorcar idled for a moment in front of the house, then, as if waiting upon a signal, slowly maneuvered down the narrow laneway that led to the rear of the building.

"Now quietly drive us over to the other side of the street—that's it. Just stay behind here and give me a minute."

Ursula got out of the car and carefully made her way down the lane. When she got to the iron bars of the rear stairway that led to the kitchens, she paused and slowly peered round the side of the building.

A tall, dark-suited man was standing with his back to her, opening the rear door of the motorcar. Jeffries, Christopher Dobbs's butler, hastened up the basement stairs, whispered in the man's ear, and then looked nervously around. Ursula ducked her head back quickly and waited before edging her way back round the wall. The tall muscular man appeared to be dragging something from the rear seat of the car. Whatever it was, it was about the size of a man, but looked little more than a wraith covered in dark filthy rags. Ursula looked on with growing horror as the bundle struggled for a moment, bare arms suddenly exposed and flailing, until exhausted, seemingly lifeless, it collapsed and went limp. The tall man then turned and, with an ease that suggested whoever it was weighed little more than a child, carried the bundle down the back stairs into Dobbs's basement kitchen.

Jeffries remained in the laneway with his head bowed. Ursula took a step back, conscious that her presence could easily be revealed should he look up. Back on the street, Ursula hurried back to Bertie and Samuels, shaken by what she had just witnessed, conscious that without her suit jacket, she would soon attract the attention of passersby.

* * *

"Are you sure it was a person?" Winifred cupped her tea in her hand.

"Absolutely sure," Ursula replied bleakly.

They were sitting in a tea shop near Euston Station, waiting for Ursula's train to the North.

"God, who do you think it was?"

Ursula shivered. "I have no idea, but the thought of someone in that condition being taken down there . . . it doesn't bear thinking about."

Winifred looked grim. "You need to tell someone about this, Sully."

Ursula shook her head. "Who would I tell, Freddie? Who's going to believe me? It's sounds like something out of a Dickens novel, and I'm sure if someone were to go and investigate, this mysterious person would be long gone."

Winifred put her tea down and moved her plate aside.

"I've lost my appetite just thinking about it."

"I thought Obadiah Dobbs was bad enough, but this, this smacks of kidnapping, degradation, and I don't know what. I almost wish Chief Inspector Harrison was back here in London. At least he might believe me."

"Is there no way you can get in contact with him at all?"

"I don't know—I'm not even sure he's still in Egypt. Maybe Oliver would know. . . ." Preoccupied as she was, Ursula didn't even notice she had referred to Lord Wrotham by his first name.

"Well, maybe you should ask him. Oh, God, I can't believe I just said that. Me, recommending that you ask Lord Wrotham for advice. If our sisters at Clements Inn could hear me now!"

"Freddie, do be serious!" Ursula exclaimed.

"I am being serious," Winifred said quietly. "I think it could be dangerous to act alone on this."

Ursula closed her eyes and breathed slowly.

"I don't know," she said. "I need time to think this through."

"Then do so," Winifred recommended. "And now, I'd better tell you what I found out about the letter fragments."

In the past Ursula would have insisted on acting immediately, but now she understood the need for restraint as well as patience. She would help no one if she acted rashly.

Winifred wiped her hands, slid the plate out of reach, and dug out a yellow envelope from her coat pocket. "I put the fragments in here for safekeeping. And I wrote out what we could decipher." She laid the fragments out carefully on the table.

Ursula leaned in closer.

"As you can see, none of it makes any sense."

Ursula took a look at the paper and shook her head.

"Why would Arina have a letter written in some kind of code?"

Winifred shrugged. "Is it political, perhaps?" she asked. "You said Arina was involved with the Bolsheviks."

"Possibly," Ursula answered, but she was noncommittal. "But my gut tells me this had something to do with her death."

"Well, the police obviously didn't think so—they missed finding it entirely."

"Yes, which makes me wonder how seriously they are taking the case. When I visited the station, I got the feeling that Arina's death was going to be treated just like any other industrial 'accident.' It was as if her life was of such little consequence that it wasn't worth properly investigating her death." Ursula could not hide her bitterness.

"Are you going to take the letter fragments to the police?"

"Do I have any other choice? Maybe it will finally make them sit up and take notice."

"More likely they'll put the whole matter down to a political act of the Bolsheviks and ignore it," Winifred responded

Ursula sighed. "I hope not but I'm going to keep the copy of what was written. Who knows, maybe we'll find the key and be able to decipher what the fragment says."

"Which reminds me," Winifred said. "Lady Winterton has been doing some research on codes for the WSPU. Now that our old codes are likely to be made public in the trial, we're obviously anxious. Maybe Lady Winterton could help us decipher this?"

Ursula bit her lip. "Maybe, but I don't want to involve anyone I cannot completely trust as yet. I'd rather keep this to ourselves. It's bad enough that we have to keep an eye on Alexei."

"Speaking of which," Winifred replied, "what do you want me to do about him?"

Alexei, thought Ursula, was an added complication she could have well done without. "Keep a close watch on him. I want to talk to him further about Arina, but first let's see what happens at the coroner's inquest." She rubbed her eyes.

"I did ask him what happened the night Arina died," Winifred said.

"And?"

"I agree, he's holding something back."

"Do you think his mother knows he's back in England?" Ursula asked tentatively.

"I'm not sure but it's best to leave that issue well enough alone. You know how Anna blames you for Alexei leaving England in the first place. Imagine what she'd do if she found out Alexei had returned, and no one had told her."

"Hmm . . . Well, I'll leave you to deal with Anna."

"I think that can wait till we have this all resolved. Anna has enough to worry about without Alexei. But, Sully—"

"Yes?"

"Don't make the mistake of thinking he's changed."

Twelve

Oldham Coroner's Court

Ursula entered the Oldham coroner's court trying to appear as inconspicuous as possible, her small, narrow-brimmed hat pulled down low. Unlike other courtrooms she had been in, this one did not have a dock, only a raised dais at which the coroner was to sit with a witness stand on the left and a jury box on the right. The long rows of benches reserved for witnesses, the press, and the general public were filled to capacity. The noise in the courtroom was deafening. There were some twenty girls, many of whom Ursula knew from the Oldham factory and mill; George Aldwych and his family; and sundry other locals Ursula vaguely recognized from visits with her father. Ursula hesitated for a moment, looking for somewhere to sit.

"Miss Marlow." A young police constable came forward. "The coroner wishes you to come to the table up front. That's where all interested parties sit. Family, lawyers, and the like. We're just waiting on the factory inspector and union representative t'come."

Ursula eyes traveled to where the young constable was pointing. Directly in front of the coroner was a long wooden table. Ursula bit her lip; she hadn't planned on making such a public display.

"Please, follow me," the constable urged as he started walking down the aisle of the public gallery. Ursula followed him reluctantly, then sat down, demurely removed her gloves, and readjusted her hat. She had deliberately chosen a somber black dress, but she was hardly inconspicuous sitting at an otherwise empty table. She could just make out, through an open door that led to a small antechamber, the silhouette of the coroner, Ainsley Mortimer, standing in profile, straightening his jacket. Eustacia was standing next to him, organizing his papers.

Ursula turned round and spied a couple of men in the back of the courtroom, obviously members of the press, already scribbling notes furiously. Ursula sighed. No doubt tomorrow's newspaper's would be filled with inane stories about her—what she wore, what she said—rather than anything to do with the true matter at hand, the tragic death of a young girl in a factory fire. Before long Ursula was joined by Eric Duckworth, the local county factory inspector and Reg Slater, the textile workers union representative. Having already met with both men about the fire there was no need for introductions. With a curt nod and a tip of a hat they sat down at the end of the table in silence.

With a clang the main courtroom doors were closed, and the police constable who had escorted her to her place made his way toward the dais. The door to the coroner's antechamber was closed in preparation for the coroner's official entry into the courtroom. The public in the gallery jostled to take their seats. No one sat beside Ursula until, barely a minute before the police constable rose to officially open the inquest, a tall, dark-haired man entered with glorious solemnity and took the place next to Ursula. The room fell silent. Only Lord Wrotham, Ursula reflected drily, could make such an entrance without the slightest appearance of deliberation or theatrics.

Lord Wrotham took off his black felt derby hat and black leather gloves and placed them on the table. Ursula noticed how his long, sensitive fingers drummed a beat for just a second, betraying a flicker of emotion beneath his unruffled exterior.

"Lord Wrotham," Ursula murmured without making eye contact.

"Miss Marlow," he replied.

The policeman stood at the front of the court and cleared his throat.

"Oyez, oyez, oyez . . ."

The inquest began.

Ursula drew a notebook and gold-nibbed fountain pen out of the deep side pocket of her dress. As she started to write, she realized, a little wistfully, that the pen was one that Lord Wrotham had lent to her last summer, and which she had forgotten to return. She stole a sideways glance at Lord Wrotham, but he was staring straight ahead, eyes fixed, jaw set.

Dr. Mortimer began the proceedings with a calm, almost gentle description of the circumstances surrounding the death of Arina Petrenko. The jury were mesmerized as he provided in detailed medical terms the results of the postmortem examination. Ursula had to look away, however, when the young police constable brought and laid out various exhibits that illustrated to the jury the condition of the body when found. The police constable called out each exhibit in turn, and as the coroner described the items, he displayed each on a wooden tray before the jury:

Exhibit 1: Photograph of woman's body found in situ.
Exhibit 2: Photographs of woman's bodily remains including head and throat and charred torso, taken during autopsy.
Exhibit 3: Fragment of dress.
Exhibit 4: Fragment of left boot.

Dr. Mortimer then read out a summary of the forensic pathologist's report, concluding that all evidence thus far pointed to death occuring prior to the fire. The microscopic analysis suggested possible asphyxia but the lack of further examinable bodily remains precluded a definitive assessment.

The public gallery was deathly quiet as everyone strained to see and hear the gory details. Ursula's hand trembled, but she continued taking her notes.

Dr. Mortimer called the chief of the Oldham fire brigade, Superintendent Harry Boardman, who described how the brigade had attended the fire at the Oldham Garment Factory and how, in the early hours of the morning, he had discovered the body of a young woman lying dead in the smoking ruins.

"Can you indicate on this drawing of the factory where the body was found?"

The police constable stood in front of the jury, holding up a hand-drawn plan of the garment factory. The superintendent pointed to a spot on the map beneath the doorway that linked the sewing room to the nursery annex.

"And you found the body in the doorway?"

"Yes. Or at least, what was left of her."

A ripple went through the courtroom.

Ainsley resumed his examination of Superintendent Boardman. "Can you describe what else you found at the scene? Was there any indication of how the fire started?"

"At first we weren't sure, but when me and the boys started siftin' through the debris, we found evidence of what we believe was used to start the fire."

"Which was?"

"Spilled petrol and petrol-soaked cotton rags. We found scraps in the sewing room. We think these were lit, causing a chain reaction across the factory. You know how these places are—fabric and the like everywhere. Almost as bad as a mill."

"So in your view the fire was not an accident?"

"No—whoever did it probably thought they'd be nothin' left to find, but he were wrong."

"Thank you, Superintendent. Now, as the jury has heard from my postmortem results, Arina Petrenko did not die as a result of the fire, so the jury must bear in mind that evidence of arson may or may not be relevant in terms of the cause of her death."

"Damn suspicious, mind you," the superintendent muttered.

"That will be all, Superintendent. Remember, this is not a criminal trial. This is just an inquest to determine cause of death."

The jury looked a little mystified by this, but Dr. Mortimer continued, calling upon Sergeant Barden to provide details of the Oldham police investigation.

Sergeant Barden took the witness stand, outlining the events of that night and the following morning. He was careful, given the nature of the inquest, not to provide any extraneous information beyond the questions asked. A short, stocky man with a bushy mustache and fluffy hair, he was taciturn on the stand, and much to Ursula's disappointment, he provided little in the way of supposition as to what really happened that night.

He described his visit to Back Gladstone Street, where Arina's roommate, Natasha Desislava, identified a piece of clothing (Exhibit 3) retrieved from the dead woman's body.

"But Natasha refused to come and view the body, is that correct?"

"Yes, we 'ad to 'ave Nellie Ackroyd come t'station for that."

"And she confirmed it was Arina?"

"As best she could; there weren't much left of 'er—"

"Yes, I think we can spare everyone the details of that again; we heard quite enough about that earlier. . . . Oh, there is one final matter, and that is the question of Natasha Desislava. Have you any idea of her present whereabouts?"

"No. When we returned that afternoon, she had already left. Despite makin' enquiries in London last week, we've been unable to locate her." A stickler for procedure, Ainsley Mortimer asked the constable to call Natasha Desislava three times to the witness stand before recording her failure to appear in his coroner's notes.

"Thank you, Sergeant Barden," Dr. Mortimer said. "Please remain in the courtroom, as we will require your services again when we return to the question of the police investigation later in the inquest."

Dr. Mortimer then called four witnesses in quick succession. There was Mr. Frank Pickersgill, the driver of the Oldham Metropolitan Tramway Corporation's electric tram running from Hollinwood to Chadderton, who confirmed he had seen Arina board and alight from the five forty-five tram bound for Chadderton at Oldham Edge. Then there was Len Bolton, who reluctantly told the coroner's court about the alleged break-in at Arina's cottage. He told little else of importance, and Ursula's mind started to wander. Was it truly possible that no one had seen Arina after she boarded the tram from the factory?

The next witness to be called, Mr. Lewis Heagney, turned out to be a red-faced sot, whose words were already slurred at barely three o'clock. He provided a disjointed and not entirely believable account of having seen what he termed "a swarthy-looking foreigner" skulking around the factory at close to nine o'clock that night.

"Can you describe him in any greater detail?" Dr. Mortimer asked in frustrated tones.

"As I told the sergeant, he was dark-like. Curly hair. Looked a right one, 'e did—" Ursula shifted in her seat uncertain over her decision to trust Alexei.

"They'll be seeing German spies next," she heard Lord Wrotham mutter under his breath, and indeed, when the landlord of the Imperial Railway Hotel took the stand, he did mention that he thought one of the men who booked a room that day could have met Lewis's description. "I woulda said 'e were a German all right," he concluded.

Lord Wrotham groaned.

Dr. Mortimer looked down and shuffled his papers before calling Nellie Ackroyd to the witness stand. Nellie, a seamstress who worked with Arina at the factory, was a woman who in her youth must have been considered quite the beauty. Now, although Ursula guessed she was barely thirty-five, she looked like a doll worn and tattered after years of misuse. Her blond hair was obviously dyed, and her rosebud mouth now seemed pinched and drawn. There were jeers from the public gallery. Someone shouted "trollop" and the resultant fracas between the girls of the Oldham factory and other locals caused at least five women to be removed from the courtroom by the young police constable. It dawned on Ursula just how fraught tensions were over her factory.

Nellie's eyes were brimming with tears, and Ainsley allowed her a moment to compose herself before asking her his questions.

Ursula leaned forward. Up until now Arina had been little more than a tragic figure in a play, and she hoped Nellie's testimony would help form a clearer picture of who Arina, the person, really was.

Nellie Ackroyd had three young children, and after her husband deserted her, she spent a year in the Oldham workhouse before managing to find work in Ursula's factory. Nellie's eyes glistened with tears as she described the impact of the factory's closure. She was now back in the workhouse, and her children had been taken to a Dr. Barnado's home in Rochdale. Dr. Mortimer listened with compassion before directing her to focus on the issue at hand, namely the death of Arina Petrenko.

"I'm sorry to have to put you through this once more, but it was you, was it not, who identified Arina's body at the morgue?"

"Yeah. It were me," Nellie mumbled.

"You'll need to speak up so the jury can hear you. Remember, this inquest is just a formality—so we can determine how Arina died. You mustn't feel nervous or ill at ease."

Nellie nodded and scrubbed her eyes with her handkerchief.

"Yes," she said loudly. "I saw the body and told Sergeant Barden I thought it was Arina."

"Thank you, Nellie. Now can you please tell the jury what happened the day of the fire?"

"Arina and I was at the factory, same as usual. At lunch she and I sat together—then we had a bit o' play with my Eliza and Daniel. They were in the nursery annex. Eliza's not yet two, and Danny, well, he's but a babby. My eldest, Ian's his name, he's now at school."

"Yes, that's very nice to know, but can you focus on Arina for a moment?"

Nellie wiped her eyes once more.

"So after lunch you and Arina . . . ," Ainsley prompted gently.

"Me and Arina were operatin' the sewing machines. She were acting just as she normally did. For her anyway. Quiet. We 'ad our break at two, and then the whistle sounded at half five. Same as always. We left together, and she caught the tram to Chadderton and I walked to the bus."

"How would you describe her state of mind on the day in question?" Dr. Mortimer asked.

"You what?" Nellie replied.

Lord Wrotham's fingertips began to drum on the table.

"How did Arina seem—was she happy? Was she sad? Did she seem preoccupied or concerned about anything that day?"

"No."

"Can you think of any reason Arina may have been in the factory the night of the fire?"

"No."

"Can you think of anyone who may have wished to harm Arina? Did she have a boyfriend?"

"No, she talked about a boyfriend but said 'e were in Europe. I never saw 'er with any other feller."

"Was there anyone she may have quarreled with recently?"

"No."

"Did Arina have many other friends at the factory?"

"No. She were quiet like. Didn't mix with many of the other girls. But she were a good sort to me. She were kind to my little 'uns . . . givin' them little trinkets and chocolate. . . . I can't believe this coulda happened to her. . . ."

Dr. Mortimer looked at Nellie kindly. "You can step down now," he said. "Unless you have any other information you'd like to tell the jury that may be of assistance."

Nellie scrubbed her eyes with a grimy handkerchief. "No."

Dr. Mortimer motioned for Sergeant Barden to help Nellie out of the courtroom. Lord Wrotham shifted in his seat as Ainsley Mortimer called George Aldwych to the stand. Ursula put down her pen and stretched her fingers for a moment before George proceeded to tell the jury the same information he had imparted to Ursula the previous week. Absently she jotted down some of the times he mentioned, making a mental note to ask Alexei to confirm what time he had been "lurking" about the factory, when she was suddenly struck by an inconsistency in George's story. She was sure George had told her that he left the Dog and Duck around half past seven or eight, but now he told the jury he was definitely home before seven, after downing only one pint at the pub. Ursula circled the time in her notes and then noticed that Lord Wrotham was leaning forward in his chair, his piercing blue-gray eyes watching intently as George continued his testimony.

"Is there anyone who can confirm that you were indeed at home on the night in question?" Dr. Mortimer asked as George concluded.

George tugged his beard. "Me wife was visitin' her mam with the kids—but you can ask anyone in the pub, and they'll tell you I left before seven."

"Please, Mr. Aldwych, no one here is suggesting otherwise," Dr. Mortimer responded. "It is merely for the jury's benefit that I ask this question."

Ursula experienced a strange pricking sensation on the skin of her arm, as if a draught of cold air had suddenly entered the courtroom. She shivered involuntarily, and Lord Wrotham looked at her sharply. Ursula had always been particularly susceptible to influenza, and since her mother had died of tuberculosis, there was always anxiety she too might succumb to the disease.

"I'm fine," she assured him in low tones. Lord Wrotham removed his jacket and placed it over her shoulders. Ursula caught sight of one of the reporters nudging his neighbor. This would definitely be in all the newspapers tomorrow.

Ursula turned her head to look at the public gallery. Mrs. Aldwych was sitting in the middle of one of the rows, one of her little redheaded children in her lap. Ursula tried to catch her eye, but Mrs. Aldwych studiously ignored her.

Dr. Mortimer pulled the fob watch from his waistcoat pocket and called for a fifteen-minute recess. As a measure of formality, everyone stood in the courtroom as he left, but as soon as he had closed the door behind him, the public galleries began to ring with chatter. Lord Wrotham got to his feet abruptly. "I must see if I can have a word with the coroner."

"Why, are you planning on cross-examining someone?" Ursula asked with a note of sarcasm. Looking distracted, he ignored her comment and walked over to the constable officiating over the proceedings. They spoke at length, and then Lord Wrotham left the courtroom, returning some five minutes later without explanation.

He returned to the table, still thoughtful.

"What is it?" she asked, this time seriously.

"George Aldwych is lying."

Ursula had opened her mouth to speak when a knock at the rear door signaled that the coroner was returning. Lord Wrotham took his seat.

It was now Eustacia Mortimer's opportunity to take the stand. Her nose twitched as her brother asked her with all formality, "You were Arina Petrenko's personal physician, were you not?"

"I was," she answered.

"And can you give the jury an assessment of her physical condition—was she a well woman?"

"She was a normal, healthy twenty-three-year-old woman. I saw her no more than three times since she moved to Oldham, each time for a merely routine matter. In my view there was no physical ailment or preexisting medical condition that could account for Arina's death."

"What about her mental state?"

"I have no reason to believe Arina's mental state was anything but completely normal. I certainly saw no sign of a neurological condition that may have indicated suicidal tendencies."

"Thank you, Dr. Mortimer that will be all."

Sergeant Barden was recalled to the witness stand to provide further details of the police investigation. With a nod of his head, the constable brought out and placed on a wooden table some of the belongings collected from Arina's house the day after her death. These items included the letter fragments that Ursula had found and taken to the police, but to Ursula's dismay, they were just laid out alongside the most trivial of other items. There were two day dresses, a pinafore, a gray knitted shawl, a sets of underclothes and stockings, and one pair of tan walking shoes. Otherwise, Arina's life could be measured in small details: An ivory-handled hairbrush. A photograph of a young man (whom Ursula assumed was Kolya) in front of Brighton pier. A book of Pushkin's poetry with an inscription in Cyrillic. Some jewelry in a small velvet box. There was one photograph, in a silver frame, that caught Ursula's attention. Dr. Mortimer held it up for the jurors to see. The photograph was of two young girls posing for a formal studio portrait. By the look of their white pinafore dresses and dark stockings, they could have only been about twelve at the time the photograph was taken. Ursula stared at the girls' faces in shocked recognition. The girl on the right was unmistakably Katya Vilensky.

"Good God!" Ursula cried out involuntarily.

Lord Wrotham placed a hand on hers. "Don't . . . ," he said under his breath. Ursula shot him a furious look and got to her feet.

"I'm sorry, Miss Marlow?" Dr. Mortimer asked, bemused.

"Do you know who that other woman is?" she asked hoarsely. The jurors leaned forward. Ainsley pulled out his spectacles from a pocket and put them on.

"Yes, Sergeant Barden said it was thought it was her sister. But we haven't had anyone come forward who knows her full name. Nellie Ackroyd seems to believe she is traveling on the Continent, but so far we've been unable to contact her. Once again, jurors, that is not something that you should take into consideration in any negative way. People travel all the time, and it is often difficult to make contact."

Ursula sat down on the wooden chair with a thud. Arina Petrenko and Katya Vilensky were sisters. The coincidence was startling enough. But what on earth, Ursula wondered, was the link between the death of the wife of a rich London banker in Cairo and the death of a poor factory worker in Oldham?

"Miss Marlow, are you sure you're all right?" Dr. Mortimer asked.

The courtroom door opened, and a man in a gray overcoat entered. Ursula spun around to see Chief Inspector Harrison take a seat in the last row of the public benches. She turned back and replied, with some confusion, "Yes, it's just that I recognized the other girl. The sister in the photograph."

"Really?"

"Yes."

"And so where is she, Arina's sister?"

"She's . . . she's dead."

Thirteen

Eustacia Mortimer hurried in with a cup of tea, while Ainsley fussed around Ursula in his flannels and brown cardigan, like an anxious dog.

"I'm fine, truly," Ursula said, accepting the cup from Eustacia. "Thank you."

The inquest had ended in an uproar. Not only had Ursula's dramatic pronouncement sent the jury into disarray and reporters scurrying off to telephone their editors, but Chief Inspector Harrison had then calmly announced that Scotland Yard was now in charge of the investigation, and the inquest was temporarily suspended. After this the courtroom lost any semblance of order. Ainsley Mortimer shouted himself hoarse trying to restore calm, but to no avail, and the young police constable officiating the proceedings almost came to blows with two young weavers who decided to use the occasion to shout their support for Ursula and the "votes for women" campaign.

"What a complete debacle," Lord Wrotham commented once he, Ursula, and the chief inspector were safely ensconced in the Mortimers' parlor. Ursula still had Lord Wrotham's jacket tucked about her shoulders, and Lord Wrotham was standing in his shirtsleeves beside the coal fire. Eustacia bustled past, bringing in a plate of toasted tea cakes.

"Those look good," Chief Inspector Harrison said, reaching over to grab one. He bit in, and butter dripped down his hand. Eustacia handed him a napkin with a grin.

Lord Wrotham flipped open his fob watch with disdain.

"Five o'clock already," he muttered. Ursula suspected he had been planning to return to London that evening.

Eustacia perched next to Ursula on the sofa.

"The coincidence, Ains, you must admit, is startling. And shocking, of course." Eustacia patted Ursula's hand. "You poor thing. To have witnessed that poor woman's death. And now to find out that it was her sister who died in your factory. It's too awful for words!"

"Stacie, I think Miss Marlow has probably heard enough about it all for one day," Ainsley gently chided. He was standing by the fire next to Lord Wrotham, looking decidedly crumpled, a mug of tea in one hand and a toasted tea cake in the other.

"Did you know Arina was in danger?" Ursula asked Harrison quietly.

"You mean, because of what happened to Katya?" Harrison asked, washing down his mouthful of tea cake with a quick swig of tea. "No, I assure you. There was nothing about Katya's death that suggested that her sister was in danger. But as soon as we found out Arina Petrenko was Katya's sister, I insisted that Scotland Yard assume responsibility for investigating both cases. I only returned from Egypt yesterday, and I assure you I came as soon as I could. Who knows? This may be merely an unfortunate coincidence."

Ursula shot him a contemptuous look, and Harrison hurriedly concluded, "Not that we aren't paying full regard to the seriousness of the case."

Lord Wrotham brushed an imaginary crumb off his gray silk waistcoat as Ainsley finished his tea cake.

"As you can see," Lord Wrotham said to Ursula with barely disguised irritation, "the matter is now in good hands. Not before we had to endure that local circus, of course. But now, I assure you, Arina's death will be properly investigated."

"Really?" Ursula responded skeptically. "And yet Chief Inspector Harrison here continues to believe that Katya's death was the work of Egyptian nationalists. No doubt he will attribute Arina's death to Bolsheviks, and the farce will be complete!" Ursula was finding it difficult to keep her frustration in check.

Ainsley wiped his mouth with a napkin. "Miss Marlow, you needn't . . . needn't be concerned. I am fully committed to finding out the truth in this case, no matter who it may involve."

"See," Eustacia said with a smile. "Ains, at least, is on your side."

Harrison adjusted his shirt collar, looking uncomfortable.

"It's certainly one of the most puzzling cases I've dealt with," Ainsley Mortimer confessed.

"Didn't you know?" Chief Inspector Harrison said dryly. "Puzzling cases are Miss Marlow's specialty."

Ursula flushed, but before she could retort, Harrison put down his plate and cup and cleared his throat. "Look, I understand how difficult this must be and how frustrating, but as I told you in Cairo, you must learn to leave these matters to those who can deal with them best."

"And in this case, that would be Scotland Yard," Lord Wrotham interjected.

"You have my assurance," Harrison continued, "that this matter and any possible connection to what happened in Egypt will be fully investigated." In his attempt to sound reassuring, Harrison came off as condescending. But by now, Ursula knew better than to resist either man—openly, at least. She merely nodded wearily while mentally resolving to continue her investigations. A man of Harrison's caliber did not investigate simple murder cases anymore. No, he was Special Branch, which meant there was much more to Katya's and Arina's deaths than first appeared.

After an awkward pause, Harrison turned to Ainsley and, with unusual deference, asked whether he could have copies of all the postmortem reports.

"Sergeant Barden is sending his case notes to me at my hotel, but I think it would be best if you and I work together on this. I was particularly impressed by the thoroughness of your initial postmortem examination and your foresight in sending samples to a forensic pathologist for further examination. Many coroners would have just assumed the fire was the cause of death."

Ainsley Mortimer went pink.

"I think the first thing we should do," Harrison continued, "is bring George Aldwych down to the station for further questioning. Lord Wrotham is convinced he was lying when he gave his testimony today. I was not in the courtroom at the time—my train unfortunately was running late—but what do you think, Dr. Mortimer? How reliable a witness did George appear to you?"

Ainsley prevaricated for a moment, looking at Ursula as if guessing the matter of whether her own factory manager could have been involved would be a delicate one.

"It's all right, Ainsley," Ursula responded, noting with satisfaction that Lord Wrotham looked piqued by the familiarity with which she addressed Dr. Mortimer. "George told me before that he didn't leave the pub until half past seven or eight that night, but on the witness stand he said he was home by seven. It's only a minor discrepancy, I know, but it does seem strange. George is known for being a stickler for details."

"Yes, but I know George and I cannot believe he would have any reason to lie." Ainsley responded.

"People lie for a good many reasons," Lord Wrotham said coldly. "Not all of which are readily apparent."

Ursula wondered if there wasn't a double meaning to Lord Wrotham's words. She looked at him questioningly, but after meeting her gaze for a brief instant, he looked away.

The porcelain clock on the mantel chimed six o'clock.

Eustacia picked up some of the plates and cups and placed them on a tray.

"Perhaps you would care to stay for supper, Chief Inspector, then you and Ains can review the case."

"Why, Miss Mortimer, that would be lovely."

It was Eustacia's turn to go pink. She quickly turned to Ursula.

"Of course, if you and His Lordship wish to stay . . . ," she began, but Ursula caught sight of Lord Wrotham's face and shook her head.

"Thank you all the same, but I really think I should get back to Gray House." A weariness had descended upon her, and with all the anxiety of the inquest, Ursula hadn't realized until now just how drained she felt.

"I took the liberty of sending Samuels back earlier this afternoon. James is waiting in the Daimler outside," Lord Wrotham said, and though Ursula would have thought him high-handed for making such a presumption in the past, tonight she was grateful. The car ride back to Whalley would give them a chance to talk.

Eustacia reached over and took Ursula's hand. "You do look a little peaky to me," she said. "Ains, what do you think?"

Ainsley put his mug down on the mantel and looked at Ursula with concern. "You look awfully pale. Can I get you some aspirin, perhaps?"

Ursula stood up and pulled Lord Wrotham's jacket closer around her. Although it was May, and the late-afternoon light would be with them till late, the coal fire had dulled to little more than a faint glow in the grate, and the room seemed chill and damp.

"No, I think I'm fine," Ursula assured them. "Just a little tired."

Ainsley and Eustacia accompanied Ursula through the parlor door and down the hallway. Ursula shook hands with Eustacia before turning to bid Chief Inspector Harrison and Ainsley Mortimer good-bye.

Lord Wrotham picked up Ursula's notebook and pen from the hall table. He turned the fountain pen around in his fingers and, with a faint smile, put it in his top pocket before joining them on the steps that led down to the street.

"I'll call you tomorrow," Chief Inspector Harrison said in low tones as James helped Ursula into the car. Lord Wrotham responded with a brusque nod. He then turned to Eustacia and Ainsley and extended them a cool but courteous good evening before climbing into the back of his gray Daimler.

"That man really is a cold fish," Eustacia said as the motorcar drew away from the curb.

"Yes," Ainsley replied with a wistful sigh. "But Miss Marlow doesn't seem to mind."

The first part of the journey back to Whalley was spent in uneasy silence. Ursula stared out at green fields and gray clouds blurred by an early-evening mist, thankful for a respite from the day. She ran her fingers absently along the fringe of the plaid blanket James had placed around her knees. Lord Wrotham sat beside her, his arms folded and his head bowed, apparently deep in thought.

"I went to see you yesterday," Ursula announced, just as James turned at the Accrington Road intersection. "At your chambers."

Lord Wrotham looked up and contemplated her face with guarded eyes.

"You were busy," Ursula said. "Returning from court with Eyres and Fenway. I didn't like to bother you."

"I assume you saw Vilensky, then."

"Yes."

"His being there had nothing to do with his wife's death—or, for that matter, Arina's."

"I know."

Lord Wrotham frowned.

"I trust that you would have told me if it had," she responded simply.

"Vilensky had been referred to me by an associate of his, to inquire as to whether the Foreign Office had any information regarding the fate of some passengers aboard a ship that sailed from Alexandria in December. I told him I would pass on his request. The ship in question was the *Bregenz*, carrying settlers bound for Palestine. . . . I see that this may be of interest after all," he said frankly, as Ursula's eyes had widened. "Can you trust me enough to tell me why?"

"In Alexandria, I discovered that Katya Vilensky had made inquiries about this ship the *Bregenz*. I spoke to a shipping clerk there, and he became quite agitated when I questioned him about it. I'm not sure what happened to the *Bregenz*, but it may have something to do with Katya's death."

"I'm not sure I understand."

"Neither do I, but the clerk was found dead a few hours after I spoke to him, so I suspect"—Ursula inhaled deeply—"I suspect his death may have been because of me."

Lord Wrotham looked at her intently.

"There was another man, someone I saw as I was leaving the customs house—his name was Ambrose Whittaker."

"That name isn't familiar to me."

"He works in the Ministry of Interior, and there were rumors that he was possibly involved in the trade of armaments. My investigations were cut short by Arina's death, and I returned to England without finding out anything more."

"I passed on Vilensky's request to a friend at the Foreign Office. I could also make discreet inquiries about this man Whittaker." Ursula detected the reproach in his voice. Lord Wrotham was clearly disappointed that she had not confided all this in him earlier.

Ursula sighed. "I would have told you all this before if things had not been so . . . well, if I hadn't made such a mess of it all the other night." Lord Wrotham's eyes flicked to James, but he made no comment.

"That was why I went to see you. . . ."

Lord Wrotham face remained inscrutable. After a moment of silence, in which Ursula felt decidedly uncomfortable, he bent over and pulled a file out from an attaché case beneath his seat.

"Speaking of trust," he said, tossing the file over to her. It was labeled "SIS Intelligence Report—Syndicalist-Bolshevik Relations with Trade Unions in Britain."

"What is it?" she asked warily.

"Open it."

She opened the file carefully, trying to keep the papers together as the Daimler bounced along the rough road. She caught sight of the typewritten name at the top of the first page, and her stomach dropped.

Ursula read the first paragraph.

"He has been under surveillance ever since he arrived in London."

"I can explain," Ursula started to say.

"Then do so," came Lord Wrotham's curt reply. He reached over and, in a rare display of anger, snatched the file from her.

Ursula caught sight of James in the rearview mirror. He made no sign of acknowledgment, but merely focused once more on the road ahead.

"Alexei approached me on Wednesday night. Said he needed help and had nowhere else to go."

"Did he tell you about his relationship with Arina?"

"He told me he had returned to England to find her. Her lover, Kolya Menkovich, was Alexei's good friend, and he felt obliged to tell Arina that Kolya was dead."

"Did he tell you he was also once Arina's lover?"

Ursula's knee jerked involuntarily.

"No," she responded. "But I wasn't idiotic enough to believe he had told me everything. I knew he was holding something back."

"And yet you still protected him—"

Ursula bit her lip. "He told me he went to the factory the night of the fire—just to see it—he never went inside."

"So he was the 'dark swarthy chap' seen lurking around."

"So it would seem." She faltered. "He said that he saw nothing at the factory though and he was back in his hotel room before the fire started. He never even saw Arina."

"Do you believe him?"

"I thought I did . . ."

"And still you refused to tell the authorities?"

Ursula fell silent.

Lord Wrotham handed the file back to her.

"I can't let you have everything, as it may compromise the investigation, but you may as well see who you're dealing with. SIS, that's the Secret Intelligence Service, was alerted to his arrival by an Okhrana agent. As you no doubt remember from your time with Alexei, Okhrana, the tsar's imperial police, have long been interested in the activities of the Bolsheviks."

"I remember," Ursula said somberly.

"Well, it seems that Alexei's mission in England wasn't just to find Arina. While in Poland, he has been helping to establish an armed clandestine group within the Russian Social Democratic Labour Party to undertake targeted assassinations. They hope to not only disrupt the tsarist regime but also encourage workers to mobilize for a global revolution. Russia is in an uproar at the moment—there are strikes and protests across the country after the Lena gold mine incident. It has provided a catalyst that men like Alexei are hoping to exploit. The SIS believes he has come to England to meet with trade unionists and set up a similar armed group here in the UK. The last thing the British government wants is for militant trade unionists here to consider a similar form of campaign to that in Russia."

"Why are you telling me this?" Ursula demanded. "If you've had him under surveillance, I assume you know where he is. Why not just tell Scotland Yard and have him picked up and questioned?"

Lord Wrotham rubbed his eyes. "At this stage, the government would prefer to keep him under observation. It's more important that we find out who he's dealing with in England. If there are militant trade unionists who are considering similar action, we want to know."

"I won't turn informer, if that's what you're asking," Ursula said defiantly.

Lord Wrotham sighed. "You really think that's why I showed you the file?"

Ursula fell silent.

"What I've told you is extremely sensitive—the possibility of an assassination campaign in Britain could undermine the very fabric of our society. It could be worse than the Fenian threat. I have to trust you won't alert Alexei to what we suspect. No matter where your politics lie, Ursula, you cannot sanction murder. For all we know, if there was a campaign in England, it could very well target employers just like yourself."

"A clandestine group proposing a systematic campaign of assassination? Sounds like an Erskine Childers novel!" Ursula replied, but her skepticism was muted by a real sense of unease. Lord Wrotham was hardly the sort of man who bandied about words like *assassination* and *murder* without real foundation.

"My contacts in the government don't think so. You are only seeing this file because I convinced them that you would tread carefully."

There was a sudden bang and a jolt as the Daimler skidded into the hedgerow, tossing them both back against the seat.

"Sorry, my lord," James said, and Ursula envied his calm. "I believe we may have punctured a tire."

They had stopped along the narrow roadway that led across the moors to Clitheroe. Lord Wrotham got out of the car and joined James in inspecting the front wheel.

Ursula waited for a moment and then, seeing James take off his chauffeur jacket and roll up his shirtsleeves, she too alighted from the motorcar. She grabbed the plaid blanket and swung it around her shoulders. While James fixed the wheel, Ursula wandered over to the stone wall, climbed the stile, and looked out over the valley.

Lord Wrotham joined her, and they both stood watching the sun make its slow descent behind the misty outline of trees at the edge of the field. A couple of sheep startled and scattered, bleating their indignation.

"So why did you really show me the file." she asked.

He continued to gaze ahead. "I very nearly didn't. I wasn't sure how you would react to Alexei's return."

"You can't really think—" Ursula halted. Lord Wrotham's face had become inscrutable once more. She wasn't sure what to say, so instead she leaned on her elbows, gazed out at the sunset, and tried to clear her mind.

"What of Arina—do you think Alexei was involved in her death?" Ursula's voice was little more than a whisper.

"I don't know the man," was all Lord Wrotham would say.

"No." Ursula paused. "I guess from what you've just told me, neither do I."

They both stood, lost in their own thoughts.

"You know what's so hard about being back up here?" Ursula said suddenly. "It's that I feel a total stranger here. I may have grown up here as a child, but now it's as foreign to me as it is to you. These people who work in my father's mills and factories, they don't know me, they don't trust me as they did him. I'm nothing more than a London society girl trying to fill her father's shoes. And yet in London . . ."

Lord Wrotham turned to her. "Yes?" he prompted.

Ursula dropped her head. "God," she sighed. "I just seem to be making a mess of it all. Don't you see I need to stand on my own for a while? Prove that I can do it."

"With or without me?"

Ursula stared at him bleakly. This was not how she had intended the conversation to end.

"I don't know," she answered hoarsely. As she looked up, she caught sight of his eyes. They smoldered with barely restrained anger.

"My lord!" James called out, and his voice jolted them both. "The wheel is repaired. Shall I start the engine?"

Ursula pulled her hand away and drew the blanket around her tight. Lord Wrotham was all cold officiousness once more.

"Thank you, James. Yes. We should probably get Miss Marlow back to Gray House as soon as possible."

Lord Wrotham opened the passenger door and helped Ursula in before seating himself. Ursula leaned her head against the small rear window and closed her eyes. She felt sapped of all her strength, small and insignificant compared to the worries that weighed upon her.

Lord Wrotham stared ahead angrily. She wanted to turn, she wanted to face him and give him the answer he needed, but she couldn't. The struggle was too great within her. She had to master the effect he had on her, tame the emotions that only became confused and tangled when she was around him.

An hour later it was dark as James drew up outside the stone wall that surrounded Gray House. Ursula leaned forward in her seat, blinking as she grew accustomed to the glare of the streetlamps after the darkness of the country roads. Lurking about the gates were two reporters, who, as soon as they saw the Daimler approach, ran up, clamoring questions. Ursula shielded her eyes. Biggs and Samuels opened the tall wrought-iron gates and tried to fend off the reporters. They had seen Lord Wrotham, however, and, sensing the possibility of scandal, refused to hold back. Ursula was bundled out of the motorcar unceremoniously and escorted inside by Biggs as quickly as possible. It wasn't until she was inside the entrance hall of Gray House and Bridget was fussing around her with a knitted shawl and a cup of hot cocoa that she realized that Lord Wrotham had not accompanied her inside. She walked to the window to see the Daimler's headlamps retreating through the gates. With a with a pang of regret, she realized he was gone.

Fourteen

Rising early the next morning, Ursula sat at the bureau in her bedroom, still clad in her batiste nightgown and silk dressing gown, gazing down at a blank sheet of writing paper. A china cup of tea and a plate of thin arrowroot biscuits lay untouched on the side table beside her bed. Her mind was still reeling from the events of yesterday—the coroner's inquest, the connection between Arina and Katya, the whole vexatious question of Alexei. She needed to get more answers not questions. Perhaps Hugh Carmichael would now be more forthcoming—he might even provide her with a possible clue that could link Katya's and Arina's deaths. There was also the issue of Dobbs and his offer for Marlow Industries to contend with. Ursula wasted no time in formulating a letter to Hugh Carmichael. Ursula was planning to be in Newcastle on Thursday to meet Julia, who was returning with the Lawrences at last from Egypt. She finished her letter with a suggestion that they meet for lunch in Newcastle and then tapped the end of her fountain pen against her lips, trying to decide what else needed to be addressed.

She started a letter to Winifred but couldn't think of the right words to say. How could she warn her about Alexei without disclosing all that Lord Wrotham had told her? She wasn't sure where to even begin, but she knew she had to try and send a discreet message to Winifred, telling her to keep a close watch on Alexei.

Instead, she dashed off a rather cryptic note that read,

> *Dearest Freddie,*
>
> *Well, the coroner's inquest was a nightmare. Turns out that Arina was Katya's sister, but I have no idea whether (or how) their deaths are connected. Harrison is advising me to keep out of the investigation—yes, you heard right—Chief Inspector Harrison is now on the case. I'm not sure things could get any worse. But then I remember Dobbs and Alexei . . . and then there's always the question of Lord W . . . To top it all off I've got reporters buzzing about me like flies (vultures, more like!).*
>
> *Oh, Winifred, what an appalling mess I'm in. I can only hope to return to London next week and try to regain some semblance of control. On top of everything I have Mrs. P-S's Empire Day ball to attend. I need to go to keep an eye on Dobbs. After everything that's happened I have to get Arina's letter fragments decoded. When I return, we need to find someone who can help us decode it.*
>
> *In the meantime, please take extra special care. There's more to Alexei's story than meets the eye.*
>
> *Yours, etc. . . . .*

Ursula placed the letter in an envelope and then paused, her hand hovering above the telephone. She took a deep breath, lifted the receiver, and asked the operator to connect her to Shepherd's Hotel.

"This is Miss Ursula Marlow, calling from Gray House. I was wondering if Lord Wrotham was available. I believe he is a guest of yours."

"I'm afraid His Lordship has already left for London, Miss Marlow. Would you like me to take a message for you? He said he would be back at the weekend, likely as not. . . ."

"No, that's all right. I'll try and contact him in London."

"Right you are, then, Miss."

Ursula replaced the receiver and sighed. A knock on the bedroom door from Bridget signaled that it was time for her to get dressed for the day. Ursula stared at herself in the mirror. She looked like the tragic figure in an opera, with her auburn hair coiled about her shoulders and her eyes dark in the dim morning light.

"I need to pull myself together," she murmured to her reflection before calling out for Bridget to come in.

"Here's some of the post that was addressed to London, Miss. Mrs. Stewart had it sent up here just in case there was anything important."

"Thank you, Bridget. I can look at it while the bath is being run."

"I've laid out your navy suit and your green blouse, Miss. I didn't think you'd want any of the other summer suits. Seein' as how you'll be visitin' all them dirty mills and factories. And," Bridget noted as she peered out of the window, "with all this rain we've been havin', you may not get to wear 'em at all this season."

Ursula merely nodded in reply as she concentrating on opening the mail that had arrived.

One of the letters was from Eugenie Mahfouz, telling her that Chief Inspector Harrison had left Egypt. "It would have been helpful to know before he arrived," Ursula muttered as she continued reading. Eugenie wrote that all information surrounding the death of Katya Vilenksy's had been totally suppressed. She had found nothing more on the *Bregenz* or Hartuv. She couldn't even get the commander of the Egyptian police to admit that Chief Inspector Harrison had concluded his investigation. No arrests had certainly been made, and almost all of the nationalists who had been brought in for questioning had been released. As a final note, Eugenie wrote that Ambrose Whittaker had resigned his post and was rumored to be returning to India, where he had spent many years as a local magistrate.

Ursula spent the following two days visiting her mills in Oldham, Blackburn, and Rishton to try and reassure workers about their safety and the future of Marlow Industries. It was difficult, and she had to convince the trade union leaders to hold off on any threatened strike action for the results of a full inquiry she was undertaking into the spate of recent accidents. Ursula returned to Gray House Tuesday night, but there were still no messages from either Chief Inspector Harrison or Lord Wrotham.

She was reading the *Lancashire Telegraph* over her breakfast on Wednesday when she saw a small notice stating that this evening the prominent financier Mr. P. Vilensky would be attending a public meeting to discuss the issue at the Jewish Working Men's Club in Cheetham near Manchester. Ursula tore the notice out of the paper and placed it in the pocket of her knitted cardigan.

Samuels drove Ursula to Cheetham later that day and waited with her outside as the meeting at the Working Men's Club concluded and the men began to exit the red-brick building in droves at around nine that evening.

Ursula remained in the car, on the lookout for Peter Vilensky. He was one of the last to leave, walking out with a man who looked to be his personal secretary and who held an umbrella to ward off the rain that had just begun to fall.

"Mr. Vilensky," Ursula called out, climbing out of the car.

Peter Vilensky halted once he saw her.

"I need to talk to you," Ursula said. "Since you refuse to answer my letters or telephone calls in London, I had no choice but to come here."

"What do you want to talk to me about?" Peter replied, crossing his arms. "As you can see, I'm a busy man; I haven't got time for trifles." The hostility that he had shown to her in Egypt was muted beneath a thin veneer of civility.

"I want to talk about Arina Petrenko," Ursula responded.

This gave him pause. "Not here," he said with a small jerk of his head. "Inside."

Peter Vilensky turned and murmured something in the secretary's ear. The man nodded and headed back up the stairs.

"Does Lord Wrotham know you're here?" Vilensky asked as Ursula and he climbed the stairs.

"No, why? Should he?" Ursula answered.

Peter Vilensky looked confused for a moment but made no further comment.

The secretary led them into a small, windowless office adjacent to the public meeting hall.

Ursula steeled herself before starting to speak. "You've heard about Arina's death, of course."

"How could I not? I was her brother-in-law." Vilensky stood in the center of the room with his arms folded.

"Then you know it was in one of my factories."

"Yes, what of it? Accidents happen all the time."

"Is that why you didn't bother to attend the inquest?"

"I cannot be expected to attend everything."

"Did you know that Arina was killed before the fire?" Ursula chose her words deliberately, watching to see how Peter would react.

"I heard . . ." Peter Vilensky fiddled with his hands. "But surely you must realize I could have had nothing to do with it—I was sailing home from Egypt at the time. Unless I grew wings and flew, I hardly think I could have been involved."

"I wasn't here to suggest that you were," Ursula replied coolly.

"So why are you here?"

"Are you not concerned? Your wife dies in Egypt, and then in England her sister is killed—suspicious, don't you think? I would have thought a man in your position would have moved heaven and earth to find out what really happened."

"Miss Marlow, Chief Inspector Harrison is now handling both cases. I am sure he will advise me of anything significant in either case. I fail to see why I should need to speak with you!"

"I was with Katya when she died, and Arina was killed in my factory. I didn't choose to be involved, but now that I am, I think I have every right to find out the truth!" Ursula was shocked by her own vehemence. The anger that had remained suppressed since she arrived in England had suddenly announced its presence. Taking a moment to compose herself, Ursula knew she had to continue in more moderate tones if she was to get any information out of Peter Vilensky.

"If you weren't concerned about the inquiry into Katya's death, why then did you go to Lord Wrotham and inquire about the *Bregenz?*"

Peter Vilensky eyed her warily. "Lord Wrotham told you this?"

"Yes," Ursula lied, hoping that if he believed she had Lord Wrotham's confidence, he would trust her.

"Then you must know that there is no further information on the *Bregenz.* I received a note just this morning. All the Foreign Office could tell us was that the *Bregenz* reportedly sank in the Mediterranean two months ago."

"And the crew?" Ursula prompted in low tones.

"Presumed lost," Peter Vilensky replied.

Ursula was determined to take advantage of the trust Vilensky believed she shared with Lord Wrotham. "Is there any link between what happened to the *Bregenz* and your wife?"

Vilensky frowned. "None that I'm aware of. I have no idea what prompted her to investigate."

"Did she say anything to you about the settlement at Hartuv?"

"Hartuv is not a settlement funded by me or Baron Rothschild. I don't recall my wife ever mentioning it."

"I found a postcard in one of the books I lent her—she had written Hartuv on the back."

Peter Vilensky rubbed his eyes. "I cannot think what interest Katya had in it. . . . Miss Marlow, don't you think you should leave these questions to Scotland Yard? You are an amateur and Hartuv may be an irrelevancy."

Ursula hated to think he might be right but she knew that there must be some connection between the sisters' deaths. "Was Arina in contact with Katya before her death?" she asked.

"They were sisters. Of course they were in contact."

"But were there any letters exchanged in Egypt?"

Vilensky shrugged. "I cannot remember, but I expect there was the obligatory postcard."

"Can I assume that Arina was not someone *you* were close to?" Ursula asked, trying to hide her impatience with his lack of cooperation.

Vilensky shifted his weight from one foot to the other. "No doubt you have already heard that I did not approve of Arina or her friends. I tried to limit Katya's contact with her sister as much as I could."

"Because she was associated with Bolsheviks?"

"No, because she only ever approached Katya when she needed money. I grew tired of subsidizing her and her so called 'comrades.'"

Ursula eyes narrowed.

"Don't you dare presume to judge me! You didn't know Arina," Peter Vilensky snapped angrily. "She never could extricate herself from those parasites. She even shunned her own community for them, and what good were their socialist ideals? All they did was keep her down. What did she end up as? A seamstress in a factory, abandoned by her so-called lover, and an outcast to her own people!"

Ursula bit her lip. The last thing she wanted was for Peter Vilensky to refuse to answer her questions.

"My apologies," she ventured. "I intended no disrespect."

Vilensky's anger died as quickly as it had risen. He continued speaking, but this time his tone had moderated. He sounded less bitter, more regretful.

"Arina wouldn't speak to her sister in months, and then we'd find her on the doorstep, asking once more for money. Katya was too indulgent—she felt responsible for looking after her sister since they were left orphaned in France, but her kindness was misplaced. Arina grew dependent, and so I insisted that Katya supply no more funds—after that, the sisters saw each other only infrequently."

"But Katya maintained a correspondence with her sister?" Ursula pressed.

"Yes, though I tried to limit that too—Katya still felt the pull of her sister's affection."

"Did Arina write to Katya in Egypt?"

"I don't remember."

"Please try, it could be important."

Ursula drew out the piece of paper Winifred had given her, outlining the words found in the letter fragment at Arina's.

"Among the belongings found in Arina's room, there were some pieces of a letter found in the stove." Ursula handed the piece of paper to Vilensky. "I tried to have them translated, but it appears to be in some kind of code."

Peter Vilensky looked at the paper. "This letter would not have come from Katya—nor was it from Arina."

"Why do you say that?"

"Because they always corresponded in English. Katya insisted on it."

Vilensky handed the piece of paper back to Ursula.

"I'm sorry," he said with what appeared to be genuine regret. "I cannot help you with this."

Ursula tucked the paper back in her skirt pocket. "I'm sorry, too."

They both remained silent for a moment before Vilensky, running his fingers through his dark hair, suddenly said, "I do recall a letter from Arina that arrived a couple of days after Katya's death." Ursula looked at him expectantly, but Vilensky averted his gaze. "I returned it unopened, with a note explaining the circumstances of Katya's death," he said.

"You didn't read Arina's letter?"

"As I said, it remained unopened. I was sure it contained a plea for money. Her letters always did."

"Wasn't that a bit harsh?" Ursula queried. "You hadn't thought to notify Arina before then? Katya was her sister!"

"What do *you* know?" Peter Vilensky blurted out bitterly.

"I know full well what it is like to lose one of your family—a loved one. It is almost unendurable."

Vilensky flushed. "I'm sorry, Miss Marlow," he resumed in quieter tones. "I should not have said that—it was tactless of me. I realize, of course, that with your father's death you would know what it is like to have someone you love murdered."

"And Katya was with me—," Ursula began, but she choked on the words.

Peter sat down heavily on the folding wooden chair. "I know." He seemed confused for a moment, as his bitterness dissipated and his grief rose to the surface.

"Why did you not tell Arina before you received her letter?"

"I had decided to wait until I was back in England. I couldn't bring myself to tell everyone—it was too much. But then her letter arrived, and it angered me that she would be asking for money at such a time. Katya had already received a letter when we first arrived in Jaffa—it distressed her greatly, and she pleaded with me to send funds to Arina. I . . . I refused. I merely believed Arina's second letter repeated the plea, and I couldn't bring myself to open it. I blamed Arina's influence for Katya's betrayal. . . ."

"Why do you persist in believing your wife betrayed you?" Ursula asked quietly. "I spent a great deal of time with your wife, and I know she loved you and you alone. Despite the rumors, I'm sure there was nothing going on between Katya and Hugh Carmichael."

"What do you know of such things?" Vilensky responded sharply.

Ursula gave a soft, sad smile. "I just know."

Fifteen

Thursday morning, Ursula left Gray House early in order to catch the train to Manchester and connect to the ten-thirty train bound for Newcastle. Samuels had left the previous night with Bertie, and Ursula was planning to travel back with Julia by motorcar later that day.

Samuels was waiting at the Newcastle Central Station, rugged up against the unseasonably wet weather. The steamer from Antwerp carrying Julia, Mrs. Millicent Lawrence, her husband the vicar, and her two missionary friends, Misses Norton and Stanley, had been due to dock earlier in the morning, but bad weather in the Channel had delayed it by two hours. Julia, not a good sailor at the best of times, was still a little green when she disembarked and made her way down the gangplank to greet her mistress.

"Mrs. Lawrence, I must thank you again for agreeing to let Julia join you all on the voyage home. I do hope she could be of service," Ursula said.

Millicent Lawrence looked as hale and healthy as ever, despite the long journey home across the Continent. They had been obliged to break up their return by stopping frequently so as not to exacerbate Millicent's husband's lumbago (which, according to his wife, flared up when he was exposed to "papists and foreigners").

"Julia performed most admirably," Millicent Lawrence replied robustly. "What with my maid running off with the purser in Cyprus and Violet coming down with food poisoning in Marseilles, we needed all hands on deck, I can tell you!"

Ursula's lips twitched.

"The fact of the matter is that good help is hard to come by these days," Millicent continued. "And we'd be quite happy to make it a more permanent arrangement."

"Oh, Mrs. Lawrence, I couldn't give up Julia! But I am so awfully glad it all worked out for the best."

"Well, we certainly knocked the heathen out of her! Why, when she was first aboard the *Esperante*, she didn't even know her Old Testament from her New. Now you'll find she can recite the Lord's Prayer by heart and can list all ten Commandments. She'll be quite the addition downstairs at Sunday Bible reading, I can tell you."

"Yes, I'm sure she will," Ursula murmured, picturing the look of horror on Biggs's face should Julia dare to suggest *she* prepare the Sunday reading.

"So how are you holding up?" Ursula asked Julia after Mrs. Lawrence and her party had left and while Samuels arranged with the porter to bring Julia's small trunk over to where Bertie was parked.

"Ooh, I was terribly sick, Miss, all the way across the Channel. But I'm much better now, thank you—and well pleased to be back on dry land, and in England!"

"Well, I know Mrs. Norris has prepared a meat and potato pie for you for supper. I asked her to make your favorite. Samuels, why don't you and Julia see if there's a tea shop in that new arcade where you can grab yourselves some luncheon? I'm meeting Mr. Carmichael at twelve, and expect I should be done by half past one."

"Yes, Miss," Samuels replied, lashing Julia's small trunk to the back of the motorcar.

Ursula and Julia climbed in.

"Do you know where this Blue Anchor is?"

Samuels barely repressed a grin. "Yes, Miss. I've heard tell from some of the locals this morning that it's famous for its fish pie and brown ale."

"Oh, wonderful," Ursula responded dryly. "Sounds like just my kind of place."

Hugh Carmichael was meant to meet Ursula outside the Blue Anchor. Ursula, wearing a peach-and-white-striped linen suit with a Peter Pan collar and a wide-brimmed straw hat, couldn't have looked more conspicuous or more "bourgeois" (as Alexei once told her). As she waited, a motley assortment of clientele walked into the pub: a couple of sailors in their Royal Navy uniforms; a man in a brown frock coat, smelling of spice; a young clerk with ink-stained fingers; and an older man with long, white whiskers, in a grubby navy surplus overcoat and knitted cap.

There was a smell of petrol and a squeal of tires as Hugh Carmichael came barreling along the cobbled street on his Douglas motorbike. He wore a long leather coat and hat and a pair of goggles. The motorbike spluttered to a stop outside the pub, and Ursula instinctively took a step back and covered her nose with her lavender-scented handkerchief.

"Hugh, you are a menace!"

"Hello, sweetheart!" Hugh responded with a grin. He took off his hat to reveal a shock of gray-black hair. "Never mind old Daisy here—"

Ursula wrinkled her nose.

Hugh climbed off the motorbike stiffly.

"Are you all right?" Ursula queried.

"Yeah . . . just had a bit of an accident last week. Brakes failed coming down from Marley Hill. I was lucky it was only a few bruises, nothing more."

"Hugh, you need to be more careful."

"Sweetheart, when my time's up, it's up."

"I wish you wouldn't say things like that. Not after all that's happened."

"Sorry." Hugh's face was suddenly sober.

"Shall we?" Ursula prompted.

"Are you ready to sample the Blue Anchor's famous fish pie?"

"After seeing some of the . . . er . . . clientele entering the place, I think I might wait and eat luncheon on the way home."

"Miss Marlow, I'm shocked. Where's your sense of adventure?!"

Hugh held open the ancient wooden door, and with some reluctance Ursula ducked her head and went inside.

The publican found them a seat at the back beneath paneled Elizabethan windows that looked out onto the lane behind the pub. Ladies weren't allowed at the bar, so Ursula had to remain in the dining room while Hugh went to purchase drinks for them. Ignoring the curious stares of some of the other patrons, she contented herself with watching how the light refracted through the tiny hexagonal panes of glass set in the wrought-iron-framed windows.

Ursula slid her hat off and placed it gingerly down on the window seat beside her. Hugh returned, carrying a pint of brown ale in one hand and a Pimm's and lemonade in the other.

"The inquest must have been a bit of a shock," Hugh began.

"It certainly had its moments."

"So this girl who died in your factory, she was Katya's sister?"

"Yes, not that Peter Vilensky seems to care, but yes."

"And that chief inspector from Egypt, he's now handling the case."

"Yes, and his involvement indicates to me that there's something bigger going on—I don't know what, but it links to Katya's and Arina's deaths, of that I'm sure. . . . If only I could prove it."

Hugh's face remained impassive.

"You're still not going to tell me what happened between you and Katya in Egypt, are you?"

Hugh did not reply.

"You don't have to protect me, you know," Ursula said.

Hugh took a swig of ale.

"I can't believe you—," Ursula started to say, but Hugh gestured her to stop.

"It's not that I don't want to find out what happened. I just cannot help you at the moment. I'm fighting for my business here—my very livelihood—and Iris's inheritance. The shipyard was her family's business, don't forget. And Dobbs is forcing my hand. I've got the bankers breathing down by neck, Vilensky baying for blood—I'll spare you any more metaphors, but the long and short of it is, I cannot help you."

"But two women have died!" Ursula exclaimed. Some of the other patrons started exchanging uneasy glances, and Ursula had to stifle her frustration.

"And there's nothing that you or I can do to change that. You'd be best to keep well out of it and let this man Harrison do his job."

Ursula's pursed her lips, and Hugh drained his glass.

"It's not that I don't admire your sense of justice. I do. But people are dying, Ursula—and you need to stop playing Lady Molly of Scotland Yard."

Lady Molly was Baroness Orczy's fictional female sleuth.

"You haven't been talking to Lord Wrotham, have you?" Ursula asked swiftly.

Hugh Carmichael smiled. "No such luck, sweetheart. But I'll tell you what I really think. I think you should fight for your business just as hard as I damn well am. Fight for your father's empire. Be the businesswoman I know you can be and rub Dobbs's nose in it like he was a dog. Then, when you've proven all that to society, marry Lord Wrotham, be happy, have lots of children, and godammit, forget about Katya and Arina!"

Ursula dined alone at Gray House that evening, sitting at the small dining room table she and her father had shared while she was growing up. Mrs. Norris was no substitute for Cook, but she did prepare a good pie. Served with pickled red cabbage, it brought back memories of her childhood, and for once this provided a comfort rather than a sad reminder of the mother and father she had lost.

Ursula had just finished eating dessert, Mrs. Norris's sticky date pudding, when Biggs entered the dining room, looking somber.

"Yes, Biggs? What is it?" Ursula asked as she put down her silver spoon.

"Dr. Mortimer to see you."

"At this time?" Ursula replied with a glance at the grandfather clock in the corner of the room.

"I've placed him in the Blue Room."

Ursula pushed her plate back and rose to her feet, patting her mouth with the linen napkin. "I guess I'd better go to him. You may as well serve coffee in there."

"Yes, Miss."

Ursula hurried down the hallway and into the Blue Room.

"Dr. Mortimer!" Ursula exclaimed as she entered. "Is everything all right?"

Ainsley Mortimer jumped to his feet. "Miss Marlow, I'm so sorry to trouble you at such an hour."

"Please sit down, and there's no need to apologize. Tell me quickly, though—is it bad news?"

"Nothing . . . nothing like that!" Seeing Ursula's stricken face, Dr. Mortimer stumbled over his words. "I didn't mean to alarm you. . . . But I thought you should know—"

Ursula took a seat.

"Should know what?" she asked quietly, dread filling her heart.

"Chief Inspector Harrison has just arrested George Aldwych."

Ursula sat very still.

"Tell me."

"George was brought in for questioning yesterday—and the chief inspector, well, he spent hours with him, and then . . . just around six this evening, I received a telephone call. George confessed to lighting the factory fire."

Biggs entered the room quietly and placed a silver coffeepot and two china cups down on the table.

"I . . . I didn't like to telephone . . . I wanted to tell you in person, knowing how much of shock it was likely to be."

"I see. Thank you," Ursula said hoarsely.

"I would have brought Stacie—but she's at one of her debating meetings. I'm sure you must think me terribly improper, coming at this hour, alone."

"Not at all," Ursula responded mechanically.

"Chief Inspector Harrison wanted to wait till morning but I . . . I . . . thought you needed to know."

The coffeepot remained untouched.

"What about Arina?" Ursula asked quietly. "Did George—" She couldn't finish the question.

Ainsley chewed his lip. "The chief inspector told me that George maintains he had no idea that she was in the factory, for what that's worth . . . "

Recovering from the initial shock, Ursula offered Ainsley some coffee. He reddened and shook his head, saying, "No, really, I'm fine."

Ursula was too preoccupied to notice his discomfit. Slowly she poured herself a cup and sat back down.

"What possible motive could George have for lighting the fire?" she eventually asked. "He was always so loyal to my father."

Ainsley looked even more uncomfortable.

"Did the chief inspector say whether George told him why he did it?" she asked.

Ainsley hesitated.

"Please, Ainsley, I need to know," Ursula urged.

"George told him he was angry about the kind of women being employed. Called it an abomination. Taking jobs away from decent local women."

Ursula shrank back in the chair.

"I can't believe it," she said softly, more to herself than to Dr. Mortimer. "I mean, he never expressed any of that to me. . . . I even walked through the factory with him—he seemed so shocked. I never, never suspected he could have been involved."

"I know, these things are so often unexpected."

Ursula got to her feet abruptly and walked over to the windows that overlooked the back garden of Gray House. It was a clear night, and in the moonlight she could see the wild roses in the hedgerow bobbing their budding heads, almost mocking her in the night breeze.

"Can I speak to him?" Ursula asked suddenly.

"Pardon?"

She turned away from the window.

"Do you think if I went down to the station tomorrow, Chief Inspector Harrison would let me speak to George?"

"I'm not sure I understand," Ainsley replied.

"I want to speak to George. I need—I need to hear it from him."

"It could be very upsetting for you—are you sure you want to?"

"There's something bigger at stake than just this factory." Ursula continued. "You know what's been happening. I have to find out if this is more widespread—whether there's a conspiracy to set fire to any more of my mills and factories. George may be able to provide me with the information I need to find out whether I have any more traitors in my midst."

She had to steady her hand as she lifted the coffee cup to her lips.

Ainsley's brown eyes grew soft. "I . . . I understand. I can try to speak to the chief inspector."

Ursula put down her cup slowly.

"Ainsley," she started to say with a gulp, "do you think George killed Arina?"

"If George is to be believed, the cause of Arina's death remains unknown. . . . But now of course he must be a suspect—all I can say is you should prepare yourself for the worst."

"You can't honestly believe George could have murdered a young girl."

Dr. Mortimer shook his head. "I would never have believed he was capable of arson, either."

Sixteen

Samuels drove Ursula down to the Oldham police station the following afternoon. Arraigned and waiting for trial, George Aldwych was being kept in one of the jail cells in the back of the police station. After a long debate that morning, Chief Inspector Harrison, with urging from Dr. Mortimer, had agreed that Ursula could speak to George in one of the tiny windowless interview rooms that lined the corridor leading to the rear of the station.

George sat at the table, handcuffed to the chair, his head bent low. He looked sullen and withdrawn. Ursula pulled up another chair and sat down opposite him.

"George . . . ," she started to say, but he refused to look up.

"George, what about your family? Who's going to provide for your wife? Your children? I can't believe you would do such a thing. Not to them. Not to me. Not to my father."

George kept his head down and said nothing.

Chief Inspector Harrison stood in the corner of the room with his arms folded tight across his chest. Ursula wiped a tear from the corner of her eye. "I expected more from you. If you had a problem with what I was trying to achieve at Oldham, you should have spoken up. But now, now I have to ask you something I never thought I'd ever

have to ask. Did you have anything to do with what happened to the other mills and factories? The accident at Great Harwood, the strikes at Victoria and Jubilee Mills? Do you know who was involved?"

George remained mute.

Ursula rubbed her temples. Chief Inspector Harrison tapped her lightly on the arm, as if asking if she wanted to leave. She shook her head furiously.

"Why?" she asked George again. "Why did you do it?"

George shrugged his shoulders, still refusing to look up.

"These were women just like Arina. They had nothing. Why would you destroy that? I would have thought you more than any-one would have had compassion for such women. All I was offering them was hope. I cannot believe that—" Ursula choked. "I cannot believe you were responsible."

George continued to sit, head down, refusing to meet her eyes or speak with her.

"Did you hate these women enough to kill one of them?" Harrison's voice seemed loud in the small room. "Were you angry that night? Had you been drinking?"

George made no sign that he was even listening to Harrison.

"Did someone tell you to do this, George?"

"George—" Chief Inspector Harrison leaned over the desk. "If someone else forced you to do this, you have to let us know."

Ursula was surprised by his vehemence.

"Was the man that was seen outside the factory your accomplice? Did he force you to light the fire to cover up the death of Arina Petrenko? Damn it, man! You need to speak up in your own defense. You need to tell me what happened—otherwise, by God, you *will* find yourself standing trial for murder!"

Ursula had never seen Harrison be so confrontational. He seemed genuinely angry and frustrated, but George was immune to his plea. He merely stared at his feet and continued to say nothing.

Harrison ran his fingers through his hair and exhaled noisily.

Ursula sighed and, after a weary glance at George, rose to her feet.

"I've seen enough," she said, barely disguising the contempt in her voice.

Harrison held open the office door, and she walked through. As she was leaving, George muttered something under his breath. She turned and looked at him sharply, but George had fallen silent once more.

Harrison closed the door behind them and escorted her to where Ainsley Mortimer was waiting.

"I must thank you, Dr. Mortimer," Ursula said, "for convincing the chief inspector. George wouldn't say anything, but at least I tried."

"It's strange," Ainsley said as Samuels pulled up in Bertie, "the chief inspector has been questioning him for well over a day and is even transferring him down to London for further questioning. That's a great deal of effort. . . ." Ainsley's voice trailed off, and Ursula sensed a slight rebuke. If Ursula wasn't who she was, would a young factory girl's death have ever garnered such attention? The case had certainly not been a priority until Ursula's outburst in the coroner's court and the chief inspector's arrival. Ainsley Mortimer had probably seen hundreds of deaths, many of which the police simply ignored—but then, what was the value of a poor woman's life when measured against the power and wealth of a woman like Ursula Marlow?

Later that afternoon, Ursula decided to pay Mrs. Aldwych a visit. George and his family lived in a modest stone house that Ursula's father had provided when George was foreman of the Oldham mill. When she appointed him manager of the factory, Ursula had maintained this arrangement. The house lay on the corner of Linney and Beal Lanes, close to the mill and the factory, but a few streets away from the rows of workers' cottages that lined Victoria and Spring Streets.

Ursula knocked on the black-painted door. The door opened, and Mrs. Aldwych stood, feet apart, her wide frame filling the doorway. She wore a plain dove-gray dress with a striped wraparound pinafore tied across the middle. "Miss Marlow!" she exclaimed. "Well, I never!" She glanced quickly down the street. "Please come in."

"Thank you, Mrs. Aldwych. I thought I'd come by and see how you were managing."

Mrs. Aldwych fiddled with the ties of her apron. "Well, we're doin' the best we can," she replied. "Will you not take a seat, Miss Marlow?"

"Thank you." Ursula chose the armchair beneath the window and sat down. She looked about the room curiously. There was a surfeit of ornaments littered across every conceivable surface. From the porcelain shepherdess and row of diminutive brass carriages on the mantelshelf to the row of miniature cups and saucers across the window sill and the cheap figurines on the small table next to Ursula, everything felt claustrophobic and overcrowded. There were lace doilies on the backs of the chairs and settee, florid pink wallpaper, and a faded framed photograph of the North Promenade in Blackpool. The gas lamp on the wall hissed, while the coal fire smoked in the grate.

"Bessie," Mrs. Aldwych called out as she caught sight of a young girl in a grubby pinafore peering round the doorway, "make us some tea, there's a pet. And change out of that filthy smock—you look a right ragamuffin."

The girl nodded, and with a flick of her plaits she disappeared into the back room that Ursula assumed was the kitchen.

Mrs. Aldwych perched herself on the edge of the sofa, as if ready to get up at any moment. Her hands hovered above her lap but never quite came to rest.

Ursula took off her gloves and, with a tug, pulled out her hat pin and removed her hat. "No, this is quite all right," she responded as Mrs. Aldwych motioned to take her hat and gloves, instead placing them on the wide arm of the chair.

"I know this must be very awkward, Mrs. Aldwych," Ursula began.

"No, no," Mrs. Aldwych interceded.

"I still can't quite believe that George would have done such a thing," Ursula continued.

Mrs. Aldwych dropped her eyes.

"He woulda never done it in your father's day."

"Then why would he have done it now?" Ursula asked.

Mrs. Aldwych didn't respond for a minute or two before replying, in measured tones. "I canna say . . ."

"You can't say what, Mrs. Aldwych?" Ursula asked more gently.

"I think 'e were just a bit disappointed," Mrs. Aldwych replied.

"Disappointed?" Ursula exclaimed involuntarily. "Whatever do you mean?"

Mrs. Aldwych mumbled something inaudible in reply before getting up and making an excuse that she had to go "and see about that tea."

Ursula remained seated, trying to understand why George Aldwych would have felt disappointed. George had been luckier than many. He had started in one of Robert Marlow's mills as a piecer at the age of fourteen. By sixteen he was a mule spinner, and by eighteen an overlooker. As a reward for his diligence and dedication, Robert Marlow had made George the manager of the Oldham mill in 1900, when George was just thirty years old. Many men would have counted themselves fortunate to be in his position, particularly with a young family to provide for.

Mrs. Aldwych returned with Bessie carrying a tray with teacups and saucers and a plate of Eccles cakes. The formality was not lost on Ursula. She knew she was being given the very best china.

"This looks lovely," she said, forcing a smile.

Mrs. Aldwych's face twisted.

"Run along, Bessie," she said to the little girl. "Leave Miss Marlow and me to talk."

"I'll not beat about the bush," Mrs. Aldwych began. "It's not me way. And I'm not excusin' what he did neither, but George did find it difficult, what with your father's death and you takin' over and all. He thought he may have been promoted, to proper management like. He's looked after your father's mills here and in Rochdale . . . and so the position of foreman at this newfangled factory of yours, well, he viewed it as a bit of a comedown. . . ."

"A bit of a comedown! But, Mrs. Aldwych, I was entrusting him with one of my most valued projects."

"Aye, and he knew it. That's why he stuck it out. But he found it hard—there's that many local women, good women who need jobs, and there you were lookin' after, well, lookin' after girls who didn't have the decency to get married, or to turn to their families for 'elp."

"I'm sorry to hear it. I really wish I'd known. It need never have come to this."

Mrs. Aldwych reddened. "Mind you," she said, "I'm not condoning what he did. I'm just sayin' this was preyin' on his mind, and when he was three parts cut—well, it may have all come out."

"May have?" Ursula said softly. "You mean, you didn't know what he was going to do?"

"Of course I didn't," Mrs. Aldwych answered, her agitation growing. "For if I had, I would have told him not to be so daft. Even if they hadn't worked out it were him, I mean, what good would it 'ave done him?"

"He could have found another position elsewhere without having to burn down the factory. What I don't understand is why he would risk it—with a family and all."

Mrs. Aldwych looked bleakly. "As I said, when he were drunk . . ."

"I didn't realize he had a drinking problem," Ursula ventured.

"Until the last few months or so I wouldn't have said he did—but the last few months he's been down at the Dog and Duck more times than not in the evening. Wasn't like him. Wasn't like him at all."

"So George had changed recently?"

"Yes," Mrs. Aldwych admitted reluctantly. "And I don't know who it was at the pub fillin' his head with stuff, but I'm sure that's where the idea musta come from. Why, he hadn't mentioned anything about the factory for months—not since December last year. Then all of a sudden, the last month 'e was broodin' about summat."

Mrs. Aldwych noticed Ursula hadn't finished her tea. Not wishing to offend her, Ursula gulped downed the last dregs. She sensed her time here was drawing to a close.

"Well," Ursula said, putting down her cup and saucer on the side table, "I just wanted to say how shocked and sorry I am that things turned out this way. Thank you so much for the tea, and for taking the time to talk to me. I'd best be leaving."

Mrs. Aldwych stood up.

"Did you know Arina Petrenko?" Ursula asked as she gathered up her hat and gloves.

"Aye, she came round 'ere a few times with that Nellie Ackroyd. Always askin' for money, made me right angry, it did."

"What did George think?"

"He felt sorry for 'em first off, and then he were right mad an' all."

There was another awkward pause as Mrs. Aldwych walked Ursula to the door.

Now came the worst part of all. "You know I can't let you stay here," Ursula said sadly.

Mrs. Aldwych looked at her squarely. "I know."

"But I will give you a month."

Mrs. Aldwych tugged at her apron, clearly trying to rein in her emotions. A month's notice was more than generous in the circumstances, and Mrs. Aldwych knew it.

"Where will you go?" Ursula asked softly.

"To me mam's."

"And how will you manage?"

"Well, I've got my position at Kirby's Bakery, and our Stan's down t'mill. Tommy has taken an apprenticeship at the brick works, and Irene can start making herself useful at last. She's sixteen, you know, and it's time she left her books and helped support her family."

"Oh, please don't pull her out of school!" Ursula exclaimed. She remembered Irene, and was dismayed that such an obviously intelligent and eager student would be denied the chance for a proper education.

"She'll muck in with the rest of us," Mrs. Aldwych responded firmly. "As George always said, what's the point in filling her head with books and the like? She's been mollycoddled enough. Education is a luxury girls like her can nay afford."

Ursula opened her mouth to speak. She dearly wanted to intervene—to offer Mrs. Aldwych something to stop her from ruining Irene's chance of escaping this life, of making something of herself. But it was hopeless—she could see that in Mrs. Aldwych's eyes. They were like cold, hard cobblestones. Ursula was reminded of a story her father often told her, how when he bought his first barrow and was trying to sell firewood in the back streets of Blackburn, his own father had turned to him and said with a bitter tongue, "No use trying to rise above your station, lad. It'll only bring you grief."

The Oldham Union Workhouse fronted onto Sheepfoot Lane, and Ursula had to be escorted through the imbecile wards by the matron as they made their way to the main building. There she was met by Nellie Ackroyd, who had been assigned to the kitchens that day.

Matron agreed to let Nellie speak with Ursula for a few minutes in one of the female dormitories, away from the poor ventilation and sickening smell of the kitchen.

Nellie sat on the edge of one of the narrow beds, head bent, fiddling with her apron string.

"Nellie," Ursula began. "I wanted to let you know that we're planning to rebuild the factory as soon as we can. In the meantime, I have a position at the mill, cleaning the spindles."

Nellie coughed loudly. "I used t'work a'mills, but me lungs gave out."

"Oh . . ." Ursula wasn't sure what to else to say. She put aside the question of finding another opportunity to get Nellie out of the workhouse and reunited with her children, and proceeded to ask Nellie about Arina.

"I wanted to ask you a couple of questions about Arina," Ursula said.

Nellie nodded her head and sniffed.

"You told the coroner's court that she was very kind to you."

"That she were. . . ."

"Did she ever speak of her childhood in Russia?"

"Nay. She didn't like to talk about it. Said it were that long ago, she didn't remember much anyway. I never 'eard her even speak Russian. Told me a bit about Paris, though. That's where she learned 'ow to sew."

"Yes." Ursula remembered Katya telling her about the garment factory in the Marais district of Paris.

"Did she speak about her sister, Katya?"

"Yes." Nellie hesitated. "She said she were really rich."

"You heard in the court, though, didn't you, that Katya, Arina's sister, was dead?"

Nellie nodded.

"She died in Egypt, and my worry—which is why I've come to see you," Ursula said gently, "is that Arina's and her sister's deaths were related in some way. So that's why I'm asking you some questions. You see, I was a good friend of Katya's, and as I'm sure you know, it's hard to lose a friend."

Nellie's eyes swam with tears.

"Did Arina ever say anything about Katya? Anything that sounded strange or which upset her?"

Nellie shook her head.

"Are you sure there was nothing? She didn't receive a letter, maybe?"

Nellie looked thoughtful.

"Just take a moment and see if you can remember," Ursula urged her.

"Well, she did seem a bit upset—teary, like—a few months back . . . but we all thought it were because she hadn't heard from her feller. The Russian—"

"Kolya?"

"Summat like that. Arina weren't one to say much about that sorta thing. None of us did. We'd all had it wi' men."

Ursula, sensing Nellie was thinking about her own unfortunate love life, reached over and took Nellie's hand.

"I'm sure it's been hard for you."

Nellie snatched her hand away and wiped the tears off her cheek with the back of her hand. "I aint 'ere to ask for no pity o' yours."

"No, of course not," Ursula said hurriedly. "Can you remember anything else? Any other letter Arina may have mentioned from her sister?"

"No . . . only a note from 'er brother-in-law tellin' her about her sister. She were right upset about that, of course."

"Nothing else? Nothing strange or odd about Arina's behavior? No mention of any other letters?"

"Well, she did tell me she thought a few of her letters 'ad gone missing, after the break-in. She seemed right cut up about it, but she didn't want the police around about it."

"But she seemed upset—about the letters going missing?"

Nellie screwed up her nose. "Not upset . . . more . . ."

"More what?"

"Scared."

Seventeen

Ursula reluctantly returned to London the following Thursday to attend Friday's Empire Day ball at Mrs. Pomfrey-Smith's. As she sat on the train, she composed a list of all the information she had gathered thus far, and the key questions that remained regarding Katya's and Arina's deaths. She leaned back on the red leather seat and propped her leather-bound notebook on her lap. Tapping the end of the pencil on her chin, she stared at the blank white page and was soon lost in thought. By the time the guard knocked on the carriage door to tell her that luncheon was being served in the first-class dining car, she had compiled a long list of items, almost all questions that still needed to be addressed.

"I'm convinced," Ursula later told Winifred as they sat together in the front parlor in Chester Square, "that the letter we found was sent to Arina in the last few days before her death. It wasn't one of the letters she spoke of to Nellie Ackroyd—not one of the ones that went missing. I believe that those are likely to be letters from Katya. I'm not sure what they contained, but what if Katya wrote to Arina telling her of her investigations into the *Bregenz*? What if that's why Katya was murdered? What if she told Arina, and that was why Arina was killed?"

"That's a lot of what-ifs, Sully. Are you sure there's a connection between Katya's and Arina's deaths?"

"If there wasn't a connection, why would Chief Inspector Harrison be involved?"

"True," Winifred admitted.

"So," Ursula continued, "if the fragments we found are from the killer—most likely they are his or her instructions to Arina to meet her at the factory that night—then we need to focus on decoding these. That could be our strongest chance of discovering the connection between Arina's and Katya's deaths."

"And what about Chief Inspector Harrison?"

"He's not about to help me. In his mind, I'm just an interfering girl sticking my nose in where it's not wanted."

"And Alexei?" Winifred asked. "What's his role in all this?"

"Maybe the letter will tell us," Ursula answered.

"Perhaps," Winifred mused. "It's certainly a place to start. Perhaps it will help us understand George Aldwych's role in all this. From all you've told me, I still think there's more to his so-called confession than meets the eye."

"You may be right, Freddie, but I also need to work out why Katya was so interested in this ship, the *Bregenz,* and what that damned man Whittaker was up to in Egypt. I simply don't understand what the significance of that ship could possibly be. Was it something to do with the cargo, the passengers?"

Winifred eyed her friend closely. "What about Lord Wrotham? Could his Foreign Office contacts help?"

"I can't ask him anything more," Ursula interrupted swiftly. "Things are too . . . too muddled between us. I can't think straight when he's around. And besides," she ended, "I think I need to work this out for myself."

"I'm sure if he learns anything further about the *Bregenz* or Whittaker, he'll let you know," Winifred replied.

Ursula shrugged. "Perhaps,"

"What about Dobbs?" Winifred ventured.

"Oh, I haven't forgotten about him, or what I saw that day. I just don't know what I can do about it or his offer. If I'm to stop his destroying Hugh Carmichael's business, I'd better have darn good evidence. Telling Harrison, or Lord Wrotham, that I think Dobbs is holding some poor man prisoner in his basement is more likely to get me sent to the nearest asylum."

"Well," Winifred said sensibly, "we just have to focus on the evidence we do have, and I really think if we're to have any chance of deciphering this letter, we need Lady Winterton. She's the one who has spent the most time researching all this code stuff. I really think she's become quite the expert. Besides, neither of us know enough Russian. How are we to even know if we've succeeded in decoding it?"

Ursula still looked unconvinced.

"We wouldn't have to tell her anything except the bare details. And, Sully, she's one of us. I think we can trust her."

An hour later Lady Winterton entered Ursula's study and sat down with an expectant smile.

"So," she said, "why all the cloak and dagger? I'm assuming this is not WSPU business."

"No, it's of a more personal nature," Winifred began before Ursula cut in.

"We have some pieces of a letter. Written in Russian, and written, we suspect, in code."

"Can I ask what the letter is about?"

"It's a love letter," Ursula blurted out, ignoring Winifred's raised eyebrows. "At least, that's what a mutual friend of ours is worried about. She wants to know if her fiancé is involved in an improper liaison, and she came to us for help."

Lady Winterton looked surprised, but appeared to accept Ursula's explanation.

Ursula drew the curtains in the study as Winifred moved a chair for Lady Winterton up against the mahogany desk. Ursula laid out the copy of the letter fragments that Winifred had drawn up.

Lady Winterton drew out a pair of pince-nez glasses from a beaded bag that hung from her skirt and peered over it.

"I've been reading some very interesting texts," she said as she drew out her notebook and fountain pen and proceeded to start writing. "One, *Le Cryptographie militaire*, was most enlightening. I've also been reading Kasiski's famous treatise on solving the Vigenère cipher, of course, *Die Geheimschiffer und Die Dechiffir Kunst*." Lady Winterton looked up expectantly. "I have you to thank, Ursula, for that; your mention of the Vigenère cipher was very helpful." Both Ursula and Winifred regarded her blankly. Lady Winterton laughed, took off her glasses, and sat back in her chair. She then proceeded to explain the various forms of codes and ciphers she had discovered in her research. Both Ursula and Winifred listened closely.

"I don't think that this is a substitution cipher," Lady Winterton concluded. "The Cyrillic letters used don't follow any pattern likely for that. I also doubt that a really elaborate cipher would have been used for something like a love letter. I mean, you wouldn't expect someone to have the necessary skill to develop or unscramble such an effort."

Ursula and Winifred exchanged glances, but Lady Winterton didn't seem to notice. She merely instructed them to remain quiet while she tried some alternative methods of deciphering what was written. Ursula waited anxiously, but in the end, after nearly two hours, Lady Winterton sat back on her chair with a resigned sigh. "It's no good," she said. "I can't get anything to work. Nothing translates into anything that even resembles actual Russian words. I'm sorry, but I'm not sure I can help you."

Ursula unhooked her collar and sat back in her chair. She felt stiff and uncomfortably hot from being in the overheated study for so long.

"I must confess," Lady Winterton continued, "it seems strange that such an elaborate cipher, whatever it may be, was used for a love letter. But I guess I'm just a novice at this after all."

Winifred got to her feet, stretched, and yawned loudly.

"I'll at least leave you my Russian dictionary, just in case you can use it," Lady Winterton said. "And I'll send over some of my books in case you want to do some research yourselves."

"Thank you," Ursula replied before Winifred exclaimed, "Crikey! It's nearly midnight."

"Time obviously ran away with us," Lady Winterton responded with a smile as she too got to her feet. She looked unruffled as always.

"I expect I will be seeing you at the Empire Day ball tomorrow night, Ursula," Lady Winterton said.

"Yes," Ursula replied, rising and ringing the bell for Biggs.

"I assume you and Lord Wrotham will be arriving together."

"No," Ursula replied. "I will be going alone."

"Lord Wrotham is out of town?"

"No, I don't believe so."

"Oh, I'm sorry, I didn't realize that you and Lord Wrotham were . . ." Lady Winterton left the question hanging in the air.

"It's late, and I'm sure everyone's very tired!" Winifred interrupted, sparing Ursula the need to reply.

Biggs entered bearing Lady Winterton's hat, coat, and gloves. He calmly informed her that Samuels was already waiting outside to drive her home. Ursula gave Biggs a grateful smile. Even in the dead of night, he could be relied upon to behave impeccably.

"I hope to see you tomorrow evening," Lady Winterton said. "I'm only sorry I could not help you more."

The next morning, bleary-eyed and pensive, Ursula sat in the front parlor, trying to decide on her next steps. She resisted the temptation to call Lord Wrotham, knowing that to do so was likely to raise only further confusion as to the nature of their relationship. Lady Winterton had unsettled her enough in this regard.

Tapping her fingers lightly, she gazed out over Chester Square. Presently she rang the bell for Biggs.

"Yes, Miss."

"I'd like you to telephone Christopher Dobbs's residence. Tell his butler or whomever it is that answers that I'd like to set up a meeting with him. Preferably today."

"Of course, Miss." Biggs replied and exited the room. Ursula sat on the Mackmurdo sofa and stared out the window.

A few minutes later Biggs returned.

"I'm afraid Jeffries informs me that Mr. Dobbs is otherwise engaged this morning. He is expecting visitors apparently. I inquired whether Mr. Dobbs would be available by Monday or Tuesday, but Jeffries was decidedly noncommittal."

"Never mind, Biggs," Ursula replied, but she was intrigued by the reference to visitors. It was too enticing to ignore. "Actually," Ursula called out as Biggs was about to leave, "ask Samuels to bring Bertie round right away. I need to go out for a few hours."

"Shall I tell Cook to expect you back in time for luncheon?"

"Yes," Ursula answered distractedly. "Oh, and tell Julia not to worry. I promise to leave plenty of time to get ready for tonight's ball."

"Very well," Biggs responded, and left to find Samuels.

Ursula jumped to her feet and grabbed her notebook and pencil. As she opened the door to the hallway, Julia approached, carrying her suit jacket, hat, and gloves.

"I heard you were going out, Miss."

"One step ahead of me, as always," Ursula replied with a smile. "Thank you."

Julia helped Ursula put on the navy and white jacket, the matching straw hat, and her white gloves.

Ursula heard the familiar sound of Samuels driving Bertie to the front door and bid Julia good-bye. Once inside the motorcar, she leaned forward and said, in a tone that broached no argument, "Forty-five Bletchley Avenue, Holland Park."

Samuels cast a glance in the rearview mirror but made no comment.

Ursula had Samuels drive Bertie round the block and come to a halt on the periphery of Holland Park, keeping Dobbs's house just in sight.

"Just wait here," she told Samuels. He looked at her quizzically, but she gave no explanation. They waited nearly an hour, during which time Ursula nervously fidgeted with her gloves and hat. She was just about to tell Samuels to return to Chester Square when she saw a motorcar pull up outside Christopher's house.

Ursula watched closely. The first man to alight from the car was tall, muscular, and dark-haired. He filled out his frock coat to the point where it looked tight and uncomfortable. He stood with his back to Ursula, holding open the car door as another man alighted. This man Ursula recognized immediately. From the florid countenance, the portly figure, and the thinning hair, there was no mistaking Mr. Ambrose Whittaker. Whittaker quickly pulled on his hat, gazing at the sky for a brief moment as if he half expected rain. The first man brushed his mustache with his fingers and, mimicking Whittaker, tilted his head back to look up as well. Whittaker made some comment, and the man laughed, his face now clearly visible to Ursula. A tremor of recognition shook her entire body. The way he laughed, the cut of his tall muscular figure—all he needed was a monkey on his shoulder. At first her mind rebelled against the possibility, but her body had viscerally betrayed the truth. This was the same man she had seen in the Khan el-Khalili the day Katya Vilensky was killed.

Eighteen

That night, Samuels pulled up at the rear of a long line of motorcars outside Mrs. Pomfrey-Smith's Mayfair residence as guests arrived. There was a red carpet laid out to the pavement, and a striped awning framed by two footmen waiting in attendance. This ball was one of the highlights of the London season and began, fashionably, at ten in the evening.

Ursula, with more pressing concerns, found it difficult to remain patient as she waited for the footman to take her coat and gloves. She was apprehensive and anxious to know whether Christopher Dobbs was going to attend, and if so, how she was going to approach finding out the nature of his relationship with Whittaker and the man who had been in the Cairo bazaar. She was so preoccupied by these concerns, she hardly noticed the other guests as she entered.

"Ursula!" Elizabeth Anderson tugged at the kimono sleeve of Ursula's dark blue chinchilla-trimmed gown. She spun around. "Mrs. Anderson," she exclaimed. "I'm sorry—I was quite lost in my thoughts."

"Gerard told me you were in the North—but I felt sure you wouldn't miss out on all the season! My girls are here tonight. See, there's Emily over in the corner there, near the punch bowl. And where is my Marianne?—oh, there she is! Did you see the engagement notice in the *Times*? She got engaged just last week. Such a wonderful match, even if he is an American. From North Carolina—made his fortune in tobacco."

"That must be very ... nice ... for her. My congratulations," Ursula responded with a tense smile. Elizabeth Anderson fiddled with her necklace.

"How are you doing?" she asked.

"Mmm?" Ursula responded, preoccupied, as she watched Christopher Dobbs enter the room, accompanied by a dark, exotic-looking lady. Her eyes followed Dobbs as he walked across the room. Much to her irritation, he noticed and flashed her a smile.

"Miss Marlow." A voice made her jump. Ursula turned to find herself face to face with Lady Winterton. Elizabeth Anderson drifted away with a faint look of alarm, as if suffragism was a disease she was in danger of catching if she stood too close.

"Don't mind Mrs. Anderson," Ursula explained. "After what happened with Freddie, she thinks all members of the WSPU are either insane or dangerous."

Lady Winterton laughed. "That explains a great deal." She was wearing an elegant sapphire blue dress that set off the delicate paleness of her skin and accentuated her eyes. "I am sorry I couldn't be of more assistance last night."

Ursula, mulling over what she had seen this afternoon, regarded her blankly.

"I hope your friend discovers whether her fiancé has remained true to her," Lady Winterton then ventured.

"What? Oh, yes," Ursula replied. "I'm sure she'll work it out."

"I'm glad to hear it. One should know within, I mean deep inside, whether a man is true. If she does not, then I'm afraid she might be right to suspect him."

Ursula rubbed her nose. "I suppose so," was all she could think of by way of reply.

Lady Winterton laughed again. "Sully, you are always so serious! No wonder you find the concept of marriage so baffling!"

Ursula regained her equanimity. "I just think society has created marriage to ensure that women remain subjugated all their lives," she replied.

"You can't really believe that, can you?" Lady Winterton replied. "Surely we women aren't as weak-willed as all that,"

"I'm not saying that we are. I just wish marriage could be about an equal partnership—which it isn't, yet."

"My dear, with your wealth and independent nature, I find it startling that you have such little confidence in yourself."

Ursula flushed. This conversation was straying too close to her relationship with Lord Wrotham for comfort. Lady Winterton, with consummate tact, immediately moved the conversation into less controversial waters and onto the subject of Mrs. Pomfrey-Smith's new French chef, Monsieur Decassé. Ursula and Lady Winterton were soon joined by Daniel Abbott and Gerard Anderson, and as Ursula caught Mrs. Pomfrey-Smith's eye, she knew she had to start the pretense of enjoying the charade that was a society ball. Reluctantly she excused herself, saying, "I'd better go and pay my respects to our hostess."

Christopher Dobbs was regaling a group of guests, including Mrs. Pomfrey-Smith, with his adventures in the West Indies aboard the steamer the *Ulysses* in the summer of '07. Ursula took the opportunity to walk up to the group, thanking Mrs. Pomfrey-Smith for "as fine an Empire Day ball as ever I did attend."

Mrs. Pomfrey-Smith flushed with pleasure. "Ursula, it is so good to see you here! I was beginning to fear you would be spending the entire season in the North—which wouldn't be the done thing at all. Your father would have wanted me to keep an eye on you." Mrs. Pomfrey-Smith squeezed Ursula's arm. "Which I have every intention of doing."

Ursula forced a smile.

"I didn't know Miss Marlow needed keeping an eye on," Christopher Dobbs interjected.

"Oh you know me, Topper," Ursula replied with a sanguine smile. "Always getting myself into trouble."

Ursula pulled Mrs. Pomfrey-Smith aside on the pretext of seeking her guidance with respect to some upcoming charity events. After she had satisfied Mrs. Pomfrey-Smith's urge to provide advice on all things related to "polite society," she began the real questioning. "I was wondering, Dolly . . ." She cast her eye back to Dobbs, who was now dancing with Anderson's youngest daughter, Emily.

"Yes, dear?" Mrs. Pomfrey-Smith replied distractedly; she had caught sight of herself in one of the mirrored doors, and was checking the position of an ostrich feather in her hair.

"Does Dobbs happen to know a man by the name of Ambrose Whittaker? I thought I saw him this morning and remembered him from Egypt. I'd really like to get in touch with him while he's in London, as he gave me some terrific advice on collecting Alexandrian art. Now, I know you're the best person to ask about connections. So have you heard anything? Is he a close friend of Christopher's?"

"You say his name's Whittaker . . . hmm, let me think. I seem to recall that name from India. Could that be him? Obadiah would have known him—although come to think of it, Topper probably did as well. I don't know for sure, but I can easily find out."

"No need to go to any trouble." Ursula said hurriedly. "But if you could find out where Whittaker is staying while he's in London, I'd be most grateful. I don't like to bother Christopher—not with all the unpleasantness surrounding his offer for Marlow Industries."

"I quite understand. And I support you one hundred percent, my dear!" Ursula raised her eyebrows. "Your father would never have sold his business, no matter how tough things got, and besides, Topper should know you'll soon be married—"

"Ah." Mrs. Pomfrey-Smith was still deluding herself that Ursula's marriage prospects were best served with Marlow Industries intact. "Thank you anyway, I appreciate all your help. I know how close you are to Christopher and his family."

"They have been very good to me, since your father died. Oh, look, my dear, Lord Wrotham has arrived—and he's brought his mother with him. How absolutely splendid!"

Despite her murmured protests, Ursula soon found herself accompanying Mrs. Pomfrey-Smith to the far side of the room, past a group of guests gaily dancing to the quartet.

"Adela!" Mrs. Pomfrey-Smith descended upon them in a cloud of ruffled chiffon.

"Dolly, what a pleasure to be here!" Dowager Lady Adela Wrotham replied. "I was beginning to think my son would keep me trapped in the country for the entire season. Oh, and Miss Marlow, too," the dowager continued, her tone cooling. "But how delightful." She said the word *delightful* as if she had just tasted spoiled food. Despite Ursula's fortune, the dowager still regarded her as nothing more than a "chit of an upstart." If she had her way, Lord Wrotham would have been married off by now to a pliable American railway heiress, not brooding about the daughter of a coal miner's son.

"Lady Wrotham," Ursula replied, determined to remain courteous in her presence. "What a pleasure it is to see you again. It's been far too long."

"Well, since my son insists that I see out my days at beastly Bromley Hall, it's hardly surprising. Dolly, you really must come and visit me again soon. I fear I shall die of boredom if you don't! Oliver has only let me come to London for the week because I begged and pleaded."

"Mother, please."

Mrs. Pomfrey-Smith tucked her arm inside the dowager's, eager to placate her as always. "Come with me, Adela. I've got so many people I want you to meet! Brigadier Galbraith is here; y'know, his wife died last month . . . oh, and do you remember how I told you last summer that I'd made the acquaintance of the renowned psychoanalyst Herr Hubert? Well, he is here too—and he's brought one of his patients with him, no less!" Mrs. Pomfrey-Smith led the dowager off through the crowd, leaving Lord Wrotham and Ursula standing near the doorway.

Lord Wrotham grabbed two glasses of champagne from a passing footman and handed Ursula a glass. "With any luck, by the time this ball's over, she'll either be married off to the brigadier or committed to an asylum."

Ursula took a sip. "The asylum sounds good to me."

For the remainder of the ball Lord Wrotham and Ursula kept their distance. He busied himself talking with friends and colleagues from the Carlton Club, while Ursula tried to pretend that she was enjoying herself. She caught sight of Lady Winterton talking to Lord Wrotham and felt a surge of jealousy. Lady Winterton seemed so at ease in her surroundings, so much a part of her class, that Ursula could not help but envy her. With her easy laugh and exemplary manners, she demonstrated all the self-restraint and assurance that Ursula so often failed to display. Lord Wrotham, his head bowed, seemed to be listening intently, and after a few moments Ursula saw him give one of his rare, sweet smiles. He then raised his eyes, and Ursula quickly averted her gaze, lest he notice her watching him.

Amid all the chatter, music, and dancing, it was hard for her to relax and enjoy herself after what she had witnessed that morning. She spent the next hour walking around in a daze, tossing around all the clues she had amassed so far in her mind, failing to create any sort of discernible pattern. She was just about to bid Mrs. Pomfrey-Smith good night when she caught sight of Lord Wrotham, this time alone, standing in the corner of the room. In his well-tailored evening dress, smoothed-back hair, and polished black shoes, he reminded her of a sleek black panther in a Gauguin painting, watching her from behind the palm.

"Careful," Christopher Dobbs whispered. "You don't want to set tongues wagging again, now do you?" He had managed to steal up on her unawares.

"And you think that somehow I care?"

"Oh, I know he cares. How could he not? Respected member of the House of Lords. Famous barrister and King's Counsel. 'Friend' of the Foreign Office. Reputation's all he's got."

"Well, then, he need not worry about me." Ursula replied.

"Oh, I think we both know that's a lie. Why, Miss Marlow, you are like a firecracker. Who knows when you might explode in his face? Of course, that's not to say you aren't a decoration that's worth having around. But we all know that educated girls like yourself don't make suitable society wives."

"If you have a point, please come to it quickly."

Christopher Dobbs smiled. "I just want you to be realistic, that's all. Mrs. Pomfrey-Smith may still fuss around you, but once your fortune's gone, well . . ."

Ursula raised one eyebrow. "If you're trying to scare or intimidate me into accepting your offer, it's not going to work."

Christopher Dobbs raised his whiskey glass to his lips with a smile.

"How's your friend Alexei Prosnitz?" he asked with maddening calm. "I'm sure the society pages would be very interested in him . . . more grist for the Marlow rumor mill."

Ursula watched Dobbs closely. "How's your friend Whittaker?" she asked coldly, testing the waters. "You and he been arranging the deaths of any more young women?"

Christopher Dobbs's face went white.

Ursula extricated herself from the ball as soon as she was able. Once seated in Bertie, she chastised herself for being so reckless and impulsive. Though Dobbs's reaction was enough to convince her of his involvement in Katya's death, she was afraid she had been too hasty, too premature in alerting him to her suspicions.

"Home?" Samuels asked.

"Not yet," Ursula replied.

"Brook Street?" Samuels responded after a momentary hesitation.

"Hmmm?" Ursula looked up. "No . . . no . . . Freddie's place. Woburn Square."

Ursula looked at her pocket watch. It was nearly midnight. She knew Winifred refused to celebrate Empire Day on principle, but would it be too much to expect her to be home at this hour on a Friday night? She decided it was worth trying.

Samuels stopped at the front of Winifred's house, and Ursula instructed him to wait while she got out and hurried up the stairs, still clad in her ball gown and cloak. She banged on the knocker frantically, praying that Winifred was home. The lights were on in the front parlor; the curtains opened, Winifred peered out, and a minute later the door opened. Winifred was wearing a pair of gray flannel breeches, a striped shirt, and a long brown cardigan, and was holding her pipe in her hands.

"Sully, what's the matter? Is everything all right?"

"I'm not disturbing you, am I?"

"No, you needn't worry. No ex-lover inside—well, no ex-lover of *mine*, at least." Winifred stuck the pipe in her mouth and grinned. "Actually," she said, "I was just finishing a lecture I'm giving on Tuesday. Come on in."

Ursula waved to Samuels, signaling him to leave.

"Is Alexei downstairs?"

"Yes, of course . . . why, what is it?" Winifred replied as Ursula hurried in.

"I think it's time we had a little chat with him."

Winifred rubbed her nose. "I was wondering when that was going to happen," she said with a grim look of satisfaction.

Ursula took off her cloak and hung it up on the coat stand.

"Nice dress," Winifred commented.

"Not now, Freddie. . . ."

"Is that real chinchilla?" Winifred asked as they made their way down the stairs.

Alexei was sitting beside the stove with his feet propped up on the kitchen table, to all appearances engrossed in Winifred's copy of the final volume of Havelock Ellis's *Studies in the Psychology of Sex.*

"I heard you," he said, placing the book down on the table. "What is it that you want to chat about?"

"Let's start with the part where you lied to me about why you were in England."

Alexei studied her face. "It wasn't a lie. I just didn't want to burden you with everything else."

"Like the fact you're here to set up some armed revolutionary group, or maybe you just left out some of the minor details, like the fact that you and Arina were lovers?"

Alexei swung his feet off the table and leaned forward in the chair.

"That was a long time ago. Before I met you, *lapushka*. . . ."

"I need to know why you're really in England." Ursula continued, ignoring his reply.

"Sounds to me like someone has already been talking to you."

Ursula knew she had to tread carefully. "Yes, well, I don't like being sent anonymous notes," she lied.

"What did this note say?" Alexei asked carefully.

Winifred looked baffled.

"It was a warning. It said that you were arranging an armament shipment for your comrades and stirring up trouble with the English unions," Ursula continued with the charade.

"And who was this note from?" Alexei asked, his eyes never leaving hers.

"I told you, it was anonymous. But then at tonight's ball I received a thinly disguised threat to reveal to reporters that I am helping harbor you in England."

"And I suppose you won't tell me who made this threat?"

"What would be the point?" Ursula retorted. "I need to be able to trust you before I tell you anything more."

Alexei ran his fingers through his curly dark hair and sighed.

"What do you want me to say?"

"I want you to start by telling me what really happened that night at the Oldham factory."

Alexei took off his spectacles and rubbed his eyes. "There's really not much more to tell. So I failed to tell you that Arina was there when I arrived at her house—it makes little difference. I spoke to her when she returned from work, and I told her about Kolya. She was obviously upset, but she also didn't want me around. She asked me to leave. She was angry. So I left. Everything else is just as I told you."

Ursula regarded him skeptically.

"That's the truth," he countered.

"Do you know where Arina's roommate, Natasha, is?"

Alexei hesitated for a moment and then replied with a shrug, "Perhaps . . ."

Ursula crossed her arms.

"I can take you to a place. There are no guarantees, but she might be there tonight."

"Sully . . ." Winifred placed a warning hand on her arm.

"Natasha really doesn't know anything," Alexei protested. "She had nothing to do with Arina's death."

"I'd like to talk to her all the same."

Alexei looked Ursula up and down. "You might want to consider changing, unless you want to be mistaken for a tsarina."

"Why don't you go upstairs?" Winifred suggested. "Help yourself to whatever you can find to fit. I can stay and watch Alexei."

"Don't worry," Alexei said. "I still need somewhere safe to stay, so I'm hardly likely to leave. Besides, I cannot risk Okhrana finding out where I am. Whatever you may suspect about me, you know I am telling the truth when I say I cannot allow them to find me."

Ursula and Winifred exchanged glances.

"I am still the same man that I was," Alexei said, looking at Ursula. "You know I am loyal to the party and to my comrades. If I am in England, it is to serve them. You once believed in what we stood for. You believed in me. I am not the one who has changed, *lapushka*."

Ursula's eyelids flickered. She wanted to believe him. It was hard not to feel the pull of the past, of what she had once felt so deeply.

Winifred tugged her sleeve. "Come on, we'd best get upstairs. It's late—if we're going, we'd better go soon."

Alexei picked up his book and, pushing his glasses back, started to read once more.

Winifred and Ursula climbed the stairs to the bedroom. In Winifred's previous house, the bedroom had been a richly furnished, bohemian boudoir, full of vermilion-and-black oriental cushions and heavy gold brocade bedclothes. Winifred's taste's had become subdued and muted since Laura Radcliffe's death. Aside from the dark curvaceous wardrobe and chest of drawers in the corner, there was only a simple marble-topped washstand with a basin and ewer, a single wrought-iron bed, and an armchair beneath the window. There was no central chandelier, just two brass wall sconces that emitted a soft glow of light when Winifred flicked the light switch next to the door.

Winifred opened the wardrobe and pulled out a simple brown serge wool skirt and mannish striped shirt.

"I don't have much that will fit you. But this might do. Here, let me help unhook you."

Ursula stood in the center of the room, struggling with both her dress and her tears.

"I told you to be careful," Winifred said gently. "You and Alexei were always such a volatile combination."

Winifred finished unhooking Ursula's dress and let it slide to the floor. Ursula stepped out, picked up the dress, and laid it on the armchair.

"And what of me and—" She left the sentence unfinished. She grabbed the shirt and skirt and got dressed quickly.

Winifred helped button the back of the shirt and draw in the skirt.

"Now, that's a volatility of quite a different kind."

Ursula turned and faced her, and together they struggled to hitch up the skirt and readjust the waist with a belt, for Winifred was a good deal taller than Ursula and had little in the way of her curves.

"What do you mean?"

"You and Alexei are both idealists, impetuous and reckless. Together you just consume and destroy each other. Whereas you and Lord Wrotham, well, that's quite a different matter."

"Because we're so different?"

Winifred also removed Ursula's delicate hairband and tied a gray scarf to hide the Parisian styling of Ursula's hair.

"Is that what you think?" Winifred probed.

Ursula regarded her quizzically.

"Let's put it this way," Winifred said with a smile as she stepped back and regarded her handiwork. "You could be in a room full of Labour Party supporters—from social reformers to revolutionaries, men dedicated to the female suffrage cause, even passionate radicals like Alexei—and there'd still be just one man in the room as far as you're concerned, and that would be Lord Wrotham."

Ursula sat on the bed and pulled on a pair on Winifred's boots.

"Freddie, don't be daft. . . ."

"Here, let me help you. It'll be a miracle if you can walk in these—mind you, I can't see you getting very far in those fine satin slippers of yours, either."

When they were done, Ursula regarded herself in the wardrobe mirror.

"What do you think?"

"You'll do. Not that you'll ever look exactly poor, m'dear. What do you want me to do with your earrings?" Ursula's necklace was hidden under her shirt.

"Best leave them here."

Winifred placed them carefully in the small trinket tray on the chest of drawers.

"And the ring?" Winifred pointed to Ursula's right hand.

Ursula took off the filigree moonstone ring and placed it beside the earrings.

They made their way out of the bedroom and down the stairs.

"Well, here goes," Winifred said as she opened the door that led to the kitchen stairs from the main hallway. "Let's see how many more of Alexei's little secrets we uncover."

Winifred, Alexei, and Ursula left by the servant's entrance and hurried to the Euston Street tube station to catch the last underground train on the Metropolitan line to the Farringdon station. From there, they walked to the Rose and Anchor public house, well known for its associations with Lenin and the Russian Social Democratic Labour Party. Although the pub officially closed at eleven o'clock, and from all outward appearances was dark and empty, down in the basement there was a crowd of people, all standing, smoking, and shouting out in various languages. There were Russian revolutionaries standing next to Italian anarchists, Irish nationalists and French syndicalists all arguing loudly, while laborers and intellectuals sat along the low wooden benches drinking their pints.

The publican, a huge, barrel-chested man with a long dark beard, greeted Alexei with a roaring torrent of Russian and a bearlike hug. Alexei leaned over and shouted in his ear. The publican nodded, and Alexei returned to Winifred and Ursula, who were still standing in the doorway.

"He's going to check, but he thinks Natasha was here earlier. She may be in one of the back rooms."

Alexei led Ursula and Winifred through the front room and found them a place to sit, squeezed in alongside a group of Italian men engaged in deep conversation. The men didn't even pause or look up as Winifred and Ursula sat down.

Alexei leaned over and whispered in Ursula's ear, "Takes you back, doesn't it?"

Ursula was indeed reminded of one of the first meetings Alexei had taken her to. It was May 1907, and Alexei had brought her to a RSDLP meeting to meet his friends. Unfortunately, as the entire meeting was conducted in Russian, Ursula had hardly found it edifying, but she still remembered vividly how exciting it felt to be sitting among people filled with such passion.

Alexei's hand ran lightly down Ursula's back, and she flinched slightly.

"I'll go and see what I can find out. Wait here," Alexei said and disappeared into the crowd.

"Typical," Winifred said. "Didn't even buy us a drink. Shall I go?"

Ursula shrugged—she was too anxious to speak with Arina's roommate.

Winifred got up, stuck her pipe in her mouth, and walked over to the makeshift bar that was set up in the corner of the front room. A young barwoman was standing there, wiping a glass dry on her apron. Winifred ordered four vodkas and returned, balancing them in both hands. She sat down and handed a glass to Ursula.

Alexei appeared beside them, accompanied by a frail-looking young woman with wide dark eyes and wispy blond hair. He was carrying a pint of beer in his hand.

"This is Arina's roommate, Natasha."

"Please sit down," Ursula said, moving along the bench to make room. Natasha slunk into the seat next to her.

"Why is she so frightened?" Ursula asked Alexei under her breath as he also squeezed in alongside her.

"She isn't sure whether to trust you or not. She thinks Arina's death was the work of Okhrana, and she's convinced their spies will come after her next."

"It's all right," Ursula told Natasha. "I only want to know what happened to Arina that night. Can you tell me?"

Natasha looked nervous.

Alexei spoke to her in Russian, hoping to reassure her.

Natasha remained wary but began to speak. "Arina told me that morning she was planning to go to the Garden Suburb after work, so I was surprised to see her when I got home. But she was distracted and upset, so I didn't ask her any more about it. Alexei was already there when I arrived, and he had told her about Kolya."

"And she was very upset about his death?" Ursula prompted. She had to shout to be heard over the din.

"Yes," Natasha nodded. "And she insisted that Alexei and I leave her alone. Alexei told me he would return to the hotel, and I, I had to go to the colliery. I work two shifts on a Tuesday. When I returned early the next morning, I heard about the fire. . . . Alexei arrived, and then the police came. . . ." Natasha's voice broke.

Ursula clasped her hand. "It's all right," she said. "You're safe here. We just want to try and work out what happened to Arina, that's all."

Natasha turned to Alexei and asked him something in a stream of Russian.

Alexei shook his head.

"She was asking me whether the coroner's inquest had determined who killed Arina."

"Natasha," Ursula said leaning in close so she could hear her. "Why would Arina go to Garden Suburb? Was there someone she used to visit there?"

Natasha shook her head. "No, but there was a walk she told me about. Along Green Lane and through Green Wood. She liked to do it when things got . . . got . . . hard for her. She said it was peaceful, and it reminded her of the village she grew up in."

"Oh, I see . . . but Arina was home, so she hadn't gone to Garden Suburb. Do you know if she was planning to meet anyone that night? Had she ever spoken of a man called Christopher Dobbs, or Ambrose Whittaker?"

Natasha shook her head. Out of the corner of her eye, Ursula saw a tall, thin man watching them from beneath his bowler hat. Ursula was about to speak when she saw Alexei's reaction to the man's entry. He whispered urgently in Natasha's ear, and she blanched. Alexei then leaned in and said to Ursula and Winifred, "Don't look, but I am sure the man who just came in is an Okhrana agent. I think it's time we were going." Alexei tipped the contents of the vodka glass into his mouth and placed the glass back down with a bang.

"But I still have questions," Ursula protested. Winifred hastily downed her glass and pulled Ursula to her feet.

"Then they will have to wait," Alexei responded sharply.

Winifred, Ursula, and Alexei walked along Clerkenwell Road toward Bloomsbury. It was now close to two o'clock in the morning, and there were few taxicabs to be found in the area at this hour. The Empire Day concerts and plays were over, and they were far from the elaborate balls of Mayfair and Belgravia. A soft rain had started to fall, misting over the streetlamps and forming a fine, damp film across Ursula's face. As they turned down Southampton Row a motorcar skidded past, sending mud flying. The driver and his passenger shouted "Hooroo!" as they drove away, waving gaily.

Ursula shook out her skirt, viewing with horror her muddy hem and boots.

Alexei laughed. "I must take you with me to Siberia some day . . . there you can really appreciate mud and filth."

Winifred craned her neck, looking for taxicabs. "Still no luck," she commented and looked at the sky. "Rain's getting worse. . . ."

Alexei took off his jacket and moved in to hold it over Ursula's head. She felt suddenly conscious of his closeness; it felt strangely uncomfortable.

Winifred pulled her hat down low, and together they hurried back to Woburn Place.

Winifred pulled her key out of her waistcoat pocket and opened the front door.

"I'll get the fire going!" she called out as she dashed inside.

Alexei held the door open for Ursula with his elbow, still holding his jacket over her head.

Once inside the doorway, Ursula took off her scarf and tossed her head, sending a fine spray of raindrops across her shoulders. Alexei propped the door open with his foot as he shook out his jacket.

"Shut the door, for heaven's sake," Winifred shouted out from the drawing room. She was on all fours, lighting the fire in the grate.

Through the open doorway, the golden glow of the streetlamps bathed Alexei in a soft, misty halo. Ursula stood in the hallway, shivering. He reached out to wipe the rain from her cheeks. The cuff of his shirt was rough against her skin. It was such an intimate gesture, Ursula held her breath. Alexei leaned in and kissed her. At first she tasted only cool, wet rain on his lips. He cupped her face in his hands, and the first hesitant kiss turned deeper. It tasted of cigarette smoke and bitter brown ale. It was like revisiting a taste from childhood, something long remembered and yearned for—like crab apples stolen from the orchard next to Gray House, or the treacle tart Mrs. Norris used to make. The first taste brought her memories of Alexei back, but it was curiously unsatisfying. After the passage of time, the memory grew false. The return was too cloying or too bitter, too unsatisfying after the time without him.

Ursula pulled away. She was suddenly aware of how exposed she was, standing in an open doorway. If Lord Wrotham was correct and Alexei was under surveillance, then she had just provided an unplanned exhibition.

Alexei ran his tongue along his lips.

"You taste of honey."

"You taste of the past."

Alexei jerked away, and the front door swung shut.

Nineteen

It was early Saturday morning, and the weak, pale morning light drew across Ursula's face as she lay in her four-poster bed, gazing at the canopy. She blinked and slowly propped herself up against the goose-feather pillow. Her mouth was dry, and she gingerly reached over to the bedside table and poured herself a glass of water from an earthenware jug. She tasted fine particles of dust and salt on her tongue before replacing the glass and leaning back once more.

She lay there for nearly an hour, simply waiting and reflecting on the past. She glanced over at the photograph that stood on her dressing table. It was of her mother and father on their wedding day.

There was a light rap on the bedroom door, and Julia peered inside.

"God bless you, I thought you were up early, Miss. Would you like a cup of tea?"

Ursula wiped her eyes. "Thank you, Julia. Give me just a few minutes."

"Of course, Miss," Julia replied and quickly disappeared.

Ursula rose from the bed and slipped on her silk dressing gown and slippers. She walked over to the window and carefully opened the curtains. Chester Square remained bathed in misty morning light. Ursula leaned against the cool windowpane. After what she'd said to Dobbs last night, she knew that she had to act quickly. Hugh Carmichael had warned her before that everyone associated with Katya Vilensky's murder was dead. It was only a matter of time before her own life was threatened, and this time she was determined to be the one to confront the truth.

"I need to find out what Dobbs is up to," Ursula said.

"I know, I know . . . but Sully, if you should get caught . . . then what? You don't even know if there's anything worth finding there."

Winifred drummed her fingers along the edge of the Mackmurdo sofa.

"I don't like this plan, Sully. It sounds too dangerous. Why not go to Harrison now?"

"I need more evidence—I can't fit the pieces together yet."

Ursula took out the letter she had just received that morning from Mrs. Pomfrey-Smith. "Read this."

Winifred took the letter and starting reading it aloud.

> Topper has invited me to join him at a shooting party at his great friend Rufus Sandforth's in Cambridgeshire this coming weekend. He's closing up the house and sending his valet on ahead. Most of the servants are going to Shrewsbury Grange, a magnificent country home that Topper has just leased, so that it can be shipshape for a hunt he is planning to host the following weekend (and which to my delight I am also invited).

"It may be my only chance," Ursula urged. "Dobbs is going to be away all weekend."

Winifred exhaled noisily. She had already made it clear to Ursula that she was uncomfortable about using the WSPU's legitimate tactics to achieve suffrage as a diversion for what amounted to little more than breaking and entry. Nevertheless, after a moment of silence, she reluctantly agreed.

"I shall merely pretend to be undertaking a political act of vandalism," Ursula said. "I mean, if Emily Davison can pour oil through pillar-boxes, I'm sure I can convince them I'm up to something similar. Dobbs is known for his antisuffrage views."

"Still, I'd rather you let me come with you, or better yet, let me do this for you. It doesn't matter as much if I'm arrested."

"Freddie, after all that happened to you after Laura's Radcliffe's death, I won't hear of you taking that risk. No, I need to rely on you to create the diversion. Can you get some of our WSPU sisters involved?"

"Of course! It won't take much to convince others. Sir Henry Plymouth lives just up the road, and we've been planning on targeting his house for months after that speech he gave in the Commons denouncing women as being incapable of the level of thinking necessary for political discourse."

"Then we should be all set for Sunday night?"

"Yes, I'll make sure we're ready."

"It's best if we don't meet that night—that way you can honestly say you weren't directly involved, should the worst happen and I'm arrested."

Winifred nodded, but she was grave.

As arranged, Ursula took a taxicab to the Holland Street Underground station and then walked the remaining few blocks to Christopher Dobbs's house on Bletchley Avenue. She waited in the park until she heard the Kensington Church clock strike midnight. Then she made her way across the street and down the front servants' entrance stairs. The house was all dark, but Ursula wasn't about to risk alerting any servants who might still be there, sleeping in the attic level of the house. Ursula heard the crash of windowpanes breaking a few houses along. A cheer erupted, and at that exact moment she used the rock she was carrying in her khaki backpack to smash the kitchen window. She reached in to unlock the servants' door and squeezed through the doorway, closing the door as quietly as she could behind her. She stood for a moment listening, but there was no sound of movement above.

Taking off her shoes and tying them around her neck by the laces, she pulled out a flashlight just in case, but made her way in the half-light cast by the streetlamp outside through the kitchen and up the stairs to the main floor of the house. She paused once more, straining to hear, but everything remained quiet. From there she passed the front parlor and entered the large living room that had served as a ballroom the night of Christopher Dobbs's cocktail party. She then tiptoed up the wide staircase to the mezzanine level.

She had never been into Christopher Dobbs's study, but remembered catching sight of a room on this level, partially hidden by the bookcases. She turned on the flashlight as she made her way along the shelves. Coming to a door, she took a deep breath and turned the door handle. The door opened with a creak, and she pointed the flashlight inside. Quickly moving over to the window, she checked that the curtains were fully drawn before setting the flashlight down on the desk and, using the ambient light, trying to orient herself to the room. Above the ornate baroque desk there was a painting of Nelson standing on the poop deck of the *Victory* at Trafalgar. In the half-light it looked decidedly sinister, while the tall leather armchairs created a circle in the middle of the room rather like the stone circle at Avebury she had visited as a child. Ursula shook off her fears—she needed to move quickly to see if she could find the papers Dobbs had been so concerned about.

First she examined the desk, using the flashlight to peer into each of the desk drawers one at a time. None contained anything more than blotting paper, pens, and, in one drawer, an ivory-handled letter opener and elephant-tusk inkwell. On top of the desk was a single stack of papers, but an examination of these revealed them to be nothing more than shipping orders.

Ursula then peered at the back of the painting hanging behind the desk.

"Damn and blast!" she muttered, seeing the unmistakable outline of a safe. She replaced the painting carefully, and sighed. Was this it, then—had she risked everything for nothing? There was no way she could break into a safe.

She sat down at Dobbs's desk in his chair and tried to think what else she could do. She didn't even know what she was looking for—she was only hoping to find something that would link Dobbs to Whittaker and Katya's death.

Absentmindedly she fidgeted with the brass replica of the HMS *Victory*, trying to work out where else Dobbs might keep important papers. The rest of the study's furnishings consisted of more bookshelves (which seemed to have more sextants and other nautical paraphernalia than actual books) and a telescope on a brass stand. There really weren't many places for Dobbs to hide anything. Ursula turned the oversize paperweight around in her hand, feeling its weight, and remembering how Dobbs had been doing the same the day they had met. The paperweight must have then been in the front parlor, and it struck Ursula as decidedly odd that he should have removed it now to his study. She replaced the paperweight, and suddenly all her senses were on edge. She picked it up once more and examined it under the flashlight. At first she could see nothing out of the ordinary, until she turned it upside down. It seemed solid enough, but when she took a closer look, she noticed a small cylindrical hole. There seemed to be paper folded tightly and wedged inside.

Ursula pulled the paper out and flattened the sheets on top of the desk. The first was a letter.

> My dearest Arina,
> I write to you from Eretz Yisrael with great urgency and despair. I dare not tell anyone what I have learned, not even Peter. But you, my dearest sister, you are the only one I can trust. It is you I must confide in.
> What I have just discovered could get me killed. . . .

Twenty

Ursula continued reading the letter in horror.

> There can be no denying that the settlers never reached
> Hartuv. I visited the small moshav, and this was confirmed. As
> you can imagine, my anxiety deepened when I realized that no one
> could account for the settlers' movements since the Bregenz had
> landed in Jaffa five weeks ago. I know you are desperate to hear
> news of Kolya but no one can even confirm he left Poland, let alone
> boarded the Bregenz. You know how Peter can be; so I daren't ask
> him for help. Yet I owed it to you to discover the truth.
>
> I have seen the grave. Eleven souls, all laid to rest in an
> unmarked mound of sand and dirt off the road to Jerusalem. I
> discovered that there was one survivor, Baruh, whom I found in
> hiding and in fear of his life. Having heard his story, I knew he
> could not remain here, and so I secretly arranged passage for him
> to go to England. The horrors he spoke of must be told. The men
> who did this must be held to account. No matter that they are some
> of my husband's closest business allies.
>
> Peter seems so distant from me now; his jealousy has become
> an obsession, and I can no longer confide in him. He views all that

*I do with suspicion and anger. I do not think he would even believe
me if I told him the true fate of the Bregenz.*

*I trust you, my only sister, with this burden. Perhaps Baruh will
lead us to learn the truth about poor Kolya's fate also. But first,
you must tell the authorities that Dobbs is illegally selling armaments to the Ottoman Turks, and that he has the blood of eleven
Jewish settlers on his hands.*

If I fail to return, you will know that I am dead.

Numbly Ursula unfolded the other sheet. It was Anna's reply,
which Peter had never bothered to open.

A police whistle suddenly sounded, and Ursula nearly jumped
out of her skin. She quickly turned off the flashlight, plunging the
study into darkness. The police whistles retreated down the street,
followed by shouts and disgruntled voices. Winifred had completed
her part of the scheme. Ursula waited a few minutes, her heart
pounding so loudly that she was sure it must be echoing throughout
the house. But there was only the sound of the wind in the branches
of the oak tree outside, and the leaves brushing the windowpane.

Ursula turned the flashlight on and carefully tucked the letter into
the pocket of her skirt. She had to make sure it reached the authorities. She was just about to resume her search for evidence when she
heard the creak of a floorboard overhead. It sounded as if one of the
servants had been woken by the police whistles and was coming down
to investigate. Ursula quickly switched off the flashlight and crept out
of the study onto the landing and down the stairs.

She reached the kitchen and was just picking up her khaki knapsack when she heard a low moan. Ursula froze. She thought quickly—
the servants, one of whom appeared to now be awake, usually slept
upstairs on the top floor or the attic. With Christopher Dobbs away
and the house shut up, it was unlikely that any of the servants would
be down in the kitchen, but she couldn't be sure. There was another
moan, and the rustle of something moving. It seemed to be coming
from behind the door that led down to the wine cellar.

A terrible thought suddenly dawned on her. Was it possible that the person she had seen being dragged in here all those weeks ago was still here, being held captive in the cellar?

Ursula crept along to the foot of the kitchen stairs and listened intently. There was no further sound from above. Perhaps the servant who was disturbed from his sleep had retired once more to bed.

She made her way to the thick wooden door to the cellar and placed her ear against it. She could still hear the soft, low moans of a man in pain. Ursula reached out and turned the door handle. It was locked.

She turned on the flashlight and scanned the kitchen. Mrs. Stewart always kept all the keys to the Chester Square house on a hook by the scullery. Ursula followed the beam of light and scanned the kitchen, scullery, and pantry walls in search of a similar place. She found a set of keys hanging just below the wall-mounted bell rack used to summon the servants. As quietly as she could, she lifted the iron ring of keys off the hook and hastened back to the door. The rest of the house was still silent.

The third key Ursula tried turned the lock, and with a tiny push, she opened the cellar door.

"Hello?" she whispered loudly. "Is anyone down here?"

The moans ceased, and there was an expectant silence.

Ursula shone the flashlight down the stairs and caught sight of a shadow, nothing more than a heap of rags, shrinking away from the light into the corner of the room.

"I'm not here to hurt you," she whispered again, taking two hesitant steps down the stairs. The shadow remained curled up in a fetal position and did not move.

Ursula's breathing quickened as she descended the remaining steps into the cellar. She reached out to the shadow.

"I'm here to help you." She spoke in her normal voice this time, and the man, as she could now tell the shadow was, turned his face toward her. His eyes widened as a hand reached out from the rags and grabbed her arm. He spoke to her in a torrent of words. The language sounded strange and alien, like no language she had heard before.

"I can't understand you!" Ursula cried out. The man spoke again, and this time the language sounded vaguely familiar. It was that which she had heard many times, walking in London's East End to her father's factories. It was Yiddish.

"I'm sorry," she said. "I don't speak that either. Do you speak any English?"

The man looked at her with dark eyes.

"A little," he croaked. "On the ship. I learned on the ship,"

"Which ship?" Ursula asked. "The one coming that brought you to England? The one Katya Vilensky arranged for you?"

The man's eyes widened once more, and she saw a flash of suspicion cross his face.

"I was a friend of Katya's," Ursula urged. "A friend. I'm going to get you out of here. Do you understand?"

The man fell back against the wall, tears pooling in his eyes.

"It's all right." Ursula reached out and clasped his arm, which felt bony beneath the thin layer of cloth that surrounded it. "I know you're ill. I know you are scared. But I have to help you, and I will."

The man convulsed into sobs.

"Katya?" was all she could hear him say, and she knew, with a terrible sense of finality, that whatever had happened here had broken him. Ursula thought quickly. It was going to be almost impossible for her to carry him out of here on her own. She would need to find out what had happened to him, and then hope to enlist the help of Chief Inspector Harrison in the morning.

She took Katya's letter out of her pocket and held it up in the light.

The man recoiled as if she had slapped him. Ursula hastily reassured him that she had taken the letter from Dobbs's study and was not one of his associates. It was difficult, and the man still looked unconvinced when she spoke again.

"You were on the *Bregenz*? Are you Baruh?" Ursula pressed.

Baruh nodded wearily.

Ursula moved closer, her compassion stirred by his frailty and despair.

"Tell me," she urged. "What happened?"

"We found out. The cargo. On the *Bregenz*. Machine guns and rifles. Bayonets and grenades. All bound for Smyrna and the Ottoman Turks," he began in broken English.

"The *Bregenz* was carrying armaments?"

"Yes. To be used one day against us. Bulgarians like us."

"So what did you do?"

"We tried to take the ship. Tell the British what we knew."

The man stopped speaking as a racking cough took hold of his body and shook him. Ursula stared around anxiously. She needed to get him out quickly, but was afraid she might never learn the truth.

"And?" she prompted gently.

"We were too few."

Ursula remembered Katya's letter—*I have seen the grave*—and shivered.

Baruh fell back against the wall. "We spent three days in the ship's hold. No sun. No food. No water. The heat . . ." His voice trailed off as Ursula looked on in horror. "Then they took us to shore. We were on a train. Then in the darkness they lined us up. Women, children, as well as men. I was shot in the leg. The body of another man, Avraam, fell on top of me. That is how I lived."

Ursula thought she heard a sound from the top of the stairs, and she held up a warning hand. Baruh looked terrified. Ursula stood up and made her way to the bottom of the cellar stairs. With a final glance at Baruh, she placed her fingers to her lips and turned off the flashlight.

Slowly, feeling her way along the wall, she climbed the stairs and opened the door.

It took a while for her eyes to adjust to the darkness after being guided by the flashlight, but by the time she reached the kitchen, she could make out some of the familiar shapes and shadows. Ursula hesitated in the doorway. There was no further sound, and she began to wonder if she had been mistaken. She was turning to descend the stairway once more when she was grabbed from behind. A hand was quickly and firmly placed over her mouth.

"Quiet!" It was Chief Inspector Harrison's harsh whisper in her ear. He held on to her tight as he dragged her away from the stairs. Ursula struggled. "Wait!" she tried to say. Harrison ignored her. "No!" She struggled against him. "He's down there!" But the words could not escape.

Harrison forced Ursula out of the house and dragged her up the outside stairs to the street. He then threw her into the backseat of a motorcar without explanation. Harrison hopped into the car beside her and commanded the driver, "Go!"

Ursula struggled and tried to open the car door.

"He's still in there!" she cried out.

"I know!" Harrison hissed.

The driver pulled out quickly, and with a squeal the wheels skimmed the pavement, headed down Abbotsbury Street.

"What on earth?" Ursula cried out. Harrison craned his neck to see if anyone was behind them. The car spun round the corner and onto Kensington High Street.

"Are you totally mad?" Harrison turned to her and exclaimed. "Do you have any idea what you have just done?"

Ursula took the letter out of her pocket and threw it at him. "I've just uncovered the truth."

"You've just ruined months of investigation—that's what you've done."

They drove out of London, continuing west through Ealing before turning south to cross the river Thames. Ursula's throat was hoarse from insisting that Harrison stop the car. All her demands for explanation had been ignored; even as they passed through Richmond and Shepperton, Harrison refused to tell her anything more. He communicated with the driver in short, swift commands in between bouts of sullen rumination. Ursula became more and more uneasy—even at his most surly during the investigation into her father's murder, Harrison had never before seemed this concerned.

She observed him as he read Katya's and Arina's letters and then told him, her voice choking with emotion, all that Baruh had said in the cellar.

Harrison handed her the letters back without comment.

"Promise me," Ursula urged. "No matter what it is that you've been investigating. Promise me you'll take care of that poor man."

Harrison remained silent.

Everything started to blur and pitch in the night as the motorcar made its furious way along the rudimentary roads of Surrey, past tiny towns that comprised little more than a stone church and a couple of farms. Finally, after nearly two hours, the motorcar bumped along a small lane cut through the hedgerows and stopped at the entrance of a narrow driveway. The moon peeked out from behind the clouds, and she caught sight of a dilapidated two-story stone farmhouse nestled behind a copse of tall oak trees. Harrison got out of the car and opened the wooden gate, and the driver edged the car through the opening and up to the house.

Ursula got out and stretched her legs. She felt stiff from being huddled in the seat for so long. "Where are we?" she demanded.

"Somewhere remote enough, I hope, at least for the time being," Harrison replied.

Ursula rubbed her hands together to try and keep warm. "Don't you think we've had enough drama for one evening? I need to get back. I need to free that man. You can hardly expect Dobbs to come leaping out from behind any bushes. Do you really think all this is necessary?"

"I do," Harrison responded tersely, silencing Ursula.

"Do you think we were followed?" Ursula asked hesitantly. Suddenly the situation didn't seem absurd as much as terrifying.

"No, but I had two of my men trailing us, just to be sure. There should be here shortly . . . yes, here they are." Harrison reached into the rear seat of the car and grabbed his flashlight, which he then used to signal, with three short bursts of light, the motorcar that came to a halt at the gates at the end of the lane. The car headlamps flashed on and off before the engine was turned off and the countryside was suddenly quiet. Two men got out of the car and walked over to join Harrison. They barely acknowledged Ursula except with a short nod and a mumbled "Miss" as they passed her.

Harrison drew out a key from his trouser pocket and opened the farmhouse door.

Ursula checked to see if Katya's letter was still safely tucked in her skirt pocket before following Harrison into the farmhouse. She gingerly stepped over the threshold and into a large old stone kitchen. It was clear no one had been in the house for many months. It was cold and musty.

The two men spoke to Harrison in low tones before taking up position outside the front and back doors to the farmhouse.

"I'd rather not risk lighting a fire, so here—" Harrison threw her a thick, scratchy woolen blanket. "You'll have to make do with this. In the morning I'll make arrangements for some provisions to be dropped off." He turned on the flashlight and hunted round in one of the kitchen cabinets. "Last time I was here, I believe there were some crackers and anchovy paste." Harrison handed her a tin of stale crackers and a small earthenware jar. "Here, have this, potted shrimp, I think. I'm afraid mice got to the anchovy paste. I can't risk lighting a fire to heat a kettle. So no tea . . . but here's a glass, if you need some water."

Ursula nodded, her eyes now accustomed to the darkness from the drive down. She took the glass, went over to the wide sink, and filled it with water, using the wooden-handled pump. It made a terrible grating sound, but after a few minutes of vigorous pumping a gush of ice-cold water cascaded out and into the ceramic sink. Ursula drank quickly and replaced the glass on the stone windowsill.

Harrison instructed her to sit down, and Ursula hugged the blanket around her as she perched on a rocking chair next to the empty fireplace. She shook her head when he again proffered the food. She had no appetite.

"Now," Harrison commanded, "show me the letter again."

Ursula handed it to him and, using the flashlight, Harrison

crouched down on the stone floor and started to read. Ursula said nothing until he had finished.

Harrison stood up abruptly and began pacing the room.

"Now we know why Katya died," Ursula said.

"I have to return to London and speak to my superiors," Harrison replied.

"Did you know about the *Bregenz?*" Ursula demanded.

"We suspected about Dobbs trading in armaments aboard the *Bregenz*, but nothing about the passengers."

"Is that what your investigation has been about? His involvement in arms trading?" Ursula asked.

"We're been watching Dobbs for the last six months—ever since he started using his father's shipping business to transport arms. In the current climate we obviously need to watch that kind of thing carefully—check that British armaments don't end up in the wrong hands—"

"Like Egyptian nationalists?"

"Yes, or Indian independence seekers. . . . But more important at the moment, we don't want our armaments ending up in our enemies' hands. Everyone is mobilizing for a possible war. We need to know who is building or buying what."

"Do you think Dobbs is supplying arms to our enemies?"

"That's what we've been trying to ascertain. He certainly is selling to the Turks—who knows where the arms end up after that? As you can see from this letter, this is a sensitive matter."

"One worth killing for to keep quiet?"

"So it would appear."

"I saw Whittaker two days ago at Dobbs's house. He was accompanied by one of the men I saw in the Khan el-Khalili the day Katya was killed." Harrison's eyes flickered.

"Lord Wrotham told me that Whittaker was present at the customs house in Alexandria. I alerted officials in Egypt, but by then Whittaker was already en route to England."

"I should have told you earlier, but I didn't think you would believe me without further evidence."

Harrison face was shrouded in shadows. He made no reply.

"I think Dobbs's men stole this letter the night Arina's house was broken into. I think that's why she died."

"Maybe." Harrison was noncommittal.

"As I said, I must return to London and speak to my superiors. My men will keep an eye out here. You really are very reckless, Miss Marlow. You realize that anyone who has the slightest knowledge of the matters contained in this letter is dead? Katya, Hugh Carmichael's copilot, the shipping clerk, Arina. Even her roommate."

"Arina's roommate has been killed?" Ursula cried out.

"They fished her body out of the Thames on Friday night."

Ursula went pale. That was the night she, Alexei, and Winifred had spoken to Natasha at the Rose and Anchor. Had they led Dobbs's men to her?

"And still you insist on playing detective!" Harrison retorted. "I hope you realize you could have been killed tonight. Dobbs has a man there—he checks on Baruh every two hours. If he had found you there . . ."

Ursula nodded mutely. Her mind was still trying to process everything she had heard and read.

"You should try and sleep, at least," Harrison said brusquely. "While I try and figure out what the next step will be."

"Wouldn't that be arresting Christopher Dobbs and Whittaker in connection with the murder of Katya Vilensky?" Ursula demanded.

"If only it was that simple. No, Ursula, I'm not in the mood to discuss this. It's nearly three o'clock in the morning. Anything further will have to wait till daylight. I must leave London but should be back here by late morning—and please, Miss Marlow, don't do anything rash until then."

Despite all the anxiety and excitement of the evening, Ursula eventually found herself drifting into an uneasy sleep. Her head nodded forward, her eyes stung, and a heavy, dreamless sleep consumed her. She had decided to try and make herself comfortable next to the far side of the fireplace, propping her feet up on a second wooden chair.

Here, she was protected from the draft coming from under the front door and hallway and from the windows, which rattled in the night breeze.

She must have been asleep an hour or so when she awoke suddenly, her nerves prickling with the certainty that something was terribly wrong. There was no moonlight visible, and the house was pitch-black and quiet. Sensing danger, Ursula silently unfurled her legs and gently placed the blanket on the floor as she rose to her feet. There was still no sound at all, not even the shuffle of feet or the strike of a match. She knew Harrison had posted two policemen as guards, and it seemed strange that there should be absolutely no sound from either of them. She unlaced her shoes and held them in her hands as she crept in her stockinged feet across the stone kitchen floor and peered through the doorway that led to the hallway. The moon slid out from behind the clouds, and a shaft of silvery light revealed the body of one of Harrison's guards, sprawled across the foot of the stairs. Another was propped up against the wall and from the awkward and unnatural angle of his body, Ursula knew he was already dead. There was a murmur of voices above, and Ursula's heart began to race.

Ursula lifted up her skirt so she wouldn't alert anyone to the sound of it rustling along the floor. The clouds moved across the moon once more, plunging the house into darkness. Ursula felt her way to the front door, and found it ajar. She opened it further, and took a tentative step outside. The moon slid back out behind the clouds, casting an eerie sliver light across the farmhouse grounds. She could see no one, but above she spotted the thin beam of flashlights and knew she didn't have much time. Carefully she closed the door behind her, keeping it slightly ajar so as not to make any sound. She placed one shoe on and then the second, lacing them up with trembling fingers. A fine drizzle, the threat of rain, hung in the air. She heard one man shout above, and without waiting to hear anything further, she gathered up her skirts and started to run.

Twenty-one

Ursula had no idea where she was. In the haphazard moonlight, the fields and fences seemed to be little more than pools of dark and light, and obstacles of rough wood and wire. All she knew was that she had to keep running.

She kept to the fields, too scared to travel by road. She reached a small farmhouse about a mile away and was greeted by two barking dogs. Terrified lest they give away her position to anyone following her, Ursula bypassed the main farmhouse altogether. Instead she crept along the back of the large barn at the rear at the property. The dogs continued to bark, knowing she was still close. Ursula nearly tripped over an old bicycle propped up against the barn. As quietly as she could, she wheeled it away, then carried it as far as she could before exhaustion nearly caused her knees to give way. Winded, she rested beneath a large oak tree, laying the bicycle down beside her. She caught her breath for a moment, trying to decide the best course of action. Now she had the bicycle, it would probably be best to travel by road, though at this time in the morning a young woman on a bicycle would hardly be inconspicuous. Still, she knew she couldn't continue running through the fields. It was too exposed, and she was growing tired. She needed a plan. She needed somewhere to go.

Suddenly she heard the dogs barking furiously again, and she jumped to her feet. She took the bicycle and heaved it over the hedgerow, then swung herself over indecorously, jumping the final three feet to land beside the bicycle on a mud-splattered lane. She awkwardly tucked her dress between her legs and climbed on. It creaked and groaned under her weight as she began to pedal. She hadn't been on a bicycle since she was fifteen years old, and it felt cumbersome and uncouth to be trying to ride again now. The bicycle's threadbare seat was hard and uncomfortable and the wheels wobbled precariously, but as she pedaled, she felt a slow grinding progress was finally being made.

After another mile or so, making slow headway along the rutted and muddy road in the darkness and misty fog, she came to a T junction and halted to catch her breath. She squinted hard, trying to make out the signage in the darkness. One sign pointed to Guildford, the other to Godalming. Ursula took a deep breath, tossed a mental coin, and decided to head for Guildford.

This road was much smoother here, and she started feeling as if, finally, she might be widening the distance between herself and her pursuers. She came to the outskirts of Guildford and felt some measure of relief. By now her legs were aching, and her hands chafed from gripping the bicycle's metal handles. She followed the signs to the railway station, craning her neck now and again to see if there was anyone following, but the town was deserted and quiet.

Once at the station, Ursula dismounted, hid the bicycle behind the luggage cart, and turned out her pockets. The decision to travel by taxicab and underground to Christopher Dobbs's house had been a fortuitous one—it had forced her to carry change in her pocket for the return fare. She counted out the coins, hoping she would have enough for the train fare to London. Katya's letter was still stuffed into the pocket of her skirt, but she knew that this might be her only opportunity to protect the secrets it contained. Ursula spied the night porter strolling along the platform, whistling in the early-morning fog.

"Excuse me, when's the first train to London?" Ursula asked. The night porter looked at her curiously and answered, "Blimey, the first train that will get you to London ain't till five. There's a local coming through in about ten minutes or so that has a couple of passenger carriages. No first-class coach, though, Miss. But it would take you to Woking, and you could connect to the four-thirty train to Waterloo."

Ursula wriggled her nose. She rarely traveled by train these days, and only when traveling to the North. "I'm sure this must look very odd indeed, but I really must get to London as soon as I can. . . . Do I have to change platforms at Woking to catch the London train?"

"Aye, but it's just the opposite platform, so you'll have no trouble at all, Miss."

He looked at her with a fatherly smile.

"Thank you," Ursula replied, still feeling embarrassed. "I'm sure this is going to sound a little strange, too, but is there a pillar-box near here?"

"Why, yes, Miss. Just round the corner on Coronation Street."

Ursula looked down and realized she had no stamp.

"I need this to get to someone urgently . . . ," she began.

The night porter hunted around in his jacket pocket. "Hang on a minute," he said, pulling our some keys. "Let me 'ave a quick look in the stationmaster's desk."

"Would you really?" Ursula asked.

"Of course, just hold on there, luv, and let's see what we can do." The night porter disappeared into the stationmaster's office. Ursula shifted from foot to foot, hugging her arms around her.

"You're in luck!" the night porter cried. " 'Ere's a half-penny stamp—there, that should do the trick."

"I don't suppose the stationmaster has an envelope in there, does he? I'd pay you for it, of course—"

"Oh, don't be daft—'ere take it. Looks like you're in need of some 'elp."

"Thank you, I really am most grateful."

Ursula leaned over one of the benches and scrawled the address on the envelope, leaning it against one of the wooden slats. Once she had finished, she affixed the stamp and then looked at the night porter urgently. "Do I have time?"

He flipped open his fob watch. "I reckon you've got a good five minutes. You should be able to do it. I can put it in the pillar-box for you if you'd like."

"No, I think I should make sure. It really is most urgent."

Ursula, half expecting to see the men from the farmhouse leap out of the shadows, hastened across the bridge over the platform, and down and along Coronation Street. She held the letter for just a moment, gazing at the address before depositing it in the pillar-box and hurrying back toward the station. She could hear the train approaching. She ascended the stairs and was halfway across the bridge when she noticed two men speaking with the night porter. Ursula froze. Their voices carried easily in the thin early-morning air.

"Excuse me, have you seen a young woman round here?"

"A young woman, eh?" the night porter replied. "Can't say as I have. . . . No."

Ursula didn't know which way to turn. She stood rooted to the spot.

"Although," the night porter continued, "I did see a young lass on a bicycle maybe ten minutes ago, heading back along Hanlon Street. Looked like she was heading for the Southampton road."

The two men barely even nodded before they hurried out of the station.

The night porter looked up at Ursula, the whistle poised in his mouth. Giving a gesture to the engine driver to hold the train for a moment, he signaled her to come down. Ursula, having little choice but to trust him, hastened down the stairs.

The night porter inclined his head toward the train. "Best be gettin' on this, Miss."

"Those men—," Ursula started to say.

The night porter opened the carriage door. "Didn't like the look of 'em meself. Best get on to London as soon as you can."

"I can't thank you enough," Ursula said gratefully as she closed the door. The porter blew his whistle, and the train lurched to a start. Ursula quickly bent down to pretend to fix her shoe, terrified lest she be seen by the very men she had just managed to avoid.

Her heart thumping wildly, she finally allowed herself to exhale slowly once the train reached Woking and she was on her way to London.

Ursula alighted from the train at Waterloo station just as the sun was starting to rise, sending slivers of light across the vault of the station hall. She joined the early commuters making their way down to the London Underground and took the Bakerloo line to the Russell Square station.

She sat down in the carriage, feeling immeasurably exhausted. Her brain didn't seem to be able to function properly anymore. Lack of sleep had taken its toll, and she felt sure she must look a fright beneath the strong electric lights of the underground. Ursula stifled a yawn, fussed with her hair for a moment, and then gave up, slumping back in her seat until the train reached the Russell Square station and she got off, eager to walk to Woburn Place and find Winifred.

Ursula arrived at Winifred's house and knocked on the front door. She looked around nervously, expecting the worst, but Woburn Square remained quiet, with only the sounds of the milkman with his horse and cart breaking the eerie early-morning quiet. The fog hung low and thick, muffling the sounds of the waking city.

No one answered the front door despite her furious knocking. Ursula scurried down the servants' stairs and proceeded to knock again and again, with growing desperation.

"Come on, Mary," Ursula muttered under her breath. "Surely you're here by now."

Still no answer. Panic was starting to grip her.

She knocked a third and final time.

The door opened slightly, and Alexei peered out. He was disheveled and unshaven.

"Ursula?" he exclaimed, and opened the door fully. Dressed in his gray flannel trousers and a collarless striped shirt, Alexei was bleary-eyed without his glasses on. As Ursula hurried inside and closed the door behind her, he tucked in his shirt.

"Where's Mary? Where's Freddie?" Ursula demanded in quick succession.

"Monday is Mary's day off, and Freddie hasn't returned from her little 'outing' last night."

Ursula paced up and down the kitchen. "Damn and blast!"

Alexei picked up his glasses and shoved them on.

"What's the matter?"

"You haven't heard from Freddie at all?" Ursula asked with growing concern.

"Well, not since around one o'clock this morning, when she had the gall to telephone to tell me she was staying at Lady Catherine's. I don't know why she bothered." Alexei yawned loudly.

Ursula sighed with relief. "Thank God. I thought the worst."

Alexei raised his eyebrows. "What's all this about?"

"It's nothing," Ursula said quickly. She didn't want to say anything until she had contacted Winifred. "But I need to use the telephone. I need Freddie to come home as soon as possible."

"You look dreadfully tired. Let me telephone her. Put the kettle on and make yourself a cup of tea—isn't that what the English always do in a crisis? I'll tell Freddie to come right away." He reached over and stroked her cheek. "You look like you're in a terrible state, *lapushka*."

"Oh, Alexei," Ursula said, ignoring the gesture and rubbing her temples furiously with her fingertips, "if you knew the half of it."

"Do you have time to tell me?"

"Later. Perhaps. You telephone Freddie. I just need some time to wrap my mind around things. Alexei, I've discovered letters—"

"Letters?" Alexei asked. "Do you have them with you now?"

Ursula was too preoccupied with her own thoughts to answer.

"Never mind," Alexei said. "Let me go upstairs and telephone first; you can explain everything while we're waiting for Freddie to return."

Alexei went up the stairs, leaving Ursula standing next to the deep cast-iron sink, kettle in hand, absentmindedly running water into the top. She placed the kettle on the Aga stove and then returned to the sink to splash her face with the ice-cold water.

Alexei returned a few minutes later.

"Freddie's on her way back now."

Ursula finally relaxed, crumpling her weary body into one of the wooden kitchen chairs.

"So tell me more about this letter," Alexei asked, "while I finish making your tea."

Ursula hesitated, for she still remained unsure of Alexei's motives. But she was inclined to trust him at least in so far as Katya and Dobbs were concerned. She recounted part of the story, censoring what she felt was necessary, and although it sounded incoherent and confusing, Alexei continued to listen, his dark eyes curiously impenetrable.

Ursula drained her cup of tea and walked over to the sink to rinse out her cup.

"So this letter you found, what are you going to do with it?" Alexei asked.

"Well," Ursula started, but a low rap at the kitchen door stopped her.

"That'll be Freddie now," Alexei said and walked over to the back door. Ursula was still standing by the sink, dishcloth in hand, when it occurred to her that it would be very odd for Winifred to knock at her own servants' entrance door. That thought was cut short as she was seized from behind. A handkerchief was thrust under her nose and over her mouth. "Alexei!" she tried to call out, but her body started to collapse beneath her. Her vision became grainy and blurred. She stumbled over her feet and, as the ether numbed all her senses, swooned, unconscious, onto the floor.

"Forgive me, *lapuskha*," she heard Alexei say. "But I had no choice."

Twenty-two

I n her dream she was being buried alive beneath the sand. She struggled, arms flailing. Her mouth opened to scream, but the sand caved in. It was hot and gritty, pouring into her ears, mouth, and nostrils, drowning her. She fought and fought, desperate to rise to the surface, when suddenly her eyes opened and she awoke to find herself looking up at a vaulted ceiling painted with cherubs and seraphim.

"Where is the letter?" Dobbs asked.

All along one wall was a row of heavy brocade curtains over a series of French windows. The curtains were all drawn, so the room was dark. Between each Ursula could see chinks of light. Wherever she was, it was daylight.

Ursula, in her half-conscious state, murmured "No . . ."

"Ursula, wake up and tell me where the letter is," Dobbs ordered.

Ursula opened her eyes. "No," she repeated. This time it was a deliberate response. It was then that she realized she was sitting in a chair in nothing more than her undergarments. Her hands were bound behind her back and tied to the chair with thick rope.

"As you can see, we have searched you and know you don't have the letter about your person. So I ask once more, where is it?"

Ursula knew her only chance of staying alive was keeping the letter safely out of his reach, but she also had to play for as much time as she could, to enable the letter to reach its intended recipient. She closed her eyes and slumped forward in the chair. Rudely started by a wave of cold water thrown over her head, she sat upright, blinking back the water from her eyes.

Christopher Dobbs crouched down and stared her in the eye. "No more games, Ursula. Do you want to live, or do you want to die?"

"Aren't I dead already? I mean, you've killed everyone who saw the contents of that letter . . . ," Ursula responded.

"You may prove useful in other ways," Dobbs responded calmly. "So if you tell me where the letter is, I may be inclined to spare your life."

And pigs might fly, Ursula thought, before another realization hit her in the gut. Alexei had betrayed her to Dobbs.

The man she had recognized from that day with Katya in the Khan al-Khalili stepped forward. "Would you like me to take over now, Sahib? I have skills that may come in handy."

"See," Dobbs said, "Harsha is as eager as ever—he's missed having Baruh to torture. I don't believe we need to resort to such methods just yet. I think you'll succumb and tell me soon enough."

Ursula looked at him defiantly.

Dobbs laughed. "Do you imagine that I'd think twice about killing you? It can be so easily arranged. What do you think the newspapers would say? Ursula Marlow commits suicide over the collapse of her father's empire. Who's to say any different?"

"Is that what you thought with Katya? That you could get away with blaming Egyptian nationalists, and no one would say any differently?"

"Well, they didn't, did they? Apart from you."

"And how about Arina—how did you expect that to look? An accident? The work of George, my disgruntled manager?"

Dobbs laughed. "George really was most obliging. Oh, he professed his loyalty to your family, of course, but it didn't take much.

The threat of exposing his little indiscretion with Nellie Ackroyd was all it took. Have you met his wife? Well, then, you'd know why he didn't want her to find out. Stupid what some men do after just a couple of pints. And Nellie, of course, was always very accommodating. . . ."

"George did it to protect his family?" Ursula asked, confused.

Dobbs merely laughed. "He did it to protect himself, and besides, I told him Marlow Industries would soon be mine, and if he wanted to still provide for his family, well, he better make sure he did what I told him."

Ursula looked at Dobbs in disgust.

Dobbs grinned and, as if guessing her thoughts, responded, "Of course I couldn't trust him to actually kill the girl. We had to arrange that ourselves. Harsha really is very efficient. . . . How did you do it again?"

"Strangulation, Sahib."

"So simple, and the fire almost succeeding in disguising it all. It could have been just another 'accident' for Marlow Industries."

"You really are heartless."

"No, merely clearheaded in business. My only mistake was to keep Baruh alive. But Harsha wanted to torture him to be sure he had not told anyone else. Katya's letter proved useful in that respect. As soon as I showed it to him, he knew he had condemned not just one woman but two to death. Though after you're dead, I guess I won't need to concern myself with that anymore. Harsha can have his way with Baruh."

Ursula's eyes were blinded by her tears. Harrison must have been too late to get Baruh out. "How did you even know about Katya's letter?" she asked. Despite her fear, she was determined to keep questioning Dobbs. "I would have assumed the first person Katya would have told was her husband, yet you never tried to kill him."

Dobbs laughed. "It was Peter who warned Whittaker in the first place—not that he knew that's what he was doing. His obsession with his wife's supposed infidelity came in very useful. He was worried enough in London, but when Katya met Hugh in Palestine his obsession became paranoia. Peter confessed to Whittaker that he was concerned about Katya's mysterious trips and investigations. It didn't take Whittaker long to realize what Katya was doing and by then Peter could think of nothing but her alleged affair with Hugh."

"And Hugh, of course, realized the danger and refused to ask any questions."

"I also needed him alive if I was to get hold of his shipyards," Dobbs answered as if by way of explanation.

"Yes, what a real credit to your father you are!" Ursula spat out.

Dobbs's eyes narrowed. "My father would be proud, I'm sure. He'll certainly be pleased when I manage to bring Marlow Industries to its knees."

"You've failed so far. Did you really think I didn't suspect who was behind all of the attacks and unrest? I will never sell to you, and neither will Hugh Carmichael. Your dreams of building dread-noughts and armaments are already over."

"You think so? I don't know—with your death, I think it will all be pretty easy. Hugh Carmichael's close to the brink—and I doubt even the indomitable Lord Wrotham will oppose me once you're gone."

"You think it'll be that easy."

"Oh, Miss Marlow, once I'm finished with you, everything will be very easy. So tell me, if I'm to even contemplate sparing your life, where is Katya's letter?"

"I posted it," Ursula replied simply. "To Peter Vilensky."

Ursula started to come to. Her neck was stiff, and her mouth was bloody from the blow she had received. Christopher Dobbs was pac-ing the room while Whittaker watched.

"Your father told us not to underestimate her," Whittaker said.

Dobbs ignored him, walking over to the rosewood chiffonier near the door and pulling a pistol from the top drawer. Without a word he approached Ursula and held the gun to her forehead.

"Wait!" Whittaker called out. "She may be useful to us alive!"

"I can't imagine how," Dobbs responded coldly.

"If she dies now, how will you get Marlow Industries? We need to set the stage—plan it so that we can achieve all our aims. Peter Vilensky is not indispensable—perhaps we can implicate them both in some sordid affair and then stage a double suicide. Use their deaths to our advantage. What do you say, old boy?"

"I say you need to shut up and let me think!" Dobbs spat out in reply.

Ursula groaned as she sat up.

"Glad you could join us again, Miss Marlow." Dobbs said. "Even if it won't be for long."

"I don't understand why you would even keep it," Ursula said abruptly, feeling a strange sense of calm now that death seemed imminent. "The letter, I mean. Why not destroy it after you found it at Arina's?"

"Arrogance." Chief Inspector Harrison's voice echoed across the room.

Dobbs spun round and fired the pistol. Three shots rang out in quick succession. Whittaker dropped to his knees, clutching his chest.

Terrified, Ursula flung herself to the ground, toppling the chair.

Harsha and two other men burst in through the door at the far end of the room just as five policemen and Lord Wrotham kicked their way through the French doors. Ursula saw Dobbs lying face-down with a bullet wound to his leg. More shots rang out, and the room seemed to fill with movement and smoke and the smell of gunfire. Through it all she heard Lord Wrotham calling for her.

Out of the corner of her eye she saw Dobbs reach for Whittaker's gun on the floor. She cried out a warning, but she was too late—the shot rang out, and Lord Wrotham collapsed to the floor.

As Harrison's men rushed to Wrotham's side, ripped off his jacket, and placed it over his chest to try to staunch the blood, Harrison fought and finally overpowered Harsha. Dobbs was dragged away and handcuffed by the police. Ursula couldn't even move, bound as she still was to the chair. She knew she was screaming, but she could hear no sound. There was only the pounding of blood in her ears, the sight of blood everywhere. One of Harrison's men finally came to her and untied her wrists. She pushed him aside and ran over to Lord Wrotham. She cradled his head in her hands, but she could barely see him through the hot, stinging tears that streamed down her face.

Twenty-three

Ursula was sitting slumped against the wall in the hallway, nursing her bandaged wrists. Enveloped in a man's overcoat and wearing nothing else but her undergarments, she waited for news.

Lord Wrotham had been carried into the billiards room and was in there now, undergoing emergency surgery. His condition had been too critical, and the nearest hospital too far, for anything else to be done. The surgeon, a guest at a nearby country house, had arrived nearly two hours ago, but there was no word as yet on whether Lord Wrotham had survived the operation.

Ursula continued to stare at her wrists.

She thought, If he is dead, then I am dead.

Harrison appeared at the end of the hallway.

"Any news?"

Ursula shook her head.

Harrison ran his fingers through his hair.

Ursula closed her eyes to quell the nausea that rose in her throat. She couldn't get the words out of her mind. They simply repeated over and over again, like a gramophone record that could not be turned off. *If he's dead . . . then I am dead.*

"Miss Marlow, I should never have left you there, at the farmhouse. Dobbs's men must have followed us. I should have been more careful. We were lucky on one count, though. They were so distracted with you that my men managed to get that man Baruh out—one saving grace in all of this, I guess."

It was the closest Ursula had heard Harrison come to an apology. But she was in no mood to care.

The billiards room door swung open, and Sir Thomas Reeve, surgeon to the late King Edward himself, walked though. Dressed somberly in a black frock coat and gray trousers, he had looked more like an undertaker than a physician when he first arrived. Now, with his shirtsleeves rolled up, his hands and shirt stained with blood, he looked like a butcher. One of the police constables carried over a basin of water, and the surgeon proceeded to clean his hands and towel them dry. The water in the basin went blood red.

The surgeon then wiped his glasses with a white handkerchief he pulled from his trouser pocket.

"I removed the bullet from His Lordship's chest," he calmly informed them. "But the bleeding was extensive. I did everything that I could—"

Ursula held her head in her hands.

"But we were lucky; the bullet didn't perforate any major organs. As I said, the main concern was blood loss, but I've cauterized the wound successfully. Barring infection, he should survive."

"Thank God," Ursula whispered.

Harrison went over and shook the surgeon's hand warmly. "I'm sure I speak for all of us when I say how grateful we are."

"Well, as a good friend of Lord Wrotham's for nearly ten years—we met at Eton, don't y'know—I'm as relieved as you. Who else would I dine with in London? I can't stand anyone else at the Carlton Club." With a wink, the surgeon walked past.

"Can I go in and see him?" Ursula inquired as he passed.

The surgeon stopped, pulled out his fob watch, and flipped it open. "You'll have to wait. He could be unconscious for a while, and I've made arrangements for him to be transported to a private hospital near Southampton. An ambulance should be here within the hour. You can certainly visit him there. But just so you know, I am recommending that he return to Bromley Hall as soon as practicable. Nothing is more likely to guarantee an infection than a prolonged stay in the hospital! I must warn you—even at the hospital, I recommend no more than one or two visitors at a time."

Chief Inspector Harrison nodded.

"And on no account let his mother in."

"Ursula . . ." Winifred shook her elbow. "Sully . . ."

Ursula was slumped across Lord Wrotham's hospital bed, her hand still holding his. Her dark auburn hair was tangled and loose, and the top buttons of her dress were undone. Since she had refused to leave Lord Wrotham's side, Harrison had asked one of the nurses to arrange for someone to give her a dress to wear. She could hardly remain in his hospital room wearing nothing more than Harrison's coat and her undergarments.

"Wake up, Sully." Winifred tried to wake her once more.

Ursula started to stir.

"Come on." Winifred tried to lift her up.

"What are you doing?" Ursula asked groggily.

"I'm taking you home."

"No." Ursula pulled away.

"You need to rest, Sully. You've been here all night."

"I have to stay."

Winifred dragged Ursula to her feet. "I've come all the way from London, and believe me when I say I'm in no mood to argue. They're planning on taking him to Bromley Hall tonight, now that he is stable."

Ursula regarded her friend blankly. She felt as though she were surfacing from a dark, deep lake. Her limbs felt heavy and cold, even as she felt the reassuring warmth of Winifred's arm around her.

"I'm taking you home now," Winifred said. "Look, you can hardly even stand!"

"I need to be here when he wakes," Ursula insisted.

"It's all arranged," Winifred continued firmly. "We're on the ten o'clock train. Samuels will be waiting for us at Waterloo station. Mrs. Stewart and Julia have been running round getting everything prepared. They're all concerned for you, Sully, as am I."

Ursula had opened her mouth to argue when Lord Wrotham's eyelids flickered, and he groaned.

"I'll go tell Matron he's coming to," Winifred said quickly, and with one glance at Ursula's face, she hastened out of the room.

Ursula sat back down on the hard wooden chair by the bed and reached over to take Lord Wrotham's hand in hers. She squeezed it gently.

"It's all right," she said. "I'm here."

He opened his eyes, and for a moment he was disoriented.

"Ursula?" he croaked. She grabbed the glass of water and brought it to his lips. He struggled to sit up.

"Don't try and sit up yet," Ursula said. "You're still too weak."

"What happened?" he asked groggily.

"You were shot." she replied.

"That part I remember," he replied, still struggling to sit up. "But where am I now?"

"Southampton private hospital," Ursula replied, propping him up gently against the pillows. "They plan on moving you to Bromley Hall tonight."

Lord Wrotham lay back on the pillow and stared at the ceiling.

"Are you in any pain? Freddie's gone to tell Matron you're awake, so she should be here soon."

"I'm fine," he responded. "But what about Dobbs and Whittaker? What happened?"

"Whittaker is dead," Ursula said somberly. "Dobbs is recovering from surgery, but he may still lose his leg. They have him under guard at another hospital, and they took Harsha into custody."

"When Vilensky appeared at my door with the letter that afternoon, I feared the worst."

"I know." Ursula patted his hand. "Good thing the mail service is so efficient. I never thought I'd be so grateful for multiple deliver-ies in one day. But truly, you needn't worry. I'm fine. . . ."

Lord Wrotham closed his eyes for a moment. "Yes," he muttered. "I'm sure you are." Ursula frowned, for his tone was curiously bitter.

Ursula held his hand tightly, but he pulled away. "What is it?" she asked, aware that his demeanor had suddenly altered, as if some-thing had occurred to him now that made him question something significant, something he held most dear.

"You should go," he said coldly.

"No," she responded. "I want to stay. I want to be here with you."

"Go."

"But I don't understand." Ursula said. "Why don't you want me to stay?"

"Because it only makes matters worse. I don't need you to be my nurse." His voice went cold. "And I don't want your pity. I can't have you here, knowing that as soon as this crisis has passed, it will be back to the way it was before. You pushing me away, then draw-ing me back in. I cannot love you under those conditions. Alexei may be able to. Who knows, maybe you still care for him more than me."

Ursula remembered that ill-fated kiss in the doorway and opened her mouth to explain.

"Go now," Lord Wrotham interrupted her harshly. "Save us the pain of going through all that again."

Lord Wrotham turned away.

"But . . . I . . ." Ursula choked on her words. There was a note of finality in his voice that filled her with anguish.

His back to her, Lord Wrotham remained silent.

Ursula's throat tightened. She had to take small shallow breaths as she stumbled to her feet blindly and grasped the edge of the wooden chair to steady herself.

"I think it's best if we give the patient a little peace and quiet now!" Matron instructed Ursula as she bustled through the door in her starched white dress and cap. Ursula had to step aside as Matron passed. She retreated through the doorway, her thoughts in turmoil.

She had to try and pull herself together and convince him that she must stay.

Ursula stood outside in the corridor for a moment, trying to catch her breath. Her throat was so constricted now, she found she had to gasp for air. She could hear the dull roar of the wind as it struck the windowpanes, the scrape of the chair against the linoleum floor, and then the ominous silence of the hospital corridor. Ursula searched for a sign that Winifred was returning, but the doors at the end of the corridor opened instead, and Ursula saw the image of Lady Winterton, dressed in a jaunty red hat and cape, approaching her.

"Lady Winterton?" Ursula said dazed. "What on earth are you doing here?"

Lady Winterton seemed taken aback for a moment. "I'm sorry," she said. "I understood you were heading back to London this morning."

"I am . . . at least, that's what Freddie . . . I'm sorry, I don't understand, why are you here?"

"My family's country estate isn't too far from here, and when I heard that Lord Wrotham had been taken in, I thought I ought to visit."

Ursula bit her tongue.

"Can you tell me what happened? No one seems too sure," Lady Winterton continued. She dusted off the sleeve of her cape.

"I . . ." Ursula wasn't sure what to say.

"A riding accident, I believe." Winifred's voice boomed down the corridor. She came from behind and squeezed Ursula's arm. "That's what we've been told."

"Ah, Miss Stanford-Jones. My apologies. I really did think you and Miss Marlow were on your way back to London."

"We are," Winifred answered smoothly.

Matron stalked into the corridor. "Quiet!" she said sharply. "The poor man needs rest, not the constant chatter of ladies who have nothing better to do!"

Ursula flushed darkly, but Lady Winterton merely arched one eyebrow and took the comment in her stride.

"Of course, Matron," she replied smoothly. "But tell me, how is the patient doing after his fall?"

Matron's eyes narrowed and Ursula guessed that she had been specifically instructed not to divulge the nature of Lord Wrotham's wounds to anyone.

"He'll live," came her curt reply. "But only if he is left in peace."

"Sully,"—Winifred put a hand on Ursula's arm—"we really should be getting to the station,"

Exhaustion had clouded Ursula's mind. She felt woolly-headed and slow to react. Standing there in her immaculate suit, with her basket of provisions, Lady Winterton presented a picture of all that a man of Lord Wrotham's stature would want in a wife. Ursula acknowledged for the first time to herself what an embarrassment she must be to him. Since her father's death, she had brought him nothing but scandal and disrepute.

"Miss Marlow, are you all right?" Matron asked, her grim countenance softening.

Ursula stared at her blankly without answering.

"Are you staying?" Lady Winterton asked, an impatient edge in her tone.

Winifred urged her to come home, and Ursula acquiesced numbly. She let Winifred take her arm and lead her down the corridor, concentrating all the while on simply placing one foot in front of the other as she tried to regain her self-control.

Once they were outside, Winifred turned to Ursula. She was about to speak when she encountered Ursula's gaze.

"Sully . . . what on earth is the matter?" Winifred gripped her arm. "What happened?" she asked.

"Oh, Freddie," Ursula replied, and looked at her friend with hollow eyes. "I think I've lost him for good this time."

"Alexei's gone," Winifred said gently. "Just so you know."

She had accompanied Ursula to Southampton station, and they were both standing on the platform, waiting for the London train.

Ursula was still dazed by what had happened at the hospital, and Winifred seemed determined to divert her attention by informing her what had happened the morning following her disappearance.

"I arrived yesterday morning at around eight, after spending the night at one of our sister's houses in Kensington. I was worried when I hadn't heard from you that morning. Alexei was gone, but he had left a note for me. At first I didn't know what to make of it, until I received a telephone call from Chief Inspector Harrison. Alexei's note simply said, 'Gone to Shrewsbury Grange.' I guess that was his pathetic attempt to salve his conscience." Ursula gave no indication of having heard her. "We should be grateful," Winifred continued, "that Lord Wrotham knew from Mrs. Pomfrey-Smith about Dobbs's recent real estate acquisition. Seems she may be useful for something after all."

"Alexei's gone?" Ursula asked numbly.

"I overheard Harrison talking with one of his men while you were with Lord Wrotham. Something about his evading surveillance. We can only hope Okhrana catches up with him."

Part Four

England

Twenty-four

London
AUGUST 1912

A month later, as the summer dragged into August without a sign that the wet weather would end, Ursula attended one of the last events of the London season, a garden party at Mrs. Pomfrey-Smith's. This year she had missed Royal Ascot, avoided the Eton and Harrow cricket match, and refused countless invitations to the balls and parties that punctuated the season like exclamation marks. She had been too preoccupied with recent events and too uneasy about the fate of her father's empire to care up until now. But the thought of an autumn spent without Lord Wrotham had started to wear her down. She had heard nothing from him since leaving the private hospital in Southampton. Many other people chose to keep her abreast of all developments, of course—Mrs. Pomfrey-Smith being one of the worst offenders. With every telephone call, handwritten note, and invitation she sent, she continued to remind Ursula of what she had lost.

Ursula attended the Royal Academy Summer Exhibition but missed the companionship of someone as interested in art as Lord Wrotham. She visited Hatchards booksellers regularly, but missed having someone with whom she could discuss her latest acquisitions. Even her work with the WSPU and the regular articles she was now writing for *Lady's Realm* on current political issues for women were curiously unsatisfying. After weeks of refusing Mrs. Pomfrey-Smith's invitations, Ursula finally agreed to attend her garden party; though the roses would be waterlogged and the marquees no doubt dripping with rain, Ursula put on her most dainty white lawn dress, straw hat, and gloves and went.

"Ursula, my dear!" Mrs. Pomfrey-Smith welcomed her. "Have you been burying yourself in books all summer? It'll do you no good, you know. . . . A gal's got to get out and enjoy life!"

Mrs. Pomfrey-Smith was as tactless as ever.

Her garden party was, however, a sumptuous affair. Despite the inclement weather, there were long tables filled with vases of cut roses, silver ice buckets with champagne, glass bowls filled with sherbet ices, and baskets overflowing with fresh strawberries and tiny pots of clotted cream. As a light rain began to fall and the servants hurried to produce umbrellas to protect both guests and food, Ursula ducked under the large marquee that had been set up for a string quartet that was to play later that afternoon. She was nibbling absently on an asparagus croquette when she caught sight of Christopher Dobbs making his way across the lawn, a pronounced limp in his left leg.

"Topper!" she heard Mrs. Pomfrey-Smith exclaim. "I had no idea you were back from Italy!"

Christopher Dobbs had spent the last month recovering from his injuries at a health spa outside Acqui Terme. Ursula turned away, unable to hide her disgust. Her memories of Chief Inspector Harrison calmly informing her that Christopher Dobbs was to remain free were still too vivid.

Harrison had visited Gray House almost three weeks ago to inform her that in exchange for providing details of all his contacts and their operations in the Middle East and Mediterranean, Dobbs would avoid prosecution.

"So Dobbs gets away, literally, with murder?" Ursula had responded incredulously.

"These are tense times." Harrison said. "We need to know who is supplying armaments to our enemies. Dobbs can provide a pivotal link in the chain, and we can use him to gain the intelligence we need. He has contacts from the Far East to the Balkans. He has already helped us thwart planned insurgencies in India and the Sudan. Unfortunately, we need men like Dobbs."

"Do I need to remind you that he nearly put a bullet through my head," Ursula had demanded, "and nearly killed Lord Wrotham?!"

"I need no such reminder. Believe me, if it were my choice, I would see Dobbs hang for what he has done. But we must be satisfied that the man who actually killed both Katya and Arina—Dobbs's man Harsha—will hang."

"I have no doubt that George will also be incarcerated, despite the fact that it was blackmail by Dobbs that made him light the fire."

"George made his choice. . . ."

"Yes, and so did Alexei, but I see he also managed to escape trial."

"Believe me, I and most of my colleagues would like nothing more than to put Alexei behind bars. If we had known that Dobbs was arranging to supply armaments to a group within Britain that was targeting employers for assassination, then we would have had him arrested immediately."

"Alexei all but admitted to me that was why he was in Britain. My guess is that Dobbs was going to provide armaments for all these groups across Europe. It would have been quite a coup for Alexei to have made such a deal. Imagine the chaos that could have been spread through such an assassination campaign."

"It could have caused a war," Harrison said bleakly.

"Knowing Alexei, he still can," came Ursula's caustic reply.

Ursula choked down the remaining bite of her croquette and washed it back with a swig of strong black tea. The memories of that conversation were still too raw for her to ignore. George had stood trial and received a two-year prison sentence, and Harsha was due to be sentenced next month, but here was Christopher Dobbs, the man who arranged everything, mingling with politicians and bankers as if he had not a care in the world.

"Ursula!" Mrs. Pomfrey-Smith waved her hand in the air, signaling her to come over. Ursula was horrified by the prospect of having to speak to Christopher Dobbs, but she responded with a nod and a tight smile. She wasn't about to show him how discomfited she really was.

"Topper here was just telling us about Italy," Mrs. Pomfrey-Smith said, and then turned back to Dobbs. "Such bad luck you taking that fall off a horse just before you left."

"Is that what happened?" Ursula asked with a deadpan expression. Mrs. Pomfrey-Smith failed to pick up the edge to her tone, but Dobbs eyed her warily.

"Yes, that's right. I was at Shrewsbury Grange trying my hand at a spot of hunting when it happened."

"Must be contagious," Ursula responded dryly. "I hear Lord Wrotham took a similar fall."

"Indeed? I guess we'd both better be more careful in the future."

Ursula was barely able to contain her fury. "*You* certainly need to be," she spat out before she managed to restrain herself. Mrs. Pomfrey-Smith looked suitably shocked but made no comment. Christopher Dobbs gave a calculated smile. "Never fear, Miss Marlow, I'm like a cat—I always land on my feet."

"Is that what creature you are, Mr. Dobbs?" Ursula asked coldly. "And here I was thinking you were the snake."

Ursula returned to Chester Square from Mrs. Pomfrey-Smith's garden party and retreated into her father's study. She curled up in his armchair and tried reading the latest installment of *The Lost World* in the *Strand Magazine*, but she couldn't concentrate. Her anger at Christopher Dobbs's ability to walk away from his invidious crimes gnawed away at her insides. She had thrown down the magazine and was pacing the room when Biggs knocked and entered the study.

"The mail arrived, Miss. There is one letter for you."

"From Bromley Hall?" Ursula asked quickly, misinterpreting Biggs's hesitation.

"No, Miss, from Mr. Anderson, I believe," Biggs replied.

Ursula's face fell. "Thank you," she said, "just place it on the desk."

Biggs complied and then calmly asked, "Would you like me to post anything for you, Miss?"

Ursula sat back down in the armchair. "No," she responded quietly. And then, as if to herself, "What would be the point?"

Ursula had sent at least four letters to Lord Wrotham, all of which had been returned unopened. She needed to accept, she told herself sternly, that things were truly over between them.

As twilight descended, Ursula stared at the coal fire and continued to reflect on the injustice of all that had happened. Beneath her feet lay a wooden box, one of the many she had shipped out from Egypt, and given all that had happened, one of the many that remained unopened. Using her father's ivory-handled letter opener, Ursula pried open the lid. Inside, packed in shavings, were some books she had bought, a brass serving tray, a box of perfume jars, and a stone tablet she had bought from a so-called dealer in antiquities. The tablet was inscribed with hieroglyphics, and as Ursula lifted it from the box, she reflected on the irony of having yet another indecipherable message in her house. She propped the stone tablet up on one of the bookshelves, opened the top drawer of the mahogany desk, and pulled out the paper that outlined the letter fragments found at Arina's house.

She looked over the Cyrillic script and sighed. The contents of the letter probably didn't even matter anymore, but still, their failure to decipher it gnawed at her. In the last couple of months she had finally had a chance to read the reference books Lady Winterton had supplied. Ursula tapped her chin with her fingers. She was remembering how Peter Vilensky had said that Arina and Katya always corresponded in English, and how Nellie Ackroyd and Len had mentioned that Arina rarely even spoke Russian—she had been in

England so long. Strange, Ursula ruminated, that the letter should then be in Russian.

With a glance at the stone tablet, a thought suddenly hit her. What if the Cyrillic letters used in the letter were really nothing more than hieroglyphics—a representation rather like a picture used as a substitution not for a Cyrillic letter but rather a letter from the English alphabet? Neither Winifred nor Ursula had even considered the possibility that the decoded message was in English, not Russian.

Ursula jumped to her feet and scanned the bookshelf for the dictionary Lady Winterton had left. She opened the front page and copied the Cyrillic alphabet across the top of one of the pages of her notebook. She knew from her early research on frequency analysis that "e" was the most commonly used letter in English, so Ursula assumed the most frequently used Cyrillic letter represented this. Soon she was drawing up tables of various alternative transpositions. After two hours and much trial and error, she stumbled upon the key. As she deciphered the words, her face contorted. There were only seven words—but that was all she needed to know the truth.

> Meet me at the factory at eight . . . Alone.
> Alexei

Ursula felt sick.

Winifred arrived later that evening and read the translation somberly.

"I guess this confirms that it was Alexei who lured Arina to the factory that night,"

As Winifred spoke, Ursula started to wonder. If she had been Arina and had received Katya's letter, what would she have done? Would she not have turned to a man like Alexei—an old lover who had once been so trusted—and told him the terrible secret Katya had entrusted her with, and sought his advice? Was that what had happened? And in return had he betrayed that trust in the worst possible way, blinded by his own needs—had he not only betrayed her to Christopher Dobbs but in doing so condemned Arina to death?

"Sully!!" Winifred cried out in exasperation.

Ursula looked at her startled.

"Don't waste any more time thinking about him!" Winifred admonished. "Alexei must have known what was going to happen to Arina that night. And there was only one possible reason Dobbs wanted you, and that was to kill you."

Ursula placed her head in her hands. "I know," she whispered. The full extent of Alexei's betrayal was evident. She just hadn't admitted it to herself until now.

Twenty-five

Oldham
AUGUST 1912

Two weeks later, Ursula returned to Gray House. London was all but deserted, with most of "society" heading off to their country homes or to their yachts off the Isle of Wight. Ursula now had energy to refocus on business once more. She busied herself overseeing the rebuilding of the Oldham factory and renegotiating key contracts with unions at all her mills and factories across the North, thereby securing earnings as well as ensuring that wages kept pace with inflation. The cotton industry was booming, but there was still considerable unemployment outside the textile towns. Ursula still found the state of much of the housing deplorable and was working with some of the local councils to build workers' cottages away from the grime and dust of the factories.

Inspired by this, she decided to visit Oldham's Garden Suburb one afternoon. It represented in many ways an idyllic housing estate, which Ursula was keen to support. As she pulled on her gloves and tied her scarf around her hat tightly, Ursula reflected that it might provide some measure of closure to walk the same streets Arina once had, and perhaps find some degree of comfort in this.

Ursula instructed Samuels to drop her at the tramway depot, and from there she decided to walk. It was the end of August, and though the summer had been wet and miserable up until now, the sun was now shining and it looked like being a glorious late-summer afternoon.

The houses of Garden Suburb were all mock Tudor in design, with fences and gardens, sidewalks, and even a common green in the center of the subdivision—a throwback to a quaint English village green from a bygone era. Women in clean tailored day dresses, straw hats, and parasols were coming out of O'Malley's butchers, or partaking in afternoon tea at Ye Olde Tea Shop on the corner opposite the green. Ursula made her way down Green Lane past the hedgerows and rosebushes, white gates and black-painted doors with brass knockers, each semidetached house identical to the next.

Ursula entered Ye Olde Tea Shop just before four o'clock, sat down at a table near the window, and ordered a small Montserrat lime juice and soda from the young girl in a frilly white cap. There was only one other customer, a lady in her middle years, in the tea shop. She was bent over the table studiously reading a Baedeker's guide to Palestine and Syria. It made Ursula wistful.

Sipping from her glass, Ursula gazed out of the window. Across the street was a small travel office, one of the new ones springing up all over the country, catering to the boom in demand for vacations and tours. In the window was a poster of Egypt depicting boats on the Nile at sunset. "Spend This Winter in Egypt Where a Perfect Climate Is to Be Obtained," the poster read. Next to it was another poster that urged, "Visit Palestine!"

Ursula sighed, for these served only to remind her of Katya. She wished she had asked Katya more about her sister, and more about their shared dreams. Her picture of Arina was incomplete—according to Peter Vilensky, she was nothing more that a leech, always demanding money. According to Nellie she was a quiet, gentle soul. Then there was the Arina of Alexei's world—full of idealism for a Bolshevik revolution. None of these images seemed to fit together.

Ursula dropped her coins upon the table and walked out of the tea shop and across the road. Aside from the posters, the shop window had a wonderfully kitsch display complete with leather suitcases, a globe, and a wooden motorcar and airplane. A banner above this read, "The Future of Travel . . ."

Ursula couldn't resist. She went in, the bell on the top of the door tinkling as she entered.

A young woman was sitting at the front desk in front of a type-writer, typing madly.

"Can I help you, Miss?" the receptionist asked with a smile.

"Oh—" Ursula hesitated. "I must confess I just came in on a whim. I spent the winter in Egypt, and I guess I just felt drawn in by your posters."

"Why, is it really you, Miss Marlow?!" A corpulent man approached from the back of the store.

Ursula frowned but answered politely, "I'm sorry, but do I know you?"

"No, no . . . I merely recognized your face from the society pages. Though I did meet your father a couple of times at the Blackburn Mechanics' Institute lecture series."

"Well, I'm sorry to have troubled you, Mr. . . . ?" Ursula looked at him inquiringly.

"Edel . . . Mr. Maurice Edel. And please feel free to ask us any questions at all. We are an authorized Thomas Cook & Sons representative—though a woman of your standing could afford to have her own private Egyptian tour, of course."

"I was thinking of Palestine, actually," Ursula responded. "A close friend of mine spoke very highly of her visit to the Holy Land."

"Why, of course—it is the dream of so many of us."

"Yes," Ursula said sadly. "I guess it is."

Ursula was thinking about the memorial to the settlers that she and Peter Vilensky planned to build on the road to Jerusalem. She fiddled absently with her white gloves.

"I read in the newspapers about the recent unpleasantness in Oldham," Mr. Edel leaned in and confided, as if it were a secret. "We don't go in for gossip, of course, not in these parts. Still, it's a terrible thing to hear about."

"Yes, yes, it was. We're rebuilding the factory, though."

"Mavis here went along to the arson trial. Shocking to think that one's own manager—entrusted with so much—could have done such a thing!"

"Yes." Ursula wasn't sure what else to say.

Mavis looked up at her expectantly. "I didn't see you at the trial, Miss."

"I was sitting at the back," Ursula replied simply. It was hard for her not to feel angry that George Aldwych was now serving a prison term while Christopher Dobbs and Alexei were free. The trial had not taken long, for George's confession led to a plea of guilty, and the jury only had to consider evidence as it related to sentencing. The lawyer for George's defense had asked Ursula if she would testify on his behalf to demonstrate his previous good character, but she had refused. Her compassion could not extend to forgiveness for his betrayal. Nevertheless, she could not help but shed a tear in court that day as she heard the details of the fire that fateful night. How George had left the Dog and Duck, gone home, and consumed a third of a bottle of Scotch to steady his nerves, before meeting Harsha at the factory at nine o'clock. Silently and systematically they had doused the cotton rags in petrol and lit the blaze. George maintained that he had no idea that the body of Arina Petrenko lay within the factory, and seeing his body physically shudder at the recollection of what happened that night, Ursula was inclined to believe him

"It's his family I feel sorry for." Mavis's voice brought Ursula back to the present.

"Yes," Ursula agreed. "It's probably hardest on the children."

"Well, especially when all that came out about 'im and that trollop Nellie Ackroyd."

"Language, Mavis!" Mr. Edel interjected. Mavis reddened.

"We should be thinkin' about the poor girl that died," Mr. Edel admonished. "Not that we knew her, of course, but Mavis reckoned she seen her a few times, wandering up and down the street."

"She liked lookin' in," Mavis said. "At the posters and such. I would see her when I was closing up some nights, just standing, like she were in a dream."

"Well, those posters are certainly enticing," Ursula replied sadly, reflecting upon the dreams that were lost for both Katya and Arina. "I suppose she never came in to ask?" she ventured.

Mr. Edel shook his head.

"Now, that's where you're wrong, Mr. Edel," Mavis announced proudly. "She did come in, just the once—oh, it must have been in February. All excited she were. Said she was expecting to get some money soon—and that she'd be back in to arrange her tickets. Poor thing. I expect she died before she ever saw hide or hair of that money."

It was then that Ursula realized that Arina had been hoping to join Kolya in Palestine—that was why Katya had initially investigated the *Bregenz*—only Kolya had died in Poland and had never even made it to the ship.

When Ursula returned to Gray House, Chief Inspector Harrison was waiting for her in the front parlor, standing by the window with his hat still in his hands.

"Chief Inspector," Ursula called from the door as she approached him. "I wasn't expecting you."

"No, don't expect you were," Harrison replied. "But I just thought I should drop by, since I was on my way to visit the Mortimers, and tell you"—he took a deep breath—"Harsha was hanged today. I wanted you to know before you saw tomorrow's newspapers."

Ursula drew back, and her hand rose to her throat.

"I . . . ," Ursula began, stumbling to take a seat. "Gosh, I didn't think I would feel this way when I heard the news."

"What way is that, Miss Marlow?"

"I'm not sure. I expected to feel relief, but instead, I just feel slightly sick, really."

Harrison shifted his weight from one foot to the other, looking uncomfortable.

"I'm fine," Ursula reassured him. "I think it's just the shock of everything that's happened—it's really just hit me now."

Ursula motioned him to take a seat and rang for Biggs to bring them some tea.

"Well, at least one good thing has come of it all," Harrison said after a pause. He pointed to the newspaper lying on the side table, folded to reveal the headline "Carmichael Shipyards and Marlow Industries in Historic Deal to Build Oil Tankers."

"Yes, Peter Vilensky was certainly eager to withdraw all his financial support from Dobbs and provide us with the money necessary to ward off any future takeover attempts. Now at least his late wife's legacy remains secure, and I—"

"I believe the *Times* said that Miss Marlow has finally demonstrated some of the business acumen her father was famous for," Eustacia Mortimer interrupted as she walked into the parlor.

"Miss Mortimer." Harrison jumped to his feet.

"I told Biggs not to worry about seeing me in, just can't get used to all that palaver, but I had to come and congratulate you when I saw the article in the *Times*."

Eustacia clasped Ursula's hand warmly.

Neither Dr. Ainsley Mortimer nor Eustacia knew the part Christopher Dobbs had played in Arina's death. They received the same story that was told to the public at George Aldwych's trial—that Arina was lured to the factory by an Indian national who murdered her on account of her sister's political activities in Egypt. Just as Ursula had feared, the newspapers blamed a band of nationalist infiltrators, hell-bent on destroying the British Empire (and not above blackmailing a poor factory manager who had had an "indiscretion" with a local girl). But Ursula was under a strict obligation of confidence now that Christopher Dobbs was assisting Scotland Yard's Special Branch—and, she suspected, the newly formed Secret Intelligence Service.

Ursula was roused from these thoughts by the image of Eustacia Mortimer crossing the room to greet Harrison with a wide smile. "Chief Inspector," she said, holding out her hand to shake his. "And remember, it's Doctor—not Miss."

A week later, Ursula met Hugh Carmichael at an airfield set up by local enthusiasts just outside Preston. Hugh flew down from Newcastle and executed a near-perfect landing along the wide strip of grass, which Ursula captured on her Brownie camera. Hugh was preparing to enter the Chicago air show later in the year, and was undertaking a series of flights designed to test the speed limits of his new experimental aircraft.

Ursula was standing among a group of onlookers, clapping, as Hugh alighted from the plane and threw his fist into the air. He had just made the journey from Newcastle to Preston in under an hour.

"Well, you've certainly inspired all the young men round here," Ursula said as she and Hugh walked along the landing site. About ten young men were busily inspecting his aircraft. Hugh accepted a steaming mug of tea from a lady standing next to a kerosene stove by a low stone wall.

"I hope so, sweetheart, I hope so!" Hugh replied with a grin.

"So when do you leave for Chicago?" Ursula asked.

"In about a week. Now that the deal with Vilensky is finalized, I can afford to take a little time off before the shipyards go into full production. I'll just leave everything in your capable hands."

"I'll try not to break anything," Ursula reassured him with a smile.

"Have you seen him yet? Dobbs, I mean," Hugh asked.

Hugh Carmichael, like Peter Vilensky, was one of the few people who knew the truth.

"Yes," Ursula replied coolly. "At a garden party in London."

"Sounds nice," Hugh responded with sarcasm.

"It was, except for his presence."

"I'll bet. Was your lord there too?"

Ursula's smile dropped. "No," she responded quickly. "He's still at Bromley Hall, recovering, I believe, from his injuries."

"You've not visited him, then?" Hugh asked lightly, but Ursula was not deceived.

"You know I haven't," she answered brusquely.

Hugh raised an eyebrow. "It's still like that, is it?"

Ursula stared out across the airstrip. She merely nodded.

Hugh seemed to know better than to pursue any further questioning. Instead it was Ursula's turn to ask him one last lingering question regarding Katya and Arina.

"Depends what it is," was Hugh's wary reply when she asked.

"I wanted to know what Katya told you in confidence in Egypt—the secret you refused to divulge to me."

Hugh ran his fingers through his graying hair. "Oh, that."

"I have to assume it was something other than the fate of those poor settlers in Palestine—for one thing, Dobbs never tried to have you killed."

"No, I guess he didn't." Hugh still seemed reluctant to say much more.

"Surely the danger to me has now passed."

"Yes, it's passed."

"So why can't you tell me?"

Hugh sighed. "All right, then." He hesitated before continuing, "Katya told me the night of the khedive's cocktail party that Vilensky had found out that she had forged his signature on some loan documents. One loan was to a small Egyptian nationalist group, another to a group of Bolshevik sympathizers in Poland, and the final one was to . . ."

"Arina?"

Hugh nodded.

"I'm also guessing the loan to the Bolsheviks was probably for Kolya Menkovich."

"Yes."

"And Vilensky found out?" Ursula prompted him again.

"Yes, and of course he saw it as yet another instance of Arina's influence over her sister. It also helped fuel his obsession that Katya was lying to him—not just about the loans, but also about her feelings. I think Vilensky sensed that Katya had confided in me, and it incensed him—just helped convince him that Katya and I were—"

"Lovers?"

"Yes—of course, that couldn't have been further from the truth. I felt more like her father confessor."

"Why did she tell you?"

"I think at first I was just someone she could tell to ease her own conscience, but the more I thought of it, the more I wondered if she wasn't trying to gain my sympathy so that should anything happen to her, I would help support and protect Arina."

"But she still didn't tell you what she had discovered in Palestine?"

Hugh shook his head. "She hinted at something, and when—when she was killed, I feared that it had something to do with the loans she had made. I couldn't work out whether it was the nationalists or the government—or even if it was Peter Vilensky himself. All I knew was that whatever Katya had been involved in was dangerous, and it likely as not got her killed."

"Why did you not—," Ursula started to ask.

"Not tell you?" Hugh interrupted. "I didn't tell you because I could see the fire in your eyes, the same fire I saw in my dear wife's, the fire of determination to find out the truth. I couldn't risk fueling that any further."

He looked at her sadly. "I lost my wife and sweetheart. I know how consuming the search for the truth can be."

Hugh gazed out over the field. A group of boys, with their fresh little faces and flat caps, were peering over the stone fence, staring in awe at the Blériot plane. "Would you look at that!" he said with a smile, breaking the awkward silence between them. Ursula knew better than to say anything further. She just patted his arm.

As they walked back across the field to the plane, Ursula couldn't help but muse, as much to herself as to anyone else, "I wonder who got the money? Arina certainly never used it to buy a ticket to Palestine, that's for sure."

Hugh didn't hear her, and as soon as Ursula spoke the words, she knew with certainty who that someone must be. Alexei. No doubt he would justify stealing Arina's money as he had justified everything else. All done in the name of the greater good—the workers' global struggle.

"Miss Marlow, are you feeling all right?" Hugh asked

"Yes," she replied slowly. "Just another reason for me to declare, once and for all, that I shall die a spinster."

"That bad, huh?" was all he said. Ursula shrugged. "Want some advice from an old romantic?" Hugh lit a cigar with a grin.

Ursula sighed. "Not really."

"Well, I'm giving it to you, whether you like it or not. When you've found true love, hold on to it. I found Iris, and she was taken away from me all too soon, so don't you dare waste the time you have. Go to him. You've shown the world you can stand on your own—now show the world you can stand next to him."

Twenty-six

Bromley Hall
SEPTEMBER · 1912

Samuels drew up in Bertie at the familiar gilded ironwork gate, got out, and turned his collar up against the wind as he dashed forward and opened the gates. They banged against the tall stone wall with a clang. Ursula leaned forward in the rear passenger seat and tilted her head up beneath her hat to catch a glimpse of the Wrotham family crest, mounted in all its medieval splendor upon the gate. *Sequere iustiam et invenias vitem*—Follow justice and find life.

Just beyond the gates, on either side of the driveway that led up to Bromley Hall, were the wild meadows that had once been the family's deer park. Even now there were deer roaming free, and as Samuels drove along the way, Ursula caught glimpses of them dotted here and there, sheltered beneath the dark green elms and grazing in the open meadow. Samuels drove past the ornamental lake with its central Italianate fountain, and they followed the curved avenue until Ursula caught a glimpse of the silver-gray limestone facade of the east wing. Samuels drew up outside the wide stone staircase at the entrance. He stopped the car, pulled down his peaked cap, and alighted to assist Ursula. Following such a wet summer, the driveway was rutted into deep trenches of mud that Ursula tried gingerly to avoid as Samuels helped her out of the car.

She gazed up at the tall windows that flanked the impressive carved doorway, took a deep breath to try and compose herself, and climbed the stairs. The door opened as she got to the top.

"Miss Marlow!" Ayres could not contain his surprise.

"Good morning, Ayres," she said, trying to keep her voice from betraying her anxiety. "Sorry to arrive unannounced, but I was wondering if Lord Wrotham was home?"

"Yes, Miss." Ayres face returned to its usual impassive state. "He is taking one of his long walks."

Ursula gave a small smile. "I thought he might be. Which route did he take?"

"The one to the edge of Rockingham Forest. He left almost an hour ago, so I expect he will be on his way back. Do you wish to wait in the Green Drawing Room?"

"No, Ayres, I'm going outside to find him."

"Very good, Miss. We shall have tea ready for your return."

Ayres, like Biggs, could always be relied upon to remain composed.

"Thank you, Ayres. I'll see myself out the back."

Ursula made her way through the vaulted entrance hall, through the old medieval receiving room, and down the long picture gallery to the end of the east wing. It felt strangely comforting to be back at Bromley Hall, and with each tap-tap of her walking shoes along the parquetry floor, Ursula was reminded of last summer, as if the memories had permeated the wood and stone, fixing them forever. She reached the end of the gallery and ducked out the French doors that led out onto the grand terrace. She walked quickly, trying to rid herself of the nervous energy that had built up during the long journey here. As the wind gathered strength, she buttoned up her tweed jacket and hurried on toward the avenue of cypress trees that formed a pathway to the edge of the Wrotham estate and Rockingham Forest.

The leaves were already turning on the giant English oak, and the wind sent showers of leaves into the air with each gust. Ursula pulled her jacket in tight, flapping her arms to try and release some of the tension as she strode along the path down between the cypresses and then into the fields beyond. The grass was wet beneath her feet, and her boots were soon sodden, but she was too intensely focused ahead to care. By the time she started to climb the low hillock that led up to the ruins of a mock Roman temple, the hem of her dress was saturated and muddy. From the top she gazed down on the ornamental lake that formed the border of the estate. On the other side was the dense, dark fringe of the forest. Just below her Lord Wrotham was standing by the edge of the lake, his two collies bounding joyfully around a stick that lay at his feet as they waited for him to make the next toss.

Now that she was here, she felt giddily nervous. The knot in her stomach had twisted in upon itself till she felt she would burst. The apprehension was almost unbearable, but with a deep breath she steadied herself.

At that moment, he turned and saw her.

Despite all her mental rehearsals, she was utterly unprepared for the impact of his gaze. He looked like Keats's knight, "alone and palely loitering," his dark hair swept back by the wind, his blue-gray eyes mirroring the bleak grim sky.

A flock of ravens wheeled above her head, and the dogs began barking madly.

"Quiet!" he ordered, and they both dropped to their haunches as she walked toward him. A gust of wind heaved and pounded the tall grass along the bank of the lake. She drew in her breath. He was waiting for her to speak.

"I'm hoping it's not too late."

The wind carried her words like a leaf.

He made no reply but remained as he was, immutable, like stone, standing before her. She approached him, slowly, as if in a dream.

"I've been a fool," she said. "Thinking that the only way I could stand on my own was to do it without you. I've been fighting my own shadow. But now"—she took a deep breath—"now I'm here, as your equal, as someone who knows for a certainty what she wants."

His eyes flickered for a moment.

"And it is you," she continued. "Always. Forever."

She hesitated in midstep. "Tell me it's not too late." This time her voice was little more than a whisper.

He looked down at the ground, and a dark lock of hair fell across his forehead. Ursula was besieged by doubts. Had she wounded him too deeply for him to trust her now? Was he weighing up the risks and deciding she wasn't worth the gamble? Had Lady Winterton found a way into his heart? The stark outline of his countenance and the rigid set of his jaw reaffirmed all her fears. Her body began to shake; she couldn't suppress the pain she felt at the prospect that all she hoped for had been destroyed.

Then his eyes met hers. Three strides, and he was beside her. She was in his arms, feeling the beat of his heart against hers, and the fierceness of his embrace.

"Marry me!" she demanded between their urgent kisses. He held her tight as they stumbled, still entwined, onto their knees in the wet grass. She gazed up at him as he took her face in his hands. He regarded her with searching eyes. "Really?" he asked. "Will you truly marry me?"

She looked him straight in the eyes and with fierce determination replied.

"Yes."

The light was fading as they made their way back to Bromley Hall. Lord Wrotham's two collies waited patiently at the door to the long picture gallery for Ayres, who opened the French doors, bearing a towel over one arm and a bowl of water in the other, to minister to their needs.

"Ayres!" Lord Wrotham called out. "Stop spoiling the dogs!"

He held Ursula's hand as they climbed the long, wide steps of the terrace. "You'll soon get used to his idiosyncrasies," Wrotham said to her with a smile. "He hid them well when you visited last summer— but be warned, once we're married, you'll soon find out that this house has a way of running itself."

"Sounds like Chester Square," Ursula replied. Then a terrible thought hit her. "Oh, God," she said. "What's going to happen when Ayres meets Biggs?!"

"Hmm," Wrotham replied as he walked through the door. "I'd better contact the Foreign Office. That requires more diplomacy than my talents allow." He then caught sight of the look of genuine concern on Ursula's face.

"My love," he said, kissing her forehead lightly, "only you would be worrying about the servants just minutes after agreeing to become Lady Wrotham."

He guided her through the door, and they followed Ayres and the dogs along the picture gallery toward the Green Drawing Room.

"The dowager has been down," Ayres informed them calmly as he opened the door to the Green Drawing Room. Lord Wrotham hesitated at the threshold.

"She decided to return to her rooms, my lord, until dinner is called," Ayres assured him. "But after hearing of Miss Marlow's arrival, she has left you one or two items on the drawing room table."

Lord Wrotham raised an eyebrow. "What could my mother have possibly—?" He left the question unfinished.

"I believe one is a draft of the betrothal notice she wishes to have placed in the *Times*," Ayres replied, a faint smile playing at the edges of his mouth. "The other is a suggested guest list for the wedding breakfast."

Ursula's eyes widened. She had half expected the dowager to take to her room in a fit of horror at the thought of her son marrying the daughter of a coal miner's son, but it seemed that the expediency of wealth won out. The entire household must have guessed what Ursula's unannounced arrival precipitated, and the dowager, ever the Machiavellian pragmatist, was determined to take advantage at once.

Lord Wrotham was unperturbed.

"See," he said with a deadpan expression. "I told you Mother would be pleased."

Twenty-seven

Ursula and Lord Wrotham sat down at a corner table in the opulent Palm Court of the Ritz Hotel. It was one of their first public outings as a betrothed couple, and it amused Ursula to see the reaction of London society, even though for most of last year the gossip mongers had already chewed over the details of their relationship until it was little more than gristle for the penny weeklies. This time was different. Although members of polite society still regarded Ursula as something of an oddity—a twenty-five-year-old heiress, suffragette, and businesswoman was certainly not the norm in Belgravia—she had garnered a modicum of respect for her deal with Peter Vilensky and Hugh Carmichael. Lord Wrotham remained the bastion of the conservative aristocracy, but the ladies were more than a little intrigued by his choice of a wife—perhaps beneath that cold exterior beat a passionate heart after all. Together they obtained a certain degree of notoriety that now appealed to society's penchant for the eccentric.

Ursula tilted her chin and gazed across at him beneath her Italian hat of black tulle with pink roses.

"I have something for you," she said with a smile, "from Mrs. Pomfrey-Smith."

He looked up from the menu, raised one eyebrow, and said, "It's not another one of her appalling lists, is it? The last one suggested a four-foot-high wedding cake, a series of betrothal dinners hosted by my mother, and a honeymoon in Monte Carlo."

"No, nothing like that. . . . It's a list of houses in Mayfair she thought we might like to look at." Ursula's lips twitched.

Lord Wrotham placed his menu down on the table and sighed.

"Mrs. Pomfrey-Smith has been talking to my mother again."

"So it would seem."

Ever since she had heard of their engagement, the dowager had been angling for Lord Wrotham to find himself a new home, one not only suitable for his new bride but also where his mother could spend the London season. Given the dowager's intemperance where money was concerned, Ursula calculated that if she came to London unrestrained, Ursula's entire wealth could be dissipated in a matter of weeks.

"So what are your plans for the afternoon?" he asked, anxious to change the subject.

Ursula wrinkled her nose.

"Well, I thought we might meet up with some suffragette friends and smash a few windows on Regent Street. I've been out of practice since the summer. Then it's afternoon tea with some Bolsheviks at the Rose and Anchor—"

"And after that?" Lord Wrotham asked dryly.

"After that," Ursula replied, "I'm all yours."

Epilogue

Ursula and Lord Wrotham returned to Chester Square after an afternoon spent wandering through the National Gallery. A shallow mist had settled along the gardens in the square, hovering above the ground, hinting that ice might form overnight.

Biggs met them at the front door and led them inside to the roaring fire set in the front parlor. Ursula shrugged off her cashmere coat and hat and handed them to Biggs before flinging her gloves on the table and sitting down with a laugh.

"I don't see what you could possibly find to object to. Eugenie Mahfouz is excellent company, and as long as we make some temporary adjustments to Bromley Hall, she and all her harem can stay for as long as they'd like."

Lord Wrotham walked over and warmed his hands over the fire.

"I suppose her husband will be giving a series of lectures while he is here. No doubt on the evils of the British Empire."

"No doubt," Ursula replied lightly.

"Well," Lord Wrotham said, "I know there's no way I'm going to change your mind, so I guess I may as well accept my fate. No chance that I could stay at the Carlton Club all spring instead, is there?"

"Not a chance. Unless you'd like to take your mother with you, of course. . . ."

Lord Wrotham shot her a withering glance.

Biggs returned with the day's mail and placed the bundle of letters down on the mahogany side table.

"Will that be all, Miss?" He addressed Ursula and she smiled. Even though she was soon to marry, he continued to acknowledge her as mistress of the house, refusing to treat Lord Wrotham as anything other than a guest until such time as the two households and two sets of servants merged.

"Yes, thank you, Biggs," Ursula replied, as she reached over and grabbed the mail. She leaned back in the chair, unbuttoned her tweed jacket, and started sorting through the letters.

"Why, there's one here from Peter Vilenksy," she exclaimed. Although her relationship with Peter Vilensky was now cordial, she would have expected him to communicate with her only via Lord Wrotham. She hoped his letter did not herald bad news.

"Has he left Palestine?" Lord Wrotham asked. Ursula shook her head, scanning the handwritten pages.

"No, he's still in Jaffa. But he says the memorial to Katya and Arina has been completed. He and Baruh have placed it in the center of the new settlement. There are nearly fifty families living there now. Isn't that wonderful?"

"Did he say when he was likely to return to England?"

Ursula shook her head, her eyes fixed on the letter. "No. . . . The letter is more of an apology, really."

Lord Wrotham raised an eyebrow. "For alerting Dobbs to Katya's inquiries?"

Ursula swallowed hard. "No, for failing to appreciate love when he had it."

A knock on the front door caught them both off guard.

"Who on earth could that be, at this time?" Ursula wondered aloud.

Biggs opened the door and entered the parlor, followed by Chief Inspector Harrsion. Through the doorway Ursula could see two policemen waiting by the front door.

"Chief Inspector," she said, rising from her seat. "This is unexpected."

"My sincere apologies, Miss Marlow, for involving you in this."

Ursula looked at him with blank incomprehension. Lord Wrotham was standing stock-still. She could feel the tension in his body even though his face remained impassive.

"My Lord, this is one of the hardest things I have ever done, but I felt it ought to be me and no one else who did it." Harrison's voice broke slightly.

"What on earth are you talking about?" Ursula demanded.

"Lord Oliver Wrotham," Harrison continued, ignoring her, "I am here to arrest you on charges of conspiracy to commit treason against his majesty's government."